FROM
THE
BOHEMIAN HILLS

RANDALL REYMAN

ISBN: 979-8-218-54935-0

Other Books by Randall Reyman:

Twister's Wake, A Cyrus Brandt Novel Bk. 1

The Path, A Cyrus Brandt Novel Bk. 2

Deadly Crop, A Cyrus Brandt Novel Bk. 3

The Talos Mandate, A Cyrus Brandt Novel, Bk. 4

Photos procured from Reyman family archives.
For more information on Randall Reyman, go to:
www.RandallReyman.com

"Give me your tired, your poor,
Your huddled masses yearning to breathe free,
The wretched refuse of your teeming shore.
Send these, the homeless, tempest-tost to me,
I lift my lamp beside the golden door!"

By Emma Lazarus, as inscribed
on the Statue of Liberty

Praise for
From the Bohemian Hills

[*From the Bohemian Hills* takes] "*the reader on the emigrant-immigrant's journey as imagined from the perspective [...] of a cast of both real and imagined characters that together, present a variety of contemporary viewpoints and thus a more greatly nuanced story. Thus, Reyman's approach gives us a primer in Czech history that further puts his fictional story into a larger historic context. Besides its not insubstantial entertainment value, his story illustrates the overwhelming poverty, a rigid (and humiliating) class system and the lack of opportunity for social and economic mobility for most people in the oppressive police state of the Hapsburg monarchy. The reader of Bohemian Hills will not soon forget its history lessons through Reyman's unforgettable characters. Its compelling plot made it hard to put down.*" D.J.B., Czechoslovak Genealogical Society International

"*Fiction and fact are nicely woven together to tell a story of the life of Bohemian villagers under kings and empires, their struggles and the difficult decision to leave Bohemia, journey across the sea, and begin new lives in a new country.*" R.L., Czech and Slovak American Genealogy Society of Illinois

PART ONE
JOSEF
1859

CHAPTER 1
BOHEMIA

THE BOHEMIAN COUNTRYSIDE IS BURNING. At least, that's how it looks from Burnt Hill. The morning mist hangs heavy, like a burial shroud, over the rolling hilltops, and the scent of columbine on a spring zephyr brushes my face. Overhead, a hawk announces its presence with a *keee-arr*, screaming in protest to—what? My presence? I'm not sure. Maybe not a protest, maybe it's a plea. If so, it goes unanswered, echoing among the hills. What response can the hawk expect? Perhaps an explanation for how this unassuming land can endure such suffering? And to what end is this suffering? Just to assure the filling of the lord's coffers and to bring more unfortunate souls into this wretched world? Where's the good in that?

I've been sitting on this hillside since midnight, my Lorenz musket leaning against a large oak as if standing guard, protecting something important. But there's nothing important here—certainly not me. I'm as insignificant as every other cottager in Krouna, that miserable village, scarcely discernable in the mist below.

On the horizon, a diffident sun emerges, and then all at once it dazzles with its first brilliance. I bury my face in the refuge of cupped hands, and it feels good to be concealed in this false darkness. I wish I could hide in it forever, free of the burdens awaiting me down in the village where I've lived my entire life. It's a pitiful town, this pathetic collection of about fifty humble huts made of stone, wood, and mud, made ever more insignificant under the heavy hand of the Habsburgs who've ruled here for centuries.

But Frantiska tells me that progressive political winds are beginning to blow and that our lives are soon to improve. What a foolish woman she is; her optimism is disgusting. Don't invent false hope, I say. Can't she see we're still beholden to the estate lord? He owns our property, our house even. Still, Frantiska insists I should be satisfied with the contentment a wife and children provide. But any contentment she and the children might offer doesn't conceal the harsh realities of death. Two deaths, actually—the passing of our first child some years ago, and now the death of our youngest, Josef Jr. How does one find contentment in that? What is contentment, anyway, but a relative thing measured in the degree to which it distances itself from suffering?

Just last evening, I cradled the limp body of my little Josef Jr. in my arms. Only two years old, the boy struggled mightily to endure the frigid winter as if spring were a better time to die. We watched as he slowly wasted away, and yet we failed to comprehend the reality of the boy's inevitable passing. Little Josef's death was a senseless loss in this nonsensical life—a vicious blow, callous in its indifference and lack of meaning.

Staring out into the mist, I can just make out my house sitting a short distance from the base of Burnt Hill. What a pathetic single-room structure it is—dirt floor, two shuttered windows, and a crude wooden door. Frantiska's there now with the children. Vincencie and Antonin are probably just waking up, but I'm sure Frantiska's been up all night, sitting with little Josef's body. I wonder how his death will affect her. Will she muster enough of that optimism to move on with her life? I wonder. She's the strong one, after all. While she seems to confront life armed with her undaunted faith, I tend to do so with resignation and the belief that nothing will ever change.

I hold my face in my hands for a while longer, but I know when I open my eyes, everything will remain as before, two children already dead and two more—well, who knows? Frantiska may have her faith, but all I have is this old musket and the measly twelve kreuzers in my trouser pocket, intended to purchase goat milk and flour. This is the sum of my existence, the total holdings of a life embarked upon some nine years ago when Frantiska and I wed. Even my carpentry and masonry tools belong to the estate, to the lord living high and mighty in his château so far away.

It's no use. Covering my face can't protect me from my problems. Hiding is pointless. It's somewhat cowardly too, I suppose. I slowly lift my head from the refuge of my hands and look out onto the floating mist below. Does God see what I'm seeing? Does he witness our misery? Does he care? Does he even exist?

Glancing toward my rifle, I wonder why I carried the thing all the way up here. For protection from dangerous creatures roaming these hills? I doubt there's much chance of that. Suddenly, an ominous thought enters my mind, and I reach for the weapon, holding it in front of me. It feels heavy, heavier than I've noticed before, and my arms now struggle under its weight. As if directed by something dark within me, I quickly pull back the hammer and insert the firing cap. Turning the weapon around, I place it between my legs, with the barrel tip pressed under my jaw. Gazing out over the valley below, I'm at once overcome with an overwhelming sense of well-being. This will solve everything. And it will be easy. I feel my slumped shoulders straightening and my lips assuming a slight smile. When was the last time I smiled? I can't remember.

With the rifle in its current position, the distance necessary to discharge the weapon is beyond my reach, so I remove the ramrod and extend it, its wavering tip now stretching toward the trigger. The decision before me seems simple enough. Is there any reason to continue in this wretched life? Even Frantiska often considers me a source of irritation. She'll be better off without me, won't she? Indeed, no one will miss Josef Zach.

The notion of exiting this painful existence is an oddly calming one, even pleasant. But how will Frantiska remember me? If she is left to face the future alone, she will certainly hate me. And what of the children? No, this isn't so simple after all. It occurs to me that I've made very few decisions of any import throughout my life. I've always been told what to do and when to do it. How can I expect to so easily make this decision—this final decision? My ramrod inches ever closer to the trigger, shaking as it reaches out, begging for my final consent. Finally, paralyzed by my indecisiveness, my fatigued grip on the ramrod fails, and the ramrod falls to the ground.

That's when I hear it. Something walking in the leaves further up the hill behind me. From the sound of the slow, methodical footsteps, it must be something bigger than just a squirrel or a foraging bird—perhaps a wild boar? Certainly not another person; I've never seen anyone wandering these hills. I lower the rifle from my chin and twist my head toward the sound. It takes several moments for my eyes to focus as I stare up the slope toward a dense stand of trees. Then I see it: a movement beyond one of the larger tree trunks, hidden in the shadow of the tree canopy above. Suddenly, I realize what I'm looking at. A head and then shoulders appear from behind the tree. It's a large buck with an antler rack I estimate to be around eight tines.

This is private land belonging to the estate's lord. I shouldn't even be here. And while trespassing on this property isn't such a serious offense, I know poaching on it would be. If I take down this buck, I could at the least incur a hefty fine, and at most? Well, I don't want to think about that. All I can think about now is that this buck might provide enough meat to sustain my hungry family for a long stretch. The icehouse would see to that. I might even earn some money if my neighbors want to share in the spoils. Does the buck know I'm here? I think not. Not yet, anyway. I glance into the valley to assess my distance from the village. Will anyone hear a gunshot from here? I'm not sure. But my family is hungry. What choice do I really have?

The buck is still about two hundred paces up the slope from where I sit. I need to be closer to increase my chances for a clean hit. If I don't drop the animal with my first shot, it will most likely run a good distance before going down. Maybe if I stay where I am, the buck will come right to me. Otherwise, I'll have to move, increasing the chances the buck might see me and bolt up the hillside. I watch the animal feed on some early spring buds on the thin branches reaching down around him. The buck shifts toward a branch in the opposite direction, and I stealthily rise to my feet, positioning myself behind the oak tree. Holding my rifle, my feet steadied, I train the weapon on my prey.

I'm not a crack shot, but I'm not a bad shot either. My training with the Imperial Army has seen to that. Fortunately, I've not been called up for any serious combat since my conscription nine years ago. I'm not sure I could bolster the courage to kill another man. That would take a far better reason than simple loyalty to the Crown. However, the target in front of me doesn't present any such dilemma beyond the lord's claim to this land. As I grip the rifle, I plan my next move. My Lorenz gun is fairly accurate, but I still need to shorten the distance to the buck if I'm going to be assured of success.

The buck's moving closer now. Closer. Closer still. And I continue to hold the Lorenz in firing position, cocked and ready to take my shot. I try to concentrate on my breathing, keeping it slow and regular. Five counts in, five counts out, just like they taught us on the firing range. The buck is now about fifty paces away. Five counts in, five counts out. I'm sure of my accuracy at this distance, yet there's a problem. The buck is facing me, and I decide to wait, hoping for a clean body shot. Five counts in, five counts out. Finally, it plucks something delectable off a nearby branch, giving me a much better angle for my attempt. I hold my breath and squeeze the trigger.

The gun kicks, and for a moment, I'm disoriented. I can taste gunpowder and I blink, trying to focus on my target, or at least where my target was standing a moment ago. I can't see it. "*Sakra!*" I blurt, as I race in the direction my bullet has just taken. I know I'll be in trouble if the buck runs very far, especially if it falls in the open valley where someone might see it. But most likely, the injured animal has bolted for the protection of the trees and underbrush. That could present a different problem. I might have trouble finding it when it finally collapses.

Breathing hard, I arrive at the spot where the buck just stood and gaze hopefully toward the trees to my right. I'm relieved to see the animal lying among some small saplings, its antlers tangled in the thicket and its legs crumpled beneath its still body. It was a successful hit.

Giving a yank on the animal's antlers, I see that the buck is much larger than I'd estimated earlier. Now I have an additional problem. Although my hands are strong from years of working with wood and stone, and my legs are sturdy enough, it will be difficult to drag my quarry down Burnt Hill. And besides, the task will take me far too long to accomplish, making it likely that someone might see me struggling to do it. I release my grasp on the antlers and let the buck's head fall to the ground. With my rifle thrown over my shoulder, I leave the downed animal where it fell and start downhill out of the woods and onto the plain opening up toward Krouna.

How will Frantiska react to what I've done? Certainly, she will understand. And if she doesn't, so what? I did it for the good of the family. She will just have to accept it. She's a reasonable woman. That's what people always said about her before we were married. Capable and reasonable, that's what people said. That would make for an acceptable wife, was my thinking. And it was good that I didn't find her unattractive, nor possessing a vexing disposition.

The sun has done its job, and the morning mist has mostly dispersed as I reach the corner of the house. My neighbor, Anton, suddenly emerges from the shadows of his own stone home, still wearing his long brown nightshirt, imbued with clinging fragments of straw from their old stuffed mattress.

Anton and his wife, Rose, have been living next door ever since we first moved here. I consider Anton, some years older than myself, the prosperous one. He's a man of agriculture, who has over the years been able to purchase some of the estate land he had been renting. This makes him a man of means, or at least that's how I've always seen him. In actuality, now that I think about it, Anton is just another peasant scratching out an existence in this depressed village. He just owns a few miserable hectares of rocky ground, with a second room attached to his house where he stables his two mules and a few goats. A man of means? In a pig's eye!

Still, compared to his, my home is more modest, boasting just one room like many other dwellings in Krouna. I was at first embarrassed to begin life with my new bride in such a place. But Frantiska was the practical one, insisting that this humble structure was all we could afford. Besides, I wasn't a farmer who needed extra space to shelter livestock. I was just a stonemason and carpenter requiring only a small space for my family and my meager set of tools. Perhaps, we could build another room onto the house as we prospered, she had said. Of course, we haven't been able to prosper, and almost ten years hence, the place has enjoyed no improvements.

"G'morning, Anton," I offer blandly, leaning my rifle against the outside wall of my hovel.

"What're you doing out here, Josef?"

"Why?"

"Well, I heard a gunshot earlier, and here you are with your rifle. What should I make of that?" he asks.

I furtively glance around to see if anyone else is about. There's no point in denying my actions to Anton. He'll know soon enough. I ask, "Do you think anyone else heard it?"

"It wasn't very loud, but it echoed around the valley a bit. I was lying awake when I heard it. I figured some of the lord's hunters might be up in the hills today, but now I find you here with your gun."

Anton's the only person I can trust to help me. I could deny everything, I suppose, but I need his help to retrieve the buck. What's the point in feigning innocence?

"Yes, Anton, that was me," I admit bluntly. "I shot a buck up on Burnt Hill, and I could use some help to get it down here."

My bluntness surprises Anton, who nervously scans up and down the dirt path running through our village. "What have you done, Josef?" he whispers accusingly.

"I know, I know," I answer. "But I had a choice, Anton. Either risk penalty or watch my family starve. What else was I to do?"

"You could have asked for help from your neighbors. That's what you could have done."

"Do you have food to spare? Does anyone?" I counter.

Anton knows I have a point and shakes his head. "No, I guess not. It's been a hard winter," he admits. "But you shouldn't be up in the woods hunting. You know better than to do that."

"Well, I really didn't intend to shoot that buck. It just sort of happened."

"Then why were you up there in the first place?"

I pause before looking Anton in the eyes. I say, "Little Josef died last night."

He meets my statement with a sudden gasp and then silence, as our eyes meet in stoic countenance. "Oh, I'm so sorry, Josef," Anton finally says solemnly. "That's just terrible. Rose and I knew he wasn't well, but . . . that's just terrible," he repeats. "And Frantiska?"

"I think she's OK, though I left her before midnight. I've been up on the hillside since then," I reply without further explanation.

Anton stares at me for a moment. He looks confused and asks, "You left her and the other children here all night with little Josef?"

"I had to leave. It was just too much, Anton," I answer unashamedly. My son died last night. Surely, Anton knows how that might make a man do unexpected things.

"Wait here, Josef," he says calmly. "I'll be right back." He re-enters his house and soon emerges holding a sack of tools and a shovel. "Let's go take care of that buck," he says in a low voice. "Rose will check on Frantiska while we're gone."

It takes most of the morning to dress the buck. We bury its entrails and carry the edible portions of the carcass down the hillside, slinking along a tree line to avoid detection. After three trips, the job is done.

Anton objects when I insist on bringing the buck's eight-point rack with us. "What if someone discovers the antlers?" he queries. "How would you ever explain having this in your possession?"

"It's a perfectly good trophy don't you think, Anton? Maybe I can sell it to someone. I'll be careful, don't you worry," I say, attempting to assure him.

"At least let me store it in my house for a while," offers Anton. "Your place is much too small to hide something like that. Later, maybe we can figure out what to do with it."

With the meat stored safely in the icehouse, I think about how Anton and I filled it with large chunks of ice we dragged from a nearby pond last January. That showed an optimism that perhaps overreached the reality of our situation. Neither of us expected to acquire any perishables to store in the small structure, our efforts being more a labor of hope than expectation. Both families will now have some reserves to get us at least partway through the spring months. But first, Anton and I will need to salt and cure the rest to preserve it for the future. The trick will be doing this without notice from the village judge, Emil Spacek, or his scoundrel son, Thomas, whom I and most of the other villagers despise.

CHAPTER 2

THROUGH THE WOODEN DOOR, Rose can hear the rhythmic sound of Frantiska's loom, a contraption she inherited at the passing of her dear father. It's a sound Rose hears almost every day—a sound she's learned to expect whenever she ventures near Frantiska's house. The sound of that loom has become so familiar that on the occasional day that Rose doesn't hear it, she wonders if something might be wrong, and she rushes to check on her friend. But today, she can't understand why Frantiska would be working at her loom—not this soon after little Josef's death. Rose has second thoughts about interrupting Frantiska at this moment. Is this Frantiska's way of coping with her loss, her way perhaps to bring normalcy back into her life? With trepidation, Rose weakly raps on the door. Hearing nothing beyond the constant working of the loom, she hesitantly pushes it open and lets it swing inward.

"I-I-I was just wondering how you were doing, Frannie," Rose stutters apologetically as she pokes her head in.

Frantiska is a woman of slight proportions, but Rose has always marveled at her strength to push and pull the apparatus, producing the most intricate of linen and woolen cloth designs. Despite her slight frame, Frantiska's wide face, penetrating dark eyes, and prominent, almost masculine chin project a kind of undeterred determination. Since Frantiska and Josef came to live next door almost ten years ago, Rose considers Frannie to be the perfect match for Josef, possessing not only a remarkable physical strength, but also an inner strength that Josef seems to lack. Rose knows this family will need to draw upon Frannie's strength if they are to endure the death of another child.

"Come in, Rose," mutters Frantiska, her voice flat.

Rose steps into the house and immediately spots the covered form of the deceased boy on a small pallet on the other side of the room. She averts her eyes downward, letting her chin fall to her chest as she slips onto a stool Josef fashioned from oak. It's a stout, plain seat, suited for its purpose like the three matching stools arranged around Frantiska's table.

"I heard about little Josef. I'm so sorry, Frannie," Rose offers.

With a puffy face and wet, dull eyes, Frantiska looks up at her friend. "I'm weaving this cradle sheet for Josef's burial," she says, her voice scratchy and her chin trembling.

"It's beautiful, Frannie. Just beautiful," says Rose with a little too much emotion.

For a long moment, Frantiska studies the fine weave of her linen cloth in silence. She's worked on this all night, holding back her grief, trying to control herself. But with Rose watching her, she can't hold back any longer. She wipes her nose with her hand and then looks at Rose, opening her mouth to speak. Giving up, she presses her lips together and crosses her arms, grabbing her shoulders tightly with tense hands, her shoulders heaving slightly as she begins to moan. Rose is at Frantiska's side in an instant, pulling her friend into her own body and holding her tightly as she grieves.

Frantiska looks up, glancing toward the window, and Rose, reading her mind, says, "Don't worry. I saw the children playing outside. They're fine."

"We haven't told them yet," Frantiska whimpers.

"They'll be fine. They're young. Don't worry, Frannie."

"And what of Josef? Have you seen him? He's been gone since the middle of the night."

"He's up on the hill with Anton," replies Rose, trying not to sound judgmental. "Apparently, Josef shot a buck up there early this morning."

"What?" Frantiska blurts incredulously through her tears. "Is he trying to ruin this family?"

"Anton doesn't think anybody will find out," Rose reassures her. "They're going to dress it up in the woods and put the meat in the icehouse. They'll be careful. And there'll be meat for your family!"

The prospect of food for her children tempers Frantiska's grief, and she regains her poise, blinking away her tears. "That man is going to be my downfall," she whispers.

"Oh, Frannie. He's a good man. Don't lose faith in him. Things will get better."

Frantiska doesn't reply, but sits sniffling, staring down at little Josef's burial sheet. It's true, she thinks. Josef *is* a good man. Well, good enough, anyway. She is well aware of Josef's limitations, and she's also aware of his positive traits. She agreed to marry him after putting all these considerations through a rigorous process of weights and balances. Though Josef was short in stature, she recognized his muscular build and strong hands. Frantiska recognized that he was capable of arduous work, and she was confident he'd be a good provider. However, she also recognized that Josef had a definite stubborn streak. This, and the fact that he didn't seem particularly grounded in his Christian beliefs, made for a persistent tension that often intruded on their daily interactions. Still, she found him to be mostly gentle with her and sometimes quite witty, with a disarming ability to make her laugh even at the most unexpected moments. The sum of all these considerations, plus the lack of other suitors, was enough for her to commit to a life with Josef Zach.

Two days later, Josef Jr.'s ceremony takes place in the cemetery next to the plain wooden structure where the town's small group of Evangelical Reformed Protestants occasionally meets. The burial is performed with the usual efficiency, an efficiency that's customary for the deaths of children in these hard times. Diseases are common in the peasant villages, and the vulnerable children are no match for maladies that hover about, randomly selecting new, and often young, victims. Indeed, the graves of children litter Bohemian cemeteries, and few people besides the closest relatives and friends ever take the time to attend these funerals anymore.

Other than Josef Jr.'s family, the only people present are Rose, Anton, and Pastor Košút, a small, stooped man who clutches his Bible with bony, prominently veined hands, and wears a frozen smile, belying the psychological scars he bears from conducting so many of these affairs. It's a simple ceremony, and after the pastor's well-rehearsed words, Josef and Anton slowly lower the casket into the ground. After the small group stumbles halfheartedly through a couple of hymn verses, Pastor Košút concludes the ceremony with a rather long, rambling prayer. As the group stands nearby watching, Josef and Anton fill the grave with loose soil, patting it down with their shovels, making the ground uniformly symmetrical and smooth.

Finally, Frantiska leads her family home in silence holding Vincencie's small hand, with her husband toting a sleeping Antonin following close behind. The afternoon is bright and warm—a perfect spring day—and spirits would under other circumstances be running high. But this is a slow, solemn walk, and they shuffle past neighbors' homes, noticing people receding from open windows in deference to the privacy of the family's grief. In this place where death is so common, it is still death—not a trivial thing, especially when it's the death of a child. As Frantiska knows all too well, a child's death takes a part of you, a chunk of your soul never to be replaced. The injury will eventually heal, the sadness will finally fade, and the dark memory will move to the back of her mind—only to reappear later when she least expects it, reconstructing itself like it happened only yesterday.

CHAPTER 3

IT'S MIDMORNING as I check on the meat in the icehouse. Securing the door behind me, I make my way around the side of our small home and discover Thomas Spacek standing at my front door. Thomas is a large-framed, rather fleshy man with a long, slender nose and small eyes set close together. He seems to resemble a raccoon with a manner just as menacing. Even at our first meeting some years ago, I pegged him as a man who values power above all else—a man who enjoys taking every advantage of his higher station, granted him by his father, the town judge. Give him any excuse, and he's quick to prove his superiority to another person's unworthiness—as if we need any reminders of that! Upon seeing me approaching, Spacek offers not the slightest greeting. "Is Frantiska around?" he asks.

"What's it to you, Spacek?" I answer tersely.

"Now, Josef. Why are you so rude to me? I would think you would want to stay on the right side of me and my father."

"I offer the village judge ample respect. It's you I can't stand. What do you want?" I ask sharply. I do not conceal my contempt for him. Thomas and Frantiska grew up together in Jarošov, a simple village just over the hills to the north. Early in our marriage, Frantiska admitted that Thomas showed considerable interest in her back when they were teenagers. Although Frantiska rejected Thomas's overtures in those days, when his father became Krouna's village administrator eight years ago, it didn't take him long to seek Frantiska out and continue his rather forward and unsolicited behavior. Even now, after all this time, Thomas persists in seizing every opportunity to flirt with her, sometimes discreetly, other times openly.

"Two things, Josef. First, there is some stonework to be done on two homes on the other side of the village, lot numbers ten and thirteen. My father will pay you your usual rate to make those repairs. Interested?" Thomas says wryly, smiling because he has me at a disadvantage.

"I guess I can do that," I answer, concealing my disdain. "When does he want it completed?"

"Soon as possible. I'm sure you can fit it into your very busy schedule," he says, seething in sarcasm. "And make sure it's done right if you want any more work coming your way."

"I'll do it right, Spacek—just like I always do."

"Just so you do. I'll be inspecting it when you're done."

"Great," I answer mockingly as I turn to walk toward the back of the house.

"There's one more thing," Thomas adds, calling after me.

I stop and turn. "What would that be?" I ask impatiently.

"The lord will ride through here tomorrow afternoon."

"All the way from the Crown Château?"

"Actually, he's been staying closer, at Rychmburk Castle. He's riding down here to examine parts of his estate," Thomas says as he looks around disparagingly. "Make sure you get this place cleaned up and have things around here looking their best. Also, when he rides through, you and the missus should be outside by the road with the rest of the townspeople showing your respect."

I grunt as I turn, again walking away from Spacek. "Respect, my ass," I mutter venomously. "I'll show him respect when I drop my pants and show him my Bohemian ass."

"What was that, Josef?" calls Thomas.

"I said I'll get to those jobs just as you ask," I say without turning back.

When I'm sure Thomas is finally gone, I go into the house, where Frantiska is at her loom. "That ass Thomas was just here," I say derisively.

"What did he want?" she replies over the rhythm of the machine.

"What he really wanted was to see you, I suppose. He was sniffing around, looking for you like a bull stud on a heifer. One of these days, when I've had enough of him, I'll drag him up Burnt Hill, and you'll never have to worry about him again."

"Don't talk like that, Josef. I can handle Thomas. Don't worry. He's just a blowhard with a big opinion of himself. He's nothing, really. And I don't want you doing anything else shameful up on Burnt Hill. You did plenty when you shot that buck. You should've known better," she reminds me accusingly.

Duly reprimanded, I say, "OK, OK, Frannie. I'll behave, I promise." I pause before adding, "He said he had a couple jobs for me. I'm going to get to 'em this afternoon."

Frantiska abruptly stops weaving and turns to me in surprise. "That's wonderful, Josef. Maybe that's a sign that things will pick up, as I predicted."

"I hope so. There was something else, too. That horse shit of a man also told me—"

"Josef Zach!" Frantiska shouts reproachingly. "Such language!"

"Sorry," I reply, again duly chastised. "Anyway, Thomas also said we're getting visitors tomorrow afternoon. Prince Ferdinand is coming."

"The lord's coming to our little village?"

"Yes, Prince Bonaventura himself, in all his wondrous glory," I spit with scorn. "He's coming from Hrad Rychmburk. Spacek thinks we should all be out at the road cheering and waving flags for the prince like he's a god incarnate."

"Hush, Josef. Don't talk like that. Please tell me you won't do anything to embarrass us in front of the prince. We should show him respect, don't you think? He owns our home, after all."

I smile as I imagine myself showing him respect, waving cheerfully to him just before dropping my britches and revealing my blanched Bohemian buttocks. "That's right," I say. "He owns our home, the land it sits on, and everything else, Frannie. It's like he owns us."

The masonry work on the two homes is completed in good time. Perhaps too efficiently, I realize. I don't want Judge Spacek and his raccoon-like son Thomas to think these jobs are too easy. At the second job site, I dawdle awhile after I've finished, taking time to clean my tools and meticulously arrange them in their crude wooden toolbox. Finally, by midafternoon, I pick up my toolbox and head for the village center. I'm eager for my payment and hope to catch the village judge before he leaves for the day. I hope I haven't dillydallied too long. No, I decide, gauging the sun's position overhead. This should be just about right.

It doesn't take me long to reach the building in the middle of town, and I stride up the steps into the old stone structure. The woman at the massive desk is stamping some kind of forms, and I patiently stand in front of her as she stamps one page, then turns it over to stamp the next page, turns, stamps, turns, stamps, turns. She never even looks up at me but continues stamping, even when the door to a rear office finally opens and Thomas walks through to the front.

"What is it, Josef?" he asks impersonally. "Do you need something?"

"I just finished the work on those houses. Took me all morning and into the afternoon. That foundation was in pretty awful shape. I stopped by for my pay on my way home."

"What did I tell you, Josef?"

"Huh? What d'you mean?"

"I told you I need to inspect it. I should be able to get over there late tomorrow morning."

I know Frantiska expects that money, and I answer, "I know, but I thought I could get paid today if that's OK with you."

"Sorry, Josef. As I said, I'll inspect it tomorrow. You can stop by around noon to get your money," Thomas says as he stands there with that same smug grin I've learned to despise.

What can I do? Nothing. Not if I want more work coming my way from Spacek. "Alright. I'll come back tomorrow," I concede. Then I add, "Don't forget. It was almost a full day's work."

"I'll remember," he replies before turning and retreating into the back office.

I look down at the woman still working at the desk. Stamp, turn, stamp, turn, stamp, turn. "Thanks for your help," I mumble sarcastically as I continue past her and out the door.

The next day, I wait as long as my patience allows before I leave for the village center. The late morning air is cool, and the sun is edging upward, foretelling a much warmer afternoon. The village folk scurry about in their preparations for the prince's arrival, gathering fallen leaves and branches, storing implements and tools, and taking in their hanging laundry. I have done little to clean up around my yard, feeling no need to win the lord's favor. Why should I? What more can the lord do to diminish me than he has done already? Frantiska is most likely tidying up the place herself at this very moment, doing the work she would have expected me to do. A tinge of guilt grabs me, but I shrug it off. If cleaning up makes her feel better, let her have at it, I figure.

When I ascend the steps into the large stone building, a different woman sits at the desk. She gazes up to greet me, albeit impersonally.

"*Hallo. Kann ich Ihnen helfen?*" she asks. German—that figures, I think. I don't know the language well, but I've gained a rudimentary knowledge of it over time, mostly from random travelers occasionally happening through Krouna. But to say those encounters are occasional is not quite accurate. Those encounters have been rare indeed.

I reply, "My name is Josef Zach. I came for my money."

"*Ja*, Herr Zach. *Hier ist es.*" She reaches into a side drawer and withdraws several coins, handing them to me with a practiced smile.

Holding out my hand to receive the coins, I stare at them as they lay sparse and cool in my palm. Twenty-five kreuzers. It isn't much, but it'll hold us over for the immediate future. "Thanks," I say coldly as I turn to leave.

"*Bitte schön*," replies the woman, who is already looking down, jotting some notation on a piece of paper.

I stand for a moment outside the building with my money gripped in my fist, and then shove it into my pocket, jangling the coins for good measure. This makes me feel good. Turning for home, I notice the tavern just across the street. Do I deserve a midday refreshment? I wonder. Oh, why not? A midday brew won't set me back too far—maybe a kreuzer or two. I stride across the street and walk through the tavern entry. The door is lashed open with an old leather strap, an invitation to potential clientele. It's surprising to see the place empty except for Jakub, the wizened and very bald proprietor.

"Hello, Josef. It's good to see you," Jakub greets me as he grabs a mug off the shelf. Without asking what I would like, he fills the mug with brew. There is only one option available, so no asking is necessary. Drinking heartily, I consume half of its contents before slamming it down noisily on the tabletop where I sit. "Ah, that is a wonderful thing," I exclaim. Noting again that I am Jakub's lone customer, I ask, "Where is everybody, Jakub?"

"Haven't you heard? The lord is coming this afternoon."

"Ah. The great lord," I say, nodding irreverently. "I almost forgot. Well, I suppose one less flag-waver won't be missed, right?" I add before downing the rest of my beer. "I think I'll have another, Jakub, if you please."

CHAPTER 4

FRANTISKA GAZES DOWN disapprovingly at her dress. It's the dress her mother made for her when she married Josef almost ten years ago. She wishes she had tried it on yesterday, for she suspected it might no longer fit. Her shape has considerably diminished in its womanly curvature, she realizes, due to years of the nutritional deprivation that poverty imparts. Then, with the arrival of her children, it had become necessary to relinquish a portion of her meals, as scant as they were, to them, for seeing her children go hungry was too painful, making her own suffering far less important and even tolerable.

The dress hangs loose on her now, but she doesn't have time to take it in. Even so, with the dress's white puffed sleeves trimmed in red lace, and a full-filigreed skirt reaching to the floor, it makes her feel better than she's felt in a long time. And the smaller dress she made recently for little Vincencie is just as charming. Frantiska's dress may hang a bit loose on her shriveled frame, but she decides she and Vincencie will still look just fine standing there next to the road, waving, welcoming the prince to their village.

Examining Vincencie one last time to make sure she's presentable, Frantiska gathers Antonin up into her arms, and the three of them make their way to the road to wait. She pauses briefly to see that everything in her yard is in its proper place. "It will have to do," she whispers, as she gazes down the village road toward the middle of town, nervously looking for Josef. He's nowhere in sight, and she wonders what could possibly be taking him so long.

Suddenly, she hears a commotion from far down the road in the other direction. Someone is yelling something she can't make out, but she assumes they are announcing the prince's arrival. Once more, she glances down at her dress and gently lays her hand on it smoothing down the linen that is wafting gently in the spring breeze. Then, pulling Vincencie close to her side in readiness, she stands, holding Antonin, her shoulders back, her prominent chin raised, her eyes bright.

Soon, Frantiska can see the horses drawing near. First, two soldiers ride by, proudly adorned in the colors of the house of Kinsky: red, gold, and white, with the emblem of three large wolf's teeth emblazoned on the front of their uniforms. They each have a jewel-handled saber proudly displayed in a scabbard, ready to be put to service if a threat presents itself. As finely as the two horsemen are attired, though, it isn't their uniforms that impress Frantiska as much as it is the beautiful steeds the men are riding. They are the most exquisite golden color, perfectly matched, as they proudly strut in a rhythm of near-exact synchrony. A single soldier, dressed like the others, follows close behind, carrying a banner displaying the official Kinsky coat of arms. He rides a similar golden horse, as does the prince, who rides just behind him.

Oh, the prince, Frantiska thinks. How grand—how regal! She has seen the prince's father, Rudolf the Sixth, once before, but that was when she was just a child in Jarošov. But this prince, Rudolf's heir, Ferdinand, is much more—how to describe it?—beautiful. That's the only word that comes to mind. He looks so young, younger than Frantiska herself. But with an air of superiority, the countenance of his breeding, that she finds reassuring rather than off-putting. The prince sits confidently erect on his golden mount, wearing a pristine red jacket and light-colored riding slacks. His long boots, extending almost to his knees, are a lustrous black, causing Frantiska to doubt they have ventured anywhere close to the ground. On his coat, he displays multiple colorful ribbons and sparkling medals–

–too many to have been meritoriously conferred upon a man so young. But his magnificent hat is the most elaborate part of his uniform, extending high above his head and topped by a tall white plume flapping from side to side in rhythm with the horse's gait.

Behind the prince walk two more of the impressive golden horses carrying attendants who are far less grandly attired. And following the attendants are four more horsemen, identically dressed in the Kinsky coat of arms and fully armed with saber and rifle. Frantiska understands the need for such protection on travels between towns and villages where bandits often lay in wait for the unsuspecting traveler. For as long as she can remember, most roads in the rural areas have been unpatrolled and dangerous. Crime is widespread and has become more so in these difficult economic times.

Finally, at the end of the procession, riding far less impressive steeds, are Emil Spacek, the village judge, and of course Thomas, both of whom must have ridden out of town to meet the entourage. Frantiska notes that Judge Spacek stares straight ahead as he rides, while Thomas looks out at the people alongside the road, as if to make sure they are noticing him. As Thomas passes Frantiska's house, his gaze falls for an especially long duration upon her, and then he scrutinizes the house and the surrounding area. He is looking for Josef, and Frantiska can sense it.

CHAPTER 5

IT'S LATE IN THE AFTERNOON when I finally come through the front door with a fatuous smile smelling of brew. Frantiska ignores me as she sits, repairing a loose stitch in Vincencie's new dress. She's probably angry I wasn't here when the prince came by, and my smell of alcohol isn't helping. She must now realize where I've been. I can see from her bearing that she's dissatisfied with me. She'll get over it. I pull my hand out of my pocket and lay the coins cautiously on the table.

"I got paid for my work," I say guardedly, hoping for a favorable response. No response comes, so I push on. "Then I stopped for a beer at Jakub's place. I guess I stayed there a bit too long, didn't I? It appears I missed the prince's big arrival."

"Yes, you certainly did," she replies curtly as she continues to work.

"That's too bad. I was hoping to salute him with my ass," I say, chuckling to myself, hoping Frantiska's mood will improve with my humor. I am to be disappointed.

"The children!" she reprimands. "I asked you not to speak like that, remember?"

"I remember, Frantiska. That's why it's just as well that I wasn't here when the prince passed by. I might have said something quite rude to his grand highness."

Frantiska stops her sewing and glares at me, saying, "I don't know why you insist on being so defiant. It serves no purpose—no purpose at all, Josef."

"No purpose? What purpose is there?" I shoot back angrily. "Do I have a purpose? Do you? We work our fingers to the bone, we live with the scantest of conveniences, and we suffer the death of our . . . children." My voice falters as

I'm shaken by my own words. I swallow hard and then continue. "If we go on like this, we'll still be here thirty years from now with no more to show for our lives than what we have now, which is practically nothing."

Frantiska has resumed her sewing and calmly says, "God has a plan."

It's just a simple statement, a statement of naïve faith, but it is all I need to lash out in frustration.

"God? You mean the same god who put my son in the ground? The same god who makes me beg that misfit Thomas for every shitty job, so I can buy food scraps for my family?"

I'm raising my voice, expressing the dark thoughts the beer now allows me to unleash. I push further, saying, "You mean the same god who offers no hope for the future? Is that the god you think has a plan for us? That god doesn't give a shit about us, woman. That god won't provide for us any more than that peacock lord who rode through here today. That god doesn't—"

"Stop it! Just stop," Frantiska shouts as she leaps to her feet, her voice trembling with unchecked emotion. Through tears of rage, she spits her words brutally at me as I stand there dumbfounded. I've never seen her like this before. With rancor, she insists, "If I cannot believe God will help us, then what do I have to believe in? That's all I have, Josef. My faith is all there is. How else can I get myself up every morning to face the day? That faith serves me a lot better than your anger and defiance have been serving you—that's for sure." Her harangue stops abruptly, devolving into a coda of sobs as she sits at the table with her head down on folded arms, weeping.

"You're a fool," I say softly but without compassion. "Go ahead. Worship your god. That god has done me no favors. He's of no use to me."

This is enough to bring Frantiska back to her full fury, and she again springs from her stool, knocking it over noisily. She stands facing me, pointing at the door, summoning up all the rage that's been building within her, and shouts, "Then get out! This is a home where God abides. I will not have you here talking words so vile!"

"You can't mean—" I protest.

"Go. I've had enough of you!" Frantiska marches to the door and yanks it open, waiting for me to leave.

"But—"

"I said, GO!"

Sighing forcibly through my nose, I slog toward the door. Stopping suddenly, I turn back to retrieve a few of the kreuzers from the table, shoving them into my pocket. Then, after one last contemptuous look at my spiteful wife, I stomp out and proceed up the village road. Several of my neighbors are staring at me through their windows. I know they've plainly heard the exchange between us, for there aren't many secrets in this village. "*Sakra všichni!* Damn you all!" I shout at them as I trudge toward the village center, heading for Jakub's tavern. I'm already looking forward to finding refuge in another one of his sudsy brews.

The sun's getting low in the western sky before I start back toward home. My few coins are spent, an expenditure amply justified by the heightened self-confidence the brew has provided. Certainly, Frantiska will have calmed down by now, I think. If not, I'm not sure what I'll do.

As I pass Anton and Rose's house, I'm annoyed to see Thomas again standing at our front door, this time talking to Frantiska. I also see that Frantiska is gazing over Thomas's shoulder at me, and she points in my direction as I approach. Thomas turns toward me and says, "Ah, there you are, Josef. My father would like a word with you."

"Why is that?" I snap.

"He's disappointed in your behavior and your disrespect. He understands you were in the tavern when you should have been standing here on the road showing your deference to His Lordship."

"Screw His Lordship, Thomas. And screw you, too. There's no law that says I must bow before His Highness, is there?" The front door slams shut and Frantiska's face vanishes from sight.

"We are losing our patience with you, Josef. There are other carpenters and stoneworkers whom we can employ around here. You may soon find yourself with no income for your family if you continue this way."

"Stop bothering him, Thomas. Don't you have anything better to do with your time? Why don't you go collect some rent money or something?" It's Anton who's been listening from his doorway. Over the last couple of years, he's witnessed many interactions between me and Thomas. While I may have been somewhat careless in my dealings with the man, Anton has finally had enough of Thomas's goading me.

"You should mind your own damn business, peasant!" Thomas walks the few steps over to Anton's house, shoving him viciously back through the entry and onto the floor where Rose stands, rigid and wide-eyed. "Keep your nose out of this," Thomas scolds as Anton struggles to get back on his feet. Thomas scans the modest living space, and his gaze suddenly fixes on something partly hidden behind a stack of firewood in the corner of the room. He walks over to it and lifts the buck's antlers into the air. "What do we have here?" he asks, staring accusingly in Anton's direction. "Where did you get this?"

"I-I got it from . . . a friend," replies Anton hesitantly.

"Is that so?" Thomas replies suspiciously. "Who?"

"Oh, it's just a friend from another town. You wouldn't know him."

Thomas pivots and marches, antlers and all, out the door, and I watch as he begins searching behind Anton's home, looking for something. I know what he's looking for. It doesn't take long for Thomas to see the icehouse. He glances reprovingly at Anton and then plods toward the icehouse door. The entrance is nothing more than a small, crude door, positioned more horizontally than vertically upon a large mound of dirt, resulting from its excavation. Icehouses like this are common around Krouna, and I'm sure Thomas has seen plenty of them. He leans down, pulling on the door, pausing as his eyes adjust to the darkness inside. He lets the door fall open and, without hesitation, drops the antlers on the ground, stepping into the darkness. It doesn't take him long to find the salted deer meat covered with ice and straw, and moments later, Thomas's head pops back out into the sunlight.

"Just as I suspected," he says, walking up to Anton. "Poaching is a serious crime on this estate. You're coming with me, Anton." Thomas grabs the antlers, takes hold of Anton's shirtsleeve, and shoves him in the direction of the village center. "Let's go," he mutters.

Watching all of this unfold, I realize Anton is about to accept the blame for my crime. Being slightly drunk from my visit to Jakub's tavern, I first have the satisfying thought that I'm about to evade prosecution for my misdeed. But then, just as suddenly, I realize I can't let Anton take the blame. Not my friend of so many years. Why would Anton do that, anyway? To protect me, Frantiska, and the children? Anton and Rose have no children to care for, so he might reason that the damage caused to their life will be considerably less than the harm it would bring my family. Is that what Anton is thinking? I wonder. Finally, I muster all my confidence and shout, "Wait!"

Thomas stops and turns. "What is it?" he asks impatiently.

"Anton didn't do it. I did. I shot the buck," I announce, at first confidently, but then I add more submissively, "It's me you want."

Thomas smiles as he looks from Anton to me, saying, "Well, aren't you two a real pair?" He turns back to Anton. "Is that so? You didn't kill that buck?"

"I guess that's right," Anton meekly answers, looking apologetically at me.

"OK, then," says Thomas. "Let's go, the both of you."

"And if we don't want to go? Then what?" I ask, always defiant.

"Well then, I'll just have to come back later with some of the judge's men. They might not be as polite as I am. You choose, Josef," Thomas says, waiting, smiling wryly.

I know he's right, and I fear what might happen to the two women and the children if those armed men were to return after we were hauled off. "Let's go, Anton. Let's get this over with," I say, submitting to the inevitable.

It's almost sunset as Thomas shoves us up the steps into the stone administrative building in the center of Krouna. Thomas opens the door leading to the back office and holds it open as the two of us shuffle by him through the portal. I have never been in this rear office before, and I'm surprised to find it much smaller than I'd imagined. It's a stark room, with only a wooden file cabinet and a desk that seems large compared to the small space around it. The setting sun glares through a single window located behind the desk on the far side of the room where someone is seated. I can't see a face, shadowed by the brilliant illumination from the outside, but I hear a man speak.

"What's this, Thomas?" the shadow asks.

Thomas gives me a shove, and I lose my balance, stumbling forward. "This is Josef Zach," he says. "This other one is his neighbor, Anton Novak. I caught them poaching." Thomas tosses the antler rack onto the floor in front of the judge, saying, "Josef here shot a buck, and it appears the two of them stored the meat in their icehouse."

Thomas's father bolts upright with a look of surprise. "Poaching, you say?"

My eyes have adjusted to the room's light, and I now can more clearly see the judge squinting over small, round spectacles. Though draped over an aging frame, Judge Spacek's features mirror his son's—the same raccoon eyes, the same cunning countenance, the same menacing manner. The judge wears a grimace on his stubbly face, which reveals a set of rapidly decaying teeth when he opens his mouth to speak. I become strangely mesmerized as I watch those teeth moving up and down, querying Thomas about the details of the crime. Does the judge suffer much discomfort from that mouthful of deterioration? I hope so—I hope he is suffering right now.

"Josef!" Thomas shouts. "The judge is talking to you!"

I wake from my trance, letting my gaze move from the judge's mouth up to his eyes. "What?" I utter without emotion.

"I said, what do you have to say for yourself?" the judge repeats impatiently.

"I needed to feed my family. That's all. Anton had nothin' to do with it. It was just a measly deer. I'm sure the prince won't miss it," I say with a slight smirk on my face, a smirk that's not lost on the judge.

Anton shakes his head. "Stop it, Josef," he whispers discreetly to me. "What are you doing? Don't make things worse!"

"You don't think the prince will miss it, do you?" Spacek shouts angrily. "Do you think this is a joke? No, this isn't a joke. This is a serious crime. This is thievery. You stole from the prince!" He pauses to let me think about that.

I am indeed thinking about it. I haven't considered it that way before. I didn't really think of it as stealing. I'd never heard of anyone being caught, let alone punished, for such a deed, and I now realize my punishment might be far greater than I'd expected.

The judge is speaking to Thomas, who has taken a position next to his father's desk. I have difficulty hearing them as they speak privately in German, but I hear Thomas mentioning Frantiska's name and *zwei Kinder*.

Eventually, Thomas steps away from the desk, and the judge says to Anton, "Anton, I understand that your complicity in this crime only extends to the concealment of the meat in your icehouse. For that, your fine is twenty guldens, to be deducted from your pay this fall in the fields. Do you understand?"

Anton sighs, letting his chin drop to his chest as he mutters, "Yes, I understand."

The judge continues, "And you will return the meat you have stolen."

"Yes, sir," Anton replies compliantly.

The judge then turns his attention back to me, saying, "You seem to be a bit of a troublemaker, wouldn't you agree, Herr Zach?"

I don't think the question requires an answer, so I remain silent.

"First, you disrespect the prince when he comes through the village, and now this," Judge Spacek says as he waves his hand dismissively in my direction. "We haven't had a poacher since I've been here in Krouna. In fact, the last time I had to deal with a poacher was back in Jarošov about twenty years ago. As I recall, I sentenced the offender to a few years in the Vítkovice iron mine, though I don't believe he actually survived to finish his sentence."

This is looking bleaker and bleaker, I realize. I think about Frantiska, Vincencie, and Antonin. How will they survive without me? Will Anton and Rose watch over them? I can only hope so. But what if I never come back from that iron mine? What then? What a fool I've been—a careless, defiant fool.

"There may be another way, however," I hear the judge say. I look up hopefully as the old man continues, "I understand you've almost completed your military obligation in the Imperial Army. Is that right?"

"Yes. Come July, my obligation will be complete."

"Have you seen any combat in those years?" asks the judge.

"Nope. Thankfully."

"Well, that may change."

"What's that mean?" I ask, afraid of where this is going.

"I will give you a choice, Herr Zach," says the judge. I hate being called that. I'm not an Austrian, and I find the term *Herr* to be offensive.

The judge goes on. "Emperor Franz Joseph requested reinforcements for his little war in Sardinia. Prince Bonaventura needs to fill a quota of conscripts for the 47th Kinsky Regiment. They are needed immediately at the front."

I've felt fortunate to avoid any military action thus far, and I'm not keen on going into battle now. "And if I don't wanna do that?"

"Well, Herr Zach, how do you feel about working the mine? It's your choice."

I consider this. As much as I fear combat, I'm not hopeful I'll survive years of hard labor in the mine at Vítkovice. Besides, won't this little war in Sardinia be over rather quickly, considering the strength and size of the Austrian Empire's military machine? And who are these Sardinians anyway? Do they really think they can stand up against Franz Joseph's army? I have no idea where Sardinia even is. It certainly can't be a very big kingdom, I think, if I've never even heard of it. Certainly, these Sardinians will be defeated in a matter of days, and I'll be back home before I know it. That sounds a lot better to me than several years in the mine.

Finally, I mumble, "I guess I'll join the regiment in Sardinia . . . wherever that is."

"Very well then," declares the judge. Turning toward Anton, he says, "Anton, go back to Josef's house and secure his rifle and uniform. Bring them here first thing in the morning."

"Can't I go get 'em?" I protest.

"No, you'll be held here until the other conscripts come from the surrounding villages," the judge says before turning to Thomas. "Lock him up, Thomas."

"With pleasure," his son replies, smiling smugly.

CHAPTER 6

FRANTISKA EXPECTS THE WORST when she sees Anton standing alone at her door, biting at his lower lip and unwilling to look her in the eyes. "Where's Josef?" she asks.

"Maybe we should sit down, Frantiska," he says hesitantly.

Now she is all but certain the worst is coming. She walks numbly to her table and sits down on one of Josef's stools.

"Where is he?" she repeats as Anton sits across the table from her.

"They kept him," Anton replies somberly.

"What do you mean, *kept him?*"

Anton carefully explains what occurred in Judge Spacek's office, but when he finishes, Frantiska sits stone-faced. Her eyes move toward the window, blinking nervously. To Anton, it seems as if Frantiska's mind is somewhere else, far from her small hovel. He doesn't speak for a long moment before he asks, "Frantiska? Did you hear what I said?"

"Yes, I heard you," she utters matter-of-factly, staring out the window. "If there's nothing else, I'll see you out," Frantiska says as she abruptly rises to her feet and marches stoically to the door, opening it wide.

Anton studies her carefully, finding her behavior strange and quite concerning. Rising from his seat, he retrieves Josef's uniform from the hook on the wall, grabs the rifle, and adds, "Rose or I will check on you in the morning if you'd like."

"No need, Anton," she replies indifferently as she closes the wooden door behind him.

The following morning, Frantiska busies herself preparing two sacks for Josef. One holds bread and dried meat, and a second, larger one contains extra clothing and supplies. She leaves Vincencie and Antonin with Rose and begins her trek toward the center of town. She wonders how Josef will fare in battle. He's just a stoneworker and carpenter, after all. She prays that he'll be strong enough to survive the ordeal and make his way back to her. She wants him back, even though she banished him from the house just yesterday. Certainly, he knows her true feelings, doesn't he? Frantiska shudders at the thought of Josef going off to fight thinking she doesn't want him back. She's determined to take these bags of food and supplies to him and tell him how she really feels. Otherwise, how will either of them survive their separation?

Frantiska has almost reached the administration building when she meets Anton, who is walking in the opposite direction. Anton is oddly silent, and she looks up at him questioningly.

"He's gone," Anton utters, almost inaudibly.

"Gone?" Frantiska asks, her voice breaking.

"I got there just in time to give Josef his gear and watch him leave with the other conscripts."

"So soon? Did he say anything? Did you talk to him?" she asks, with tears beginning to pool in her dark eyes.

"No, Frantiska, Josef didn't say a thing, and I didn't really know what to say either."

"But how could he leave so soon? I have food and supplies for him, and I need to tell him . . ." She coughs, her despair gripping at her throat, and she falls to her knees, her face buried in moist, stiff hands. "I need . . . to tell him that I . . . ," she moans softly.

"He knows, Frantiska. He knows," Anton assures her. He reaches down to pick up her bags and with some effort, helps Frantiska to her feet. With his arm around her for support, he walks her back home.

Frantiska sits at her table for a long time, trying to make sense of it all. Her earlier worries continue to haunt her. Does Josef think she is still angry with him? Does he think she doesn't love him? If she could only have seen him today before he left, she could have told him that all was forgiven.

Suddenly, she stands up to retrieve a small box from a cabinet in the corner of the room, a cabinet Josef built just after they were married. Frantiska sets the tin box on the table and opens it. Inside is something else that Josef made for her. It's a quill pen he fashioned out of a goose feather he found down by the pond. He secretly worked on the tip to harden it by heating it in hot ashes, flattening it out, and then rolling it firmly together with his fingers to create a durable point. He also arranged a trade with one of the village merchants for a small container of black ink, in exchange for some carpentry work. All of this, he proudly presented to her on her birthday four years ago. The pen is crudely made, but it is quite functional and is one of Frantiska's most prized possessions.

Returning to the corner cabinet she retrieves an envelope and some paper she's been judiciously hoarding. She addresses the envelope to the 47th Kinsky Regiment, Imperial Army, Wien, Austria—the regiment Anton told her Josef is joining. Then, from the small stack of coarse paper, she selects a single page and writes "My Dearest Josef, . . ."

CHAPTER 7

WE TRUDGE ALONG the dirt road moving south from Krouna. We've been told our destination—first Brno for two days of training, and then on to Wien by train. From there, we'll be traveling southwest toward Milan in northern Italia to be deployed with our regiment in the field. None of this holds any meaning for me. I've never been to Brno, let alone Wien or Milan, and I've only just heard of the contraptions they call trains. I've never actually seen one.

How I miss my Frantiska. Is she still angry with me? If so, I can hardly blame her. I've been stupid and careless. I let her down, her and the children. What a fool I've been. I wonder if they might be better off without me. Perhaps it would be best if I never came home at all. Maybe if my body is left rotting on the battlefield, Anton and Rose will take better care of my family. But what if that viper Thomas Spacek worms his way into the lives of Frantiska and the children? Thomas raising my children? The thought infuriates me, and I intensify my grip on my rifle, swallowing hard as I revel in my raging hate for the man. No, I can't let that happen. Thomas can't have her, and he certainly can't have my children. It occurs to me I have something to live for after all. Perhaps Frantiska won't take me back, but I'll be damned if I let Thomas have her. I'll kill Thomas first. I'll survive these next few weeks, if for no other reason than the satisfaction of feeling my grip around Thomas's fleshy neck.

For the first time, I look around to scrutinize the men marching with me. Besides the horseman, I count ten soldiers, all clad in their Austrian military uniforms: light blue slacks, dark blue coats, and tall medallioned hats.

Several appear to be experienced, exhibiting at least a modicum of military training like myself. These men are carrying their rifles with confidence, as if they know how to use them. About half the men, however, don't even have a weapon. Several of them look anxious, even frightened. How will two days of training in Brno prepare these green recruits to fight effectively? And why is the infantry in such a hurry to get these men to the front line? Certainly, a few more days or weeks of drills would be a good idea. Otherwise, they'll be little more than target practice for the enemy. I hope for their sake they won't have to face the enemy anytime soon, or at all. Hopefully, the fighting in Sardinia will be over by the time we get there. Certainly, the massive power of the Austrian Empire will prevail once again, and do it in short order.

Our training in Brno is short, and we are soon readying ourselves for travel. On a crisp morning, they shove us into five boxcars originally used for transporting vegetables, linens, and glassware. But the empire is at war, and soldiers are in these cars today. I'm at once fascinated by this train machine. How could man have invented such a thing? It's truly an otherworldly contraption. Everything about it is beyond my imagination and description, a fantastical apparatus that must be experienced to be appreciated fully–
–the acrid smell of the belching stacks, the deafening squeal of the braking iron wheels, the explosive discharges of pressurized steam, the incredible speed. It's a magical thing, this mechanical beast charging across the countryside—a remarkable intersection of iron wheel and iron track.

The time passes quickly as the train rolls along with its human cargo, making stops to pick up more units in Wien, and onward to places like Graz and Klangenfurt. Awed by the countryside flying by, we take turns standing near the open door to gaze in amazement at the spectacle. I feel like

I'm flying. Such speed I've never imagined. In two days, the train makes its way into Italia, where it stops in Mestre and Padua. Then it's on toward Vicenza and Verona, eventually arriving at our final destination in Milan with brakes screeching and smoke belching, the iron beast shuddering to a clanging halt.

Explosions erupt to the west, far beyond the front of the train, and I hear what sounds like gunfire much closer. Grabbing my weapon I cautiously peer out the boxcar door. Surprisingly, the train has stopped well short of the train station, and when I look down the tracks, I can see why. The station appears to be under siege, with men in close combat with their sabers and bayonets. Some of our unit clamber off the train and stand by the tracks, wondering what we should do. Gunfire hits the boxcar, and some of the younger recruits shrink back into the safety of the interior. Suddenly, the line of Austrian defense breaks, and blue-coated enemy combatants charge forward toward the train, firing as they come.

No Austrian officers are in sight, and I know that if we stay here without leadership, we'll soon be victims of a massacre. Looking in the other direction, I notice Austrian troops already fleeing the area, and I scream, "Run!" pushing men away from the oncoming attackers. "That way!" I point. "Move!"

The men now understand the direness of our situation and begin running with heads down, dodging incoming gunfire behind us. The sound of ricocheting bullets, the screaming of the injured and dying, and the frenzied retreat of the desperate men paint a chaotic scene. Fortunately, most of my comrades find cover behind houses and shops. Our training finally kicks in, and we return fire to slow the enemy's approach along the tracks. There's adequate cover behind a boxcar at the end of the train, so I stop to watch the enemy troops reach the open boxcar where I stood just moments earlier. Several of the young recruits still cowering in the boxcar are being thrown out upon the ground and executed where they lie, and I shudder at the sight. Those poor souls, I think. But there's no time to linger.

I hear shouting behind me, and I can see an Austrian officer on horseback waving his saber, yelling in German. I doubt my company of Bohemian soldiers understand a word he's saying, but they all recognize the motion of his saber. It signals a retreat, and they're more than ready to run in the officer's direction. I look back once more toward the oncoming assault and see one of my young comrades lying on the ground next to the train. An officer clad in red and blue pulls his saber from its scabbard, and I know he intends to bring it down on the frightened young soldier. I should be retreating with the rest of my unit, but I raise my rifle, steadying it against the corner of the boxcar, taking careful aim, breathing five counts in, five out. My mind slides back to that moment up on Burnt Hill when I stood next to the large oak, taking aim at the buck. That was an animal; this is a man. I'm about to shoot a human being. I find it ironic that my decision to shoot that buck led directly to this moment—this moment when I am to make a similar decision. But this is a very different target—a human target. What would Frantiska say to this? Will she ever forgive me for what I'm about to do? Five counts in, five out. The officer raises his saber high over his head and begins to bring the blade down. My aim is a bit high, but the slug still hits the officer on the side of his neck, and he collapses, his saber clattering to the ground some distance away. I hesitate, watching longer in morbid fascination as the officer lies there writhing on the ground in his own blood.

I continue watching just long enough to see another soldier finish the slain officer's job. He runs his bayonet into the young Bohemian lad still lying on the ground. There's little I can do but turn and run with the rest of the men as they follow the mounted officer along the tracks, away from the attack. There is gunfire now coming from various vantage points ahead of me, and I realize Austrian riflemen are providing cover for us as we try to move out of harm's way. Perhaps we'll get out of this alive after all, I think. The officer leads us past a barricade that's been hastily constructed on the street. Behind the barricade are about fifty riflemen and two big artillery guns. One of the cannons discharges with a deafening blast just as I run past the fortification to safety. The blast almost knocks me to the ground, but I keep my balance and stand in a protected spot behind the fortification, where I hurriedly reload my musket.

The rifleman standing at the barricade next to me is one of the soldiers who arrived with me on the train. Like me, he remained behind to join the fray. As I reload my weapon, I yell to my co-fighter, "Who are these Sardinians? They're fierce bastards, aren't they?"

"Those aren't Sardinian soldiers," he replies. "Those are French soldiers. And yes, they're damned good."

French soldiers? No one told me I'd fight both Sardinia and France. I stand to fire into the mass of blue and red uniforms in front of me, but the French line is firing with such intensity I can hardly get off a shot. The other men at the barricade are having trouble returning fire too, and I know the barricade will not hold for long. Thankfully, two teams of horses arrive with caissons and limbers. Soon, they hook up to drag the big guns to safety, and as they pull away, we are all eager to make our retreat as well.

The fighting is chaotic as we retreat through the town. Doorway to doorway, street corner to street corner, the battle rages as we fall back. Firing as we run, we step over dead and bloodied comrades in our retreat. This is not the fighting they have trained me for. There's no orderliness or strategy in this kind of engagement. Only individual survival—every man for himself. I've but one goal: to get as far away as I can from the French fighters firing at me. I tell myself that I'm an Austrian soldier brought here to help put down a Sardinian uprising, not defeat France. At this moment, I only want to live to see another day, and if that requires more running than fighting, so be it.

It takes the Austrian force far too long to retreat and take a position on the east edge of town, on the east bank of a small river. Finally, I get a good look at the size of our force. Regiment after regiment of infantry and cavalry, thousands of men, and more cannons than I can count. How can a force this large be taking such a beating? I wonder.

Evening thankfully falls, and the darkness brings a welcome respite from the fighting. I wander about in search of my fellow Bohemians from the train. Eventually, I approach an officer to ask about the 47th Kinsky Regiment. The officer speaks only German, and I struggle to use the very few German words I know. I somehow make him understand, and he finds a piece of paper to write my plight down in German to aid me in finding my regiment. The officer then points in the direction I should begin my search for the 47th.

I walk along the river bank, venturing into a mass of injured and tired troops, many lying on the ground, all of them eating what food they can find and tending to their wounds and those of their comrades. A general calm has fallen over the camp, and I notice that the big guns are being drawn down a dirt road away from the encampment, heading east, away from Milan. So this huge fighting force is giving up and retreating?

As I continue in search of my regiment, I see more and more companies of men regrouping to march east under the veil of darkness. My hopes of joining my regiment dwindle as more and more troops move out, so I join one of the Austrian units and march eastward. By sunrise, the riverbank is abandoned. The Austrian army is in full retreat, relinquishing Lombardy to the enemy and falling back toward Venetia.

Near sunset the following day, the huge columns of men finally halt and encamp on a defensible ridge offering a clear view of the Italian countryside. The massive Austrian force has now consolidated in numbers close to a hundred thousand, all scattered along the ridge and around it in the woodland areas.

It's far into the night before I finally encounter someone who speaks my language. He's a captain in my regiment, the 47th Kinsky Regiment. And although he's a Bohemian like me, he's a man of much higher breeding and station. Captain Brodsky speaks both German and Bohemian, and he's tall and lean, holding himself with a striking confidence. He seems younger than me, probably gifted his position by political appointment, and I assume he's the product of one of those transplanted Austrian families bequeathed an estate in Bohemia generations ago. I doubt the man has had much fighting experience, Still, who am I to judge? I myself just killed my first enemy combatant the previous day.

Saluting, I say, "Sir, my name is Josef Zach. I just arrived from Bohemia to join the 47th Regiment."

"Ah, yes. You're one of those unfortunates who were involved in that mess near the train depot."

"Yep. That was us, sir," I respond.

"The rest of your friends, or what's left of them, have been straggling in all evening. Most of them are over there," the captain says as he points. "You'll be serving in Lieutenant Barta's company."

"Barta? Yes sir," I say as I walk in that direction. I stop, turning back to the captain. "Sir? May I ask where we're headed?"

He says, "We got quite a thrashing from Foyer's French division today, as you know. So General Gyulai is taking us east to regroup at the Quadrilateral. Hopefully, we can counterattack from there if the general has the stomach for it, which I seriously doubt."

"The Quadrilateral?" I ask.

"Four forts that defend Venetia, and ultimately the Austrian border," he explains. "We'll most likely end up in the fortification of Verona or Padua. One of those two, or maybe both, I would imagine."

None of that information is particularly helpful to me. But the mention of Venetia tells me I am headed back in the direction I came from the day before, and that sounds good to me.

"How far away is that?" I ask.

"I'd say around a five-day march. We'll be trying to move fast to stay ahead of the French, who you can bet are on our tail."

"Why are the French in this war, anyway? I thought we were fighting Sardinians."

"Well, I guess Napoleon III has as much thirst for conquest as his wretched uncle did," the captain answers.

That doesn't answer my question, but I've taxed the officer's attention far too long already. "*Danke schön, Hauptmann*," I say in my rudimentary German before heading to join my company.

It seems to take forever for our massive army to reach its destination. The Italian countryside, with its woodlands, fields, hills, and vineyards, makes for difficult going. Occasionally, we're brought to a near-standstill as we confront bottlenecks in the difficult terrain. But if it's slow going for our Austrian force, it must be just as difficult for the French/Sardinian divisions chasing us. Our march is arduous, and we trudge from early morning well into the evening. It takes a full week for our massive force to finally reach Solferino, a small village just outside Verona.

As we set up camp, I can sense nervousness from several of the officers. And soon, I hear rumors about the officers' lack of confidence in Gyulai's leadership ability. I even hear that Gyulai might soon be relieved of his duties, considering the army's poor showing in the earlier battles at Montebello and Magenta. I wonder how an army under such leadership can successfully fight any war, let alone one against the combined French and Sardinian forces.

I'm exhausted from the march, and I can see my comrades feel the same. One of them is Jan Havel, my comrade from the barricade. Jan is from the town of Pardubice and is the son of a clothing merchant. We have little in common beyond our Bohemian origins, but I find the man to be informed about political affairs, or at least much more informed than myself. Over the previous days of the march, Jan explained what he knew of the events leading up to the war we now fight. I understood most of what Jan told me. But this has little effect on my commitment to the conflict between the warring nations. Why can't France just mind its own damn business? If it wasn't for the French support, the Sardinians would probably be soundly defeated by now. I'd already be on the train back toward Brno, and then home to Krouna.

"When do you think we'll finish this thing?" I ask Jan.

Shrugging, he answers, "Hard to tell. I'm just a pissant soldier like you, Josef. How would I know what Franz Joseph or Napoleon has in store for us?"

The following morning, as my unit sits around our campfires, we hear from the officers that General Gyulai has indeed been relieved of duty. The second bit of news is that Emperor Franz Joseph himself has arrived to personally lead the army from this point forward. This news is well received by the officers, for they hold little regard for Gyulai's abilities to lead. Still, according to Jan, the emperor's lack of military experience doesn't leave his officers with high hopes either. While Franz Joseph fought well as an officer against the Italians in 1848, he's never commanded an entire army in battle before. What will happen when Franz Joseph attempts to lead them against the fierce fighting machine that has ably handled his forces thus far in this war?

Two days later, our army remains near Verona, licking our wounds and regaining our strength, if not our confidence. Finally, on the third day, I notice a nervousness about the encampment, and soon, rumors surface of a new offensive in the making. Late that morning, Lieutenant Barta rides in among the trees where we're bivouacked. He dismounts, secures his horse to a nearby tree, and strides purposefully toward Jan, me, and several others in the company. We all spring to our feet as he approaches.

"We have new orders, men," the lieutenant declares. "We received word that the French have halted their progress and are now encamped near Brescia. This is our chance to make our counterattack, and maybe surprise 'em. Spread the word to the company that we march tomorrow at daybreak."

When he finishes, he waits for neither comment nor question, but turns and walks quickly toward his mount. As he pulls himself up on the animal, he turns back toward us, pulling out his saber, and shouting, "This time, let's show those Frenchies some steel!" His enthusiasm brings staccato shouts from many of the men, but I'm not one of them. Haven't these men seen enough killing? I've watched a French officer fall from my bullet. I think about the way his blood gushed from his neck, congealing with dirt and gravel on the ground, and the image of it still sickens me. I also think about the boy bayoneted on the ground afterward.

There has already been too much bloodshed, and I wonder how I'll be able to continue the killing tomorrow.

CHAPTER 8
BOHEMIA

ANNA KREJSA COMES from undistinguished Bohemian stock, born to undistinguished peasants from an undistinguished village. Her exaggerated Slavic features, more rounded than chiseled, might have brought her ridicule had she been born elsewhere. But in the village of Jarošov, most of the children looked just like her. They all eventually outgrew their rotund juvenile features upon reaching puberty. All of them except for Anna, that is, who took a few years more to shed the corpulent veneer of her youth. Now, at twenty-one, she's still rather round and somewhat awkward in her carriage. But she's an intelligent woman with a bright disposition who learned to read at an early age and longs to explore the world beyond Jarošov.

And so, with no serious suitors at her father's door, Anna ventures out to see what life might grant her. This decision, of course, is not received well by her parents, simple farm laborers living on a small acreage of potatoes and beets. They see little future for a young woman out in the world alone. Still, Anna is a bit of a burden on the household, another mouth to feed for a family struggling in poverty. Indeed, her father has mixed feelings when she tells him about the opportunity to take a parish teaching position in a village called Krouna.

On the twenty-third of June, the same day Josef's company is readying for battle near Solferino, Anna enters Krouna, sitting atop a horse-drawn dray driven by her father. In her hands is the wrinkled piece of paper she received weeks ago from her pastor in Jarošov. The paper announced the job opening and its meager benefits, and Anna now intends to discuss each of these benefits with her prospective employer. Her salary is to be paid by donations from the children's families, and her housing allowance is next to nothing. Still, it's employment, and Anna is resolved to succeed in this first chapter of her adulthood. As Anna and her father arrive in Krouna, it's already midday. They pull to a stop in front of a modest building where Pastor Košút stands by the road, taking stock of his wilting flower garden.

"Hello. Are you the reverend?" asks Anna's father.

"Yes. May I be of service to you?" the pastor replies.

"I'm Johann Krejsa, and this is my daughter, Anna. She's here about the teaching position."

"Ah, Miss Krejsa. Of course. Welcome. I've been expecting you. Would you two wish to come inside?" Pastor Košút asks as he points toward the building.

Bordered on one side by a small cemetery, the pastor's church is a simple structure, with no steeple—just a two-room log building. If not for the adjacent cemetery and the man standing outside in clerical attire, it would have been difficult for Anna to identify this structure as anything other than a haybarn or a shed for storage. But as Anna and her father follow the pastor into the building, she now sees crude benches set up in rows and a small, rough-hewn cross on the front wall. Further on, there's an attached smaller room, a classroom by the looks of it. Small, dusty desks and stools are shoved to one side, and a small, distressed teacher's desk sits in front of the chalkboard at the far end. Anna doesn't see any teaching materials except for a few worn books clumsily arranged on a shelf by the wall. Pastor Košút watches Anna as she examines the classroom. She hasn't spoken a word yet, and he wonders what she thinks of the facility.

He says, "I think once we get all the desks and stools arranged, it'll look a lot more like a classroom. We haven't been able to hold classes here for quite a while. I just can't find a teacher. The parents can't help much. Many can't read nor write themselves, and the ones who can just don't seem to have the time. I'd do it myself, but I don't feel I can give the children the attention they deserve. That's why we're so glad you're interested. You are interested, aren't you?"

Anna looks at him and smiles, answering, "Yes, I'm very interested." Then she adds, more confidently, "This room will be just fine."

"Can you tell me about your experience? Have you taught children before?"

"Well, no. Not exactly. Unless you count my little cousin. I'm teaching him to read and write."

"Hmm. Is that the extent of it?" Pastor Košút had hoped for more. "Tell me about your schooling, Miss Krejsa."

"The pastor's wife in Jarošov took me through all the primary levels," Anna answers.

Her father, who stands several paces away, interjects, "Anna's very smart. She reads well, and her handwriting is beautiful. You saw her letter, right?"

"Yes, I did. It was very well written indeed," replies the pastor. This girl seems so young, and he wonders if she can handle a class of students, keeping them on task and behaving. But, of course, how much choice does he have? He's been trying for over a year to find someone interested in this position. She'll just have to do. If she doesn't work out, he can always send her packing back to Jarošov, he figures.

"If you'd like the job, we'd be happy to have you," he says finally. "Do you have questions?"

Anna ponders for a moment and then says, "I was wondering how many students I'll have in my class."

"Well, that depends on you. I have a list of families with children. You'll need to visit them to see if they want their children to attend or not. Some may not be able to afford the small donation we are asking for, and maybe others won't think reading and writing are important. You'll have to convince them."

"I suppose I can try to do that. And about my living allowance?"

"That's negotiable, but it should cover most of your housing costs."

Her father walks up to join them and says, "I'm wondering about Anna's immediate living arrangements."

"Oh, you don't need to worry. She can stay with my wife and me until we can find her other accommodations. We'll take good care of her."

Anna's father seems to be satisfied with that and turns to Anna, asking, "Well, Anna, what do you think? Shall we get your bags from the wagon?"

"*Ano, Tatínku.* Yes, Father, let's do that."

The next day, Anna wastes no time getting started. Soon she's walking down the path that bisects Krouna, intent on visiting all the families the pastor has included on her list. Going door-to-door, she finds many of these people rather standoffish, reluctant to engage in conversation, and when Anna knocks on their doors she figures they might at first think she is one of those itinerate types who occasionally wander through town asking for handouts. After all, her simple attire doesn't set her above any other commoner who might happen by. But when she identifies herself as the new teacher, she's happy to find that most of the cottagers of Krouna warm up to her and eagerly welcome her inside.

It's close to noon when she walks up to the home of Josef and Frantiska Zach. Standing at the door, she can hear the sound of a loom working at a steady rhythm within. A girl plays nearby under the meager shade of a small tree, and Anna approaches the girl, careful not to frighten her.

"*Dobrý den*! Hello. What's your name?" asks Anna cheerfully.

"I'm Vincencie," the little girl replies with trepidation. "Are you here to see my mother?"

"Yes, and your father too, if possible."

"He's not here. He's in a war," Vincencie replies matter-of-factly.

"Oh, my. That's too bad. I bet you miss him, don't you?" Anna asks, trying to put the child at ease.

"Sometimes, I guess."

Anna converses with the girl for a while longer before the front door suddenly swings open, and Frantiska steps out into the sunlight, eyeing the stranger suspiciously.

"Is there something you need?" she asks firmly.

Looking up at Frantiska, Anna hesitates, her brow furrowed as she takes a step closer. "Do I know you from somewhere?" Anna asks, looking down at the name on her list and reading the woman's first name aloud. "Frantiska," she whispers. Looking back at Frantiska, she exclaims, "I do know you! You're Frantiska Kosina, aren't you? From Jarošov, right?"

"Why, yes," Frantiska exclaims, eyeing the woman in puzzlement.

"Well, don't you recognize me? I'm Anna Krejsa. You used to know my older sister."

Frantiska's mouth falls open as she takes in a breath of surprise. "You're little Anna Krejsa? Last time I saw you, you were what?—ten years old?"

"Yes, that's me. I'm the new teacher at the parish," Anna says, letting her inflection rise as if it is a question to be answered.

Frantiska relaxes, smiling. "Of course you are! How wonderful! Won't you come in?"

Frantiska leads Anna into the modest abode. The large loom occupies most of the space in the one-room home, and the family's table and crude beds take up the rest, but Anna notes that the place is clean and tidy. There is much to talk about: catching up on mutual childhood friends, reminiscing about the parish school where they both studied with the pastor's wife in Jarošov, and their life histories since last they saw each other.

Frantiska notices that both her children take an immediate liking to this young woman. Soon, Anna is holding Antonin on her lap while helping Vincencie dress her small doll.

"Vincencie looks to be around six, is that right?" Anna asks.

"Yes, well, almost. Next month she will be."

"Will you be sending her to my class, then?" Anna inquires, then adds, "It really shouldn't cost you too much."

Frantiska hesitates, looking down into her lap, her cheerful disposition turning at once to disappointment. "I wish I could. I just don't know how I can afford it," she says sadly. "With my husband gone, it's been very difficult. I'm surviving on whatever I can make from my weaving trade, which isn't much. So I don't think Vincencie can attend, I'm afraid. I've just been teaching her myself when I find the time."

Frantiska realizes she has unloaded far too many of her concerns on Anna. Embarrassed, she looks contritely at Anna, adding, "I'm sorry. I didn't mean to burden you with my problems."

"Don't give it any mind, Frantiska. But I would love to have Vincencie in my class. Perhaps you and I can work something out. Let me finish visiting the families on my list," Anna says, lifting her list from the table. "Then perhaps, in a couple of days, after I secure a place to live, I can come back to talk again."

"I won't take charity, Anna."

"I understand," replies the woman, "but maybe there is some other way you can pay me. Perhaps in linens or blankets, or . . ." Anna pauses and glances around the room. "Would you consider letting me live here in return for Vincencie's schooling?"

"Are you serious? In this little place? How would we fit?"

"I don't know. Maybe I could sleep on the floor, or—"

"Or," interrupts Frantiska, with the excitement of discovery in her eyes, "Vincencie could sleep with me and you could have her bed."

"That would be perfect. My living allowance isn't much, but it would easily cover Vincencie's school obligation, and maybe even let you earn a little profit as well."

Frantiska looks at her two small children, asking, "How do you two feel about that? Would you like to have Miss Krejsa living here with us?" They both nod their heads with ample enthusiasm.

"Then it's settled," declares Anna, smiling broadly.

CHAPTER 9
ITALIA

I CAN'T SLEEP, and it's obvious from the evening disquiet around the camp that many other men in the 47th Kinsky Regiment can't either. The Austrian army, one hundred thousand strong, is gearing up to meet a force of similar magnitude. I don't want to think about the carnage that will result from the ensuing battle. I know I'll be lucky to live to see another nightfall, and my thoughts turn to Frantiska. I want to hold her one more time, but all I have are memories of the smell of her hair and the sound of her soft voice. Still, I know that when the sun ascends in the morning, all reveries of Frantiska will need to move to the background of my thoughts. Tomorrow, I must concentrate only on survival. Otherwise, I will have no hope of ever seeing Frantiska again.

I sit in the dark, my face illuminated only by the flames licking up through the spent logs of the campfire, waiting for the sun to make its unwelcome appearance. If only it would stay low beyond the eastern Italian hills. But I shake my head at the absurdity of that.

Suddenly, it occurs to me that I could probably escape from the camp under the cover of night. No one would notice, would they? I'd look like a soldier walking to join my regiment bivouacked on the edge of the encampment, and then I could slip away through the trees without being noticed. It'd be easy. This isn't my war, anyway. What do I care if the Austrian Empire maintains control here in Italia? Besides, there aren't any members of the Habsburg family out here getting ready for battle, that's for sure. They're all back in their palaces sipping fancy wine or whatever they drink waiting to hear of their great victory over the French forces. Why am I the one who must fight their battles? Should I have to risk my life for them?

Jan has dozed off, sitting by the fire across from me with his chin now fallen to his chest. Several other men from my unit are also nearby, sitting by their fading fires, either sleeping or lost in their thoughts. As quietly as possible, I roll my blanket and secure my satchel. Slowly getting to my feet, I reach for my rifle and turn to walk away.

"Where do you think you're going?" Jan has awakened and is now stoking the fire with a long stick. His gaze doesn't meet my eyes but is trained on the fading coals before him.

"Uh…I'm just heading over…"

"You're not leaving, are you?" he asks, finally looking up at me.

"I was thinking about it," I admit as I glare at him unapologetically.

"You probably think you're going to get away with it. You probably think no one will miss you and that you'll make your way home and live your life peacefully, right?"

"Something like that," I say, realizing it all sounds a little naïve.

"You'll be a deserter, Josef."

"Not if they don't notice I'm missing," I answer. "You're not going to tell 'em are you?"

"No, Josef, I won't. But you can be sure Lieutenant Barta will notice. And so will the other men you've left behind to fight this battle without you."

A tinge of guilt shoots through my mind, but it's only a tinge. "So what if they notice? What do I really care as long as I get as far from here as I can?"

"Why are you running? Are you afraid?"

What a stupid question, I'm thinking. Of course, I'm afraid. But I'm not about to give him the satisfaction of hearing me admit it. "Afraid? No," I answer. "But I have no stake in this war. Why should I die for no reason? You should come with me."

He continues poking at the fire for several seconds before saying, "So you're not afraid, huh? Well, I sure as hell am. That's why I won't be going with you, Josef," he answers.

"What's that supposed to mean," I ask, confused.

"If you run and make your way home, I guarantee that the news of your desertion will reach the authorities there before you even arrive. They might not arrest you on the first day, but by the second, you'll surely be in their custody. And by the third day? You'll most likely be dead. Now, if you're not afraid to die, go ahead—make a run for it. But if you want to live, you will at least have a chance if you stay and fight with the rest of us."

I look up through the airborne ashes of the fire considering my options. Slowly, I shuffle over to Jan. I lay my rifle, satchel, and blanket on the ground, and sit down, cross-legged, next to him. We sit there together in silence for a while before I speak.

"OK, I'm afraid; I admit it, Jan. It's one thing to be thrown into a battle like in Milan, but this is different. It's the waiting that's unbearable. It gives me time to realize just how fearful I am of dying, never to see Frantiska and the children ever again," I finally say, gazing into the flames.

A moment passes, and I wonder if Jan has heard me speaking to him, but soon, he offers, "My uncle fought in an uprising in Kraków. I think it was in '45 or '46. I remember him describing his fear as he sat through a night just like we are now, waiting to do battle, worried he would not be up to the task. My uncle had no ill feelings toward the Poles, he told me. In fact, he respected their desire for independence. But he knew he had to be ready to fight them. He told me he realized something that night as he sat there. He realized that if he wanted to survive the battle, he would have to rid himself of any thoughts of morality. He wouldn't be able to fight if he held any strong sense of right and wrong. He had been taught for his entire life that killing was morally wrong. But he knew that kind of thinking might make him hesitate at the very moment an enemy soldier was upon him, and it would be that hesitation that would most likely be the death of him. You can't bring your morals to the battlefield, Josef."

Morals? Jan is talking about morals? How does the rightness and wrongness of things matter to me? All I know is poverty and the lack of hope that goes with it. I'm not even sure morality can exist without hope—can it? Besides, what kind of moral code can possibly bring relief from my hard life?

"Morals? I've hardly ever given morals much thought," I finally respond.

Jan turns to me with surprise in his eyes. "What do you mean? Of course, you have morals. Certainly, you've been taught God's Word, have you not? Certainly, you know how to—"

"God has done me no favors, Jan," I interrupt. "I tried living by God's rules once, but look where it got me. As it turned out, God never held up his part of our bargain."

"Well, you've got to live by someone's rules."

"Hmm…well, I suppose you could say I live by my own rule. You wanna hear what it is?"

"Do I have a choice?" Jan asks. I ignore his question for I realize something. It's only now, at this moment, that I finally understand clearly what that rule is. And I'm not about to stop until I say it out loud.

"All I can do, Jan, is try to make it to the next day. That's the only rule that makes any sense to me. Making it to the next day is all I can expect from this life."

Jan is nodding heavily, and he squeezes his lips tightly together. I wonder if those lips hold back a torrent of disapproval and judgement just waiting to burst forth. But that's not what happens. Instead, he calmly says, "I understand, Josef—believe me, I do. You're talking about survival, and you know what? That desire to survive might just work for you tomorrow on the battlefield. Can you see that? There's something else, too. You're going to have to fight, and you're going to have to kill with all the brutality you can muster. And if you aren't ready to do that, you'll probably not make it. Tomorrow it will be necessary to shamelessly do whatever is necessary."

"To shamelessly do what is necessary? Hell, I've been doing that all my life. But I doubt that's all there is to it."

"Well, no, you're right about that—there is one more thing. You won't survive any battle without hatred and rage, I suppose. My uncle told me that he tried to fill himself with an intense feeling of hatred for the enemy. He said he saw the enemy soldiers as worthless and vile beings, deserving of killing, not as human beings. He tried to imagine that it would feel good to kill them—to rid the world of their existence.

"Of course, the rebels were untrained and poorly armed in that conflict," Jan continues. "The Austrian forces had little problem putting down the revolt. The battle we will face tomorrow? That's going to be much different. It'll be long and bloody. We've seen the French army fight. They're well-trained and well-armed. This won't be easy. The French will fight us fiercely because that's the way they're trained to fight. The French soldier's mind is conditioned for killing. Those Sardinians will fight fiercely because they truly hate us; we invaded their country after all. We'll have to hate them more than they hate us, I suppose."

There's only one person I truly hate: Thomas Spacek. I find it easy to see Spacek as a worthless piece of mule dung, unworthy of his next breath. It would be easy to slaughter him like any rabid vermin. This hatred is finding a home deep inside me, and I don't attempt to resist its emerging hold on me. I invite it—welcome it. In my mind, each combatant I face tomorrow will be Thomas Spacek, worthy only of the thrust of my bayonet.

It's just past daybreak when I watch two companies of Austrian grenadiers marching in four long columns on the road in the valley below. Following them is a procession of big artillery guns, hitched to caissons and limbers pulled by anxious two-horse teams. I count at least sixty of the big guns. It's an amazing sight, and I wonder how any army could stand against such firepower. Still, I've seen the Austrian army manhandled before.

Suddenly, Lieutenant Barta rides into the encampment to assess the readiness of our company. He calls out, "Let's go, men. The 47th is moving out."

The men pick up their weapons, secure their supply satchels, and hurry out of the trees and down the hill, falling into formation behind the passing artillery unit. I'm ready to fight, ready to kill any damn Frenchman or Sardinian who stands in my way. Overnight, I let hatred fester inside me, and I encouraged it—nurtured it. I now feel ready to bring that rage upon the enemy. Trotting down the hill, I am one of the first in my company to make it to the road as I take my place at the front, trudging purposefully with my eyes fixed forward. It will be quite a distance to the Chiese River where we plan to attack the opposing force, and I'm eager to get on with it.

CHAPTER 10

JAN HAVEL SLOWLY PACKS up his gear, and finally moves down toward the column to join the rear of the company. He jogs past Lieutenant Barta, who is still astride his mount, urging his men down the hillside to the road. Suddenly, another horseman appears beside the lieutenant, pulling hard on the reins to bring his mount to a standstill. Without a word, the horseman hands something to Barta. As Jan hurries past, the lieutenant shouts to him, "Havel, hold up a moment. Where is your friend Josef?"

Jan points to the front of the column, which is by now far down the road, marching westward. "There, near the front of the company, sir."

Barta thrusts the letter toward Jan, saying, "Here, this is for him. Can you get it to him?"

"Yes, sir," Jan replies, as he slings his rifle over his shoulder and reaches for the letter. He shoves it deep into his jacket pocket before he turns and continues down the hill toward his company on the road.

At that moment, the valley below erupts with the deafening explosions of an incoming artillery salvo. The erstwhile orderliness of the infantry columns now degenerates into a chaotic dash for cover. Men run in all directions, trying desperately to escape the bombardment falling like deadly rain all around them.

It's obvious to everyone that the enemy has advanced from their encampment at Brescia during the night. They are launching a preemptive strike, and their artillery is doing it with pinpoint accuracy. They inundate the valley with blasts as shell fragments and resultant human body parts scatter through the smoke in all directions.

Reacting to a nearby shell explosion, Jan Havel ducks down and glances back toward Lieutenant Barta, who is now lying on the ground, thrown from his mount. Jan rushes back to help him as another shell falls nearby, exploding into a hundred molten fragments. One of the larger fragments impales the side of Jan's head, obliterating it into flaps of flesh and brain, grotesque and unrecognizable. His limp body falls to the ground and twitches there for a time, bleeding onto the Italian hillside. Barta pulls himself off the ground, but he has little time to linger over Jan's body, or what's left of it. He rushes down the hillside, yelling orders to his men, who are near the road below, dazed and disorganized.

CHAPTER 11

LYING IN A DITCH next to an adjacent vineyard, I can hear Barta yelling and pointing his saber, and up the road I see what he's pointing at. The grenadier and artillery companies have moved ahead, beyond the area of the bombardment, and Lieutenant Barta is urging us to move in that same direction and out of harm's way. Struggling to my feet, I begin running with the rest of my comrades toward the cannoneers.

Unable to spread out among the thick grapevines bordering the road, my company races forward in two columns. Shell explosions can be heard behind me as the French guns continue to pummel the valley, and there is rifle fire ahead where I spot several officers directing their troops into the vineyards, organizing them into firing lines. Our artillery units have come to a stop in the road, and the grenadiers have taken positions in front to protect the big guns. Our artillery won't have time to unhitch and engage the enemy, and it will be up to the grenadiers and fusiliers to face the enemy without artillery support. Soon, our firing lines are bombarding the French troops, who return fire with equal intensity.

There is a collective shout in the distance. Through the smoke and gunfire, soldiers in blue and red uniforms race from the French position toward our line, firing as they come. A nearby officer screams, *"Hier kommen Sie! Feuer frei!"* and we shoot wildly at the attacking force.

The 47th Regiment has spread itself out on either side of the road among the vineyards, which extend to a hayfield just ahead. I and the rest of my company are now firing at the line of fighters charging toward us through the open field. Smoke is rising from the deafening barrage of our musket fire, and several enemy soldiers fall, lifeless, under the first fusillade. Soon, the French assault comes to a halt, and their combatants fall back to their original positions. They organize into firing lines and trade barrages according to their officers' commands.

Hurrying to reload, I hear the regiment captain shouting orders to advance on the French line. An Austrian bugle sounds and the entire line of our infantrymen bursts out of the vineyards and into the hayfield. We leave behind our artillery company, which is still scrambling to prepare the big guns for operation. I am heartened by our advance, and we continue to fire and reload as we march steadily forward.

Suddenly, war cries erupt further to my right, coming from French throats. Another enemy charge is coming to meet us. I look toward the shouting and can see a single French soldier who has stepped out in front of his own firing line. He wears baggy red pants, a short blue jacket, and an odd fez-like hat. I recognize him as a Zouave. I've heard about these Zouaves during our training in Brno. The Zouaves are fierce French fighters known for their courage on the battlefield. They fought effectively in the Crimean War and accounted for themselves bravely in the French victories in Magenta and Milan. They are a formidable foe indeed, and the French will have the advantage in this battle with fighting men like that.

The Zouave soldier raises his bayoneted rifle into the air and lets out a chilling battle cry. The company of men in the line behind him, all similarly dressed, answers in unison. They at once begin racing toward our line, yelling as they come. The Zouaves throw themselves onto our fusiliers, who have continued to fire and reload instead of preparing to engage the Zouave bayonets. Our line crumbles almost immediately, and we are helpless as the Zouaves butcher many of our recruits. Stunned by the speed and savagery of the Zouave attack, the Austrian officers bring their other companies to bear on the attackers. But the Zouave company suddenly withdraws, as fast as it has attacked. They make it back to the French line, suffering very few casualties. But they have dealt a brutal blow to our regiment, leaving almost a hundred of our men fallen and bleeding red upon the killing ground.

For the rest of the morning, the two forces of fighters advance and withdraw. Both lines eventually split into smaller skirmishes, each giving and gaining ground. The Austrian artillery units are finally ready to engage, but by this time, the close fighting of the infantry renders their support impossible for fear of killing our own troops. The officers commanding the field guns keep their cannons silent, for they can play no part in this battle.

Our company now races south behind the firing line with orders to defend the left flank, which has suffered serious losses. We arrive there just in time to face another rush of French bayonets. I detect desperation on the faces of my fellow soldiers. We realize that our French foes are far superior fighting men, in both training and resolve. As more and more of us fall under the bayonets and sabers of our adversaries, our plight becomes visibly futile, and Lieutenant Barta finally shouts for us to retreat. Bloodied and exhausted, fighting for our lives, we follow him as he attempts to lead our withdrawal back toward the vineyards.

Up to this point, I'm uncertain whether I've dispatched even a single enemy combatant. I've been firing into the French line, to be sure, but I don't know if I've hit anyone. Now, as the enemy infantry throws itself upon our company, it's all I can do to protect myself from the flashing blades of French bayonets and swords. My zest for killing, so fervently felt the night before, has all but vanished as I deflect blow after blow and watch my comrades fall all around me.

What's left of my company almost makes it to the safety of the vineyards when the French infantry ceases its attack. I feel a rush of relief, but when hooves are heard to my left, my relief is short-lived. A company of French dragoons hurls toward us to finish the job. The riders slam into our Bohemian fusiliers with full fury, horses trampling and sabers slicing. I'm in the middle of the fray, violently tossed about by the colossal beasts as deadly dragoon swords slash all around me. As I raise my bayonet toward an oncoming cavalryman, the rider turns his mount in my direction, knocking me to the ground. The horse's sharp hooves are on me now, stamping about wildly, and I drop my weapon and raise my arms to protect my head. A hoof comes down hard on my left leg, and I hear the sickening sound of the bone snapping. The searing pain is overwhelming as I scream out. The animal thrashes forward, and another hoof hits me, glancing off the side of my head to put an end to my screaming.

CHAPTER 12

HENRI DUNANT HAS TRAVELED for days, first by ship from northern Africa, up the Italian coast to Piedmont, and finally on horseback eastward through Italia. He's been trying to catch up with Napoleon III at his headquarters somewhere in Lombardy. The Swiss businessman is on a mission. Dunant has reached an impasse with the colonial authorities in Algeria regarding land and water rights. As an agent representing French development efforts there, his only recourse is to appeal in person to Napoleon III. Unfortunately, Napoleon is with his army near Solferino, fighting the Austrians. It's a bold move, to be sure—intruding on the French emperor in the middle of a war. But Dunant knows he's serving Napoleon's interests as well as his own, and he chooses the bold move over a more cautious one.

It's midafternoon on a pleasant June day in 1859 as Dunant approaches the small town of Solferino. A pungent veil of smoke hangs in the air, and he can hear explosions and gunfire to the east. He wonders if he'll need to wait until the fighting abates before he can speak with the emperor. He hopes it will end soon. As he rides along the narrow country road, he tops a small rise and pulls up hard on the reins startling his mount. The landscape ahead of him opens up into a collection of large hayfields, with hilled vineyards in the distance. On any other day, this would have presented a bucolic panorama. But what Dunant gazes upon this day is a field littered with dead and dying men as far as he can see through the smoke. Thousands of uniformed bodies lie on the ground, some in red slacks, some in blue, all strewn along a wide swath of death.

Henri rides down the hill onto the field and continues moving forward among the dead and injured soldiers. Torsos are disemboweled, heads severed, legs and arms missing or barely attached. He rides on, fighting down the bile pushing upward from his protesting stomach. He's never before come so close to this side of war. Oh, he knew people died in battle, and he was aware of the maiming that occurred on the battlefield. But he has never faced it up close as he does today.

Henri hears a moan from a victim lying somewhere nearby and brings his horse to a sudden stop. He notices a slight movement among a heap of bodies, and pauses to watch it. A soldier is trying to push himself up off the ground. The man is wearing an Austrian uniform and has a nasty gash on the side of his head, covered in blood and mud. As he tries to get to his knees, the soldier groans in pain, falling back to the ground. Quickly, Henri dismounts and steps over several mangled corpses to reach the soldier. He can see that the Austrian's leg is gravely damaged.

"Let me help you," Henri offers, reaching to help the wounded man.

The man gives a labored response. He's not speaking German, that's for sure. Perhaps it's Polish. Henri picks up what's left of the soldier's rifle, damaged and useless as a weapon, but functional as a crutch, and hands it to the man. He then grabs the man under his arm and helps him up onto one foot, dragging him away from the clutter of bodies to a nearby fence bordering the vineyard. Carefully, he eases the man back down to the ground, seating him against a fence post.

Kneeling next to the man, taking stock of his injuries, Henri ponders his next move. He knows the man will perish here without further help. He speaks to the man, doubting he'll be understood, but he speaks anyway, trying to use his hands to make his meaning clear.

"Stay here," he says. "I'll go for help."

Henri stands up and surveys the area. He sees hundreds of men who are beyond help, but he can see hundreds more who might survive if tended to. He's at once overwhelmed by the hopelessness of this task. So much wasted life, he thinks. How can these armies just leave their men behind like this? Henri looks at the impossible task before him, but he knows he has to do something. He can still hear explosions to the east, and he knows he can't find help further toward Solferino, where the fighting is still ongoing. Then he looks in the opposite direction and wonders about the town he passed a ways back. Henri mounts his horse and carefully makes his way through the maze of dead and wounded men. He is soon clear of them and now brings his heels hard against the horse's haunches. Spurred forward as fast as it can run, the horse carries its rider west toward the village of Castiglione delle Stiviere.

CHAPTER 13

SITTING FOR A LONG TIME among hundreds of dead and dying men, the time passes slowly as the moans from the injured begin to abate, life gradually draining from many of them. If help doesn't come soon, there'll be no one left to save. Leaning against the fence post, it's distressing to look at the bodies lying before me. And as the sun makes its way toward the horizon, I concentrate instead on the changing shadows of the distant landscape. There are still the sounds of fighting to be heard, but it's fainter now, indicating that the battle has moved east beyond Solferino. The Austrians must be retreating.

Touching my finger to the wound on my head, I'm surprised that it doesn't seem to be bleeding any longer, and as I gaze down at my throbbing leg, it appears to have a joint in the wrong place as it splays out unnaturally. Moving from this spot will be impossible with so serious and painful an injury. I wonder what has happened to the stranger who helped me move to this fence post. He's been gone a long time. Will he come back? I don't think I can survive here for long. Maybe the French army will come back in this direction and find me. Of course, they might just kill me. I'm an enemy combatant, after all. My prospects for survival aren't good, I realize, and my head falls despairingly back against the fence post. Scanning the sky, something now seems wrong with my vision. In my visual field are small dark dots floating about in random patterns. Has something gotten into my eyes, or has my head injury affected my eyesight? I blink desperately and gaze upward again hoping for improvement. But the dots continue to orbit above me, twisting and turning in intricate trajectories. Curiously, one of the dots separates from the others, growing larger. Not

larger—closer, and I can now identify its shape. It's a bird–
–a large bird. It finally comes to rest in the field not far away, and I can see it more clearly now. It's a vulture, and I realize those dots in the sky are dozens more of them. The large bird sits atop one of the casualties of the battle, and it is difficult not to gaze in morbid enthrallment as the vulture rips flesh from the dead man's open wounds. I'm sure that many more of the birds will soon be descending to feast upon other carcasses the battle has left behind, and I wonder if I too will be one of them. But there is little I can do but sit and wait for whatever fate awaits me. My eyes close against the morbid thought, and soon, the weight of exhaustion overtakes me, and I'm asleep as daylight fades away.

It seems like only moments after I've fallen asleep that I am startled into wakefulness once again. It's not the pain from my mangled leg that awakens me, nor is it the ringing in my ears or my excruciating headache. It's not even the fear of a hungry vulture feeding on my mangled leg. No, it's something coming from some distance across the hayfields. It's the sound of drays and hay wagons of all sizes coming over the hill, pulled by horses, oxen, and mules. Dozens of men and women accompany the procession, all moving with haste.

Soon, people are bringing wagons among the injured soldiers. People are soon lifting the wounded onto the wagons, and hauling them back up the hill and over the rise. As the battlefield succumbs to the darkness of night, the wagons haven't yet made it to where I am sitting. But the work continues, with torches lit, and I'm confident I'll receive help in short order. I spot the horseman who helped me earlier, sitting astride his mount in the middle of the activity, encouraging the people to work faster. Soon, the wagons are all around me, and four women prepare to lift me onto one of them. The horseman rides up to where I sit and smiles down at me from his mount, saying something I don't understand. Returning a forced smile, I can only guess his meaning. The women lift me onto a wagon, and I get one last look at the horseman as he spurs his mount forward, heading east through the vineyards.

My trip is far from a pleasant one. The cart bumps over ruts and large rocks in the road as it lurches this way and that, each jolt creating a rush of searing pain in my leg. Finally, after bumping along in agony, we arrive at a small village with makeshift structures constructed of cloth or canvas strewn all over town. Townspeople are scurrying about carrying blankets, bandages, and supplies. Many of them move to and from a small church building that seems to be a staging center. My wagon finally stops, and I'm soon transferred to a blanket under one of the makeshift shelters where a young peasant woman soon cleans my head wound, and two others stand over my broken leg, shaking their heads in concern.

Glancing around at the men lying beside me in the shelter, it's surreal to see them in Austrian, French, and Sardinian uniforms. They're all fighting for their lives now instead of fighting each other. Most of us are badly injured, with deep puncture wounds, sliced shoulders and limbs, gunshot injuries, and broken bones. How can these villagers treat such wounds? I see no sign of a doctor. All this effort might come to nothing if these injured men don't receive proper treatment. Most of these men will probably die, myself included, but because of these villagers' futile efforts, we'll all have to suffer a bit longer before death takes us.

I'm awakened in the dark by the sound of thirty or forty men on horseback and wagons just arriving at the scene. As they dismount, I can see from their torches that they wear both French and Austrian uniforms. The men stand together in a group, listening attentively to instructions from the man who helped me on the battlefield. With the help of an interpreter, the man talks as he points to the various shelters, and when he does this, men peel off from the group in all directions. Eventually, when one of these men enters my shelter to examine my leg, it's clear that all these men are doctors. But how can they be both Austrians and French, all working together? This seems so unlikely that I wonder if my eyes are deceiving me.

The doctor standing next to me is wearing an Austrian uniform, and I'm relieved to hear him speaking my language.

"How are you feeling?" the doctor asks.

"How d'ya think I'm feeling?" I reply roughly. "Like shit!"

"I don't doubt it, soldier," he replies without taking offense.

"You are Bohemian?"

"From Prague. And you?" the doctor asks.

"Krouna." The doctor has a look of puzzlement. "It's south, near the Moravian border," I add.

"Ah, yes," he replies as he begins to poke and prod at my leg injury.

"Ahhhh!" I protest.

"Sorry. This is a terrible break. I'll need to take care of it right away. I'll be right back." The doctor stands up to leave, but I reach to touch the man's leg.

"How did you know to speak to me in Bohemian?" I ask, puzzled.

"I recognized your uniform, from a Bohemian unit. Plus, Dunant told me there was a Slav in this shelter. He directed me here."

"Dunant?"

"Henri Dunant. He's some kind of businessman. He organized this entire operation. It's quite remarkable, actually. He even rode to the French headquarters to appeal to Napoleon for doctors. As you can probably see, many of us are Austrians, captured in the conflict. Dunant must be quite a salesman. He convinced the emperor to release us to aid in this effort. If we can repair this leg, you'll have him to thank for it."

The doctor reaches into his bag and pulls out a small bottle, emptying a portion of it into a cup. "Here, drink this. It's for the pain. You're going to need it. I'll be right back to set that bone," he says as he leaves. As he steps out of the shelter, he adds, "If we can't do that, we may have to take the leg."

I don't like the sound of that, and I begin imagining my future one-legged life. How will I be able to do my carpentry and masonry work? And how will Frantiska react? If she hates me now, how much more will she hate me if she has to tend to a cripple for the rest of her life? A one-legged future is unacceptable, I conclude. I'd rather die here on the ground than face that outcome.

The concoction the doctor gave me does an acceptable job of deadening the pain in both my head and my leg, but it proves to be nowhere near sufficient for the ordeal ahead. When the doctor comes back with two women and a crude splint, I fear what is coming. As the two women hold me down, the doctor begins to pull and twist my leg. In my elixir-induced stupor, it's distressing to hear the shriek of someone's bloodcurdling screaming. Then, as the totality of the agony grips the whole of my body, I realize the screaming is coming from my own gaping mouth. It's a red-hot, stabbing pain, unlike anything I have ever imagined. For far too long, the doctor pulls and manipulates my leg until he's tortured me enough. He stops and gently lays my leg back on the ground. We look at one another, both drenched in sweat, silently acknowledging the part each has played in this cruelty.

Finally, the doctor says, "That's about the best I can do, soldier. I'm not sure if it'll be enough. You can't move from here for a while—not if you hope to walk again."

He then applies the splint, and adds, "There's still a good chance you're going to lose this leg. Time will tell."

"How much time?" I ask, still breathing hard from the ordeal.

"Weeks, but if we need to remove the leg, we'll know sooner than that," replies the doctor as he stands and abruptly walks away.

For the next few days, I lie there, impatient with my inability to will myself back to normalcy. Still, I'm thankful I'm alive as I watch other men die, their bodies carried to wagons and hauled out of town to where their graves will litter a constantly expanding graveyard. The caretakers and doctors working in the encampment remain vigilant in their efforts. But eventually, the doctoring is over, and they're all just waiting to see who will succumb next.

I'm waiting, too. But just when I think the worst is over, I awaken in a cold sweat. When the doctor approaches me, I hardly know who he is. I feel weak, and my mind seems muddled. Where am I? Who is this person attending to me? Why am I unable to move? Confused and bewildered by my thoughts and circumstances, I soon pass into a world far beyond my physical reality. *I'm floating high above the ground, like a bird soaring on an obliging air current. But for the sound of the gentle airflow, it is so very quiet, and a feeling of calm and well-being envelopes me. I look at my outstretched arms and notice that they have turned into large beautiful wings, hardly moving as they keep me aloft on the unwavering updraft. The vast countryside below me extends in all directions, revealing a wonderous patchwork of forests and fields and vineyards, and I hope to soar over this magnificent vista forever. But soon, I begin to descend in easy zigzag paths before smoothly alighting on the ground. But it isn't the ground. It's a man's leg—a misshapen leg—and I begin viciously tearing flesh from its bloody open wound, swallowing the bloody repast and then repeatedly thrusting my beak back into the leg for more. I momentarily glance up from the man's leg to his face. It is my face that I see, and the man is shrieking in terror.*

I awaken, screaming. The doctor is standing there with two attending women, all of them holding me down with some effort so that I won't do further injury to my leg. It's all they can do to get me calmed down and covered once again with blankets. Soon I am asleep, untroubled by further visions of horror, and I remember little after that.

After a couple days, I awaken feeling clearheaded again. The fever has finally broken, and thankfully, the doctor thinks I'll keep my leg after all. I know I'm lucky, and although he says I'll find it difficult to walk normally, I'm looking forward to the prospect of going home, albeit with a pronounced limp.

Two weeks later, the Austro-Sardinian War is over, and a truce has been signed in a town called Villafranca. Apparently, Napoleon III was satisfied with the conquest of Lombardy and left Venetia to the Austrians. I wonder how the people there feel about that.

We are all pleased that the truce between Napoleon and Franz Joseph includes an exchange of prisoners. This includes amnesty for the injured Austrian wounded and their doctors in this little town. By the middle of July, many survivors in the encampment in Castiglione delle Stiviere prepare to travel back to their respective homelands. The French and Sardinian soldiers head west on wagons and horseback. The Austrians travel eastward, mostly in small groups or alone on foot. Only a few remain behind, not yet ready for travel, and I am among them. My doctor makes me promise to remain for at least another month before attempting to walk, and two of my caretakers vow to make sure I comply with that promise.

It's a full month, almost to the day, after the battle near Solferino before I try to stand on weakened legs for the first time, aided by a crudely constructed crutch. The pain is an immediate indicator that I'm not yet ready to walk on my own, and I'm disappointed that I'll need to remain here in Castiglione delle Stiviere for a while longer. Fortunately, I am under the care of Maria and Alberto Ricci, two shopkeepers who live in the middle of town and have attended to me since the day of my arrival. I have observed the inordinate generosity and patience the Riccis have shown me and the many other soldiers under their care. Now it's just me, the only one left who can't leave town under my own power, and the Riccis show no apprehension at taking me in as a welcome guest in their modest home.

CHAPTER 14
BOHEMIA

NEWS TRAVELS AT A SNAIL'S PACE throughout the Bohemian hills. Written accounts of current happenings around the empire are almost nonexistent here, and why should they not be, with so many illiterates in this land? The peasants in and around Krouna rely primarily on word-of-mouth reports from travelers passing through town on their way someplace else. It should come as no surprise that the accuracy of such reporting is dubious at best and prone to exaggeration and vagueness. In the end, most people end up believing or rejecting new information as they see fit, thereby formulating their own personal view of the world, a view that enables them to live from day to day in the bliss of ignorance.

But in the case of the Austro-Sardinian War, everyone eventually learns of the Austrian defeat at the hands of the Franco/Sardinian alliance. Everyone hears of the twenty-three thousand Austrian troops killed, wounded, or missing in the battle at Solferino. Everyone also hears about the empire's relinquishing of the Lombardy, Nice, and Savoy regions. With Louis Napoleon's victory at Solferino, he easily pushed Franz Joseph's army back across the Mincio River into Venetia. He could very well have pushed them further, people say, but his army suffered almost as many casualties at Solferino as Franz Joseph's. And the unimaginable carnage left on the battlefield convinced Napoleon III to join the Austrians at the negotiating table.

Frantiska has heard of the truce ratified on the eighth of July. But what does she care? What does it matter if the Austrians lose part of northern Italia to the French? Or all of Italia, for that matter? She doesn't care a whit. And why would she care if the French are far superior to the Austrians in fighting prowess? She takes no stock in the wars of men, led by bloodthirsty generals and vain emperors. Wars are senseless wastes of human lives. No, she has no interest in the spoils of wars: the defeats or victories, the acts of heroism or cowardice, the generals' strategies, or any of the rest of it. Frantiska's interests are of no nationalistic or patriotic concern to her. Austria isn't her country, anyway. No, she doesn't care that Austria will lose face. The only thing she cares about is having Josef back home. But the number of reported casualties is sobering. And though Frantiska continues to pray each day, and again each night, her fear of a future without him looms ever larger in her thoughts.

It's late July, and the heat hangs heavy in the house as Frantiska sits at her loom. Her front door hangs wide open to invite any passing breeze that might offer relief. But no relief comes, and she wipes her brow, thinking about Josef. Even with Anton and Rose next door, and Anna and the children close at hand, she is so lonely. "Josef—just come home," she pleads. Dreaming will do her no good, she knows. Why even bother?

She resumes her work at her loom, trying to complete a colorful blanket for a local burgher's wife. At least this is something within her control, she thinks. It's a Saturday, and Anna has taken Vincencie and Antonin to the parish classroom, leaving Frantiska to do her weaving. Undisturbed by the children, perhaps she can finish this blanket by tomorrow and receive payment for it so that she can feed the children.

Suddenly, Frantiska sees Thomas Spacek standing at her open door. She can see that he has something in his hand—a few pages of paper. But he makes no move, simply standing there in silence watching her work.

"What do you want, Thomas?" Frantiska asks impatiently, wondering how long he's been standing there in the doorway watching her.

Finally, he hands Frantiska the paper items. One, in particular, catches her eye, and she looks at it more closely. She sees her own handwriting. It's the letter she wrote to Josef. She quickly turns it over and can see that it's unopened.

"What's this about, Thomas? Weren't they able to deliver it?" she asks.

"I'm sorry, Frantiska, but they delivered it, alright," he answers. He swallows hard and continues, "They found it on his body, Frantiska. It seems artillery fire killed Josef near Solferino. I'm so sorry."

Frantiska glares up at Thomas's face. Something about his expression makes her doubt his sincerity. She sees the same smugness that is always etched there. And she is enraged. Her words come, reeking of brutal contempt. "You're sorry? You bastard!" she hisses and slaps him viciously across his smug face. The savagery of her blow throws Thomas back, knocking him off balance. Thomas raises his hand in protest just as she slams the door in his face.

For several moments, she stands inside the door, wondering what she should do next. Should she scream? Cry? She doesn't know. Finally, she leans against the door, letting her legs collapse until she sits on the dirt floor with the papers gripped in her trembling hand. She studies the envelope. Why is it unopened? Josef is not much of a reader, she knows. She tried to teach him years ago, but he was never a very serious student. Certainly, though, he could have found someone in his company to read it to him, she surmises. Why didn't he? Was he afraid of what she might have written there? The thought brings a wash of acute sadness as she holds the envelope to her forehead, feeling a weightiness in her arms and tightness in her chest. Oh, poor Josef. Didn't he know how she really felt about him?

She lays Josef's letter on the floor and examines the other items. One of them looks to be some sort of certificate. Printed in German, it includes the phrase *tapferer Service* and *patriotische Pflicht*. She doesn't know exactly what those words mean, but she wonders if this is some sort of commendation for Josef's service to the empire. She wrenches it aside in disgust and looks to see what the last piece of paper can reveal. Some numbers near the bottom specify an amount of money, stated in Austrian guldens. On one line is the word *Servicezahlung*, followed by *100*. Is this a voucher for Josef's military pay? Is that the value of Josef's life? One hundred guldens? Is this money supposed to ease her grief and repay her for her loss? Frantiska violently flings the papers aside and collapses back against the door, staring straight ahead at nothing in particular. What will she do now? she asks herself.

CHAPTER 15

SADNESS? ANGER? FEAR? NEED? LOSS? FUTILITY? It's none of those. None of those describe how she feels. Emptiness. That's what it is! Frantiska realizes that her life feels empty now. It's like she's feeling nothing at all. Just a void—an emptiness so profound that even the air around her seems empty, making it difficult for her tight chest even to take the air in and out. She's been sitting here on the floor, trying to understand this feeling. Yes, she's sad, and yes, she is angry, and yes, she feels those other things, too. But all those feelings are secondary to the immense hole at the center of it all. Those other feelings are moths flitting about a lit candle, flying perilously close to the flame, the void attracting them. It's only her awareness of those secondary feelings—the sadness and anger—that somehow protect her from a descent into this emptiness which she fears may offer no escape.

Thankfully, her thoughts soon turn to more practical things, things that provide a distraction from her gloom. What should she do to move on, to make up for Josef's absence, to support her family? But is it right to contemplate such practical things now—to move on with her life so easily? No, it's wrong to think about those things at this moment. She's determined not to just shrug off Josef's death. Frantiska will sit here a while longer—perhaps much longer—and let herself wallow in her grief. Josef's passing deserves at least that, doesn't it?

Returning from her classroom, Anna walks down the dusty path through Krouna, a child yanking on each hand. She wonders if Frantiska has finished her loom work. She hopes so because her own afternoon hasn't been especially productive. At least she's been successful in entertaining Antonin and Vincencie for a little while. That's fine with her. It's been fun spending time with the children.

As the three of them walk past the mercantile shop, Anna stops, having spotted a rather ornate poster tacked next to the shop door. With her curiosity piqued, she steps up to the poster, children in tow, and reads:

AMERICA
WANTS WOMEN
FOR HOUSEHOLD WORK
Assisted Passages
For Approved Applicants
GOOD WAGES
EMPLOYMENT GUARANTEED
Apply to
Any Employment Exchange,
The Superintendent of Emigration for U.S.A

Anna's heard about the opportunities in America. She's heard of the way the United States has thrown off the shackles of English tyranny to begin a new and free nation. She wonders what it would be like to travel to such a place to start a new life. Would America be like Bohemia? She hopes not. Certainly, it would be better, without the never-ending poverty and hopelessness. In America, she could do housework if she had to, she supposes, or maybe she could be a teacher there, too. Certainly, many Bohemians who emigrated to America are looking for teachers for their children, aren't they? She wonders about the cost of passage from Bohemia to America, and if she could save up enough from the income of her new position to afford the voyage. Anna can't know the answers to any of these questions. But as she stands there with Vincencie and Antonin at her side, she's transfixed by this pondering. She allows it to plant the seeds of a burgeoning dream—a dream of a better life. And as Anna, Antonin, and Vincencie proceed onward toward home, Anna walks in silence. She imagines what it would be like to leave her homeland and embark on such a grand adventure. It's pleasant to dream, at least, she thinks.

Her whimsical mood comes to an abrupt halt as she and the children arrive home. Anna struggles to push the door open and finds Frantiska sitting on the floor with paper items strewn all around her. Anna isn't sure what to make of it. She has never seen Frantiska this despondent before. Frantiska has always been the strong one, the one with the strong faith, the one propping up others in times of need. As the children stand and watch with concern, Anna tries to move her friend to one of the stools, but she refuses to be budged. Without a word, Frantiska simply grabs the paper items and thrusts them at Anna.

It doesn't take Anna long to understand what's happened. Her ability to read German is superior to Frantiska's, and the writing on the pages is painfully clear in its meaning. The children don't yet know why their mother is so upset, but Anna can see they are worried about her. She pushes them toward the door, imploring them to play out in the yard for the time being. Then she hastens to bring a cup of water to Frantiska, sitting down next to her on the floor, holding her friend's limp hand. All of Anna's thoughts about America at once vanish, and she considers the brutal realities of this oppressive life. Will this be the only life she ever knows? The only one she deserves? She feels a pang of guilt run through her as she feels sorry for herself. What kind of friend am I? she asks herself. She should be concerned for Frantiska right now. Her dreams of America far behind her, Anna turns her attention back to her broken friend.

Widowhood is not a lifestyle Frantiska wears easily. She doesn't consider it a badge of honor, nor does she consider it a cause for pity. It's simply a condition lesser than her previous life, the life in which she and Josef together could eke out a modest survival. She wonders what she should do now. How will she take care of Antonin and Vincencie? What if she becomes destitute, unable to feed her children? She'll most likely have to give them up to neighbors who can take better care of them. If that happens, she knows the chances of Antonin and Vincencie staying together are not good. She's seen it happen before, and it's broken her heart to see families split apart like that. But what is she to do? She feels helpless among these uncertainties, and as she does regularly throughout her days now, she closes her eyes and whispers aloud, "Please Lord, give me strength."

In the weeks that follow, as Frantiska continues to mourn Josef's death, Anna shows herself to be a true and loyal friend, assuming many of the duties associated with the children, keeping them at a distance from Frantiska. This allows her friend to mourn alone, without distraction. Frantiska wants it that way, and Anna has sensed this desire early on. Through it all, Anna maintains as cheerful a manner as possible without being excessively so. And with the school session not yet upon her, she can assume many of the housekeeping duties Frantiska either chooses not to do or forgets to do.

None of this is lost on Frantiska. In the throes of her grief, she recognizes a profound depth of friendship developing between herself and Anna. And as the days pass, with Anna's help, Frantiska feels herself regaining her compass, moving away from the darkness toward a brighter place. Anna can feel it too, as her friend becomes more communicative and, occasionally, even rather sunny. As Frantiska's mood improves, she opens up more and more, sharing both her feelings of loss and her worries about the future of her family.

During one of their conversations, Anna mentions her dream of traveling to America. Frantiska at first scoffs at such a notion. But the more Anna talks about it, the more Frantiska allows Anna's dream to grow from a grain of remote plausibility into a dream of her own. The two women speak often about this dream and imagine how it can come to pass. What will it require of them? What will it cost? Will this be possible with just the two of them and the children? What will the journey be like? What will America be like? All these questions are at once frightening and exhilarating. But before long, a plan begins to emerge.

This dream of America will require money, and the first thing Frantiska does is convert Josef's pay voucher into cash. Then she finds a suitable container and buries the one hundred guldens behind the icehouse. Next, she undertakes something quite distasteful, even perhaps dangerous, but necessary. She goes to ask Thomas Spacek for a temporary reduction in her house rent until she gets back on her feet. To accomplish this, she has to apologize for slapping him. She has to ask forgiveness for doing something she doesn't regret. But it's all designed to soften him up, and she finds Thomas to be an easy target for her wiles. As distasteful as this is for her, it works.

These steps are all part of a carefully devised strategy. Saving their money and increasing Frantiska's weaving production will hopefully make their dream of emigration possible. Anna's teaching income will help, too. Amid this planning, neither of them will admit it, but deep down they both genuinely doubt it can ever happen. Still, it gives them a purpose, something to work toward, something to help Frantiska put her grief behind her and help her envision a brighter future.

CHAPTER 16
MEANWHILE, IN AMERICA

ANETA KUN AWAKENS to Karel's crying. She opens her eyes, and the darkness of her slumber now yields to another field of black. She has always feared the dark, and this awakening from one darkness into another is at once distressing. On the brink of panic, she jerks her head in the direction of Karel's wailing and, failing to see him, scans the blackness pressing in on her. Gratefully, she spots the faint glow of a few spent coals in the fireplace, and she realizes that her deep sleep has prevented her from stoking the fire.

Feeling her way to the fireplace, she pokes at the reluctant embers—her only defense against the cool night temperature—trying to bring the fire back to life. The sun will warm the log cabin, but that won't happen until the sun clears the tree line to the east. Until then, Aneta hopes to encourage the fire with the help of two more logs that she lays on the fading coals. She glances over at Julie to check if Karel's cries have stirred her. The girl is still sleeping in her sling, so Aneta tends to Karel, changing his diaper and taking his soiled one outside to rinse and dry on the line.

Two years ago, in the summer of '57, she had moved into this decrepit cabin in Tama County when she and Francis married. To be sure, this wasn't the home she'd envisioned when he proposed to her. After all, Francis Kun was an impressive man: intelligent, educated, talented, and striking in his appearance. And above all, he was a man of the cloth, a man of God, whose self-declared mission was to bolster the faith of those he called the *lost sheep of the Iowa plains*. In Francis, Aneta saw a man of potential who'd not only provide for their family but also provide proper guidance in their faith.

But Aneta had overestimated the man's potential. Of course, Francis hadn't made himself out to be someone he wasn't. He was all those things: intelligent, learned, engaging, and religious. He was a native of Moravia, where he was born into a long line of religious men, men steeped in the teachings of the great theologian Jan Hus. All these things had impressed Aneta. And what nineteen-year-old wouldn't be impressed? She'd thought she was marrying the finest man in all of Tama County and beyond.

In some ways, she was correct. When Aneta first heard Francis preach the Word, she recognized his talent as an orator. She recognized the passion he held for his beliefs. More impressive was the fact that he was a remarkable linguist. Francis was fluent in German, Greek, Latin, and Hebrew—skills unheard of in this land of illiterate commoners. Yes, Aneta could see that Francis was an extraordinary man. And it came as no surprise that her father thought as much, too. So with her father's enthusiastic approval, her name soon changed from Aneta Budka to Aneta Kun.

All of this had greatly pleased Aneta. Why would it not? Still, there were two things she hadn't counted on. Two things quite unexpected, but now apparent to her. Two things that continue to trouble her to this day, causing her to wonder if she chose wisely.

The morning light creeps through the window now as she sits holding Karel and Julie in her lap, thinking about the first of these two troublesome things. She studies the dirt floor, the irregularity of the cabin's construction, the gaps she continually tries to fill between the logs, the piteous roof that caves in each winter at the first heavy snowfall, and the meager stores of provisions generated from their dismal potato and oat crops. It's clear that Francis isn't a man suited to wilderness life. He indeed has not provided well for this family. Neither his oratory skills nor his acumen with

Latin, Greek, and Hebrew serves him well here on this paltry plot of Iowa farmland. Aneta does what she can to help. She routinely fetches water from the nearby creek, searches for firewood, checks traps, plugs cracks in the log walls, and helps with the crops. This now makes her wonder if Francis's primary motivation for marrying so soon after settling here was his need for a helper. Of course, now with the children, the burden is so much greater. This puts so much more responsibility on Francis, and even with Aneta's help, she is certain Francis won't be up to the task.

And then there's the other thing: Francis is nowhere to be seen. He should be here looking after his young family, but he's not. He's out somewhere ministering to his *lost sheep*. While his evangelical passion was at first an admirable trait, Aneta sees it now as a liability. His insistence on traveling hither and yon, spreading the Word, may seem commendable to the wayward flock, but what about Aneta and the children? It's lonely, even frightening, being stuck out here for days at a time, so far from the closest neighbor. Aneta hopes his lost sheep are profiting from her husband's presence—because she surely isn't.

Two days later, Francis makes his way up the trail leading to his homestead. He stops a moment to assess the state of his oat field. It's about ready to harvest, and he resolves to sharpen the scythe tomorrow and get to work. After that, it will be time for the potatoes. Hopefully, when the crops are in, he can head out again. Maybe he'll even head up to the Wisconsin area, where he'll find more Reformed Brethren, more lost sheep in need of a shepherd.

As Francis approaches the cabin, he sees Aneta standing with a knife in one hand and a recently snared rabbit in the other. Apparently, one of his traps was effective for a change. Little Julie is swaddled and strapped to Aneta's back, and Karel is playing nearby on the ground. Even at this distance, Francis can see that Aneta's perspiring heavily from the August heat, and he can also tell something else. She doesn't seem to be thrilled to see him.

"Is something wrong?" he asks as he approaches.

Aneta doesn't answer but walks to a nearby tree stump and begins skinning the creature on it.

"Is something wrong, Aneta?" he repeats.

She wipes her brow with the back of her knife hand, and answers, "Wrong? What could be wrong? I haven't seen you in six days. The roof is still a mess. We're short on firewood. The crops need attention. And I think there was a timber wolf prowling outside the cabin last night."

"But you and the children are all right?"

"Of course. Why would we not be? What could possibly go wrong out here in the middle of nowhere?" she answers sarcastically.

"Now, Aneta. You know how much I'm needed out there. There are so many people leaving the faith. So many are giving up on God's grace. They might all become lost souls. My preaching to them might pull them back into the fold. Don't fret, Aneta. God will look after you, and—"

"Just stop with the *God shall provide* speech!" Aneta interrupts, seething with frustration. "Don't you think maybe the work that needs doing around here is your job, not his?"

"But he will provide, Aneta," Francis replies gently.

"Then maybe you can put him to work on that roof up there," she spits as she rips off a piece of furry skin, exposing the rabbit's flesh.

Francis decides not to push it. He knows how hard this is on her. She has assumed much responsibility during his regular forays out into the countryside. But she must understand that he's been called to a greater purpose than the reaping of crops or the chopping of wood. This is the Lord's work. It's as simple as that. Nothing is more important. Indeed, Francis has to admit to himself that spreading God's word has been harder than he expected. He's found this new land to be so vast that villages aren't to be discovered over every bump in the road like back in Moravia. It can be a considerable distance between homesteads, let alone towns or villages, and trekking between them on foot can be difficult. This being the case, he hasn't served the number of believers he had hoped to serve. It's true, he has attracted decent crowds occasionally. But most often, he's preached to only five or ten ambivalent farmers at a time. And many of them have seemed dispirited by their poverty, bereft of much hope that a bolstered faith could provide.

Francis watches Aneta continue to clean the rabbit. There's nothing more he can say to his wife at this moment. It can wait until the morning. His responsibility now is to the Lord, not to his wife. It's time for Francis to assume an attitude of prayer with his Maker, a task he has repeated each evening for the entirety of his adult life. And he will also pray for his wife. He will pray for her resolve and her strength. And above all, he will pray for her patience.

Then tomorrow, he will set to work on that oat field and maybe even take a stab at fortifying the cabin roof, even though he hasn't the slightest idea how he will fix it.

CHAPTER 17
ITALIA

THE RICCIS ARE A CHILDLESS COUPLE, old enough to be my parents, exhibiting the traits of many other commoners I've observed around this village: short in stature and wide in girth. But the Riccis are well-complemented. Maria loves to cook—Alberto loves to eat. Each evening, Maria seems to produce a new variation on something she calls polenta. Neither the taste nor the texture is especially appealing, but Maria's constant encouragement and Alberto's generous servings of wine enable me to consume plenty of the stuff. Soon I'm gaining strength, as well as bulk, and though Maria sees that as a good sign, I worry the extra weight might impose strain on my healing leg.

Since moving into the Ricci home, I've recognized the motivation for the couple's limitless generosity and patience. It's the Riccis' religious fervor that stokes their bigheartedness. I'm impressed that every evening they read aloud from their Bible. It's a Bible given to them by one of the French doctors in appreciation for their help with the injured soldiers. The book is printed in common Italian, and it's no wonder the Riccis cherish the book as they do. I watch them as they handle it reverently, using care as they turn each page, reading aloud from the tome each evening. At first, it seems odd that they don't read to themselves or one another, but directly to me. They must know I can't understand a single word. Somehow, they must hope the message will get through to me regardless, and perhaps they think I should hear the message no matter what the language. But what is there to do about this nightly ritual? I am at the Riccis' mercy after all.

To my dismay, it's several days before I finally realize how these recitations are benefitting me. As they sit there reading to me, they often linger on a particular word. Then they repeat the word over and over to me, trying to reveal its meaning, and making me repeat it. Surprisingly after a few weeks, I've gained a basic understanding of their language. Even this rudimentary vocabulary, newly learned and roughly spoken, may be useful when I finally leave for Bohemia.

It's not until September that I'm ready to begin my journey home. The leg is not completely healed, but I hope it will improve as I travel. As the Riccis help me prepare, there is a sense that they don't want me to go. Do they think I'm not ready to travel yet, or is it that they'll miss me? I'm not sure. Either way, they are two of the most patient and generous people I've ever met, and I'll be sorry to say goodbye.

Maria prepares a small bag in which I can carry some dried fruits and meat she's prepared as a snack, and Alberto helps me devise a suitable cane, a replacement for the crude crutch made by the doctor. He even secures the services of a local farmer who will transport me partway eastward on my journey.

On a crisp morning, after showing ample gratitude to the Riccis, I'm finally ready to depart. Climbing aboard a dilapidated hay wagon, I ride toward the sun on the same road that brought me to Castiglione delle Stiviere two months ago.

As I ride eastward with the farmer, the ache in my leg seems almost tolerable. My military uniform has been freshly washed by Maria, and I've wrapped myself in a blanket. This will protect me from the sun during the day and the evening coolness if I'm to spend nights outdoors. We head east, but beyond that, I have no specific route in mind. How will I get to Bohemia? I don't know, beyond taking a northeastward bearing. The only thing known with certainty is that the man driving the hay wagon won't be able to take me far. Soon, he will have to let me off and head back to Castiglione delle Stiviere. And after that, I'll be on my own.

With the sun reaching its apex, the man finally pulls the wagon to a stop, saying something I can't understand. As the man speaks, he holds his arms up in a crossed position, shaking his head from side to side.

Obviously, the driver isn't willing to proceed further, and I'm not sure why. My guess is that the man doesn't want to venture anywhere near Austrian-controlled territory. I don't blame him. The man has been under their subjugation for too long. And now that his hometown is finally free of their control, he hopes to never again set foot on Austrian soil.

The man helps me off the wagon and peers at me. What does he see? Just a pathetic soldier who has nothing more than a cane, a blanket, a small bag of supplies, and a canteen hanging on a strap. He probably wonders how I will fare in a land that speaks an alien language. Suddenly, he turns and points up the road, saying, "Verona." That's plain enough. Perhaps Verona will indeed be a logical destination. I remember hearing Captain Brodsky mention the army fortification in Verona. Perhaps food and shelter can be found in the army encampment there.

"*Grazie mille*," I say, with my heavy Slavic tongue. The old man pats me gently on the shoulder before he climbs back up on the wagon and snaps the reins, moving the wagon in an arc to turn around and head home. As he drives away, I scan the surrounding panorama. This is a beautiful country. It reminds me of Bohemia. This will make for a beautiful stroll, I surmise, feeling a slight pang of hunger. I reach into my knapsack to find some of the delights Maria

Ricci has packed for me. I select two prunes and a few pieces of dried meat, which I eagerly consume along with a small drink of water from the canteen. I then begin my hike up the dirt road toward Verona.

I've greatly overestimated my ability to walk with my injury. Limping onward for a mere two hundred paces, the throbbing begins in my leg. Gazing back to where I began, I now wonder how I can make even a portion of this journey without help. Did I leave Castiglione delle Stiviere too soon? To be sure, my leg is not up to this strain. The people in Castiglione delle Stiviere were so generous to me. Hopefully, there will be other charitable folks like them who will assist me along the way. There's plenty of daylight left, and after another sip from the canteen, I push myself onward. Steeling myself against the pain, I drag my splinted leg toward Verona—walking, resting, walking, resting.

The time passes slowly, and with the sun receding over the horizon, the cool evening begins to descend upon me. I'd walk further, but the pain in my leg is too much. I'll need to stop for the evening if my journey is to continue tomorrow.

For the entire afternoon of walking, not a single traveler has come along on this road, which is quite disappointing. I've dragged myself only a short distance so far, making it difficult to imagine how I can endure this for long. How many days will it take to reach Verona at this rate? Who knows? It seems like too daunting a task. But I shake my head, trying to push that negativity from my mind.

The Lombardy hill country can become cold during the night, and I worry that my thin blanket will not provide enough warmth if I'm stranded here without shelter. My only recourse is to build a fire for warmth, or at least try. Fortunately, among my possessions is my small gunpowder satchel. I knew it would come in handy if I needed to start a fire.

Leaving the road, I move into a wooded area nearby to seek a windbreak. The temperature is already plummeting, so I begin the task of finding everything I will need for my fire. Thanks to the lack of rainfall in recent days, the ground is dry and I collect small dry sticks and leaves. In a clearing under the tree canopy, I find a place to sit and I begin digging a small indentation on a flat piece of branch and insert a thinner one at a right angle to it. Then I spin it with my palms to see if it will create enough friction to light the gunpowder. A small ribbon of smoke soon springs from the friction point, and I know what to do next. Arranging more gunpowder and dry tinder pieces around the indentation, I again spin the stick. Suddenly, the gunpowder erupts into a small flame igniting the leaves and sticks. Feeding the flames with more and more small sticks, the fire begins to burn more aggressively, and I'm confident it will continue on its own. Searching for larger pieces to add, my fire is soon ablaze. In self-satisfied comfort, I sit wrapped in my blanket, nibbling on the rest of the prunes and dried meat and staring into the flames, letting my mind wander back to Krouna.

I'm startled awake by the sun as it peeks over a rise and glares through the trees into my face. Pulling myself off the ground, squinting and blinking, I glance around to get my bearings. The fire has diminished to just a few glowing remains and pulling the blanket tightly around me, I struggle to my feet, taking stock of my damaged leg. It aches, but at least it's not throbbing as it was yesterday. Using my cane to shove dirt onto the remaining embers, they are soon rendered lifeless. Then, grabbing my meager possessions, I limp down the hill, out of the stand of trees toward the road.

My hunger has returned now. Maria's provisions are gone, and I'll need to find additional sustenance if I hope to maintain my energy. I don't know how I will make that happen, but my hopes continue to rest on the charity of the people who live in this land.

No sooner has that thought crossed my mind than I hear something coming up behind me. It's a small wagon pulled by a dray horse about a quarter mile away. As the wagon draws near, I wave to the elderly man sitting atop the farm cart until it clatters to a stop next to me.

"Verona?" I ask, pointing ahead. This is the best I can do to communicate my wishes.

The old man looks down at me, the pitiful cripple wrapped in his blanket and leaning on his cane, and replies, "*Si, signore. Salire a bordo.*" He motions for me to climb aboard. Finally! I think. Maybe my luck is changing. I may make it home after all.

I pull my blanket off to more easily pull myself up onto the wagon. Just as I hoist myself up, the man's heel hits me squarely in the chest, sending me plummeting backward onto the side of the dirt road. As I lie there confused, the old man spits at me, saying, "*Bastardo Austriaco!*" The man then whips the reins, and his rig bolts forward down the road.

What in the world has gotten into that man? Getting to my feet, I look down at my Austrian military uniform and realize what *Bastardo Austriaco* means. Apparently, the inhabitants of Venetia are no happier to be under Austrian control than the Bohemians are. And to make matters worse, I figure, most of them hoped the French and Sardinians would finish the job and drive the Imperial Army all the way out of Italia. That kick in my chest was just an expression of the old man's frustration. Who can blame him? In the future, I'll have to do a better job of concealing this Austrian army jacket when someone else comes along, *if* someone else comes along, that is.

Struggling onward along the road, one painful step leads to another. I've walked only a short way when the road tops a small rise. Suddenly, my eyes behold a welcome sight. Just beyond the rise sits a small village nestled among trees on the other side of a river, lazily snaking through a serene valley. My stomach is growling. Hopefully, one of the townspeople will offer me a meal, or at least a piece of bread. Even polenta will be acceptable. I take off my army jacket and fold it up, wrapping it in my blanket. Hopefully, that will prevent another incident like the one just moments ago. Heading for the town ahead, I move more quickly now, limping with anticipation down the hill, hurrying over the bridge and into the tiny village.

CHAPTER 18

THE SIGN ON THE SIDE of the road says Valeggio sul Mincio, and I wonder why such insignificant villages have such fanciful names. No church is to be seen, a sure indicator that this is but a minor bump in the road—a place where men gather in a barn for a friendly game of cards, or where a few women convene for a weekly prayer group. Except for one unremarkable mercantile shop and an eatery, there is nothing here but about twenty modest private domiciles.

My leg still aches from my spill off the wagon, and I survey the street for a place to sit and consider my options. Seeing no bench of any sort, I lower myself, with considerable effort, onto the ground, sitting on the side of the dirt street just opposite the small café. The place isn't yet open, but hopefully, someone will eventually show up and take pity on me, perhaps offering to buy me a meal in the humble establishment.

I now realize I'll be playing the part of a beggar for the duration of this journey. It will be impossible for me to succeed in the days to come without the help of strangers, and that means I'll be required to beg for that help. For my entire adult life, I've looked disparagingly upon beggars as they passed through Krouna. Indeed, I've considered beggars to be the dregs of society, unworthy of my charity. After all, with my reserves so scarce in the first place, why should I donate them to a complete stranger? Why can't beggars work for their own money, just like everybody else? Although Frantiska is definitely not like-minded in this matter, these are objections I've always held toward beggars. Does that make her a better person than me? Probably so.

But sitting here in the dirt, I realize I'm not just playing the part of a beggar—I *am* a beggar, and I'm no better than any of those beggars who passed by my house in Krouna. Those beggars were no lesser than me, only lesser in their circumstance, not because of their laziness or upbringing or aptitude.

There's something else, too. It will take more than just my own dire circumstances for me to be a successful beggar. Can I expect to just sit here and receive the alms of compassionate passersby without putting in some effort? No, being a beggar will not be as easy as I first thought. It will require some effort on my part if I'm to elicit sufficient pity. Certainly, my scruffy beard will help, and if I muss up my hair, that would help, too. And while my Austrian army uniform might be useful for begging in Austria, I'll keep it hidden under the blanket, for I'm now convinced it won't serve me well here in Venetia. There is one thing, however, that will be my foremost advantage in this enterprise, no matter where I am. That advantage is this damaged and splinted leg. Certainly, passersby can't ignore that, can they?

Gazing down the street, assessing whether my current location is optimal for my purposes, I find it quite acceptable. Then I shift my leg to a position extending out into the street. I make sure that the blanket is not concealing any part of it, especially the splint. Perfect, I think. With bowed head and hunched shoulders, I sit there with a wretched countenance, my hands cupped in my lap, ready to accept any generous donation from a passing charitable soul.

Soon, the owner of the eatery unlocks the front door and scowls at me from across the street. I raise my bowed head just high enough to watch the man as he sets up tables and chairs on the street outside his establishment. As the proprietor does so, he continues glancing in my direction, most likely considering me an undesirable addition to his town, sullying his street and scaring off his customers. Undeterred, I sit waiting, scanning down the street in both directions, searching for the comings and goings of townspeople.

A few people begin arriving at the café. Several of them glance my way but quickly redirect their eyes. I notice they have all chosen to take seats inside rather than out on the street, where they would have to look at me. But I hope that perhaps some of these people might offer me a few coins on their way out after their morning nosh.

I'm disappointed as the morning drags on, and soon, most of the café's customers have disappeared without offering me anything at all. Sitting there wondering what to do next, the sun rises above me, warming the surrounding street, and I soon feel drowsy. It doesn't take long before my cupped hands are lying limp and flat in my lap, and my head has fallen back against the wall behind me. I'm now sound asleep, mouth agape, snoring with impressive timbre and volume.

It would be nice to see my plight rewarded by the generosity of the people of Valeggio sul Mincio. It would be right if I, who suffered so much, would suffer no more. But perhaps it's because of my erratic faith that neither the nice nor the right outcome will come to pass. What comes to pass this afternoon is a one-horse fruit cart, clattering by on the street in front of me, with a young driver looking straight ahead, oblivious to my splinted leg splaying out into the street ahead of him.

I've been dreaming while I sleep. It's a very pleasant dream. *It is springtime, and Frantiska and I are sitting on a Bohemian hillside watching the sun descend. The western sky shines a radiant scarlet, as our children play happily in an expanse of purple clover on the hill below. Frantiska and I are speaking in low tones as lovers do, while Vincencie and Antonin roll gleefully in the clover. And little Josef is there, too. He runs to me and pulls at my sleeve. Pointing toward the sky, he says, "Look at the pretty birds, Papa." I gaze up at the creatures circling above and say, "Those aren't pretty birds. Those are——."*

The dream evaporates suddenly when I'm aroused by the pounding of the horse's hooves and the clatter of the fruit cart. I open my blinking eyes in time to see the horse pass by and the wheel of the cart strike my splinted leg, bolting the wagon suddenly into the air before it comes down and continues down the street.

A lightning bolt of white-hot pain shoots instantly through the entirety of my body. My scream follows, reverberating hideously among the surrounding buildings. It's a pain equaled only by the pain I suffered weeks earlier when the doctor set my fractured limb. Continuing to writhe and scream despairingly, I paw frantically at my tortured leg. Watching the wheel of the cart rolling over my leg has sent me into a fit of panic. My entire body stiffens with shock, and my face screws up into a tormented knot, with tears of terror bursting from my clenched-closed eyes.

At the sound of my screaming, the café owner and his only two customers come running from across the street. The fruit-cart driver jumps from his cart and attempts to gain control of his horse, which is visibly distressed by my wailing. As they watch me, the level of my agony is clear, and they stand rigid, with concerned faces. I finally open my bloodshot eyes and look up at the four souls who are taking stock of my considerable suffering. The realization hits me that the damage sustained to my leg isn't as severe as I imagined when first I saw the wheel colliding with it. In fact, it doesn't hurt much at all. That sturdy splint the doctor fabricated for my leg has protected it from any damage it might have incurred from the altercation with the fruit cart.

I have another realization, too. This is not the time to stop screaming and writhing. This is the very moment I've been waiting for, when I can extract maximum pity from these impressionable bystanders. Resuming my screaming, I allow it to continue for a suitable length of time, until I think it acceptable to reduce my expression of agony to mere grimacing and moaning, and then finally ramping it down to just heavy breaths of feigned exhaustion. My timing is exquisite. Although I've never been to Prague, it occurs to me that my performance must be every bit the equal of any that has graced the grand stages there. Soon, I allow the cart driver and a couple of bystanders to help me rise to my feet and settle into a comfortable chair outside the café. The owner, still shaken by my display, presents me with a wonderful plate of pasta and a glass of local vino rosso. I'm glad I'm not offered polenta, for the pasta dish in front of me is quite delightful, different from anything I've experienced in Bohemia.

My second helping of pasta and wine is consumed before I attempt, in my best Italian, to explain that I'm on a quest toward Verona and then onward to Bohemia. When the proper moment presents itself, I pretend to test my leg, feigning considerable discomfort. I test my acting prowess once again, convincing the cart driver, already stricken with guilt, that I am too damaged to continue on foot. My efforts prove successful, and he insists on carrying me on his wagon eastward to his hometown of Villafranca. With any luck, he'll care for me until I tell him I'm ready to move on. Maybe he'll even drive me all the way to Verona. I'm very pleased with myself now. Thanks to my exceptional acting skills, I've turned a potential disaster into a free meal and passage toward my destination. If a career in acting wasn't mostly the stuff of indigent traveling shows, I might consider taking it up professionally.

It's not long until I'm assisted onto the cart, riding comfortably out of town toward Villafranca. I've heard of Villafranca before, the town where Napoleon III and Franz

Joseph signed their truce to end the bloody conflict. I wonder if Austrian troops are still stationed there. Probably not, since the truce was signed over two months ago. But if they are, perhaps they will assist me in getting closer to home.

Villafranca is a quaint little village, larger than Valeggio sul Mincio, but not by much. The driver pulls the fruit cart up to a small home of mud and logs on the far edge of town and steps down from the dray to secure the reins to a nearby post. He helps me down from the cart, noting the considerable discomfort the leg appears to be causing his injured guest. Soon, an older man and woman, presumably my driver's parents, rush out the door to greet him, and after a short discussion, none of which I understand, the two men grip me under each arm and the woman leads us all into the house.

I'm still satiated from my meal at the village café, but when the evening meal appears before me, I eat eagerly. My meals may be few and far between after this, so I eat heartily. I'm happy to see that, once again, I'm served pasta, prepared with a savory sauce, and of course accompanied by copious amounts of red wine. While my preference would be a nice Bohemian pilsner, I am developing a taste for the wine of Italia. So much so, that this evening I imbibe just a bit too much. And soon after the meal is done, I'm snoring with great exuberance, comfortably slumbering on a cot, wrapped warmly in the blanket Maria Ricci gifted me.

Groggy from the evening's drink, I'm awakened by the woman of the house clanking about the kitchen early the next morning. Her curt demeanor indicates her readiness to see me on my way. Who can blame her? Her family has done more than enough for me. Besides, I'm not interested in tarrying any longer than necessary. I yearn for home, and, despite my morning headache, it's time to get going. Pushing myself up from the cot with my cane, I stumble slightly to catch my balance. My blanket falls to the floor, and the woman gazes upon my Austrian fusilier coat lying there in a heap. Thankfully, she picks up my blanket, wraps it around the coat, and hands it back to me without comment.

She offers me a bowl of a polenta concoction, which I politely decline. Soon, the fruit cart pulls up to the front door, and after sufficient *grazies* and *molte grazies*, I make my way out the door and up onto the cart, sitting comfortably next to the young driver.

It takes most of the morning to travel to Verona, but when we finally arrive, I'm not prepared for what I encounter in this remarkable place. The town reveals a level of sophistication I hadn't expected: grand, imposing buildings, impressive statues, bustling avenues, finely dressed people. But why wouldn't this place impress me? Before this little war, I'd never in all my thirty years ventured more than a short distance from Krouna. That being the case, everything I encounter should impress me, shouldn't it? The young cart driver, on the other hand, seems far less impressed with the town. He drops me off in the town square. And after a handshake, he heads back to Villafranca, leaving me standing and admiring the impressive spectacle that is Verona.

Taking off my blanket, I slip on my army coat in its place. There's an Austrian army fortification here somewhere, and I figure my uniform will help me find my way to it. As it turns out, I don't need any help at all. Scanning the remarkable town, I spot a structure rising above the skyline. It's a high-walled castle, and I walk unevenly with my cane in that direction, assuming I'm heading in the right direction.

It's almost noon when I finally arrive at the Castelvecchio. Entering the main gate, I notice Austrian soldiers milling about in the compound, surrounded by the tall castle walls. A line of soldiers is forming outside a doorway, men all waiting patiently, engaged in cheerful conversation. Soon, they proceed into one of the connected interior buildings, and I decide to join the queue. Hopefully, it will lead me to my first meal of the day. As the line shortens and I finally make my way past the door into the interior, I'm not disappointed. The large room is almost filled with army personnel talking loudly and gorging themselves on something unfamiliar to me. I don't care. I'm hungry, and I'll eat whatever it is, even if it's some kind of polenta.

Progressing through the line, I finally arrive at a table where a man in an apron loads my plate generously with food. Soon, I'm sitting among a group of German-speaking Austrian soldiers, feasting on a delicacy unfamiliar to me. It's a delicate white fish of some kind. I don't care what kind it is. It's delicious, and when one of the aproned men comes by to replenish my plate, I offer no protest.

As I devour my food, I notice the men around me getting up to move to other tables, and soon I'm sitting alone. That's when an officer approaches, asking, "*Was ist dein Regiment, Soldat?*"

I know well enough what he is asking and reply, "Kinsky, 47th from Bohemia, sir."

"*Ah, Böhmen. Warte einen Moment,*" he replies as he turns and walks away.

A few moments later, I'm still sitting alone enjoying my meal when the officer returns, accompanied by another soldier. The officer says something to the man, and the man turns to me, saying, "My name's Hans Huber." He speaks my language but with a rather thick Austrian accent. He continues, "The captain is wondering what you are doing here in Verona."

"I'm on my way home to Krouna. Just came from Solferino," I mumble after swallowing a mouthful of fish.

After an exchange with the officer, the man asks, "Why weren't you with the men from the 47th who passed through here a few weeks ago? Did you get lost?"

I explain the events of the last several weeks, including my recent mishap with the fruit cart. After the man translates to the officer, he confesses to me, "Some of our men are complaining about you."

"What do you mean? Complaining?" I ask, confused.

"Well, frankly, it's the odor. We need to get you cleaned up, and we should have your leg looked after. When you're done eating, I'll show you to the infirmary."

So they object to my odor, do they? Those damn, uppity Austrians! Who do they think they are? The way I suffered in their stupid war, they can just enjoy my Bohemian scent a little longer. Of course, none of this is spoken out loud. I hurriedly finish my meal and set my fork down on the table before standing and nodding formally to the captain, saying, "*Danke, Kapitän.*" Huber leads me out of the mess hall and continues to the infirmary on the other side of the compound. I can't remember the last time I had a bath, and I can hardly wait.

After cleaning up, a doctor examines my leg and replaces my crude splint with a new one. In addition, I'm given a crutch that will offer more stability than the cane I've been using to this point.

Things are looking up, and I'm confident the worst is behind me. I'll be home soon—I just know it. My thoughts wander back to my people in Krouna: my wife Frantiska, Vincencie, Antonin, Anton, and Rose. A fleeting thought crosses my mind, though distasteful, of Thomas Spacek. As I'm slipping deeper into my fantasy of home, Hans Huber appears at my bedside, saying, "The doctor thinks you should remain here awhile to let that leg heal. He said to stay off it for now. It appears your journey so far has not done it any good."

"How long does he want me to stay? I need to get home to Krouna," I insist.

"I'm not sure, but my advice would be that you do as he recommends. He knows better than you about such things."

Huber is turning to leave when I have an idea, asking, "Herr Huber, would you do me a favor?"

"If I can," he answers.

"Would you help me write a letter to my wife? I'm sure she's expecting me back soon, but now I'm stuck here in this bed for who knows how long. I'd like to let her know that I'm fine. My writing is not very good, and I could use your help if you'd be willing."

"Of course, soldier. I'll be right back," Huber says as he walks out the door. Soon, he is back with paper and a writing utensil in hand. He pulls up a chair and asks, "What would you like to say?"

I pause, looking for the proper words. "My wife's name is Frantiska, so begin with *Dear Frantiska.*"

Hans writes this down and looks up at me. He can see that I'm not sure how to begin. He finally offers a suggestion. "Do you want to say that you miss her?"

"Yes, I suppose that would be good." I don't know how she'll take that. Does she really think I miss her? Does she miss me? Who knows? I let my eyes venture up toward the ceiling, contemplating my next line.

Hans waits with patience, and then adds, "How about if we tell her about your condition—that you are all right?"

"Yes, that's good. Include that, but don't tell her about the leg. I don't want her to think I'm a cripple now." If she doesn't presently hold good thoughts about me, how will she feel about me if she thinks I'll be limping around the house for the rest of my life?

Huber continues writing, then adds, "And as you said before, we should make sure she knows you are on your way home, don't you think?"

"Yes. Add that, too. That's good," I reply.

"Anything else?" Hans asks as he looks up from his writing.

"I suppose I should say something about the children, too."

"Ah, you have children. Yes, we should indeed say that," Huber responds as he continues writing. He thinks for a moment and then finishes the letter.

"Do you want to sign it?"

"No. Just write my name there. Just write Josef, I guess. Thank you, Herr Huber."

"It was my pleasure. All I need is your wife's address, and I will get this posted for you."

"Send it to Frantiska Zach at Number 35 in Krouna, Chrudim District, Bohemia."

CHAPTER 19
BOHEMIA

IT'S BEEN JUST OVER A MONTH since Frantiska heard about Josef's death, and his absence continues to haunt her. Fortunately, the plans she and Anna have made have become an effective distraction to her ongoing mourning. As part of those plans, Frantiska is now determined to increase her weaving production of linen items, and this increased workload gives her little time to sit and ponder Josef's resting place on some distant Italian hillside. Frantiska's business has indeed flourished, and she's recently been able to peddle her wares through a local Krouna merchant who travels to several other villages. The dream of going to America seems more possible each day, and this raises her spirits markedly.

But now, with fall arriving, Anna has begun her teaching duties at the parish school, preventing her from offering as much help at home. And although Vincencie is now in school with Anna, Antonin still remains under Frantiska's care, often interrupting her work at the loom, making her self-imposed linen quotas much more difficult to meet. Still, she carries on, her determination bolstered by her resolve and ceaseless faith.

It is under these circumstances that Thomas arrives at her doorstep late one afternoon. Antonin is outside playing and Frantiska is, as usual, working relentlessly at her loom. She barely hears the knock on the door over the rhythmic working of her machine, and she's at once frustrated with the interruption, for it's been her hope to complete this particular piece of linen before Anna and Vincencie return home.

When Frantiska opens the door, she recognizes the odor immediately. It is the same stench of brew that used to follow Josef into the house from the tavern. But it is Thomas who now stands unsteadily in the doorway, and Frantiska can see he's consumed much more drink than he can handle.

"What do you want, Thomas?" she hisses with unmistakable disdain.

"I just came to see how you're doing," he answers, grasping the side of the doorframe to steady himself.

"Well, I'm doing fine, so if you'll excuse me—"

"I was just thinking," Thomas interrupts, "that maybe I could make things a little easier for you—you know, like when I halved your rent. I could maybe help out even more if you'd like."

"What does that mean? What do you have in mind?" Frantiska asks suspiciously. She knows Thomas better than to think he's being magnanimous. He is up to something, and she knows it.

"Can I come in so that we can talk about it?" he asks as he takes a clumsy step through the doorway.

"Uh, I su-suppose so," she stutters nervously, taking a step backward.

Thomas stumbles clumsily through the entry, saying, "I was thinking that in light of your hardship, I could eliminate your rent altogether until things get better for you. I realize how difficult the last weeks must have been for you and your family."

"You'd do that for us?" Frantiska asks in surprise. She begins estimating how much more money she could put away without the burden of a regular rent payment.

"I'd consider it," he says as he shuffles closer toward her. "I'd consider it, and perhaps I could assist in other ways, too."

"But why would you do that?" she asks.

"Well, Frantiska, without a man in the house anymore, I was thinking that you might have other needs that only a man can provide. I'd be willing to forgive your rent altogether if you would be willing to . . . well, you know."

Thomas lays his hand on her shoulder, but Frantiska reacts without the slightest hesitation, throwing her arm violently upward and knocking Thomas's hand away. "Get out!" she screams, pushing him toward the door. But even in his drunkenness, Thomas grabs her wrists and easily throws her back into the room. He slams the front door loudly, securing it with the crosspiece before he walks to the windows to clumsily secure the shutters, allowing only slivers of light to slice through the dimness.

"Thomas, stop this! You're drunk!" Frantiska pleads as she backs away from him.

Without a word, he is upon her. He reaches for the top of her dress and rips it viciously down to her waist, revealing her nakedness. Screaming in terror, she frantically gathers up the front of the tattered dress, attempting to cover herself.

Outside, Antonin is playing under his favorite tree when he hears the scream. He runs to the door, trying desperately to open it. "Mama, mama!" he calls as he pounds on it, crying.

Just up the road, Anna, who has dismissed the schoolchildren early as a reward for their excellent behavior, is walking home with Vincencie. As she gets closer, Anna hears Antonin crying uncontrollably and sees him beating with his small hands on the door. She clutches Vincencie's hand tightly and yanks her along as fast as the little girl's legs will carry her toward the house.

"What's wrong, Antonin?" Anna pleads as she arrives.

"Mama!" the little boy gasps, frightened.

"Help! Somebody, help me!" Anna hears Frantiska scream from inside.

Anna tries frantically to open the door, but she finds it immovable. She suddenly spots an ax that's leaning against an old stump where Frantiska sometimes beheads her chickens for eating. Anna grabs the ax and begins hacking at the closed window shutters. The shutters, which Josef so meticulously crafted years ago, begin to splinter into hundreds of pieces, and it isn't long before Anna is crawling nimbly through the destruction and over the windowsill into the house.

By the time Anna stands to gather herself, Thomas has already retreated to the door, where he is removing the crosspiece. Frantiska stands next to her straw bed on the other side of the room, grasping the fragments of her dress and trembling with equal amounts of fear and rage.

"The offer still stands, Frantiska. Just think about it," Thomas mumbles menacingly before he turns and stomps out the door, heading back toward the middle of the town.

Anna hurries to cover Frantiska with a blanket and sit her down on the edge of the bed. Sitting next to her friend, Anna wraps her arm sympathetically around Frantiska's shoulders as Vincencie stands petrified in the doorway, eyes wide, with Antonin whimpering tearfully at her side.

CHAPTER 20

ANNA HAS FOUND TEACHING to be challenging. How can it not be? Her only previous experience was her instruction of a young cousin back in Jarošov. But at the parish school, she's faced with the task of balancing the needs of thirty-two children of various ages, who have come to her with varying levels of knowledge and abilities. Her lack of teaching materials makes this undertaking even more difficult. But in spite of it all, Anna is determined, and she is beginning to develop a definite affinity for the children who come to learn from her each day.

By mid-September Anna has found her stride, and the children have easily embraced the daily routine established for them. Indeed, Anna is showing that she can be not only an effective disciplinarian but also an effective, even inspirational, teacher. This fact is becoming obvious to the parents who watch their children leave for school each morning anxious to learn and return each afternoon excited about their day's activities. Even the town judge, Emil Spacek, has heard of Anna's exemplary work.

On Monday in the third week of September, Anna looks up from her reading lesson to see three men walking in and standing, observing her in silence, in the very back of her classroom.

"Can I help you?" Anna asks with curiosity.

"We are sorry to disturb your class, Miss Krejsa," says Pastor Košút. "Please carry on. When you have a chance, we'd like a brief word with you if that's possible."

"Very well. Just give me a moment," she replies, smiling at the pastor and adding an acknowledging smile to the judge standing next to him. But when her eyes fall on the third man, her smile immediately vanishes. It is Thomas, the judge's son, and the two of them share an expressionless moment, a moment imbued with the dirty bit of knowledge about his encounter with Frantiska a few weeks earlier. Anna immediately forces her attention back to the students sitting in front of her and proceeds to assign in-class work that will occupy them for the time being. Then, when she is satisfied that all her students are suitably engaged, she walks to the back of the room to meet with her visitors.

"Is anything wrong?" Anna asks the pastor.

"Wrong? No, nothing's wrong," Pastor Košút replies with a reassuring smile. "May we step out of your classroom for a moment to speak with you?"

She glances back at her class, saying, "I guess that would be fine—just for a moment."

The four of them step outside, and the pastor goes on. "We've been hearing some very good things about your teaching, Miss Krejsa. The children seem to enjoy being here, and the parents are well pleased."

"They're nice children. I think they're learning at a good rate," is Anna's measured reply.

"I hear that you may be short of supplies. Is that correct?" the judge asks matter-of-factly.

"Why, yes, I am. We desperately need more reading books for the different levels of readers in the class, and the slate boards my students use to practice their numbers and letters are in very bad shape. It would be helpful to get some replacements for those," Anna says, looking at the judge hopefully.

"I think we can help you with that. Tell us precisely what you require, and I'll see what I can do," he says with what Anna takes to be a slight smile, a veiled expression to be sure, but one that she finds encouraging.

"Wonderful. Thank you very much, Herr Spacek," Anna replies gratefully. "I'm sure the children will really benefit from it."

"There is one other thing, Miss Krejsa," the judge adds. "I understand that the contributions from the children's parents are insufficient for your living needs. At least, that's what the pastor has told me. Is that true?"

"Oh, I'm getting by. I'm just glad that, in view of their circumstances, the parents can offer me anything at all."

"Nevertheless," says the judge, "I'm inclined to augment your pay with a small stipend that should help. We want you to be happy here. It has been difficult retaining teachers here in Krouna. We'd like you to stay, Miss Krejsa. How's that sound to you?"

"That sounds just wonderful, Herr Spacek," she replies excitedly. "Thank you very much."

Anna is already considering how she could save even more money to put aside for their dream of America. She is barely getting by at present, and though she doesn't really need the extra money for her living expenses, the prospect of this extra income suddenly brings her dream into clearer focus. Like Frantiska, Anna realizes that maybe this dream is not as far-fetched as it first seemed. Nevertheless, she has no intention of revealing any of this to these men, at least not until her departure is imminent.

As the three men turn to walk down the path toward the road, Anna can see Thomas glancing back at her. She meets his glance unabashedly and offers him a brazen look of contempt. He has nothing on her—not anymore. She knows something about Thomas that she can use against him if she so chooses—a bit of leverage she can bring to bear at some future moment, if that moment ever presents itself.

Since Thomas's assault, Frantiska has retreated into her typical mental state of reclusiveness. For all her life, this has been her way of dealing with crises. She did this years ago when her parents passed. She did this when she lost her first child, and yet again more recently when little Josef died.

And she did it with the news of her husband's death on the battlefield at Solferino. This is her way of protecting herself from further immediate harm, helping herself to regain her bearings and amass the courage to once again move forward with her hard life.

Out of necessity, however, Frantiska is still able to attend to all the things required of her as caregiver and breadwinner for her children, but she does it in relative silence, speaking only when absolutely necessary. Vincencie and Antonin are confused by all of this. They have no idea what happened to their mother that day when Thomas showed up at their door, but they know it was something of importance. It has taken their mother away from them somehow. Concerned about her, they know their mother well enough to tread lightly in her presence, and they're determined to remain on their best behavior until she returns to them.

As she has always managed to do in the past, Frantiska finally feels herself coming back to life. She feels a strength mounting inside her, a nascent force that she recognizes for its healing potential, a power that will help her accept the realities of her life as it is and move on with it. There is also something else that she doesn't recognize at first but becomes more apparent as her life comes back into focus. It is at first just a shadowy impression of scorn for Thomas, but it begins to fester and metastasize into an intensity that spreads into the far reaches of her everyday thoughts. She is at first ashamed of this. Isn't forgiveness the cornerstone of her Christian belief? Shouldn't she let God be Thomas's ultimate judge? Unfortunately, through Thomas's actions, she now fully recognizes the inherent evil of mankind, just as she once believed in its inherent goodness. Is there any going back from this dark revelation? she wonders. Has Thomas's attack somehow damaged her psychologically?

Soon something happens that convinces her of the clear veracity of these dark convictions. In the early evening of the day when Anna comes home with the good news of her pay raise, Frantiska receives a mysterious letter. It is delivered by none other than the object of her bitter contempt, the judge's son, Thomas.

The two women are at home discussing Anna's good fortune when a knock rattles the door. Frantiska opens it to find the smirking Thomas standing silently with his hand outstretched holding an envelope. Frantiska abruptly snatches it from his grasp and examines the name and address on the front. It's her name, alright, and her correct address, too. She rarely receives letters from anyone. Why would she? The only people she knows live within walking distance of her lowly hovel. She looks up at Thomas, expecting some unpleasant comment, but none is forthcoming. He simply turns and walks away without a word. Closing the door and retreating inside, Frantiska shows the letter to Anna.

"Well, aren't you going to open it?" Anna asks impatiently.

Frantiska breaks the wax seal and slips the letter out of its envelope. Her eyes immediately scan to the bottom, where she is shocked by the signature she did not expect.

"This is from Josef!" she shouts excitedly. She begins reading the letter with enthusiasm, but by the time she's at the end, her demeanor changes from exhilaration to rage. She spits, "This isn't from Josef! This is some kind of sick joke!" She thrusts the letter at Anna, saying, "It's that damn Thomas. I know it is."

Anna takes the letter and reads it with great interest:

Dear Frantiska,

I cannot begin to express the degree to which I miss you, my dearest Frantiska. You are forever in my thoughts, and I long to return home to your warm embrace once again.

Please know that I am in good health but for the pain in my heart, which longs for your touch.

Please give the children a thousand kisses for me. I miss them greatly and look forward to holding them on my knee once again.

You may anticipate my return home in very short order. You are continually and constantly in my thoughts.

Your loving and obedient husband,

Josef, August 1859

"Are you sure Josef didn't write this before he passed?" asks Anna.

"Well, he never could write well. You know that. And look at the date. That can't be right."

"Hmm—but maybe he isn't dead after all. Could that be possible?"

"No, Anna. I think this is Thomas's work. Josef didn't write this letter. That signature wasn't written by him."

Anna isn't ready to accept Frantiska's theory. She asks, "He could have dictated it to someone else, right?"

"But he would never dictate those things like *warm embrace* or the part about the pain in his heart. And that *obedient* part? That is definitely not what Josef would say! This is a cruel joke by that bastard Thomas Spacek. I just know it is. He will live to regret doing this to me."

The letter at once validates the animosity Frantiska feels toward Thomas. If she previously held any regret for harboring these hateful feelings toward him, that regret is now dispelled and forgotten.

"What do you intend to do, Frantiska?" Anna asks, concerned.

"I don't know for sure, but I certainly won't accept his charity. I'll pay every bit of the rent I owe the bastard. Then

I'll find a way to make him suffer," Frantiska says, then adding, "Maybe we should go to his father and report what he's done to me."

Anna shakes her head, saying, "We can't do that. What if he doesn't believe us? It could cost me my job. And he could bring a lot of pain down on you as well."

Frantiska thinks about this for a moment and realizes Anna is right. Judge Spacek is generally a fair man, but if his son stands accused of something as serious as this, who knows how he will react? He might try to hide it, and Frantiska wonders how far the man will go to do so. Approaching him directly with this accusation would be far too risky. No, she can't risk the welfare of Anna or the children just to settle this score with Thomas.

CHAPTER 21
ITALIA

TWO WEEKS PASS after my arrival at the troop quarters at Verona's Castelvecchio. My leg is feeling much stronger now, and I've tested it regularly on walks around the compound and along the River Adige, paralleling the north wall of the castle. On days when my leg has felt especially strong, I've also ventured away from the castle into Verona's town center. I've found Verona to be a remarkable town, and it boggles my mind to imagine living in such a place of culture and beauty. Still, I long for my homeland and my family waiting for me back in Krouna.

It's mid-September when the army doctor finally deems me well enough to be released from his care. Hans has been a fine companion during my time here, visiting my bedside almost daily, sometimes taking his meals sitting next to me, sometimes reading the poetry he's written in his journal. Hans's attention is much appreciated, and I will greatly miss my new friend when I leave.

"So, I guess you'll be heading north to Wien, Josef?" asks Hans.

"Yes, and then on through Brno toward home, I guess."

"Are you familiar with Wien?"

"Not really. Before my deployment to Italia, I'd been nowhere except Krouna. I've heard that Wien is an amazing place, though. Have you been there?" I ask.

"Indeed, I have, Josef. I was born and raised there. Many Bohemians live in and around Wien, it being so close to their border. That's how I became familiar with the language," the Austrian says. "How will you get to Wien? How will you survive once you get there?"

"I'm not quite sure. I suppose I'll walk and hope for charity along the way. It's worked pretty well for me so far."

"Well, maybe until the point when your leg was run over by that fruit cart," Hans jokes. "Let me talk to the *Kapitän*. I think some troops are moving by rail to Wien in a couple of days. Perhaps we can get you on that train. The army probably won't take you further than Wien, however. You'll be on your own after that."

"Fantastic. The ride to Wien will be a great help. This sore leg will really appreciate it."

"But when you get to Wien, I hope you don't plan to beg for food. They don't like beggars much in Wien, so I wouldn't try that same stunt you tried in Valeggio sul Mincio. There is a lot of construction going on, and I've heard there are quite a few jobs, even for people with no skills. Maybe you can get some work and save enough money to get home. Didn't you tell me you did carpentry or something like that back in Krouna?"

"Yes, carpentry and stonework. I'm pretty good at fixing things, if I do say so myself," I state proudly, for I was indeed good at what I did. That's why Thomas had continued to employ me around Krouna, despite our strained relationship.

"You know, there is a fellow in Wien who might use a man like you. He's done much construction work on my father's home there." Hans reaches for a sheet of paper nearby and begins scribbling a name and address on the page. "This's his address if my memory serves me well. Tell him that Hans Huber sent you. He should be able to find you something to do."

As promised, Hans secures a passage for me on the train to Wien. And on a beautiful autumn day, I watch the scenery fly by as I ride the train out of Verona, on through Venetia, and then into the heart of Austria. The train necessarily makes numerous stops along the way to load and unload goods, and the locomotive also needs to be replenished with water and wood for propulsion, but I don't mind at all. Not as long as I'm fed with the rest of the troops and have a place to lay my head in the boxcar. In fact, I'm having the time of my life. The fall colors are just beginning to emerge. As the train races toward Wien, I gaze out the open door of the boxcar in wonder at the way the golden and red hues of the foliage wash by the train, like the land itself is afire. I wonder if the trees in Krouna are changing as well. I imagine so, and I might even make it back home in time to enjoy the season there in its full glory.

It takes two full days for the train to make it to Wien. As it pulls into the station, I'm at once surprised by the clamor of activity. All around the station, building materials are being unloaded from the train, loaded upon large wagons, and then pulled away by horse and mule teams, making room for more wagons.

This is no charming and quaint Verona, that's for sure. Wien seems to be a city in the process of building—or perhaps rebuilding—itself. Curious, I follow one wagon carrying a load of stone, not unlike the stone I've used in my masonry work back home. The horse-drawn wagon slogs along for a long time, paralleling a tall rampart. The wall abruptly devolves into a disheveled pile of jagged rock where a section of it previously stood. It looks as if the fortification around the town center is being dismantled for some reason, and I can see hundreds of laborers, many laying stones for a grand boulevard where the wall once stood. Others are engaged in new construction in the cleared areas next to the boulevard. There are many more workers here loading and carrying off the remnants of the razed wall on the wagons that were previously unloaded.

Fishing in my pocket for the piece of paper Hans gave me, I look around to find someone who might help me. I find one nearby who appears to be a supervisor of one of the work teams, and I thrust the paper in front of him. The man squints at the writing and then points, saying something I don't understand, and I walk in the direction of the man's pointed finger.

I continue to show the paper to people as I walk, and they continue to point the way for me. Continuing on, I gaze up at the many imposing buildings of the city center, once encircled by the old ramparts. The grandeur of Wien is truly impressive. This shouldn't surprise me. After all, this is the seat of government for the Austrian Empire. I wonder if I might run into Emperor Franz Joseph on the street. Of course, I know this is a ridiculous thought. Still, if I by some chance encounter the great Franz Joseph, I'll tell the emperor what I think of his *little war* in Italia.

Eventually, I make my way beyond the din of the construction site and end up in a quieter, more residential part of the city. The homes here are quite modest, some not much nicer than my hovel back in Krouna. Finally, I come to a stop in front of one of them, this one somewhat larger than my own, and I peer down at the address Hans has written for me. Looking up at the door, I rap loudly on it. There's no answer at first, but soon the door creaks open, and a woman cautiously peeks out at me through the opening. I hold the paper up in front of her face so she can read it. She seems to be much older than me, but it's difficult to tell, seeing only the sliver of her that the door opening reveals. It's clear that she's dubious of me and won't be inviting me into her home anytime soon. But I don't blame her. I'm a rather bedraggled stranger, after all.

The woman points at a bench on the street next to the house and mumbles, "*Warten Sie hier. Alexander wird bald zu Hause sein.*"

I'm not sure what she means, but her gesture is clear. I take a seat on the hard bench and lean my crutch against the side of the house. Based upon what Hans has told me, this Alexander Hofer is a busy and capable craftsman who employs several workers. With all the construction going on in the town, I assume Hofer is most likely engaged at a work site somewhere at the moment. The sun has fallen below the rooflines of the neighboring homes, and I'm hopeful Hofer will be returning home soon.

My wait isn't a long one. Soon, a hunch-shouldered man comes trudging up the street, carrying a wooden box of tools in one hand and a shovel and pickax in the other. The man walks slowly and is breathing hard. Alexander isn't a young man by any stretch of the imagination, well beyond his most productive years, now struggling to maintain an arduous workload that in years past must have seemed much easier. He stops in front of me, sets his toolbox down, and without a word, stares at me questioningly. Struggling to my feet, I hand the man my piece of paper.

Hofer sees his own name and address scribbled near the top of the page and notices some sentences written near the bottom. As he reads, a smile appears on his wizened face.

"Ah, Hans wrote this. You are this Josef Zach from Bohemia?" he asks cheerfully.

"That's me," I reply, surprised he knows my language. "You speak Bohemian?"

"Oh, yes. I come from Gmünd originally. That's right on the Bohemian border. Do you know it?"

"I'm afraid not, Herr Hofer."

"I knew a lot of Bohemians when I lived there. And you may call me Alexander," the old man says. "Hans has written here that you are a mason and a carpenter."

"Yes. Hans thought perhaps you could find me some employment while I'm here in Wien," I say hopefully.

Alexander folds the paper and hands it back to me. "You've come at a good time," he says. "There's much work to be done here."

"Yes, I noticed that. What's going on around here?"

"They're tearing down the walls that separate the old city from the surrounding residential areas. You may have seen that they are creating a large street that will replace the ramparts. When that's complete, many new buildings will be constructed. Some of that construction has already begun."

"So, you think you can find work for me, Herr—or rather, Alexander?"

"If Hans vouches for you, I think I might find something for you, Josef," says Alexander. "Have you eaten yet?"

"Well, no. But you need not trouble yourself," I reply, wondering how Alexander's wife might react to my invading her home.

"No trouble at all. Come in and tell me all about what Hans has been doing. I haven't seen him since he left for the war. Please . . . ," Alexander says as he opens the door, motioning me to enter.

Alexander's home surprises me by its luxury. Well, perhaps luxury is a bit of an overstatement, but certainly it's a step up from my meager circumstances back home. Belied by the unremarkable appearance of its exterior, the inside features two well-appointed rooms, both with solid wood floors. Alexander and his wife may not be people of means, but they are a far cry from the impoverished souls in Krouna.

As luck would have it, Alexander's wife, Marta, turns out to be an exceedingly gracious hostess. Though her command of the Bohemian language is far inferior to her husband's, she's quick to accommodate my every need, and soon, I sit at a table teeming in Austrian culinary fare much more to my liking than the polenta of my earlier travels.

"So, Josef, what can you tell me about Hans Huber? What's he been up to?" asks Alexander, eager to hear about his friend's exploits.

I want to dig right into the delicious meal Marta has set before me, but I try to hide my disappointment at Alexander's request.

"He is doing quite well," I answer as I reach for the ladle in the large bowl in front of me. Seeing my hosts still looking at me with their hands in their laps, mine quickly retreat under the table.

I continue, "While I was in Verona, he took very good care of me at the military installation. Sometimes he even read his poetry to me."

"Ah, excellent. He's still writing poetry. I remember a few years back when I did some work for his father. Hans would read his work to me, too. I'm not much of an expert on poetry, but I thought it was pretty good."

"Well, we spent a lot of time together," I say, "and he read quite a few of his verses to me. Hans seems to have a knack for—shall we say—flowery language?"

"Indeed, he does," Alexander agrees. "I think he might be quite talented. But as I said, I'm no expert."

"*Bitte*. Please," pleads Marta to her husband. "Enough talk. Eat."

I could give Marta a huge, juicy kiss at this moment. The scrumptious aroma wafting up from the dinner table is almost too much to bear, and after Alexander utters a quick prayer, the time has come to enjoy the meal.

This is what I consider real food—goulash replete with juicy chunks of beef and delicious bread dumplings drowned in a thick dark gravy. It makes me feel closer to my homeland, and I eat voraciously. With food like this, even though I long to be home, I consider this town to be a place where I might linger for a while.

It should come as no surprise that navigating my way through Wien life is difficult. I continue to struggle with not only the language but also the customs of this strange place.

Everyone in Wien is in a big hurry to get somewhere, crisscrossing streets and boulevards, offering only fleeting impersonal glances at passing strangers, and grudgingly tolerating the many laborers occupying the construction sites. I realize it will take me some time to get used to all this hubbub.

I'm soon in Alexander's employ, working as one of his laborers laying stone for the new Ring Boulevard, or the Ringstrasse, as the locals call it. This is difficult work, but it's work I'm used to. Unlike many of his other workers, I'm an experienced mason, which puts me at a definite advantage. While many men complain about the working conditions, the only thing giving me difficulty is the inconvenience of my crutch. Despite this, I'm able to outpace the rest of the paving crew. And eventually, when I'm able to dispense with the crutch altogether, the other men working on the crew recognize me as the best of them.

Alexander recognizes my skill as well, and soon he approaches me with a work assignment of a different kind. It seems that Alexander has been contacted by a local aristocrat, originally from Prague but now living in Wien, who has need of a stoneworker and a carpenter. I can easily fulfill both these requirements, and working for a fellow Bohemian, albeit a member of the aristocracy, is a welcome prospect. To make the situation even sweeter, Count Svoboda, my new employer, can offer me a place to live on the grounds of his expansive property. It's a small one-room gardener's quarters, but it will be perfectly fine for my purposes, eliminating the need for me to find lodging elsewhere.

The next day, Alexander and I leave the Hofer home, bidding farewell to Marta and heading to the Svoboda mansion. I suspect my presence at Alexander and Marta's home has put a strain on them, especially Marta, who watches me ravenously eating through her food reserves.

Still, she remains gracious to the very end of my stay and wishes me well for the future. As I leave their house, however, she closes the door with a little too much enthusiasm. Does she slam it shut? I'm not sure. All I know for sure is that, although Marta might not miss her houseguest, I will most certainly miss her cooking.

The Count's property is in the Döbling district in the northernmost part of Wien, and it takes us a long time to reach the mansion. Alexander and I proceed through the tall iron gates and are at once struck by the immensity of the Count's home. Constructed of white stone and adorned with two tall spires, the front of the structure displays a wide staircase. It ascends from the lawn to a massive porch that extends across the entire first floor of the two-story structure. The building sports a backdrop of tall spruce and yew trees planted in rows, rimming a large green space at the rear of the property.

A servant soon spots us and hurries out to greet us as we approach. The man wastes no time and gets right to it, leading us around the property, identifying repair work to be done on the surrounding stone wall, and then taking us inside the house to note structural work and woodworking projects needing attention. There is plenty for me to do, and I know I'll be needed here for quite some time. To be sure, I'm anxious to continue my journey home, but I also feel obliged to arrive there with some money in my pockets. I know Frantiska may not be excited to see me, but she will at least be excited about the money I bring to her.

With all projects identified, we return to where we began at the front of the house, and Alexander begins negotiating with the man to determine an estimated time frame for completion as well as my pay rate. It isn't long before Alexander and I head back to Alexander's home to assemble the tools and supplies I'll need for my work. By midafternoon, I'm back at the mansion, beginning repairs on the outer stone wall as Count Svoboda's official handyman.

"You have much work to do here. That wall has been neglected for quite a while."

The voice comes from behind me, and I glance over my shoulder, curious to see who is speaking in my own language. The man is about my age and very smartly attired.

"That's fine with me," I say. "I can use the work. If you need assistance, you should probably go to the front of the house. There is a servant there who can help you."

"No, I need nothing. I just wondered if there was anything you need, Herr Zach," the man says.

I immediately drop the trowel and place my hand on the wall to steady myself as I struggle to my feet. Brushing myself off, I say, "I'm sorry. You must be the Count."

"Yes, but I'm not much for titles. Herr Svoboda will be sufficient."

I note just how far my employer will extend his informality. Apparently, not very far. Evidently, first names are out of the question here. I'm hardly surprised, judging from the man's exquisite double-breasted white jacket and fine leather footwear. I know my place and would never presume to be this man's equal.

Svoboda continues, "I hear that you're from Bohemia, so I thought I'd come out to meet you. I have very few employees who speak our language, and I thought it would be nice to hear the sound of it again. Did you get settled in the gardener's quarters?" the Count asks, gesturing toward the little hut.

"Yes, it'll be very acceptable," I answer. "Thank you, Herr Svoboda."

"Come, follow me," the Count says as he turns suddenly, walking toward the back of the mansion. I follow obediently.

We arrive at a small set of steps ascending to a rather ordinary-looking door, and the Count steps up to open it. He motions for me to enter. Inside, I can smell the pungent aromas of herbs and vegetables cooking on the very large stove. Interrupted from her work, a rather large, aproned woman turns from the stove to smile at us. Sweating from the heat of the stove, she is quite obese, with rosy cheeks, and rather pooched lips. Those lips look to be already puckered and ready to kiss me if the occasion presents itself. It won't.

"This is Sophie," the Count says. "She's our cook, and a very good one, indeed. She would be happy to make something for you when you get hungry during your time here. Also, feel free to come in during the day for a drink of water if you'd like. Though Sophie speaks only German, I'm sure she will help you as best she can."

This is far more than I could have expected, and I am pleased with the arrangement. I figure the less money I spend for food and housing, the more I'll have to take home to Frantiska.

"Thank you, Herr Svoboda. You're too kind," I say.

"Think nothing of it. Unless you have questions, I'll let you get back to work. I'll try not to bother you too much in the days to come. However, I do want to hear about Bohemia. I haven't been back there for quite some time."

The Count is leaving the kitchen area when I ask, "What's that?"

Svoboda looks back to see me staring at something in the corner. "Oh, that? That's just an old crank organ my wife purchased when we first came to Wien. It doesn't work anymore."

"A crank organ?"

"Yes, you crank the lever and it makes music. Actually, it doesn't make music. Not anymore. My wife thought it'd be nice to have for social affairs. You know, for entertainment.

But the damn thing was so loud, it drove people away—not exactly the result she had hoped for. When it stopped working, I was actually relieved."

Studying the contraption, fascinated by it, I ask, "Would you mind if I try to fix it? I won't let that interfere with my duties you can be sure."

"I suppose, if you want. Sure, take it with you. Don't get your hopes up, though. As I said, it hasn't worked for years. It's probably full of rot by now," the Count says.

I gather up the thing and retreat out the back door to my small cottage, carefully depositing it inside on the floor. I've no idea how the device works, but I'm resolved to find out. It will have to wait until later, though. There is still some time left in the afternoon, and I've much work to complete on the stone wall.

That evening, I study the crank organ. It is a remarkable contraption, made of bellows and valves, axles and rollers, air flaps and wind chambers. I've never attempted to repair anything so intricate, but I'm determined to understand how this strange thing operates. Working by the light of two candles in my small hut, it doesn't take me long to disassemble the outer shell and start poking about in the machine's innards. Thankfully, there's no indication of rot, but there is plenty of dirt and grime to be removed. Something seems to be amiss with the bellows, though I can't find a leak anywhere. Eventually, I find the problem and adjust a small leather flap that controls the air intake. I'm pleased to see that the paper rollers regulating air passage through the reeds are in reasonably good shape. After making some adjustments to the intake valve, the outer shell is soon reassembled. It's late in the evening when I finally feed the paper ribbon along the rollers and give the crank a vigorous spin.

The cacophony of sound blaring from the machine startles me, and I immediately stop, glancing out my window toward the main house, hoping no one else has heard it. Then I begin to crank much more slowly lest I awaken the people sleeping in the Count's mansion. The sound is glorious for its energy and rhythm. What is that music? Some kind of polka, I presume. A rather odd one, however. Not like any polka I've heard before.

I continue to turn the crank, my foot tapping along with the relentless beat. When the tune eventually ends, another tune immediately begins. This one I recognize as some sort of waltz. I've heard itinerant musicians who have come through Krouna from time to time, stopping at the local tavern to play polkas on their squeezeboxes for tips. Once in a while, they've performed waltzes, which they said were all the rage in Wien. I've always found these waltzes to be very odd. How can anyone dance to one of these tunes? Unlike polkas, waltzes seem much too slow for dancing. And the strangest thing about them is they seem to skip a beat at annoyingly regular intervals. But as I crank away, it becomes easier to comprehend the groupings of three beats, and I soon find myself swaying back and forth in rhythm. These waltzes are pretty catchy after all, I think. I stop my cranking when the waltz ends and rewind the roll, intending to play the entire thing again. Thinking better of it, however, I set the device aside. The wall will beckon to me early in the morning, and I need my sleep. I lie down on the straw bed and succumb to slumber with the sound of the waltz still swaying to and fro in my head.

CHAPTER 22
AMERICA

FRANCIS IS FEELING GOOD about himself. He's done some excellent work the last couple of weeks, he thinks. It's God's work. He mustn't forget that. God is ordering this—not him. Though it's late in the season, he's just fulfilled a promise he made last year to visit a group of Brethren who live about a week's walk to the north. He'd vowed to repeat the visit, and in return, they'd promised to recruit a much larger congregation for the event.

This year's visit was very well received. He delivered his sermon with his usual flair, baptized three babies, and even collected a nice donation besides. After a hearty meal and farewell pleasantries, he'd started for home. For six days he's been walking, stopping at homes along the way to gain overnight lodging in return for his spiritual guidance. Even at homes where families aren't interested in hearing the Word, he finds people at least respectful of its purveyor, rarely ever turning him away.

Francis finally enters Tama County, and he has a decision to make. He can either head home, taking the same route he came on, or he can turn in the direction of Toledo, the county seat, to see if the postmaster is holding any letters for him. It's not unusual for him to receive letters from the old country or from communities of Brethren requesting his counsel. His only worry is that he's unfamiliar with this particular trail to Toledo. He isn't sure if there will be any homes along the way where he might spend the night. Certainly, he'll find somewhere suitable, he hopes.

Francis continues onward toward Toledo, and as the sun sets, he still hasn't seen a farmhouse. Wincing at the north wind hitting his face, he pulls his hat down and his coat tight around him, sensing that a cold front must be moving in. If a storm is approaching, he knows he'll be in trouble. He hasn't come prepared for this. His light coat will be no match for colder conditions, and he has no means of building a fire. Besides, that'd be impossible with this wind whirling about. The thought occurs to him that this trail might be some minor route that's seldom used. He hopes that isn't the case, but what can he do now? Turn around and go back? It's too late for that. No, he must carry on and hope for the best. Certainly, there will be a homestead up ahead. He'll put himself in God's hands, he decides, as he mutters aloud in prayer, trudging into the forbidding wind.

Shivering, Francis walks on, clutching his arms in front of his body. Suddenly, he stumbles, losing his balance, then rights himself, looking back to see what he tripped over. There's nothing there. His knees feel weak, and he realizes how unstable he is. Perhaps if he walks faster, the exertion will help him warm up. But he stumbles again. This time, he falls to his knees and struggles to get back on his feet. What's wrong with me? he wonders. Upright once again, he staggers onward.

Francis thinks about Jesus wandering in the wilderness for forty days. He thinks about how he survived without food and shelter—how he faced temptation from the devil. If Jesus survived that wilderness, Francis is certain he can survive this one.

It begins to rain, and the insistent drops assail his face with impunity, making it difficult to see. Is the rain obscuring his view or is his vision somehow failing him? He's not sure. Maybe both. There's something else, too. He now has trouble feeling his limbs, and it isn't long before he falls again to his knees. This time he remains there, repeating, "Jesus Christ, Son of the Living God, have mercy on me. Jesus Christ, Son of the Living God, have mercy on me . . ."

As he kneels shivering in the cold mud, blinking away the rain washing across his face, he can't remember where he is or where he's going. Confusion is overtaking him. He thinks of Aneta and the children, his father in Javornik, his student days back in Debreczen, his congregation in Miroslava, and other memories prying their way into his delirium.

Suddenly, someone is lifting him, extricating him from the mire. And before Francis can understand what's happening, he's wrapped in a blanket and thrown onto the back of a horse. His vision remains blurred and his other senses dulled. But despite the numbness of his limbs, he can feel the gait of the animal moving under him and smell the unmistakable odor of wet horseflesh. He clings to the horse's neck as best he can to avoid falling off the beast, and as he looks up, he sees something he can't quite understand. Might he be hallucinating? What he sees appears to be an Indian leading the animal by a rope.

Francis has heard of Indians living close by. But he's seen one only once, when he was preaching to a group of believers last summer in a wooded area, one of God's primeval temples. He remembers the man on his horse at the back of the crowd that day. Holding a long spear and clad only in a breechcloth and leggings the man indeed cut a magnificent figure as he sat tall on his mount. Francis remembers the reaction of the people in the crowd. They whispered nervously to one another as more and more of them took notice of the savage who was observing the goings-on with much curiosity. Fortunately, to everyone's relief, the horseman must have heard enough or become bored. He soon moved on, allowing Francis to regain the crowd's full attention and resume his sermon.

Francis finds it difficult to make out the man leading the horse through the insistent rain. But he can see that the man is wearing similar leggings to the Indian Francis observed on that day last summer. On the Indian's head is a fur-rimmed cap, and a garment of rough cloth covers his broad shoulders. Where is the Indian taking me? Francis wonders. Is he going to take me into the woods, cut my throat, scalp me, and hang my scalp on his spear? Francis's vision has come back into focus now, jolted by the adrenalin that fear provides. He tests the movement in his legs and arms, but they all seem quite worthless. Besides, it's all he can do to stay atop the horse, let alone attempt to flee from his captor. He is helpless, at the mercy of this savage. Francis has read about the wickedness of such men—their thirst for blood— their heathen customs. Of all the ways he's imagined his life's end, it never occurred to him it might be at the hands of one of these godless demons.

Francis begins again, "Jesus Christ, Son of the Living God, have mercy on me. Jesus Christ, Son of the Living God, have mercy on me . . ."

The rain is still coming down hard, and as they enter Toledo, Francis hardly notices. He is much too consumed with fright, imagining his demise at the hands of this uncivilized creature. The horse finally stops, and to Francis's surprise, he's being carried over the man's shoulder up steps, onto a porch. They enter through the door into a place that seems oddly familiar.

John Zehrung, the surprised store proprietor, looks up from behind the counter where he is arranging items on the wall shelves. He gawks as Chief Meminwaneka deposits the wet and muddy preacher on the plank floor.

"Chief! Back so soon?"

"White man on Indian Road," Francis's rescuer utters in broken English.

Zehrung takes a closer look. "Reverend Kun?" he exclaims.

"You know him?" asks Meminwaneka.

"Of course, Chief. This is the preacher I was telling you about. Remember?"

"You mean one they call *man of many words*? White shaman?

"Yes. This is him."

The two men are speaking in English. Although Francis doesn't yet know the language well, he knows enough to understand this conversation. Finally, with numbed cheeks and stiffened lips, he mumbles, "I was . . . walking. I . . . so . . . cold."

"Here. Let's get you out of these clothes," Zehrung says as he pulls the wet blanket and Francis's coat off him and fetches a dry blanket from a nearby shelf. "That's a hell of a cold front that cropped up. You're fortunate the chief came along."

John Zehrung has been the town postmaster for several years. He took on the job soon after he came to town and opened his store. He hoped the extra income from handling the mail would see him through those first lean years. Nowadays, things have become easier, the store being one of the few in the area, and he's been able to thrive to the degree that anyone can expect to thrive in this land. His wife, Ingrid, and their three children help make this place feel like home. So, overall, he's satisfied with his status as a storekeeper and postmaster of the county seat.

Soon, Meminwaneka is gone, and Francis sits numbly by the store's fireplace. He's shed most of his soaked clothing and, wrapped in two dry blankets, is trying to reacquaint himself with the feeling in his fingers and legs. It takes a long time before he returns to his full senses, and he finally remembers why he wanted to come to Toledo in the first place. His mind is no longer muddled, so he asks Zehrung if the stage has delivered a letter for him. To his surprise, Zehrung produces not one, but two. One is from Racine, Wisconsin, and the other from a small settlement east of here, just south of Cedar Rapids. He'll read these later, he decides. For now, his exhaustion beckons him to sleep, and soon Francis is lying on the wood floor in front of the fireplace, snoring heartily.

The next morning, Francis is feeling much recovered. Clad in dry trousers and a shirt given him by the postmaster, Francis puts on his still-damp coat. He stares down at the blanket slung over a chair near the fireplace to dry.

"You give to Indian?" Francis asks, struggling with the English words.

"Sure," replies the postmaster. "Meminwaneka comes to town about every week. I'm sure I'll see him next week."

"Memnin…eeka…?"

"Meminwaneka is his name, but I usually just call him *Chief*. He's a good chap."

"Good chap?"

"Yes, that means he is a good man. Honest. Smart. Even funny."

"Funny?" Francis repeats with obvious doubt. After all, how could a blood-thirsty savage have a sense of humor? That couldn't possibly be true.

"You know?" says Zehrung. "Maybe you should return the blanket to him yourself. It would be a friendly gesture on your part. And you could also thank him for saving your life."

"Uh . . . I don't . . . I mean . . . is he . . . bad?" That's the only English word Francis can come up with to describe his perception of all these savages, but Zehrung understands his meaning.

"You mean dangerous? Hardly. The chief's probably the least dangerous person you'll meet in these parts. Since he brought his people back to Tama County a couple of years ago, they've attempted to exist peaceably here. They know if they cause any trouble, the government will send 'em packing back to that Kansas reservation they came from."

"I not sure I wish do this," Francis says, trying to find the sanity in visiting the chief's encampment.

"Well, it's up to you, Reverend. The Meskwaki settlement is just a short way back up Indian Road. It's not far."

Francis will think about it, but every fiber of his being advises him not to go. Still, he considers, the Lord will be with him, will he not? The chief did in fact save his life. As Francis ponders this, he recalls kneeling on that muddy road praying, asking for God's mercy, when the chief suddenly appeared to rescue him. If the Lord went to that much trouble to provide my rescuer, Francis thinks, certainly the Almighty won't let him down now.

The rain has abated, and Francis departs Toledo around noontime, determined to walk the entire way back to his cabin. Aneta may or may not be pleased to see him. Whether she's pleased won't matter, though, because he has some information from those letters that will surely brighten her mood. After he gives her that news, he'll also have to tell her he may soon travel to the Meskwaki settlement. That won't sit well with her; he's certain of that.

The sun has already set when his cabin comes into view. By the brightness of the moon, he sees a tentacle of smoke threading upward from the cabin's rock chimney, evidence that Aneta has built a fire against the outside chill. She is most likely inside tending to the children, he figures, and as he approaches, he calls out her name so as not to startle her when he pushes the door open. As Francis enters, he can see his wife tucking the children into their beds. Predictably, and to Aneta's considerable frustration, they at once clamber from their perches for their father's attention.

"There, there, now, children. Off to bed you go," Francis instructs as he kisses the toddlers and helps Aneta get them tucked in again.

"Where have you been? I expected you days ago," Aneta scolds in a whisper so as not to rile the children.

"I had some difficulty on the way back," he replies. But he knows she isn't interested in his difficulties, her difficulties being as great or greater than his own. So he explains no further, saying only, "I have something to show you," as he hands her the two letters.

"What are these?" she asks.

He doesn't tell her to read them for herself. He knows she doesn't read well, so he chooses not to embarrass her. "One is from a group of Brethren in Wisconsin, where I traveled in August. They want me to go there to be their preacher."

"It's kind of late in the season for that right now," she protests, wishing for her husband to stay close as the winter months approach.

"No. What they want is for me to move there and lead their church permanently, as their vicar."

"Really?

"Yes. Really. It's a sizeable congregation of faithful believers up there. It would mean that we could put this farm life behind us. We could get a proper home, one with a proper roof," he adds.

"That would be nice," she answers. "Where is this place?"

"It's to the northeast, up in Racine. That's in Wisconsin, right on the shore of Lake Michigan. It's beautiful, as I recall."

"Did you say north? I don't know, Francis. It's so cold here in the winter. What would it be like further north?" Aneta wonders aloud. "How far away is it? And when do they want you to come?"

"Not until next spring. It's pretty far, but we could stop along the way like I do when I do my preaching. It shouldn't take us more than a month. We could start in April or early May. This will be a marvelous opportunity for—"

"We can't go," Aneta interrupts abruptly.

"We can't?"

"No, we can't."

"But—"

"No. It will have to wait. Maybe next year would be better."

"But you hate it here, woman. This is our chance to—"

"I won't go."

"You won't go? This makes no sense. What am I to do? Leave you here and take the children?"

"That's not what I mean."

"But we might not have another chance to—"

"Francis, stop. You don't understand. Here's why we can't go. I think I'm with child again." She studies her husband, who stands with his mouth agape. "Next spring is when I'll be due. I will not give birth out on the prairie somewhere."

"We're going to have a baby?" Francis cries.

"Shhh!" she objects. "The children are trying to sleep!"

"Hmmm. Another little Kun," Francis whispers to himself as he ponders it, his eyes searching the inside of the cabin, seeing nothing but the future.

"I'm sorry, Francis," Aneta says in a gentler tone, intruding on his musings. "I know this is a wonderful job offer."

"That's true, Aneta. But we don't want to take any chances," he says under his breath, still preoccupied with this news. Then, as if he's just come out of a trance, he asks, "But instead of walking three or four weeks, what do you think about traveling only about two days?"

"What are you talking about?"

"I know it's weird, but I also got another letter. Apparently, there is another congregation, one I've never visited, that's also interested in me. Compared to the Racine job, this one isn't much. It's just five families who live south of Cedar Rapids, a short distance from a settlement called Banner Valley. I wasn't going to consider it because they'll pay me only sixty dollars."

"Sixty? What do you mean *only*? If we could get sixty dollars a month, our lives would be—"

"No. It's sixty dollars a year."

"Oh."

CHAPTER 23
BOHEMIA

IT'S OCTOBER when Anton and Rose make their big announcement. They show up together late one evening at Frantiska's door. After she shows them in, they ask if they might sit for a moment, a request indicating to Frantiska and Anna that they are about to hear some bad news. This assumption is quite logical, given that good news is such a rarity these days. The two women draw the children close, each holding one on her lap to prepare for whatever they are about to hear. Is it a health problem? Is Anton or Rose dying? They are both about ten years older than Frantiska, so a problem with their health would not be a surprise. Yet they look hale and hearty enough. Or are they losing their home for some reason? Does Thomas have something to do with this? That bastard! That's probably it, Frantiska surmises. This is probably Thomas's fault.

Anton doesn't hold them in suspense for long before he proclaims, "Rose and I have a big announcement to make. I've found a buyer for our two hectares of land, and we're leaving Krouna this coming spring."

"Where will you be going?" asks Anna, surprised and puzzled.

Rose replies, almost apologetically, "We're traveling to America."

Frantiska and Anna simultaneously take in sudden gulps of air. This is their dream, but they never imagined that Rose and Anton might share the same one. Why would a childless couple of their age decide to take such an arduous and dangerous journey? Life in Krouna has surely been difficult, but Anton and Rose have gotten by as well or better than most since they have no extra mouths to feed.

So why have they now decided to make such a drastic move? As soon as Frantiska asks herself this question, the answer becomes obvious. After all, aren't Frantiska and Anna thinking of doing the same thing? To be sure, there are undoubtedly hundreds of Bohemians of all ages with the same vision. America has declared itself open to immigration. This is clear from the many posters appearing around Krouna and throughout the realm. The lure of America is strong, and everyone can sense that an exodus from Bohemia and similar regions around Europe is inevitable.

Anna's and Frantiska's eyes meet momentarily as if reading each other's thoughts. They haven't shared their own dream of America with anyone. They've held it close, as a secret, as if afraid it would evaporate if disclosed to another soul.

"I'm so sorry," says Rose remorsefully. "We feel bad for leaving you, especially so soon after Josef's passing. Do you think you will be all right?"

Frantiska isn't thinking how she will miss them or even how this will impact her life when they're gone. No, she's realizing that this offers her an opportunity to learn and plan, to bring her closer to realizing her own dream.

"Oh, Rose. Don't worry about us," Frantiska says. "With Anna here, the children and I have been doing just fine. Don't give it a second thought. Please don't think you are deserting us. Instead, focus on the adventure ahead of you. Please, Rose. Tell us all about your plan."

Anna follows Frantiska's cue, noting that Frantiska hasn't mentioned their own intent to emigrate. Keeping their secret between them, they continue querying Anton and Rose about the specifics of the travel plans they've made. Where will they be boarding the ship? What ship will they be sailing on? How are they getting from Krouna to the port? What will the trip cost? Where will they disembark? What will they do once they arrive in America?

Anton and Rose answer all these questions as best they can, as Frantiska and Anna delve into every detail of their neighbors' upcoming adventure. Rose is relieved to see her two friends are supportive of their news. Indeed, they even seem to exhibit a level of excitement surpassing that of her and her husband.

Frantiska has heard of other families emigrating from Krouna before, but Rose and Anton will be the first ones she knows well. She's indeed happy for them. And for the first time, she envisions her own plan not as mere fantasy, but as something achievable. Frantiska feels like a weight is lifting off her. It's a buoyancy that suspends her above the hopelessness she's felt throughout her dull life. Frantiska now sees an escape from that hopelessness, and her American dream finally seems within reach.

CHAPTER 24
WIEN

MY EMPLOYMENT at the Count's mansion has extended into October, proving to be a very agreeable work assignment. In fact, it's the best job I've ever had. Over the last several days, Alexander has stopped by regularly to evaluate my work. He says it's far superior to what he considers acceptable. And the Count has also been generous in his praise for the quality of my workmanship, both on the perimeter wall and on the inside repairs I've done when rain interrupts my stonework. I've already received my third week's pay from Alexander, who contracts this work. And I've also received regular bonuses from the Count for my day-to-day efforts. So far, I've amassed about 125 guldens, all hidden safely under my straw bed, next to the crank organ.

Since bringing the crank organ back to life, I've failed to report this success to the Count, and I feel somewhat guilty about that. Still, my guilt is overshadowed by my enjoyment of listening to the thing every evening, always cranking slowly and carefully, to avoid detection by anyone nearby. Eventually, however, it is difficult to deny this guilt, and I report to the Count that the contraption is in working order once again. I'm surprised when the Count merely brushes me off, telling me to "just keep this between you and me." If the Count doesn't want the crank organ back in his house, that's fine with me, though I feel uneasy being put between the Count and his wife in this matter.

My work for the Count continues, and during my repairs inside the mansion, I occasionally cross paths with Frau Svoboda. When that happens, the matter of the crank organ is on my mind, but I will not betray the Count's trust. In my occasional encounters with the noblewoman, I find it odd that she never acknowledges my presence. Presumably, she's trying to maintain a proper distance according to her elevated station. It's just as well since neither of us can speak the other's language, making any verbal exchange rather pointless.

Although Frau Svoboda doesn't acknowledge my presence, she certainly doesn't ignore other, more worthy souls, namely members of the uppity class of the Wien social scene. On one particular weekend, I observe a steady line of these peacocks entering the front portal of the mansion. All dressed to the hilt in the finest of Wien fashion, they fill the entire house with the din of gossip and gaiety. Even the mansion itself seems to rise to the occasion with its new gas lighting, which illuminates it like the midday sun. From my little hovel, I watch through the mansion's large windows as its interior churns with the movement of highborn somebodies, brilliantly displayed in their highborn attire.

The following weekend, as I watch, the party unfolds once again, and I decide I can't just sit here pathetically watching someone else's fun. Why can't I have some fun of my own? I've taken notice of several taverns along the streets of Wien, and I can see no reason I shouldn't visit one for a stein of lager, or maybe two. I can already imagine Frantiska shaking her head at me for spending my hard-earned money on beer, and she would be right. I shouldn't be wasting my money—I should save it, as I earlier promised myself. After pondering this for a moment, an idea presents itself, and I grab my fusilier jacket against the chill of the fall evening, slipping it on. Then I pick up the crank organ and proceed past the side of the mansion, down the street toward the city center.

Emerging from the residential area, I note several small taverns, places the locals call *buschenschanks,* scattered along the street. I'm looking for someplace a bit out of the way, where my idea will have a better chance of success. On the edge of what appears to be a commercial district, I find just the spot: a tiny block building with only a handful of people hunched at the bar in silence. Walking in, I take a seat right next to the doorway. The scruffy old man behind the bar eyes me suspiciously, but I simply ignore him. And instead of ordering a drink as the bartender expects, I set the crank organ on the table in front of me and begin cranking with all my might. The blast of sound physically jolts several men leaning on the bar. One actually knocks over his cup of wine, sending a wave of the sweet nectar onto the counter and into the lap of the man seated next to him. After the grousing and moaning subside, and everyone regains their composure, they gawk in wonder as the music shrieks from my crank organ. The heads of people passing by on the street outside are now swiveling in the tavern's direction, and soon curious people step through the doorway to discover the origin of the noisy display.

In no time at all, the tiny tavern fills with customers, singing and clanking steins together in time with the raucous music. A man, who has consumed one too many drinks, brings a stein of beer to my table. Soon, other customers follow suit until tankards of brew and wine surround my crank organ.

It's early in the morning when the tavern finally clears out, and I stand to gather up my crank organ. I've consumed plenty of drink during the evening, and I wonder how I will feel at sunup. Still, I've accumulated many coins that customers tossed on my table as they exited the establishment. These additional riches will help justify any discomfort I suffer from my imbibing.

I'm about to walk out the tavern door when the proprietor hurries to stop me, asking, "*Morgen Nacht?*"

I know what he's asking, and I nod my head. "Yes, I'll be back tomorrow night." But I promise myself that, from now on, I will imbibe a bit less. Otherwise, how will I survive this burgeoning new career as a musician?

For the next three weekends, I return to the tiny tavern to work the crank organ for tips and drinks. The crank organ's two tunes are wearing on me, and I suspect the proprietor is tiring of them as well. But the customers never complain and keep walking through the door, so the man doesn't complain about it.

It's on one of these late nights that, at my invitation, my friend Alexander comes to hear me play. Soon he begins showing up regularly—so much so that I wonder how Marta feels about it. One night, Alexander walks in with some of his workers in tow. They all take seats around a corner table, becoming more boisterous as their steins are continually replenished. Soon, a man I've never seen enters the tavern and Alexander greets him, calling out, *"Johann! Hierher, mein Freund!"*

The stranger's demeanor and apparel show that he is a proper gentleman of a higher class than most of the clientele in the tavern. I wonder how Alexander knows such a man. Maybe Alexander has been hired as a contractor by this gentleman at some point, just as Count Svoboda hired me. It doesn't take long before many other men in the tavern note the fine gentleman's presence and begin congregating around his table, slapping him on the back and buying him drinks. Finding that slightly irritating, it makes me wonder how many of those free drinks might have otherwise come my way. Who is this person anyway, who deserves all this adulation? The slapping of backs and buying of drinks continues for quite some time. Finally, the gentleman rises with a wobbly effort to his unsteady feet. He bids his admirers farewell, then stumbles toward the exit, stopping momentarily to drop several coins into the tin cup I've placed on the table next to the crank organ. Grinning drunkenly at me and exclaiming loudly, *"Gute Musik!,"* he disappears onto the street and into the night.

A short time later, I take a brief break and ask Alexander about the peacock in the fine topcoat who filched the beer meant for me, the man who later commented on my music-making. "That was Johann, an old friend," Alexander says. "He's a well-known man about town."

"Well, I guess that's obvious, the way everyone was fawning over him," I say. "He told me I played good music when he walked out. He even left a very nice tip."

"It doesn't surprise me he liked that Radetzky March, Josef," Alexander notes, smiling.

"The Rad-a-what March?"

"Radetzky March. That's what you've been playing on that thing all these nights. Didn't you know that? It's a popular tune around here—it's almost a national anthem to the people in this city."

"Oh, that's good to know, I guess."

Alexander continues, "Johann's somewhat of a music composer by trade, as was his father. In fact, his father is the one who wrote that march several years ago. He may have written the waltz you've been cranking out of that thing too, but I'm not sure about that."

I think about this as I return to cranking my machine for the rest of the evening. It's fascinating that someone can make a living writing music. Did I hear that right? This is a strange and rather ridiculous notion, I think. Still, I realize that someone has to write that stuff—it doesn't just appear out of nowhere. I ponder how someone like that would fare in my little village of Krouna. It makes me smile to imagine how this Johann guy in all his finery would be the subject of considerable ridicule. He'd probably be laughed out of town. This well-adorned peacock of a man must certainly possess other skills. Perhaps, he's a bricklayer or shoemaker or something of the sort—something to put food on his table.

By the end of October, I've completed all the work at Count Svoboda's mansion, and he reports his satisfaction to Alexander when he comes for the final inspection. Soon, I gather my things from the gardener's shed, along with the crank organ, and walk to the front of the mansion where the Count waits for me. Holding the crank organ out for Svoboda to take, I say, "Thank you for the work, Herr Svoboda. I so enjoyed my time here at your home. Please thank your cook Sophie for taking such good care of me, and be sure to give my best regards to your wife, Frau Svoboda."

Holding the device out toward the Count, I'm surprised that the man makes no move to take it. "Please, Josef," Herr Svoboda says. "Take the organ as a gift. I'm sure you'll enjoy it much more than we ever will. I always hated that thing anyway. Besides, my wife still thinks it's broken and beyond repair," he says with a wink as he turns and walks up the steps onto his massive porch. I stand stunned for a moment, watching the man ascend the steps. Then, grasping the crank organ firmly with both hands, I turn and scurry quickly away for fear that the Count might change his mind.

It's time to leave Wien, and the next day is spent at Alexander and Marta's home, making preparations for my travel northward toward my beloved Bohemia. Thanks to my work at the mansion and my moonlighting at the tavern, my pockets hold 325 guldens that I will proudly bring home to Frantiska. I know the exact amount because I've counted my money every night before drifting off to sleep. I've never made this much money in such a short time. If there was no home to go back to, I might stay through the winter in Wien or perhaps much longer. But the Bohemian hills are beckoning me.

To be sure, there are compelling reasons to return to Krouna—a wife, two children, and a score to settle with Thomas Spacek. I don't know how that score will be settled. Perhaps it's not an achievable goal at all, but just a dream savored for inspiration to continue this difficult trip homeward. Either way, I continue to hold the thought in my mind, in odd juxtaposition to my longing for my dear Frantiska.

The leg is feeling much stronger now, and the wooden crutch has found a permanent home behind the gardener's quarters at the Svoboda mansion. Although I'm walking with a noticeable limp, resulting in an asymmetrical gait that will carry me to the end of my days, I can live with that. The pain is manageable, and I'm glad that, with no crutch, my hands are both free to carry the treasure the Count has bequeathed me.

That evening, I enjoy my last meal with Alexander and Marta, feasting on Marta's fabulous cooking and reminiscing with Alexander. The next morning, I depart with my crank organ to the train station, where I purchase my ticket and sit on the bench, waiting to board the train for the daylong ride to Brno. The wait is not long. The iron beast, which was sitting peacefully on the tracks, finally starts steaming and belching as if birthing itself into life. Soon, it's time to climb aboard and I choose a seat next to a window, sitting with the organ on my lap as the train moves with increasing momentum. As my car rolls along, I stare out the hazy window, transfixed, as the Austrian and eventually Bohemian countryside flies by in autumnal hues.

Nightfall is descending on the town as my train pulls into the Brno station. The evening air is chilly, and with only my coat and thin blanket to suffer the night, I pause to consider my options. I'm eager to finish my journey to Krouna, but I know that, in the days to come, I'll be traveling on foot to get home. Normally I'd sleep on a bench under the stars, but choose instead to find the nearest boardinghouse to secure lodging. My hard-earned money should not be spent on a room, but I know my damaged leg will thank me in the morning for a good night's rest.

This decision proves to be a wise one, for as the sun is just peaking above the horizon, I bound out of the bed feeling refreshed and ready to get underway. This last portion of my journey will not be easy, especially carrying the crank organ, and there's one other thing that weighs on me. After paying for my room, I'll still have an impressive stash of guldens in my possession. My biggest worry is that I might be an easy target along the road for bandits who prey upon vulnerable travelers, especially those on foot.

Of course, I no longer have my Lorenz rifle for protection. For all I know, it still lies broken near that fencepost on the Solferino battlefield. It doesn't matter, though. I'd have trouble carrying the crank organ and the rifle together anyway. But I do need some kind of protection, and I wonder if a knife would be sufficient to fend off any potential threats. Somehow, that just doesn't seem substantial enough, and what I finally settle on is an ancient French-made flintlock pistol discovered in a shop window. The price is right, being the cheapest weapon available. And I'm soon walking north out of Brno, holding the crank organ against my chest, with the weapon strapped at my waist. The pistol is old, a remnant of some previous war that these countries love to wage on one another. I'm not confident the gun can even fire. It doesn't matter, I figure. The mere sight of it will dissuade any unsavory characters along the road, and I will most likely never need to use it at all. But who's to know what to expect? I'll keep it clearly displayed just in case, I decide.

Near the end of the first day of walking, my leg convinces me to stop at a little Moravian village. The small, weathered sign by the side of the road announces the village of Doubravník. It's hardly a village at all, with only a handful of run-down homes and a small blacksmith shop. It's late afternoon already, but the blacksmith is still working when I walk through the open doors.

The short, muscular man stands sweating over an anvil, pounding repeatedly on a piece of red-hot iron, shaping it to his specifications. Pausing for a moment to retrieve a rag from his back pocket to wipe his brow, he glances at me over his raging forge and asks, "Is there something I can do for you?"

I hesitate and remind myself not to be surprised to hear my language. "I'm looking for lodging and some food," I state, and then add, "I can pay for it."

Looking back down to resume his pounding, the blacksmith replies, "None around here, I'm afraid."

Waiting a moment, expecting the man to say more, I'm met with silence as he continues with his work. After several seconds of patient waiting, the blacksmith looks up again. "None around here," he repeats, expecting me to move on down the road.

I'm not sure what to do. Exhausted from toting my crank organ through the hilly terrain, I collapse on the bench just outside the man's shop, setting the organ down next to me.

"What's that you have there?" the man asks, pointing his hammer at the crank organ.

I don't answer. Instead, I reach inside for the crank, attach it to the shaft, and begin cranking. The thing blares to life, and the blacksmith stands there stunned, with eyes wide and mouth agape.

Soon, the blacksmith is standing next to me, examining the device, fascinated by the magical workings of the machine. Like me, this man seems to possess an avid curiosity about mechanical things and the way they work. I'm happy to spend the next few moments explaining this odd little music box to him. Those few moments soon turn into a bit of shared food, drink, and an offer for me to spend the night in one of the stalls in the man's shop. Once again, the crank organ has served me well, and I'm glad I dragged the thing all this way from Wien.

The encounter with the blacksmith in Doubravník soon becomes a pattern to be duplicated in other tiny villages on my way northward. I recognize that the people living in these depressed places are not unlike my friends in Krouna. Day after day of never-ending drudgery has eventually devalued their lives into a canvas of drabness. They meet any new distraction with eager interest. It's as if their lives, otherwise colorless, are now resplendent in vibrant colors produced by my crank organ. Hearing me play the thing brings them joy indeed. What it often brings me is a warm meal and a place to lay my head where I can dream of Frantiska—and flesh-eating vultures, too.

Without the burden of the crank organ, the walk from Brno to Krouna would take about three days. But because of the added stress on my leg caused by the organ's weight, I am forced to pause at every little village that comes along. If it wasn't for the effect my music device has on the villagers, these trip interruptions would be frustrating. But I rather enjoy them. The villagers seem transfixed by the Radetzky March that I repeatedly crank out, and the generosity they heap upon me seems to increase with each repetition. And so, for the rest of my journey, I crank my way through the Moravian and Bohemian countryside as I continue toward home.

Polička lies in a region dense with forested hills and small valleys, and by the time I arrive there, it's been six days since I left Brno. I could stop for the night. Maybe even find a tavern to set up shop with my crank organ. But it's still early enough in the day that the goal of Krouna, only a short distance ahead, urges me on. So I pass through Polička, heading northwest on a dusty road lined with dense woodlands. Limping onward, I reflect on all the people I've met these last few months—my friend Jan Havel who I fear died at Solferino, Henri Dunant who organized the effort to save all those lives after the battle, the Riccis who nursed me back to health in Castiglione delle Stiviere, Hans Huber who befriended me in Verona, and Alexander Hofer, my employer in Wien.

Walking on, reminiscing about these kind and generous people, I'm suddenly roused from my reverie by a wagon drawn by a single horse approaching from behind, cutting a wide berth around to my left. As the wagon comes around, the driver glances down at me and then pulls on the reins, calling out, "Whoa there, Birdie," and bringing his rig to a dusty halt.

"Looks like you've got quite a load there, friend," notes the young man. "Where're you headed with that . . . ?" He gestures toward my large, square contraption.

"It's a crank organ. It plays music. Do you want to hear it?" I offer, hoping that once again my music-maker might bring me good fortune.

"Sure. Climb on up."

Handing the crank organ to the man, I haul myself up onto the wagon seat. The man is looking me over as I take a seat next to him. His gaze lingers on the old flintlock pistol. "Is that thing loaded?" he asks.

"Oh, don't worry about that," I assure him. "I'm not even sure if it works. I've never tried to shoot the darn thing. It's just something I picked up on my way back from Italia, where I was with the 47th Kinsky Regiment. I'm heading back to Krouna. Are you going that way?"

Satisfied I'm not intending to rob him, the young man replies, "Hmm. Not really. I was planning to take the next road north to Budislav, but maybe I could take a little detour for you. That is if you entertain me with that contraption of yours."

"It would be my pleasure, my friend," I reply, well aware that Krouna is further out of the way from Budislav than just a *little detour*.

CHAPTER 25

ANTON AND ROSE'S DECISION to start a new life in America has given Frantiska much to think about. In the month since their announcement, she's spent much time at her loom, daydreaming of her own plans to escape her life in Krouna. She has accumulated a bit of savings from her linen trade, but it's not yet enough to even think about definite travel plans. She has a vague idea of the costs for making the voyage—the train fare from Choceň to Bremen, temporary housing in Bremen, provisions for the voyage, and passage fees. It would total around 150 guldens per person, though the children would cost less, she figures. But still, Frantiska estimates she and Anna will need between 500-600 guldens to take them all to America, allowing for some funds left to start their new life there. Currently, she has saved only about half that amount, which includes the compensation for Josef's military service. She knows it will take her months or even years to save the funds necessary for such a venture.

Frantiska has now rededicated herself to working even longer stretches at her loom in order to bolster her savings. It's helpful that Vincencie is at school during the daytime, and Rose has been kind enough to watch Antonin while Frantiska is hard at work.

It's on one such day, as Frantiska is finishing an order she received from the town merchant, that Thomas again approaches her home. He's not alone this time but is accompanied by one of his cronies who regularly helps him enforce the rules around their tiny municipality. It's midafternoon, and both men have already been emboldened by drink at the local tavern. As they approach on horseback, little Antonin is playing happily outside

Rose's house. He looks up from his play to notice the men as they ride up and dismount. Without a word, Thomas makes his way toward Frantiska's door. At the same time, his accomplice sweeps Antonin up off the ground, clasping his hand over the child's mouth. Within moments the man is up on his horse, spurring it on at a hasty pace down the road as the child squirms, traumatized in the man's grasp.

Frantiska is working intently at her loom when Thomas suddenly bolts into her home and grabs her by both wrists, throwing her backward onto her straw-filled mattress. She lets out a scream just as the back of his rough hand strikes her square in the face, stunning her to silence.

"Shut up! If you make another sound, so help me, I'll hit you again," he asserts with the slurred speech of a drunkard.

Regaining her senses, she staggers to her feet, screaming, "Thomas, you can't do this. You can't just–"

"Oh, but I can, Frantiska," he interrupts. "And you're going to let me do whatever I want to do without a fuss. You see, my friend just rode away with that little peasant scamp of yours. If you don't want to see him harmed or given away to some childless gypsy couple, you will do as you're told, understand?"

"Antonin?" she gasps. "What have you done with him, you monster?" she yells as she raises her hand to strike him.

Her protest is met by a violent forehand across the side of her face, and she crumbles again onto the straw-filled mattress. Thomas lunges for her, but Frantiska adeptly slips from his grasp, and he sprawls clumsily onto the mattress. Frantiska is now on her feet looking for something, anything, to use in her defense. She grabs a stool sitting next to the table and holds it up as a barrier between her and her drunken adversary.

Next door, Rose sticks her head out the door to check on Antonin, but sees only a saddled horse grazing nearby on a clump of dead grass. Does Fransiska have a visitor? she wonders. She calls Antonin's name to see if he is close by. But not hearing any response, she searches on either side of her house with concern, and soon with increasing panic. He is nowhere to be seen, and she runs over to Frantiska's home hoping that he has made his way there to be with his mother. Reaching Frantiska's house, Rose can hear shouting. She sees movement through Frantiska's window and anxiously peers inside. What she gazes upon isn't little Antonin, but the back of Thomas, who's swatting at the stool in Frantiska's hands.

Rose steps back from the window and grabs her skirt as she races as fast as she can behind the house, scanning their two hectares of cropland. She sees her husband some distance away, digging potatoes and loading them onto his mule-drawn wagon. She runs in his direction, waving and yelling for his attention as she approaches.

Within moments of Rose reaching him, Anton drops his potato fork and sprints back toward Frantiska's house. As he approaches the rear of his own home, he hesitates, looking around, and then darts inside to grab an extra ax handle he's kept among his other tools. He hurries the short distance to Frantiska's house and finds the front door ajar. Without hesitation, he steps over the threshold to find Thomas, his pants fallen around his ankles, pushing himself down onto Frantiska.

"Hey, Spacek!" yells Anton, still breathing hard from his running.

Thomas turns with a "Wha—?" as the ax handle catches him squarely on the nose, launching him about eight feet into the adjacent wall. He lies there in a heap, motionless, with his pants still entangled about his feet.

Moments later, Rose sits on the bed, her arm around a shaken Frantiska. "Is he dead?" queries Rose, craning her neck as Anton towers over Thomas's hulk.

"God, I hope so," mutters Frantiska as she sits there shaken, her face red and swollen from Thomas's brutality.

Anton flips Thomas over with a shove of his boot, revealing a man still breathing, his face disfigured and swollen. "Damn, look at that nose, or what's left of it," Anton says, grimacing at the damage as he steps away from the mess he's created.

"Where's Antonin?" Rose asks Frantiska. "I don't see him outside."

Suddenly, Frantiska is lucid and focused. "They took him!" she cries.

"Who took him?" asks Anton.

"I don't know! Thomas said somebody took Antonin," Frantiska wails, "and he said if I didn't do everything he demanded, something would happen to him." She leaps from the bed, intending to run toward the door.

"Now hold up, Frannie," replies Anton, trying to calm her. "We'll find him. Rose, you take Frannie over to our house and bar the door in case Thomas wakes up while I go to get some help. We'll scour this area from top to bottom. Don't you worry."

With all due haste, Anton goes door-to-door, alerting his neighbors to the situation. Soon, he's enlisted the help of about twenty-five people who are searching every hovel, barn, and lean-to in and around Krouna. To their great relief, it isn't long before they find the lad sitting happily by the roadside just a quarter mile outside of town. He's playing in a clump of dead broomcorn that looms high, swaying in the breeze above his head. The boy is having a grand time there by himself. But he cries as the search party suddenly descends upon him, noisily lavishing their attention and expressing relief at his discovery. Anton lifts the child into his arms, examining him for several moments before he's satisfied the child isn't harmed.

It's late in the afternoon by the time Anton comes home with the boy in tow. He holds tightly to the boy's hand as they step through the threshold into his house. He's at once surprised to find that the women are nowhere to be seen, and he frantically rushes next door to Frantiska's house pulling Antonin behind him. Through the open door, all he sees is Frantiska's disheveled bed and a puddle of dried blood on the floor where he had left Spacek. The thought occurs to Anton that this could be a very bad development. If Thomas came back to consciousness and went off to get some of his henchmen, they could be heading his way right now. And what of Rose and Frantiska? Where could they be? This isn't good, and he considers his options.

Coming out of Frantiska's house, he cautiously scans up and down the road. Suddenly, he sees a movement at the rear of his own house near the stable area where he keeps his mules and goats. It's Rose coming out of the stable door, and when she sees Anton with the boy, she calls to Frantiska and races to pluck Antonin up into her arms. Frantiska is close behind. "Where did you find him?" she asks Anton excitedly.

"Just alongside the road, evidently unharmed. I don't think they meant to hurt him. They just wanted you to believe they would," reasons Anton.

"Well, the poor boy would have been harmed if he had been out there all night long, that's for sure," complains Rose as she bounces him up and down in her arms.

"Where's Thomas?" Anton asks nervously. "Did he leave?"

"Come with me, Anton," is Frantiska's simple reply. She looks at Rose, saying, "Can you take Antonin into the house for me?" Then she leads Anton back through the stable door, where he finds Thomas's horse unsaddled and munching oats from a bucket. Anton's mules and goats stand nearby, eyeing Thomas, whose wrists are bound to opposite stanchions. Thomas's pants are draped over a nearby stall, leaving Thomas naked from the waist down.

"What the . . . ?" Anton blurts. "What do you think you're gonna do with him now?"

"I don't quite know," Frantiska snarls, "but I wasn't about to just let him go free—not after what he did."

Soon they are back in Frantiska's house, helping her clean up the mess caused by Thomas's assault. With the house back in order, they sit around Frantiska's table, trying to decide what they should do next. They eventually come up with a plan. It's a plan only slightly more palatable than the plan Frantiska at first suggests. Frantiska wants to drag Thomas up to Burnt Hill, tie him naked to a dead tree trunk, build a fire under him, and dance around him as he twists in the flames. After all, isn't that what he deserves? He's attacked her on two separate occasions and forged that cruel letter that was supposedly from her dear deceased Josef. What was that letter supposed to have accomplished, anyway? Was it supposed to be a joke? No, it was a malicious act inflicted to bring her more suffering. Hasn't she suffered enough from poor Josef's death? She imagines that if Josef was here now, he would embrace her plan. He would agree that Thomas deserves a painful death like that. But alas, this is not the plan that is finally agreed upon. In the end, none of them has the stomach to inflict such a torturous death on Thomas, not even Frantiska.

Finally, they settle on a plan that is a bit risky, but morally acceptable to all of them. They decide they will have to release Thomas at some point, sooner rather than later, and that will be the risky part because the authorities might charge Anton with attempted murder. There is only one way for Anton to avoid this. He and Rose will need to change their plans, traveling to America not next spring, but at the first opportunity. They already secured the permits and passports from the district office a few days ago. Perhaps Thomas can be hidden in the stable for a while longer, until he and Rose finish making their preparations for passage to America. After they leave, Frantiska can release Thomas. Of course, Anton worries about the downside of this plan, which is the danger it poses for Frantiska. What might Thomas do to her after she releases him?

"You are forgetting something, Anton," Frantiska assures him. "While it may be true that it will be his word against mine in this entire affair, remember that Anna witnessed the first attack he attempted. She was also with me when he brought me that despicable letter. And half the village who searched for Antonin knows Thomas had something to do with the child's kidnapping. I figure, if Thomas doesn't want us and the rest of the townspeople telling his father about all this, he will leave us in peace."

Just at the moment their plan seems to have taken shape, Anna and Vincencie return from school, and find Anton, Frantiska, and Rose sitting at Frantiska's table, gazing oddly back at them.

"What's going on?" Anna asks.

"Oh, not much," replies Frantiska wryly, "except the fact that we'll be taking care of another boarder for a while. I tied Thomas Spacek up in Anton's stable without his pants."

"Huh?" asks Anna, confused.

"Have a seat, Anna," Anton instructs as he gestures toward an empty stool. "We have some things to tell you."

A couple of days have passed since Thomas took up residence in Anton's stable. No one has come by to ask questions of Frantiska, but she suspects that will happen soon enough. Hopefully, no one will think to look in Anton's shed.

Anton and Rose hurry to prepare for their departure. In short order, Anton records the sale of his land with the woman at Judge Spacek's office and puts all his other local affairs in order. He hitches his two mules to the wagon and, after a tearful goodbye to Frantiska, Anna, and the children, he drives off with Rose. They head toward Chrudim, where they hope to gain exit visas for their border crossing. Beyond that, they haven't divulged their itinerary to Anna or Frantiska. It's best not to burden them with information that Anton's pursuers could value. Frantiska assumes that Anton and Rose will travel to one of the few railroad connections in the area. There, they will most likely sell their mule rig and take the train to a port in Germany, maybe Hamburg or Bremen. On the day they drive off, Rose's last words are a promise to write when they finally reach the American shore.

Since Thomas's assault on Frantiska, he has been her captive. Frantiska knows that he'll have to be released eventually, and she sees no purpose in causing him additional suffering and humiliation. Tying him to the stanchions without his pants is humiliation enough, she figures. Originally, she removed his britches out of malevolence. But she's come to realize that his nakedness is a matter of practical convenience. The man needs to relieve himself occasionally, she reasons. And with his wrists tied the way they are to the stanchions she isn't about to let him do the deed in his pants. No, Thomas will just have to shit like any other naked beast in a stable—in the straw, where she can use a shovel to scoop it up daily like mule excrement.

But Frantiska can see that something is off with Thomas. He's been coming in and out of consciousness for the last couple of days. He occasionally takes in some water, but Frantiska worries about what will happen to him if he continues to refuse the food she tries to give him. She notices that even when he's awake, he doesn't seem to be very coherent. In his present condition, she wonders when and if she will be able to release him.

The early winter weather has brought a nightly chill to the interior of the stable. Frantiska throws some extra straw over Thomas for additional warmth as he sits there, noncommunicative. That's all she's willing to do for him, and if the straw causes him to itch, he doesn't show it, and Frantiska wouldn't care if he did.

It's been three days since Rose and Anton left, and a blanket of cloud cover is creeping toward Krouna in the western sky. Frantiska finishes checking on Thomas in the stable and returns inside to help Anna prepare a meal for the children. Suddenly, she notices the sound of wind picking up outside, and she worries that an evening storm might be imminent. Rushing to close the window shutters, Frantiska then steps outside her door for a look at the threatening sky. The ominous cloud bank is moving overhead and picking up speed now. Frantiska is surprised as the first snowflakes of the season spit past her face, bending in vortices as they pass the corner of the house.

Just as she turns to walk back into the house, she notices a horse-drawn wagon pulling to a stop on the road just in front of her small yard. Two men are on the wagon, and one of them struggles to climb down from the rig. Frantiska watches as the man stands motionless, facing her, his scruffy hair and wild beard angling peculiarly sideways by the force of the wind and snow. The wind is increasing in intensity, and as leaves and branches are propelled across the road, Frantiska stares in puzzlement at this ghostlike figure.

"Frantiska? It's me!" the voice calls through the roar of the wind. "It's me. Josef!"

Frantiska recognizes it as Josef's voice. What is happening? she wonders. Is this some kind of trick? How can this be? That is Josef's voice, alright. But how? Josef is dead. She's never been much of a believer in ghosts, but the sight of this eerie figure calling to her now tests that belief.

Her head is spinning, and she feels an acute weakness overtaking her legs. Before she can do anything to prevent it, she falls to her knees and faints, collapsing face-first into the snow-dusted dirt.

CHAPTER 26

"JOSEF? YOU SHOULD BE DEAD," Frantiska says weakly as her eyes finally blink open, and she stares up at me.

Chuckling, I kneel on the floor next to her and grasp her limp hand. Looking up at the man next to me, I say, "Hmm. I don't think so. Vaclav, what do you think? Do I seem dead to you?"

"No, Josef. Not really. Though you couldn't tell it from the look of you," my friend replies with a smile.

Ignoring his comment, I gaze down again at Frantiska. "I'm home, and I'm very much alive, Frannie."

Frantiska suddenly lunges upward, thrusting her arms excitedly around my neck and pulling me off balance, awkwardly down to the floor on top of her. "You're alive! You're alive!" she screams. "I thought you were dead, but here you are, thank God Almighty! It's really you! You're alive!"

I pull free of her vise-like grasp, trying to catch my breath, and ask, "Didn't you get my letter? I told you I was on my way home."

"No, Josef. They told me you were dead," she replies. "They said you were killed in Italia."

"Dead? What are you talking about? As you see, I'm definitely alive and well. I wrote to you from Verona. It was just a few weeks ago. I assumed you'd be worried about me, so I wrote to you. I wrote that I missed you and that I was OK and that I was on my way home and that I missed the children. You didn't get the letter?"

There's a sudden audible intake of air coming from the direction of the woman whom I don't recognize. She had helped me carry Frantiska into the house just moments before, and I now turn in her direction as she mutters, "Oh, no," with her hand over her mouth.

"What?" I ask, looking down at Frantiska, who is now wearing an expression of dismay similar to the other woman's.

"That letter was from you?" Frantiska asks haltingly in disbelief. "But it was written so . . . it was so . . . it was so *fancy*-sounding. I thought it was Thomas's cruel joke."

"Thomas? Of course not. A friend wrote it down for me, but it was my letter, alright. I'm home for good now, Frannie. There's so much to tell you about the last few months. I missed you so much." I put my arms around my wife and lift her to her feet. Motioning toward Vaclav, I say, "This is my friend Vaclav. He gave me a ride from Polička. He's from Budislav." Then I look questioningly at the other woman standing next to me.

"Oh, and this is Anna," offers Frantiska, following my cue. "She's living here now."

"Living here now?" I ask. How soon I can be replaced, I think.

"She's our new teacher at the parish school. She's Vincencie's teacher." I give a friendly nod toward the woman but realize that she isn't even looking in my direction. She's instead letting her gaze remain a bit too long on Vaclav.

"We should go tell Anton and Rose I've returned," I continue, "and tomorrow I want to go find that damn Thomas and give him a piece of my mind for all the hell he and his father put me through these last few months."

Frantiska and Anna say nothing for a long moment before Frantiska suggests, "Josef, maybe you should follow me. I have something to show you."

Anna stays with the children while Vaclav and I follow Frantiska through the whirling snow to the stable next door. I need a few moments for my eyes to adjust to the dark interior of the stable, and then I see a horse stabled inside, a horse I don't recognize. I turn my gaze to the other side of the enclosure, where I behold a man half-naked, wrists tied to separate stanchions, his head bowed as if sleeping.

"What the . . . ?" I exclaim. "What's going on here?"

"That's Thomas," says Frantiska matter-of-factly.

That's when I laugh. It begins as just a slight hint of a chuckle deep in my throat. But when I glance Vaclav's way, I see his mouth slung open like some witless town idiot. Looking back again at the naked man, I erupt into a torrent of full-blown laughter. Stuttering gleefully, I say, "Well . . . if it . . . isn't . . . the grand . . . Thomas Spacek!"

"Shhh, Josef!" reprimands Frantiska. "The neighbors might hear."

Frantiska immediately begins to explain the events of the last few days: Thomas's attacks on her, the ax handle Anton delivered to Thomas's nose, and Rose and Anton's subsequent departure.

"Well, what do you plan to do with Thomas?" I query, asking the first of many questions I need answered.

"We're going to let him go, but I don't think he's well enough yet."

I kneel in front of Thomas, place my hand under his chin, lift his head, and say, "I don't think you'll be letting him go."

"What d'you mean?" asks Frantiska.

"This poor bastard's dead."

At midnight, Vaclav and I go out to the shed and hoist Thomas's body up onto his horse. We tie him securely in place with his bare butt reaching for the sky. The snow continues to fall, and the wind maintains its relentless assault. These conditions will prove optimal for carrying out our plan.

We follow the tree line, heading for Burnt Hill, urging Thomas's reluctant mare along with due haste. Soon, we arrive at the edge of the valley where the hills reach upward toward our destination. The horse will be of little use now. If she was reluctant to be led in the storm along the dark tree line, there is no reason to believe we will get her to move up the hill. We pull Thomas's body off his horse, and I slap her rump, sending her off into the Krouna countryside, assuming she will find her way back to her own stable, wherever that may be.

Then Vaclav and I tie tethers to the body and begin pulling Thomas up Burnt Hill. The hill is at first easy to ascend, but our angle of ascent soon increases, requiring all our effort as we struggle to find our footing in the snow. We continue upward, taking breaks whenever necessary, but trying not to tarry too long. We want to be back home before daylight.

We pass the spot where Anton and I dressed the buck and buried its entrails, and we keep going, straining to pull the body into what soon becomes a dense wood. Just as we think we can go no further, we step out of the trees, onto the summit of Burnt Hill. I've never been to this point on the hill and looking out through the wind and snow, I try to imagine what the panorama of hills must look like in the daytime. But tonight, with the moon peeking out only intermittently through storm clouds, it is difficult to see the countryside. So I return my attention to the job at hand.

We continue some distance down the opposite side of Burnt Hill, and in a small clearing, we stop to prop Thomas's body up against a tree. Out of the sack I've been carrying on my back, I pull out Thomas's slacks, tossing them onto his lap. Also in the bag is my old muzzle-loading pistol, which I extract and examine, making sure I've wrapped it to keep it dry. Even now, I don't know if it will fire since I've never actually tried it.

"I sure hope this works," Vaclav says. "I still think we should have buried him."

"Where would we have done that? Behind my house? And the ground is pretty rocky up here. Let's just stick to the plan," I say with finality.

"Don't you think someone will hear the gunshot?"

"I'm counting on the wind to conceal the pistol's report, plus being on the opposite side of the hill should help."

"What about his pants?"

"His pants?" I ask.

"Won't they wonder why he's up here without his pants on?"

I shake my head, grinning, and say, "For anyone who knows Thomas, that probably won't come as a mystery."

Placing the pistol barrel close to his forehead near the damage inflicted by Anton's ax handle, I pull the trigger. The old pistol has more of a kick than I expect, and the gun's firing causes it to fly out of my hand onto the ground. I let it lie there as a thread of smoke twists upward from its barrel.

Examining my grizzly handiwork, my mind flashes back to the moment before I heard the buck approaching me up on Burnt Hill, the moment my trembling hand held the ramrod so close to the trigger of my rifle, the moment before I was to die. Swallowing hard to restrain myself from retching, I stumble backward trying to right myself.

"So, we just leave him here?" Vaclav asks.

"That's right, we do," I reply, trying to regain my wits. "If a search party finds him before the critters around here feast on him, they'll think it was suicide. At least, I hope it looks that way. And I really don't think they'll find him for quite some time. There won't be much left of him by then, I'm sure."

We stand for a moment, wondering if there's anything more to say. Finally, Vaclav says, "Let's get out of here. I can't stare at him a moment longer."

And with that, we walk up over the crest of Burnt Hill and down the other side toward home, pulling a large tree branch behind us to obscure any footprints left behind in the snow.

CHAPTER 27
AMERICA

LATE OCTOBER IS A WELCOME RESPITE for most Iowans when most of their harvesting is complete and their provisions put away for the winter. Like everyone else, Francis and Aneta have completed their work. They harvested their vegetables and sold off most of the oat straw to their neighbors. To be sure, their crops weren't particularly abundant this year, but when have their crops ever been abundant? Never. Francis shouldn't have taken up farming. He was never meant to work the land. These last three years have been a test, Francis figures. God's test––a test of humility to show him what it's like to fail at something. And fail he did. Well, perhaps *struggle* would be a kinder word. He struggled at the most basic of human enterprises: the coaxing of plant life from Earth's rich loam. And his efforts indeed humbled him. More than humbled—more like humiliated.

Now it seems his test is completed. And thankfully so. God has released him from this trial by sending him a sign. Two signs, actually—two letters offering him a new life away from this leaky cabin and disobedient soil. When he accepts his new calling next summer, he will be done with farming for good. At least, that's what he's hoping. Still, in the back of his mind, he suspects he could be forced back into the agrarian arts again if his meager pay proves insufficient. Perhaps God isn't finished testing him after all, he thinks. How is Francis to know? He'll pray that he doesn't have to return to farming and that he'll find some other way to support Aneta and the children. Maybe he can step up his evangelizing and receive adequate donations to make up for any shortfall. Only time will tell, and Francis can only put his trust in the Lord to set the path meant for him and his family.

Francis is well aware that it's late in the season to be trekking this far. But he can't wait until spring. He's put this off long enough. Yesterday he walked to Toledo to check on his mail. He stayed the night with the Zehrungs. And after receiving some final advice, Francis is now heading down Indian Road, the road leading to the Meskwaki settlement. Under his arm, Francis carries Meminwaneka's folded blanket.

The postmaster told him what to watch for, and soon enough Francis spots it: a small trail leading south from Indian Road, meandering up into a large area of timber. Through the trees, he can make out what he assumes to be Meskwaki lodges: large, round structures covered in white bark. Francis no sooner turns down the trail than he sees several young braves appear in front of him, barring his way. They're all wearing those same leggings he's seen before, as well as poncho-like vestures suitable to the cool October temperatures. These braves are well armed, too, with bows, arrow quivers, and spears, and well adorned in decorative feathers and beads.

Francis at once questions his reason for being here and has the sudden urge to turn and hightail it back to town. But he's come this far, and the braves are making no move toward him. They're just standing there, studying him like he's some kind of oddity from their spirit world.

"I come to see the chief," Francis finally states, nervously. The braves remain silent, standing threateningly in his path.

Francis says a quiet prayer and then, emboldened by his faith, takes a small step toward the young men, extending his hand in friendship. Suddenly, the braves erupt into whoops and howls. They hold their weapons above their heads and stand their ground, intent on barring the white man's passage. Francis is at once terrified but doesn't move. What is he to do now?

"What you want?" The deep voice comes from Francis's right side. He turns and beholds an imposing figure: a tall, magnificent man dressed only in breechcloth and leggings and bearing a stoic and unflinching expression. His bronzed head is shaven on both sides, leaving only a row of thick, wiry black hair extending from his mighty brow to the back of his skull. He seems almost regal in his appearance, Francis thinks. Is this the chief? He's not sure, since he didn't really get a good look at him when last they met. But that voice! That deep, authoritative, reverberating, unmistakable voice. That voice is what Francis remembers, and it's enough for him to know this is the man he's seeking.

"I come to see you," Francis says, uttered more like a question than a statement. He holds the blanket out to the chief, who makes no effort to take it and simply stares at him.

"This your blanket. My name Francis Kun."

"You white shaman. Man of many words. Yes, I remember. I Meminwaneka," the man states firmly.

"Memin . . . wa . . . ," Francis attempts to repeat. Then, remembering Zehrung's use of the *chief* moniker, adds, "I call you . . . Chief?"

Did Francis just notice a trace of a smile on the face of the otherwise expressionless man? He thinks so. Please let it be a smile, he says to himself.

"You call me *chief*. I call you *man of many words*," the Indian finally offers, now with a grin fully rendered. So, Zehrung was right, Francis realizes. This chief has a sense of humor after all. Thank God Almighty!

"Please, take blanket," Francis continues. "I want thank you for saving life." Francis is suddenly aware that his own rudimentary grasp of the English language is no better than the Indian's. Still, they are communicating well enough, and

Francis is glad for the opportunity to offer the man his gratitude.

The chief slowly, almost ceremonially, takes the blanket from Francis's grasp. Then he speaks in his language to the braves, who disperse as fast as they appeared. Turning back to Francis, he grunts, "Come. We talk."

The chief abruptly turns and walks down the path toward the settlement. What choice does Francis have? He follows Meminwaneka into the trees, past several lodges, and into the center of the encampment. The place is abuzz with activity. Children are playing, women attend to large pots over active fires, and men sit about lazily, studying Francis with suspicion as he passes. Soon, Francis and the chief arrive in front of a lodge, a lodge not unlike any of the other abodes in the encampment. Next to the lodge, a woman is cooking something that smells like meat. The chief wastes no time entering his lodge, and Francis follows like the obedient servant he is. Inside sits another woman, this one working on some type of beadwork, exquisitely fashioned into a piece about the size of a small scarf. The chief, having not addressed either woman, sits down on the ground and motions for Francis to take a place across from him.

The two men spend much of the morning in conversation, pausing only to partake in a midmorning nourishment of rabbit and roasted corn. Francis is wondering if the two women are both the chief's wives, but he thinks it best not to inquire about such things. Instead, they talk of their contrasting life journeys. Meminwaneka recounts two centuries of his people's migrations, evading first the French and then the Americans as the Meskwaki tried to preserve their tribe's numbers and traditions. Francis explains the oppression of his ancestors at the hands of the Habsburgs. The chief speaks of his people's recent return to the land of their ancestors, aided by the permission of white leaders in Iowa City. Francis describes the journey his countrymen endure to travel in search of similar opportunities on the plains of Iowa. These two men are really not very different from one another, and as they talk, their similar life trajectories become ever more apparent.

Reverend Kun and Chief Meminwaneka are more comfortable in each other's company now. Soon the conversation shifts to more personal topics. Francis eventually speaks of his upcoming move to serve a congregation south of Cedar Rapids, and the chief notes that many years ago, his tribe had many settlements near there. That was before they were chased further west and held captive on a Kansas reservation.

Yes, they have much in common, and they have much still to talk about. But it's already past noon, and Francis hopes to make it home before nightfall. Finally, he reluctantly bids the chief farewell and starts toward home. But that is not before the chief gifts him an amazing crimson-dyed belt made of porcupine quills. It's a generous gift, signifying a friendship founded on their brotherhood of commonality.

Francis leaves with something else, too. It's the chief's promise. A promise Francis is not sure will be well received by Aneta. But that can wait until the morning.

"He said what?" Aneta exclaims in disbelief. "This is crazy! There's no way I'll do that!"

"Now just hold up a moment, Aneta."

"No! You hold up! Are you crazy? You'll trust them with this family? No, I won't stand for it!"

"But he assured me we would be perfectly safe. They mean us no harm. God will—"

"No! God or not, I will not permit it and that's that!"

Francis realizes that an alternative approach is called for, and he softens his tone. "OK, Aneta. Then let's consider the alternatives, shall we? If we travel on foot, we won't be able to move very fast, so we'll not be able to cover much distance each day. Whether we walk in the spring when you're ripe with child or in the summer carrying a newborn, it will be an arduous and dangerous journey. Especially with the two other children."

"How about a train or even a horse?"

"The closest train connection is about as far as our final destination, and how can we afford a horse? Actually, we'd need a team and wagon for our whole family. That's out of the question. How would I pay for that?"

"Aren't we going to sell the cabin and the land? Won't that help?" Aneta asks.

Francis shakes his head, saying, "Don't you remember? We need to stay on this land for five years before the government will give us ownership of it. We've only been here three."

"Oh, that's right. I forgot about that," Aneta says dejectedly.

"Just think about it, Aneta. If they take us downriver in the canoes as the chief promised, we will be there in no time at all. It will be very safe, and won't put any unnecessary strain on you and the children."

"But they're heathens, Francis. Barely human. Who's saying they won't kill us all?"

Francis begins to chuckle, but catches himself just in time. He, too, used to believe this, but that was before he visited the Meskwaki settlement. After all, hasn't that been the stuff of newspaper stories and rumors for years? Why wouldn't she react this way? Still, Francis has explained to Aneta how the chief saved his life on the Indian Road. He's also described the Meskwaki settlement: the children, the women, the families—all living peacefully in the woods on land the tribe has purchased.

"They are landowners, for goodness' sake," he blurts. "If they are heathens, what does that make us? We own no land at all." Francis pauses abruptly, realizing he is veering off track. He continues more mildly, "They are God's children, just like us, Aneta. The chief is a fair, kindhearted man, and you can be sure his men will do as he tells them."

Aneta considers this. What choice do they have? Walking is not practical, and struggling here for two more years to own, then sell, their property in order to buy a team and rig doesn't thrill her in the least. She's had enough of this decrepit cabin and harsh lifestyle. She will do almost anything to leave this wretched place. But will she be able to entrust her family to a band of savages and their primitive canoes?

"I just don't know, Francis," she replies in a tone indicating to Francis that she'll most likely warm up to the idea by springtime.

PART TWO
VACLAV
1859–1866

CHAPTER 28
BOHEMIA

BIDDING JOSEF AND HIS FAMILY FAREWELL, I climb back up onto my wagon and snap the reins, rousing the idling Birdie to action. The wind has subsided, and the snow is now falling more vertically in large flakes. In the darkness, traveling from Krouna to Budislav through the snowfall will not be enjoyable. But once we get going, I'm sure old Birdie will trudge along with little encouragement. She's pulled this wagon to Proseč and back many times in the past to deliver my produce to markets there. Once we make it that far, she'll know the rest of the way. After this long day, she'll be eager to find her way back to the warm stall right next to her sister, Daisy.

As Birdie trudges onward, my thoughts return to the part I played in that situation in Krouna. I wonder what will happen if someone discovers the man's body. "What do you think, Birdie? If somebody discovers Thomas's remains, do you think the authorities will suspect Josef's family?" The horse gives a snort, as if in reply, and continues down the road. I don't remember when I first had conversations with Birdie. Well, they aren't actually conversations, after all. She never says anything—kind of a quiet type, I surmise. "Or what about me?" I ask. "Could I be in danger? What do you think, girl?" The mare makes no reply. "What do you make of that Josef fellow? He's kind of an odd sort, don't you think?" Still no response. "I don't know what you think about him, but he seems to have a rather careless streak, kind of unpredictable, if you ask me." I whip the reins once for encouragement. "Not like you, girl. You're about as predictable as they come, aren't you? And what about that wife of his? I bet you got a kick out of seeing her faint face-first into the snow." I pause for a reply but receive nothing but rhythmic breathing from the animal, so I continue, "She seems pretty excitable if you ask me. But capable enough, I suppose. It appears she was getting along well enough without her husband. But the way she tied that man in the stable shows her to be a bit vengeful, don't you think?

"And that other woman, what was her name? Anna, that was it. She just seems to accept things as they come, as if tying a man naked in a livestock barn is the most normal thing in the world." Riding in silence, I ponder this for a long while. "That Anna sure has a pleasant way about her," I continue. "Did you notice those beautiful dark eyes? They seemed to look right through me. I wonder what she saw. How old do you think she is? About my age, maybe younger, wouldn't you say? Maybe you can give me a ride back there someday soon, so we can see her again. That is, if you approve of her." Hearing no objections from the horse, I conclude, "OK, then. I'll take that as a *yes*."

My musings make the trip seem shorter than it is, and just before sunup, I arrive back in Budislav. Unhitching Birdie and returning her to her stall, I walk into the house where Father sits with his pipe in his limp hands as he snores resoundingly next to the spent coals of the fire.

"Hello, *Tatínku*," I offer as I brush dust and snow off my coat. "Why aren't you in bed?"

"You've been gone a long time, Vaclav. You had me worried," the old man mumbles, groggy from his sleep.

"I gave a ride to a fellow returning from the army. He lives in Krouna."

"Krouna? I don't think I've ever been there."

"I've been thinking recently about extending our reach with our produce to that area. I thought it might be worthy of a look."

"Hmm," the old man says as he begins to poke a small stick into his pipe, trying to bring it to life.

"Krouna has some odd people living there, that's for sure. But there is this one girl who kind of caught my eye," I offer to test my father's reaction.

"There are plenty of nice girls around here, you know. No sense looking across the hill country for one," he says. White smoke breathes out of his pipe, wafting upward in opaque tendrils. "What about that girl down the street who keeps coming by?"

"Marie?"

"Yes, her. She seems like a solid young woman. I think she likes you, Vaclav."

"I suppose," I reply with a sigh. "But is *solid* enough reason to court someone? After all, did you marry Mother because she was solid?"

"Why yes, I did." The corners of the old man's mouth turn down as he sucks a long breath through the pipe. He exhales a large plume of smoke, concealing his playful grin, as he adds, "Plus, she was the most beautiful creature I'd ever seen."

Father is nearing his mid-sixties. Tall and lank, he's a hardened man, skin weathered like the tired dirt he cultivates. He began his adult life as a *podruh*, a peasant laborer owning no property and enjoying no rights in the village. Since such rights included access to the town pastures for grazing privileges, he was unable to own livestock of any kind, including even a single horse for conveyance. As time passed, however, he inherited my grandfather's modest plot of rocky ground. This helped him to improve his station to become a peasant of better standing. Through the years, he and I have worked this land to at least a decent level of profitability. We even purchased some livestock and a bit more ground along the way. We now own more land than most of the other farmers in Budislav. Our farm comprises about three hectares, but only about half is tillable. The balance of it is heavily treed, where I often set snares to catch rabbits, squirrels, and an occasional game bird.

These days, I've taken over the most difficult and time-consuming tasks, seeing to the transporting of our produce—–mostly potatoes, beets, corn, oats, and cabbage—to sell in nearby town markets and the harvesting of oats and clover hay for feeding and bedding our two horses in winter. Father helps as much as he can, but he's not the man he used to be. In his declining years, he can only work for about half a day before he finds it necessary to lie down for a nap. I noticed my father taking a particular turn for the worse at the time of my mother's death. His energy never seemed the same after that, and I now realize that my mother was the old man's pillar against the daily grind of his hard life. Father carries on as best he can since her death, but his contributions in the fields continue to falter, and I'm left to pick up the slack. Overall, we thrive about as well as anyone can on land so limited in its productivity.

"Well, there it is, then," I say. "Since I don't find Marie to be the most beautiful creature I've ever seen, that settles it." With that, I figure I'm putting an end to this discussion.

"And this Krouna girl is?" Father presses, taking the pipe from his mouth and turning to look at me with eyebrows raised.

Thinking about that for a moment, I reply quietly, as if surprised by my answer. "Maybe," I whisper, more to myself than to my father.

The winter of 1859 comes on with a fury, and the residents of Budislav hurry to seal the gaps in their walls and roofs with straw and mud to protect them from the chill. No matter how well we prepare, however, the winters are indeed challenging times. Succumbing to the bitter cold, many of the very young and very old will die, their wooden caskets strewn about outside to await spring, when the ground is thawed enough to accept them.

My father and I, like all the other people in town, are busy preparing. We collect sufficient firewood for the winter months and assess our food reserves, which always seem to be insufficient. And then there's the care for the horses, which we shelter in a rough log stable, topped by a single-pitch roof, located just behind our home. Daisy and Birdie can usually generate sufficient body heat in the small shed to survive the winter months. But if the temperatures decrease to dangerously low levels, the horses will need to be brought into the house for warmth. This isn't something I enjoy, of course, but it's a necessity nevertheless.

Father and I prepare as we always have in years past and are once again resigned to spending January and February hunkered down in our small home, surviving primarily on salted meat and oat gruel we prepare with snow melted over the fire. Fortunately, this winter turns out to be less harsh than expected, and thankfully, we don't have to share our home with Birdie and Daisy, even though Birdie is a slightly better conversationalist than my father.

By March, the people of Budislav are already busying themselves outside their homes, and I'm one of the first to be out cleaning the stable and brushing down the horses. Planting is still weeks away so my attention turns to the traps that I've placed in my favorite locations up in our woods. My attention also wanders to thoughts of Krouna and that dark-eyed schoolteacher I met in the fall. Hopefully, one of these days, I can complete my chores here and take a ride south to see her again.

CHAPTER 29

THAT DAY FINALLY ARRIVES, and on a Saturday morning when no task needs immediate attention, I'm on my way to Krouna. This visit will be my chance to investigate opportunities for potential new markets to the west and south of Budislav. At least, that's what I tell my father. My real goal is to visit Josef, Frantiska, and especially that girl, Anna. And then there's that nagging curiosity about Thomas, the naked man Josef and I pulled up Burnt Hill. I wonder if anyone has found him yet, or if he's still up there providing nourishment for the wolves.

Bidding my father farewell, after suffering another of his jests about *that solid Krouna girl*, I lead Birdie from her stall and ride out of Budislav with the early morning sun on my back. The March breeze slaps me in the face, a confirmation of winter's reluctant retreat, but I breathe deeply, taking in the cool and humid air. It's still early, and I'll be arriving in the midmorning, so I let Birdie take her own leisurely pace. With Budislav just behind me, our hectares of land lie just to my left. The ground is still brown and lifeless, refusing to reveal even the slightest sign of fecundity. With the help of Birdie and Daisy, we'll be turning that soil soon enough, and by fall, Father and I will pull the yield from the earth yet again. That is, of course, if the rain spirits are kind to us. Will the rain be our friend this year? Or will it refuse us the crop we desperately need to make a decent profit, or any profit at all? Droughts have been common in recent years, and I've too often experienced the pain of watching our oats and vegetables wither under the summer sun. This is, of course, a pointless worry. I can't control the outcome, so why even think about it? But I do think about it—and often. How can I not?

Riding through Proseč, I decide not to stop, but proceed onward to Krouna. If there's time, I'll stop here on the way home, I figure. Continuing onward, the wooded hills separating the two towns soon engulf me, and I finally arrive in Krouna, taking stock of the little village. When I was here last, the conditions were quite different. It was windy and miserable then, the precipitation a mixture of snow and rain spitting sideways, clinging to Birdie's mane. But now, with the sun edging upward from the horizon, the place looks much different. Krouna is a bit larger than my village of Budislav. But it reflects the same details as every other peasant village in the region: one-room mud and log houses, a small church, a tiny store, a run-down administration building, and not much more. Except that Krouna has one other thing, a thing that Budislav lacks: a decrepit tavern in the middle of town. Riding by it, I know I won't be stopping there on my way back out of town. I'm not much of a drinker—never have been—couldn't afford it—but I have to admit that, on the rare occasion, it's proven to be quite enjoyable.

Finding Josef's house, I bring Birdie to a stop in the middle of the road, looking to see if anyone is about. Near the rear of the house, Frantiska has her sleeves rolled up and arms thrashing about as she works the laundry in a large wooden tub. The children are nearby, too, digging designs into the dirt with sticks. Lowering myself to the ground, I tether Birdie to a small tree. I've no sooner turned toward the house than the front door flies open and Anna appears. She's toting a load of something I can't identify, walking out into the yard toward the neighboring domicile.

"Would you like some help with that, miss?" I ask.

"What?" Anna answers, startled by the interruption. "No, thanks," she says dismissively as she briefly glances toward my voice and then continues walking. She abruptly comes to a halt and turns back with a look of surprise, exclaiming, "Vaclav? What are you doing here?"

"Do you remember me?" I ask. Of course, I knew she'd remember me. I recall how Anna studied me that night when Josef and I first arrived.

"Of course I do," she answers. "But I sure wasn't expecting to set eyes on you today."

Anna quickly walks toward me, and I can see that she is beginning to blush. Does she realize it? I wonder. "Is Josef around?" I ask, scanning the area around the house.

"He's still sleeping."

"He's asleep?"

"He worked late last evening. Plus, I think he had a bit to drink while he was there."

I try to make sense of this. Josef is working at night? And drinking? My bewilderment must be apparent, and Anna rushes to explain.

"He's been playing his music box at the tavern. Making a little money doing it, too, although last evening I think he spent a fair portion of it on beer. Frantiska doesn't seem too happy with him right now."

"No, she isn't too happy with the lout," interrupts Frantiska, who has just approached holding Antonin by one hand, Vincencie by the other. "Hello, Vaclav. It's good to see you. What brings you to Krouna?"

"Just stopped in to see how you're all doing. I thought I might see about selling some of my vegetables here this summer," I explain, continuing to keep my eyes on Anna as she walks on toward the house next door.

"We have a small street market every week in August. Also, you might check at the store in the village," says Frantiska.

"I'll look into it," I say gratefully. "What's Anna doing over there?"

"She's moving her things into our neighbors' old house. They left for America last fall, and no one's moved in there yet, so we figured she could stay over there. It's been pretty cramped with five of us in our little place."

I'm tempted to ask Frantiska if anyone found Thomas's body yet, but I think better of it. Instead, I call out, "Anna, would you like some help with your things?"

"Sure. Come on," Anna replies happily. "And you can call me Annie if you'd like."

The rest of the morning is spent with Annie, helping her get settled in her new home. Rose has left the place in very tidy condition, which Annie says is no surprise to anyone. I try to hide my disappointment when we eventually finish arranging things, leaving me with no further reason to hang around. We awkwardly exchange pleasantries for a while, both trying to delay my inevitable departure. Then I finally suggest, "Annie, would you like to go for a walk? It's a nice day." We both know we shouldn't spend more time in her house behind closed doors. What would people think?

Soon, we are strolling down the road toward the middle of town, chatting about topics of no real consequence. I think about asking if Thomas's body has been found yet, but again choose otherwise. Why ruin a perfectly nice walk?

Many more trips are made to Krouna in the months to come. Of course, as planting season arrives, those visits become more infrequent, and frustratingly so. I've grown quite fond of Annie, and I sense she has similar feelings toward me. Not that she's ever said so. But I can tell from her willing disposition that my relationship with her is a consensually agreeable one. And not just agreeable to Annie, but to Josef and Frantiska as well.

On one of my visits in late June, Frantiska receives a letter from America, from her friend Rose Novak. Upon receiving the letter, Frantiska gathers Josef, Annie, and the children together to hear the exciting news from America. I am arriving just in time for this excitement to unfold.

It's a rather long letter, describing Rose and Anton's trip northward to Choceň, where they continued on by train to the seaport near Bremen. The major portion of the letter describes the voyage by sea on a sailing barque, which took almost ten weeks and was fraught with considerable hardships. The letter came from New York City, where they disembarked, so she doesn't yet have a lot to say about her new country. But her description of the conditions on the voyage across the Atlantic is quite detailed and rather frightening. I wonder why anyone would want to take such a risky and unpleasant journey. It is when Josef interrupts Frantiska's reading of the letter that I realize the lure of America has already taken hold of this household.

"Oh my," whispers Josef. "What do you think, Frannie? It sounds like a dangerous voyage, and they didn't even have any children to worry about. I don't know if I feel good about taking two children on a trip like that."

"Do you think she may have exaggerated just a bit?" asks Annie. "Maybe it's not as bad as she's saying."

"I don't know," Frantiska answers. "Rose was never one to exaggerate."

I take all this in, trying to understand the significance of their conversation. When it finally dawns on me, I can't help blurting out, "You two aren't thinking of trying that, are you? Not with the children, certainly!" No sooner have I uttered it than I realize I am overstepping my bounds. You fool, I think. Stop talking. But it's too late.

Annie is at once upon me, assailing me with disapproval. "So what if they are?" she says. "It's not so far-fetched. Many people around here are leaving. You must have noticed that, even in Budislav! What is there to hold them here? Sure, the conditions on the ships are harsh, but what we have here isn't exactly the promised land, is it?"

"No, what I meant was—" I say, trying to redeem myself, but I'm interrupted as Annie continues.

"And if you must know everything, I'm going, too—if you must know." She's been glaring at me, but now she lowers her eyes, apparently embarrassed she's allowed me to get a rise out of her.

"I'm sorry," I whisper, not letting my eyes fix upon any of their faces.

Josef intervenes, saying, "I'm sure he meant nothing by it, Annie. Go ahead, Frannie; read the rest of it."

Frantiska resumes her reading, which describes a sickness that took hold during the voyage. Although the sickness infected neither Rose nor Anton, they still had to go through the worst part of the trip, which was the subsequent quarantine when they arrived at port. All of this is of considerable concern to Josef. And as his wife continues to read, he is further disturbed by the news of political strife fomenting in the United States. Rose has written of rumors of several states threatening secession.

"What's that mean?" asks Annie.

"I'm not sure, but it doesn't sound good to me," Josef says, adding, "I don't know about this, Frannie. I'm not saying we shouldn't go, but maybe we should wait to make sure there's no conflict over there. Maybe they'll reach an agreement, and it will just work itself out. But if it doesn't, we don't want to walk off a ship and right into a war. I've seen more than my share of that recently."

Annie's rebuke has hurt me, but the hurt I feel isn't to my ego as much as it is to my hope for our relationship. She has declared her intention of going to America, but what about me? She's never talked to me about it. Is she just going to abandon me someday? My mood turns dark, and I wonder if I should just go on back home to Budislav. Annie stares straight at me. Her expression is not reproachful, but more empathetic, with her brow furled and her lips somewhat pursed in worry. She subtly nods her head toward the door, indicating that we should go outside, and I discreetly exit as Josef listens to Frannie read the rest of Rose's letter.

Making my way to where Birdie is standing, I figure I've worn out my welcome and will leave soon. Annie follows me, and as she approaches where I'm standing, I'm already reaching for the horse's bridle. She lays her hand upon mine, causing me to pause and turn toward her.

"Please don't go yet," she requests.

"I think I probably should."

"I'm sorry I snapped at you. That wasn't fair."

"Why didn't you tell me?"

"I should have, I know. We've been planning it for a long time, Frannie and me."

"And you are dead set on leaving, Annie?"

"It's my dream, yes, Vaclav."

"But what about—," I pause, looking down at the ground, without finishing my thought. She finishes it for me.

"Us? You mean, what about us?"

"Yes, what about us? That's what I mean," I answer bluntly, letting my eyes come up to meet hers.

"You should come with us," Annie replies. It's a confident and direct suggestion, one that Annie means in all seriousness, nothing playful about it. I'm taken aback by her straightforwardness, her boldness, and her faith in her own sense of purpose, as if by sheer will she can make things come to pass.

"You can't be serious," I answer.

"Very serious. We could get married properly, and go with Frannie, Josef, and the children when they are ready."

This is making my head spin. Get married? We've never talked about that. We hardly know each other. Besides, how can she be so bold as to be the one doing the proposing? That isn't right. Sure, I like Annie. I like her a lot, but . . . get married? Now?

"I don't know, Annie," I finally say. I can see that she's now embarrassed she even mentioned it. "No, no, don't get the wrong idea, Annie. It's not that I wouldn't want to marry you. But . . . America? I've got my father to look after. He's rather frail, and I can't just leave him here."

It's an insoluble dilemma. Annie knows I have an obligation to my father. But I sense her dream will not, cannot, be easily dismissed. There's nothing more to say. Smiling faintly, I finally reach for Annie's hand, squeezing it gently, before I untie Birdie's bridle strap and slip deftly up onto the horse's back. Annie stands there by the small maple tree, watching as I ride off. I'm sure she expects me to look back, but I don't. Birdie is my counsel now, and I begin explaining my dilemma to her, interrupted only by an intermittent snort.

CHAPTER 30

THE REST OF THE SUMMER is spent working with my father in the fields, urging reluctant crops upward from the uncooperative rocky soil. Most of that time I spend clearing large stones from the parcel of land we most recently purchased, a parcel only modestly improved by our backbreaking toil. It's a laborious task, and I endure most of it, my father not being up to the strain. But I welcome the work, for it helps me keep my mind off Annie. And though I can't help but wonder how she is doing, I can see no reason to travel back to Krouna, encouraging a relationship not meant to be.

My mood has diminished significantly and my father isn't blind to my transformation. When he asks me about Annie, I respond with silence, a sign that she is forbidden territory for further discussion. Discussions or not, Father is concerned about me, and I'm sure one of his worries is that I'm soon to turn twenty-two, when most men in the village are already married. My father can clearly see that I'm showing a glumness incapable of attracting any prospects. Even Marie, from down the street, is tired of my disinterest. It appears she's moved on to seek the favor of other, less brooding, candidates.

Sadly, my gloom is impacting my relationship with my father. Previously amicable, it is eroding in palpable ways. Our conversations are more reserved, and humorous exchanges are now exceedingly rare. Eventually, Father spends many of his evenings elsewhere, often with aging friends more interested in lighthearted banter over friendly games of chance.

In mid-July there is some uplifting news. At any other time, I would have greeted this news with considerable elation. Upon traveling to the district office in Chrudim for the military lottery, I once again receive a high lottery number. This is my third and final time for the lottery, and my high number fulfills my military obligation.

My reaction surprises me. Instead of feeling delighted at my good fortune, I take the news in an oddly indifferent way. Is my fate of toiling forever on my rock-strewn farm plot much better than military service? Maybe it would be better to get far away from Budislav, Krouna, my father, Josef, Frantiska, and especially Annie. Maybe it would be better to test myself as a soldier on some distant battlefield. Maybe it would be better to die in combat against an armed adversary than to collapse ignobly into the dirt in a sweltering oat field. This is the nadir of despair where I now reside. I'm tired, too tired even to converse with Birdie.

As I ride home from Chrudim, my thoughts finally grind to a merciful halt as the numbness of my weariness eventually brings the welcomed intervention of sleep. Still, I somehow keep myself astride my lumbering, but steady, mount. There will be time to re-examine all this negativity in the future. And perhaps later I'll have that much-needed conversation with Birdie. But for now, I will dream pleasant dreams of better times, and dream of Annie, too.

The growing season of 1860 is kind to the farmers around Budislav, who live their lives in a perpetual state of anxious waiting—waiting for the next needed rainfall. Or waiting for the next dry spell, a sign of a beginning drought that could reduce any meager profits. But this year turns out to be a fairly good one. While this doesn't push my spirits up to previous levels, I'm heartened to know that we will at least have sufficient produce to sell at the town markets.

By August, I've already begun my weekly trips to markets in the towns surrounding Budislav. They include Desná and Proseč, two of my main selling locations in the past. My decision to include Krouna in my rotation, however, is an experiment to test the profitability of reaching more customers. Because of the greater distance necessary to get there, I plan to make the trek only a couple of times. And only later in the season, when I can manage a full load of potatoes, beets, and cabbage. If these trips prove to be more time-consuming than they're worth, I can always return to my previous routine of serving only towns closer to Budislav.

It's the first of September when I finally enter Krouna, with Daisy and Birdie pulling a wagon laden with heaping baskets of potatoes and cabbage. A few other farmers are already there. They've unhitched their animals and begun attending to townspeople who are looking for bargains. I find a large oak tree to provide cover for my produce from the summer sun. Then I settle in for a day of commercial enterprise, with the hope of returning to Budislav with an empty wagon and fatter pockets.

I busy myself arranging my produce on the ground and the wagon bed. Soon, the lady selling plums and apples right next to me walks up and says, "Did you hear the rumor going around the market?"

"Well, no. As you can see, I just got here. What kind of rumor?" I ask, irritated by the woman's intrusion.

"Just yesterday, they found a body up on a hill outside of town. The authorities think it might be the village judge's son, though the remains were pretty picked over, probably by wolves or wild boars. His name was Thomas, I think. He's been missing since last fall. Just disappeared into thin air, someone said, until now," the woman elaborates.

Acting as if I'm only mildly interested, I glance toward Birdie, who is looking at me, ears forward. "So, what do you think happened?" I ask the woman.

"They say it was a suicide. I guess they found a weapon there by the body."

I hear Birdie produce a short, discreet snort, which is odd. In all my years working with horses, I've never realized that horses have such a diverse snorting vocabulary.

The rumor about Thomas's suicide proves to be the vendors' most exciting topic of the morning. And as the sun moves to a spot directly above the big oak tree, I'm resigned to spending the afternoon engaged in the ritual of haggling with customers. I wonder if I'll see Josef or Frantiska this afternoon. Or maybe even Annie. Do I really want to see her? I'm not sure; it could just cause me more heartache.

I don't need to worry about this for long, for she soon appears, during the hottest part of the day. As she approaches my wagon, her long skirt creates small billows of road dust in her wake, and her white scarf frames her flawless round face. She stands smiling at me with that same pleasant smile I beheld when first we met. "Hi, Vaclav," she says, those dark eyes burning through me.

"Hi, Annie. How are you? And Josef and Frantiska? How are they?" I ask, spewing all my pleasantries in one nervous breath.

"We're all doing fine, thanks. I haven't seen you for a while. Josef asked about you just the other day."

"It's been really busy, you know, with the crops."

"I understand," she answers and then pauses, before adding, "We've all missed you. I've missed you."

There it is again. That same directness, that confidence I noticed before.

"Well, as I said, it's been pretty busy back home, so I couldn't spare the time to come by. Sorry."

"How's your father?" she asks.

"Fine," I answer with brevity. I was right to have been worried, for this indeed is becoming painful. In my discomfort, I now wish Annie would just continue down the road to the other vendors. But I also wish she would never leave.

My first wish is realized as Annie, sensing my discomfort and perhaps even her own, bids me farewell.

"It's good to see you, Vaclav," she says. "I'll tell Josef and Frannie that I ran into you."

She walks away, her skirt billowing in the breeze, and I whisper, "Did you hear that, Birdie? She said she missed me. You heard her, didn't you?"

I'm suddenly awash in a wave of my cruel reality. Why am I standing here pining after a woman who's leaving for America in the months to come? These implausible reveries are torture I've brought on myself, not unlike my dreams of becoming a man of means in Budislav. Neither of these scenarios will ever come to pass. I know that. And yet I continue to entertain such pointless delusions as if I can somehow force their way into reality. I'll never elevate my station in life beyond what I am: A *chalupnik*, a mere cottager, destined to work three hectares of land, struggling each season to turn a small profit. I'm as sure of that as I am that Annie will be leaving Krouna for good, leaving me alone to take care of my aging father and work that rocky plot of hilly farmland to my dying day.

CHAPTER 31
AMERICA

THE WINTER COMES AND GOES, and Francis's wife is now in her seventh month of pregnancy. To his satisfaction, Francis finds her much more agreeable to joining a Meskwaki canoe escort down the Iowa River, far away from this dismal farmstead. The winter has been a difficult one. And although Francis has done his best to make Aneta comfortable and take care of the children, he has still been hampered by heavy snow, a collapsing roof, winds encroaching through the sieve-like walls, and the ever-present lack of provisions. By the time the first robins appear outside the cabin, Francis can't wait to get in that dugout canoe. He senses Aneta feels the same way.

On a sunny morning in April, Francis and Aneta stand with their children and baggage on the east bank of the Iowa River, where Chief Meminwaneka told them to wait for the canoes. They don't wait long before they see three dugouts approaching from the north, each manned by two young braves. Francis recognizes two of the braves as the ones who stopped him on the road that day when he went to see the chief. Today, though, there's no whooping or howling. In fact, the braves utter not a sound as they beach the canoes in the muddy shallows. They immediately begin loading the Kuns's belongings. In one canoe they place the family's trunk and other baggage. In another, they help Aneta and little Karel to the middle of the craft, where Aneta sits with considerable difficulty. Soon, Francis and Julie are in the third dugout, and they are on their way with the current carrying them along.

Francis wonders how long they'll be on the river, and he asks the brave in the rear of his canoe, "Excuse me, how long it takes?" using his broken English, figuring the brave must know at least a bit of the language.

The brave remains silent—stoic even—as though he hasn't heard the question. Perhaps, he doesn't think Francis is worthy of an answer, Francis speculates.

"I said," Francis repeats more loudly, "how long we get there?"

The boy looks at him briefly and shakes his head. Francis realizes that despite his linguistic expertise, none of the languages he speaks can do him any good. These young men know only their native tongue. He wonders if the chief has given them precise and clear instructions on where his family is to disembark. He hopes so, or who knows where they'll end up?

Glancing over at Aneta, Francis notices her trying to find a more comfortable position as she fidgets on the floor of her canoe. He can't help her with that, but at least he's glad to see that she no longer has that look of terror. Now it's only a look of mild trepidation. She finally gets settled and watches with fascination as the river bank flies by. She no longer appears afraid of being scalped by these heathens with her body left floating in the river as fish bait.

The braves are expert boatsmen, Francis observes. They let the current take them smoothly downriver, rarely needing any additional propulsion with their paddles. Francis finds the trip quite enjoyable, and he's now grateful he took John Zehrung's advice to return the Chief's blanket that fateful day. Otherwise, he might be walking with his young family all the way to his new congregation.

The trip is over before it hardly starts, and Francis wishes they could continue this fascinating journey down the river a while longer. But they have somewhere to be, and soon the braves pull up to the river's bank near a crude wooden dock. Across the river on the other side, Francis can see a ferry barge tied up to another wooden structure, and a man watching them with interest.

In no time at all, Francis and his family are standing on solid ground with their baggage, watching the braves paddle back upstream. He turns to consider the rutted road stretching to the north. The Chief has told him this road links Iowa City with Cedar Rapids, and Francis knows his new congregation is located somewhere north of here on this route. The Chief has also told him about a way station nearby, where wagons take on passengers. Francis sees the place Meminwaneka was referring to, and he urges his family onward in that direction.

The way station is nothing more than a three-sided shed with a pen for two horses and a waiting area with benches for passengers. Francis wonders how long they will have to wait here for transport. Hopefully, not too long. He has a bit of money with him, saved from his sale of oat straw and also from previous donations from his preaching. But he's not sure if it'll be enough to pay for their fares. He'll just have to hope for the best. As he ponders this, he notices a stone house situated nearby behind the way station. Several outbuildings surround the house, and Josef assumes this to be the home of a prosperous farmer. Certainly, this is a farmer much more successful than he ever was or ever could hope to be. The front door of the house swings open, and Francis can see a man stepping out onto his porch, walking down the steps, and coming toward them.

"*Zdravím vás!* Greetings," the man says as he approaches, and Francis is pleased to hear the man speaking the language of his homeland.

"Hello," Francis replies.

"Can I help you?"

"Uh, yes. I'm Reverend Francis Kun, and this is Aneta and our children. We come from Tama County and are heading for a settlement called Banner Valley. Is this where we can find the transport to take us there?"

"Indeed it is. The mud wagon should be here in about an hour. Hopefully, there'll be room for you on it. Just tell the driver you want to be left off at the Jacob Shuey place. That'll get you pretty close." The man pauses and looks toward the river. "You say you're from Tama County? How did you end up on this route?" he asks, confused.

"Believe it or not, the Meskwakis brought us down the river in canoes."

"Really? That's a first for me. And you still have your scalps?" he says, chuckling. "I often see the braves floating by, but they usually avoid any contact with us white folk. It's probably just as well. My wife and a lot of other people around here are deathly afraid of 'em."

"Well, I think if you'd get to know them, you'd find them quite amiable," replies Francis. "And whom do I have the pleasure of meeting?"

"Oh, I'm very sorry. My name is Coufal, Joe Coufal. That's my place back over there," he says, pointing toward the house. "I farm most of that bottom land you see over by the river."

"I farmed up in Tama County. Never was very good at it. I'm actually better at being a preacher. Lately, I mostly travel around spreading the Word. But recently I've been called to start a church over near Banner Valley. Just a small one, only about five families, but it's a start, I suppose. Hopefully, it'll grow."

"I wish you luck. We need more churches around here. There're too many people leaving their faith. A lot of 'em call themselves freethinkers. I'm not sure what that means, exactly. Maybe not so much *free*-thinkers, but more *non*-thinkers, as far as I'm concerned. I'm sure you'll run into them eventually."

"That's fine by me. I suppose if everyone was strong in the faith, there'd be no need for people like me."

"Hmm, maybe not. That's a good point," Coufal agrees, scratching his chin in contemplation. "Say, why don't you folks come on up to the house? The mud wagon won't be here for a while. You can have some fresh water, and maybe the wife can drum up something to eat."

"That's more than kind, Mr. Coufal. We'd like that very much. And maybe I can read some scripture. Would you like that?"

"Uh . . . sure, I guess. Why not?"

CHAPTER 32
BOHEMIA

THERE IS SOLACE TO BE FOUND in the daily drudgery on my few hectares of tired soil. The summer and fall seasons bring with them many chores that, if left unfinished, will cause hardships throughout the coming winter months. I find my thoughts of Annie overtaken by the harvesting of grain and hay, the caring for my livestock, the maintaining of the house and barn, and the caring for my father. It's only in the brief moments of the late evening, between the time my head meets the pillow and sleep overtakes me, that thoughts of Annie appear. Even these treasured musings happen ever so briefly as the exhaustion of my day quickly and mercifully forces sleep upon me.

Fall soon becomes winter, and my work turns primarily to the care of my two horses and other animals in order to get them safely through the cold of the season. Our three cows and two goats, recently purchased, require daily milking and feeding, all necessary so I can sell the milk to our neighbors and help provide some income during these cold months. And then there are my traps, which provide welcomed meat from game birds and rabbits, tasty additions to an otherwise lackluster diet of gruel and beets. All these tasks are mine alone. My father has little tolerance for the cold, making him of little use with outside chores. The old man is moving about the house with the mien of declining health. It's come to where my father and I are far from equal partners in our farming enterprise. Now the old man's care has become yet another burden for me to add to my list.

Spring finally comes, and with the warmer temperatures, it is heartening to see that my father's health takes a turn for the better showing considerable improvement as April arrives. He seems to have a bit more spring to his step. But there's another problem I recognize. Though the man appears more mobile, he's having spells of forgetfulness and general confusion. So much so that I find it impossible to trust my father with even the simplest of tasks. He now requires constant supervision, a level of care that I have scant time to provide. So it's to my considerable relief that he continues to meet with his group of elderly men for a weekly game of cards. I'm encouraged by the opportunity this presents him. It provides a chance for the old man to socialize, but it also frees me to complete my chores unencumbered by worries about his care. I know that some innocent gambling is going on at these meetings, but I'm glad to see my father being entertained in the company of men his own age. I'm even willing to give my father a few coins here and there, thus encouraging the activity, and am relieved to note that he rarely asks for more.

With Father unable to contribute, the spring planting season greatly taxes my energy, but I'm still able to complete the sowing of our fields. Soon, the rains come with regularity and sprouts emerge from the gray soil. I'm hopeful this will be a good year for our crops, and as the days pass, the ample precipitation satiates our thirsty seedlings and heightens my hopes. By early July, I've taken in our first crop of oats and stored away much of the straw for livestock bedding. Our vegetables are showing satisfactory growth. But so are the surrounding weeds, forcing me to spend most of my mornings engaged in hoeing.

By mid-July, I begin my forays to neighboring towns with our bounty of vegetables. I don't include Krouna on my weekly route, for both economic and personal reasons. Most of our produce can be sold in villages closer to Budislav, and I think it best to avoid any chance meeting with Annie. I'm almost to a point now where I can direct my mind away from thoughts about her. This keeps me from falling into the depths of depression that once plagued me. Why should I take the chance of seeing her when it might cause me to dream that impossible dream all over again? Besides, for all I know, she's already on a sailing ship to America, and I'll never see her again.

It proves to be a good year for us. Our crop is bountiful, despite the rock and clay content of our fields. And I'm able to sell almost all our vegetables at the various village markets on my weekly route. After estate levies and general expenses, I can look forward to turning a small profit, most of it going toward our survival through the winter.

Alas, the winter of 1861 proves to be a severe one. Although my financial situation proves to be a bit healthier than usual, Father's health is failing, and I watch helplessly as his condition takes a precipitous turn for the worse. By late January, the man is growing weaker by the day, and I often observe him bent over, moaning from what appears to be some kind of abdominal malady. With no apothecary available, I have little recourse but to seek a local herbalist, who prescribes a concoction of such foul-smelling swill that the suffering man refuses to drink it, stating in no uncertain terms that he'd "die before putting that down my gullet!"

One week later on a frigid and windy morning, my father passes, curled up under a blanket on his straw mattress, his knees pulled up to his chest. That afternoon, I walk the half mile through town to the domicile of a local carpenter and wait as the man fashions a crude casket for my father. I drag the thing through the blowing snow all the way back home, where I place him inside, wrapped in the same blanket he clutched around him as he died. Securing the lid to the top of the casket and pulling the wooden box outside, I leave it next to the doorway. It will stay there until warm temperatures allow the ground to accept it.

In mid-March that time comes, and I finally bury my father, sending him to eternal rest as I stand over his grave with two of his card-playing friends, all mumbling the Lord's Prayer.

It takes a few days to come to grips with the fact that I am all alone. I will miss the confused old man with his ever-puffing pipe and his never-ending pleas for his son to marry, for I've never enjoyed being alone. Until now, my father has provided the companionship I needed. But now my papa is gone. And in the days following his burial, I am already yearning for a life shared with someone else. Perhaps I will go see that girl down the street, Marie. I haven't run into her lately and wonder if maybe she's already been claimed in marriage. So be it, I think. I can probably do better. There are plenty of other suitable prospects in the area who will welcome the overtures of a man who owns his own land, albeit only about three hectares.

It's about a week after my father's burial, on a blustery day, that I hear a visitor rapping at my door. I pull it open just a crack against the punishing wind and find a short, round man standing outside beneath a tiny round-brimmed hat. I've seen this man in Budislav before. I know Solomon Wise by name and by reputation, as an unsavory character from Proseč who is held in low regard even among the poorest peasants in the village. It's not that he's a beggar or a gypsy, for he has plenty of money. It's for his occupation as a local moneylender that the townspeople despise him, and many people cut a wide berth as they meet him on the road.

"What do you want?" I ask.

"I'm Solomon Wise. I'm the—"

"I know who and what you are. What do you want?" I repeat impatiently.

"Well, Herr Rejman, I received these from your father," he says as he hands several pieces of paper through the crack.

I study the papers briefly before asking, "What's this all about?"

"Those are loan documents. He's taken out several loans over these past months. I heard the gentleman died, and I'd like to offer my sincere condolences for your loss. However, business is business, and I'm here to collect what he owes me."

I open the door wider to let the man shuffle in out of the cold. Closing the door behind him, I continue to stare down at the pieces of paper, trying to tally up the numbers on the documents. Wise sees me trying to do so, and says, "It comes to thirty-five guldens, if you're wondering."

"Thirty-five?" I protest. That amounts to almost half my entire profit from last year's vegetable sales. "But these are not my loans. They were my father's. Certainly, you can't expect—"

"I'm sorry, but you are indeed responsible for his debts. We can take this to the village judge if you don't believe me."

I know I'm obligated by law to pay my father's debts. But why would my father have taken out these loans? I don't remember him purchasing anything. Then it becomes clear. It was those card games, where my father gambled away the few coins I gave him. Evidently, the stakes had become much higher than he expected, and Solomon Wise offered an easy way to replenish his stash. No wonder he seldom came back requesting more money from me. He simply got it from the moneylender. To the befuddled old man, it just seemed easier that way. No need to justify it to me.

"No, I believe you," I reply despondently. "Wait here."

I retreat from the doorway and reach for a large, round tin sitting on a shelf next to various provisions for cooking. I reach in, pull out my savings, and count out thirty-five guldens. Shaking my head, I place the tin back on the shelf and walk slowly back to Wise, thrusting out my hand at him, relinquishing the money.

"It was good doing business with you," the man says blandly as he counts the money, then turns and immediately walks back out the door.

"I'll bet it was," I grouse as I loudly slam the door behind the backside of the moneylender as he leaves.

The winter finally releases its grip on Budislav, and I'm busy preparing for planting. I miss my father greatly. But as much as I miss him, I'm grateful I'm no longer burdened by the man's care. This feeling at first fills me daily with considerable feelings of guilt. But as the weather warms and my planting requires more attention, I soon free myself of this thought, thinking of my father only occasionally in the loneliness of the late evening.

By May, with the planting progressing, I'm confident I can handle all my responsibilities. My father has taught me well, and I'm sure I know all I need to know about crop management and animal husbandry. After all, I did all this work on my own during the last year of my father's life. I can see nothing standing in my way for another bountiful and profitable crop. Except for one thing: the weather.

By mid-June, there's little left in the fields around Budislav. The drought makes sure of that. The adequate May rainfall that urged the tiny sprouts up through the reluctant soil is no more. The rain stops for good in June, leaving only tiny, limp vestiges of the grain and vegetable seedlings I so assiduously planted.

The drought strikes a crushing blow to cottagers in and around Budislav. To be sure, the village's inhabitants possess an inborn resilience against misfortune and hopelessness. After all, our ancestors for generations have lived this hard life. We've grown accustomed to the way things have always been: the poverty, subjugation, religious persecution, and precarious livelihoods. But even with this conditioning to difficulty, this merciless drought is almost too much to bear. How will people feed their families, or satisfy their obligation to the kingdom, or pay their rent to the estate landowners? Many will starve before the next growing season, and who can say whether the next year will be any better than this one?

Fortunately, I have no family to support, only myself and my livestock. But how will I do that with my food already almost depleted and my livestock scavenging for food out in scorched and lifeless pastureland? I know I could sell off the animals, something I'm not eager to do. What would I do without the income from the cows' and goats' milk, and how would I work the land for next year's crop if I have no horses? Besides, who is there in Budislav with the means to purchase any livestock amid this drought?

I continue to hope the animals will forage enough to survive until the fall, but what of next winter? I'll have no feed or bedding for them without a summer crop. And what will I find to feed myself under these circumstances?

If only my father were alive to offer his advice. I wonder what he would tell me to do. Would he tell me to leave this village to find work elsewhere? Where would I go? And what would I do? I have no skills beyond farming. No, Father would advise me to find a way through this hardship, knowing that I might recover with the next growing season. If that's what my father would have wanted me to do, that's what I'll do. But I can think of only one way forward. I'll have to go see Solomon Wise.

I've traveled to Proseč many times, selling my vegetables in the square in front of the Catholic church. But I've never stepped foot in the church itself, being more a follower of the Czech reformer, Jan Hus. Before my father died, we often attended Protestant services held by an old Magyar minister in a home on the edge of Proseč. My mother, Katharina, however, was a devout Catholic, so when she passed, we had her laid to rest behind the Catholic church.

Proseč is larger than Budislav, but besides the burial plot of my dear mother, I have little interest in the village. And as I ride into the town, the only thing that mildly interests me is the small tavern on the edge of town. It was always at my father's insistence that I avoided places like that, but now, with his passing, I take note of the place and consider stopping there on my way back home.

It's difficult to find Solomon Wise's whereabouts. But with the help of a few residents encountered in the streets along the way, I'm able to find my way to his house on the east side of town. The man's house is on the very edge of Proseč, in a respectable neighborhood where a few Jewish families live. I dismount, tie Birdie to a nearby fence post, make my way up three steps to the entrance, and rap the brass knocker twice against the door.

The door opens, and there stands the little round man, who says, "Ah, Vaclav. I was half expecting you to come to see me, and here you are," he says.

Wise's condescending tone doesn't sit well with me, but I'm at a disadvantage today and keep my disdain to myself. I'll reserve my ire for another time.

"I'd like to speak with you about a loan," I say matter-of-factly.

"Sure you would. Come in, come in," replies the man, smiling with smug satisfaction.

The meeting isn't a long one, for there're no negotiations to be conducted during this transaction. Wise states his terms, and I'm free to agree to them or not. Wise knows I have little recourse but to agree, and I soon sign the papers and shake the man's hand. I'll be required to repay Wise one-third of the loan each of the next three years, plus interest of course. I'll need to budget carefully, but I'm confident I can repay the loan and successfully get back on my feet again.

Leaving the moneylender's house with loan money in hand, I feel an odd combination of relief and worry. I've heard of people like me being duped out of their property by moneylenders. But what choice do I have? The drought has brought me close to ruin. I only hope that the next three years will bring me profit enough to repay Wise in full. If my ruin eventually comes to pass and I can't repay my debt, at least I'll have been able to delay the inevitable, and I'll cross that bridge when I come to it.

As I head out of Proseč, I ride by the square next to the grand Catholic church and soon pass the livery. Just before reaching the countryside beyond the village, I stop in front of the tavern. With the loan money I have in my pocket, I can afford a single beer to brace myself for the trip, I surmise. After all, my father won't be at home to pass judgment on the brew on my breath.

The tavern is a crude, single-room wooden structure. A small counter skirts one wall, and three small tables are scattered about the floor. Around each of them sit a couple of decrepit chairs that I eye warily for their ability to sustain my, or anyone's, weight. I decide to stand at the counter just to be on the safe side. The owner delivers the lager in very short order, and I toss a couple of coins onto the counter. The beer seems a little flat, but the flavor is satisfying. I haven't enjoyed one for quite some time. Still, I know I shouldn't get too used to it. I won't be able to enjoy many of these until I pay off the loan, that's for sure.

Sipping from my cup, I study two men sitting near the counter, drinking and talking in loud tones, their rickety chairs straining beneath their bulk. I'm not trying to eavesdrop, but I can't help but hear them occasionally invoking the word *Krouna* in their conversation. I wonder if they know Josef and Frantiska. Surely, they must know them. Krouna isn't that big. I grab my beer and make my way to their table.

"Excuse me. Sorry to interrupt, but I heard you speaking of Krouna. Would you happen to know Josef Zach?"

One man replies, "You mean that drunken musician?"

"The what? Musician?" I exclaim.

"Yes. The man with that blasted music contraption. We drink to that blaring thing most every weekend in Jakub's tavern. I'm going deaf from the clatter of it."

"That's him, alright," I say, smiling. "So he's still there in town?"

"Well, he was two days ago," answers the other man. "I guess he's still there unless someone finally ran him and his noisemaker out of the village."

I hesitate, letting an image of Annie take shape in my mind. This surprises me. I've been able to condition myself away from my longings for her. But now, there she is.

Venturing another query, "Would you happen to know if the schoolteacher, Anna, is still there?"

The first man pauses momentarily, thinking, and then replies, "Haven't seen her recently, probably because the school had to close. At least, that's what the rumor is. With the drought most people can't afford to send their children, I suppose."

The two men go back to their drinking, and I retreat to my place at the counter. As I finish my beer, questions are firing wildly in my head. So Josef and Frantiska haven't left for America yet. Why not? And what of Annie? Where is she? Has Annie avoided the enticement of her American dream, or is she already on a sailing barque to a new life across the sea?

The possibilities for my life suddenly expand in front of me. I'd given up on a life with Annie, but now my feelings for her come flooding back. If there's a chance she's still in Bohemia, I'm determined to find out. And there's but one way to do that.

Instead of turning Birdie eastward toward Budislav, I head south toward Krouna. I'm venturing further from home than I'd intended today, and I wonder if Birdie is up to the trip. I hope so. It doesn't matter, though, for I'll make it to Krouna even if I have to do it on foot, pulling her behind me. I glance skyward, realizing it's already midafternoon, and I'll most likely be returning home tonight under the cover of darkness. That is not something I'll look forward to, and neither will Birdie. In her condition, will she have the endurance to make it home? Perhaps Josef will offer me lodging. It doesn't matter. I'll sleep on the side of the road if I have to.

CHAPTER 33

I WALK INTO KROUNA, leading Birdie behind me, and the place looks deserted. The drought hasn't spared Krouna from the wrath it's inflicted on every other sad village in the district, and it looks like all of Krouna's residents have retreated into their hovels to suffer alone. The only person in sight is an elderly man slipping out a side door of his home, apparently heading behind the structure to relieve himself.

The village has the look of a town in the middle of a plague. Not a horse in sight. Even the chickens and dogs that usually roam freely in this village have apparently been eaten or perhaps died of starvation.

Birdie and I continue through the village center, passing the administrative building, the tavern, and the mercantile. It's almost sundown, and I'm not surprised to see that the tavern is the only place that appears to be open. Soon, I spot a figure walking toward me from the opposite direction, someone walking with a definite catch in his gait. As the figure approaches, I can see it's a man carrying a crank organ. I stop and wait for him to reach me, and then say, "Hello, Josef."

Josef squints through the fading light, trying to make out my face. "Well, I'll be a motherless Hungarian! Vaclav, what are you doing here?"

"Just in the area," I lie. "How are you?"

"Surviving, just like most everyone else. It's been a long time, Vaclav. The last time I heard about you being in our village, Annie mentioned she saw you at the market. Why didn't you stop in to see us?"

"It's kind of a long story, my friend. How are Frantiska and the children?"

"They're getting on fine. Frannie's still doing her weaving, although sales have really slowed down. She's been able to sell a few things in the larger towns, where people still have some money."

I set my gaze on the crank organ Josef cradles in his arms. I think back to the moment I encountered him on that road three years ago—a disheveled soldier standing there in his ragged military uniform, grasping that music machine like it was his most prized possession.

"So, where are you going with your noisemaker?" I ask with a smirk.

"No need to get smart," Josef shoots back with feigned annoyance. "I happen to be heading to my job at the tavern. I play there every Saturday night. This is Saturday, isn't it? I kind of lose track lately."

"Yes, it's Saturday, Josef."

"I used to play every Friday and Saturday, but with the drought and all, Jakub's business has fallen off a bit."

"I understand. I'm kind of surprised that he can pay you at all during these tough times."

"Well, even with the drought, men still seem to find a few coins to spend on beer. It seems that the crank organ enhances Jakub's crowd. As he says, the faster I crank, the faster they drink."

"Ah, I get it," I chuckle. I pause momentarily, and then ask, "Is Annie still in Krouna?"

"So that's why you're here," Josef says, shaking his head. "It took you two years to come asking about her? You've got some things to learn about women, Vaclav."

"Well, I thought you all were leaving for America," I plead in my defense.

"We would have, but things have been tough during this dry spell. We just didn't have enough money for the trip. Plus, there is that war I've been hearing about over there. I think it would be wise for us to make the voyage after it's over. I've had my fill of wars."

"And Annie?" I press.

"I'm afraid she's back in Jarošov, living with her parents and her sister. The school closed, and she had no means of supporting herself. We hated to see her go, but . . . you know how it is," Josef says, looking down and sighing deeply. "You should go see her, Vaclav," he says.

"Perhaps," I say.

Josef's voice takes on a brighter tone as he says, "Why don't you come to the tavern with me and hear this old musician in action?"

"I'd like to, but I should get going."

"Oh no, you don't. You can't leave without seeing Frantiska and the children. You'll stay with us tonight. That settles it! You can leave in the morning. That horse looks like it could use the night's rest. In the meantime, you're coming with me. I'm gonna show you what this thing can do," Josef says, nodding toward his contraption.

Josef and I stumble into his house late that night, talking loudly and reeking of brew. Frantiska is awake. How can she not be, with the rowdy nature of our entrance? Fortunately, her displeasure is tempered by my unexpected appearance, and she tries to get us to bed without waking the children.

My intention is to leave early in the morning, but it's not until midmorning the next day that I'm astride Birdie, heading toward home. My body hunches forward, constricting from the effects of last evening's revelry. With my head pulsating and my belly roiling, I now regret allowing Frantiska to force a small breakfast of biscuits on me. With Birdie's undulating gait, the smell of the horseflesh invading my nostrils, and a gut spasming in protest, I can't help but submit to the forces inside me. Suddenly, I lean over and purge myself of my biscuit breakfast on the dusty road. Spitting, coughing, swearing between convulsions, I finally finish my retching and use my sleeve to wipe my brow and free a bit of bile hanging from my chin. I make the vow then and there—the lie muttered by men through the years——that I will never imbibe again.

Birdie has come to a stop as I lean over and contaminate the air with the offensive smell of vomit. She waits patiently for her master to reassume command, and we're soon moving ahead, away from the repugnance left on the ground.

Weakened, but feeling relief for the moment, I push on. It will take some time to get back to Budislav, but I'll still have time to clean myself up, check on the livestock, switch horses, and head with Daisy toward the village of Jarošov. Against my better judgment, and despite my condition, I'm determined not to wait another day to continue my quest. Jarošov is a few miles north of Budislav, and with any luck, someone there will direct me to the Krejsa residence.

I ride into Jarošov feeling much better. Changing my clothes in Budislav and rinsing the foul taste from my mouth saw to that. Jarošov is even smaller than Budislav, and passing the first house on the south side of town, I can already see the last house on the far north side. Soon I find an old woman, hanging out some wet clothes on a line, and she directs me to the Krejsa home.

A young woman, much taller than Annie, answers the door. She's much too young to be Annie's mother, and I assume, judging from the likeness, that this must be her sister.

"Can I help you?" the young woman asks.

"I'm looking for Annie. Is she at home?"

An excited scream bursts from the interior of the small hovel.

"Vaclav, is that you?" comes Annie's animated voice. "Katerina, let him in, let him in!"

Annie's sister steps aside to allow me into the house just as Annie charges toward me. Startled by her enthusiasm, I think for an instant that Annie is about to throw herself into my arms, and I ready myself for the impact of the embrace. But at the last moment, she abruptly slides to a halt, regaining her composure, smoothing down her apron, and politely offering me her hand.

"It's so nice to see you, Vaclav. How are you?" she says, trying, but failing, to conceal the excitement in her voice.

"I'm fine, Annie," I reply, fixing my gaze on her. "Josef told me where you were, and I came to see you." I pause, seeking the right words, then continue. "I need to ask you something." My gaze leaves Annie and scans the room, the only room in the house. I notice bewilderment on the faces of Annie's sister and an older woman, presumably her mother.

"I need to ask you something outside . . . in private, if that's all right."

"Sure, Vaclav. Want to go for a walk? Just like we used to?" she asks.

"That'd be perfect," I say, as Annie grabs my hand, leading me out toward the road.

We exchange the proper pleasantries as we walk, holding back emotions, summoning up all the propriety we can muster, as if we're getting acquainted all over again. We talk about Josef and Frantiska. I tell her about the passing of my father. She tells me about the delay in her plans for her voyage to America. We talk about each of our lives since last we were together. Soon, the intimacy we once enjoyed in Krouna edges its way back into a much more casual and lighthearted interaction. Finally, when I think the time is right, I ask, "Annie, do you remember when you suggested we get married?"

"Yes, Vaclav, I remember that. I remember it like it was yesterday," Annie answers without hesitation.

"You said that we should get married, and you'd take me to America. Remember that?"

"Yes, I remember."

"Do you still feel that way?"

"What way? That we should get married, or that I should take you to America?" she asks.

"Well, I guess maybe both, Annie."

"Is that why you want to marry me, Vaclav?"

"What do you mean?" I ask, confused.

"Just so I'll take you to America?" she asks with a furrowed brow.

I pause to consider her query. "That's one of the reasons, I suppose." Then I add, "I just think you would make a real good wife."

"A good wife? What's that mean?"

"You know, a good, solid wife."

As soon as the words come out of my mouth, I immediately want more than anything to grab them and cram them right back where they came from. That was just about the worst thing I could have said to her. It reminds me of the way my father used to talk about marriage, the way he used to describe the slightly rotund Marie who lived down the street. Am I becoming my father? Please, not that!

"Solid?" she asks. "Did you say a *solid wife?* There are a lot of things you could have said about me, but solid? I'm not sure how to take that."

"Wait, wait! No, no, let's not . . . I mean, don't think that . . . I didn't mean—" I stammer.

"What's got your tongue, Vaclav?" She's smiling now, something I'm relieved to see. "Perhaps you'd like another chance at putting all that into a sentence, a much better sentence," she adds with considerable emphasis on the word *better*.

Gathering myself, I clear my throat and try again. "What I intended to say, Annie, before some kind of spell overtook me, was that I think you are the most beautiful creature I've ever seen, and marrying you would make me the happiest man in the empire." I know I got it right this time.

Taking my hand, she says demurely, "I like that much better, Vaclav." Then she stands on her tiptoes, wrapping her arms around my neck, and kisses me hard and long.

"See what happens when you say nice things?" she whispers into my ear. "Do you really mean all that?"

"Sure do," I reply as I hold her close. Then I joke to myself under my breath, "Plus, you feel pretty solid."

"I heard that, you oaf!" she scolds playfully. "I'll show you solid," she warns as she pushes herself away, laying a feigned punch teasingly on my chin.

CHAPTER 34

WAS THAT AN OFFICIAL PROPOSAL? I'm not sure. I told Annie I wanted to marry her, but I didn't actually ask her if she wanted to, did I? Of course, she gave me that big kiss. That means something, doesn't it?

For me, the art of courtship is somewhat of a mystery. Living alone, without a mother or father to guide me, I find myself void of any notion about courtship. And certainly, on this matter, Birdie can offer little insight. I've resigned myself to the fact that I'll need to trust my own instincts, a realization that offers little reassurance. As a boy, I was far too young to take an interest in the courtships of any of the neighbor girls. At the time, it seemed to me that they were there one day and simply gone the next. At least, that's how I remember it. I know that can't be how it happened. But as hard as I try, I can't seem to remember any pertinent details.

Is there a prescribed amount of time I'm supposed to court Annie before proposing? What about the proposal itself? Hasn't the proposal already occurred? Haven't we already come to an understanding about marriage and traveling to America? That's hardly the traditional way of proposing. I at least recognize that fact. Am I required to make a much more formal proposal? What preparations are to be made regarding wedding plans? And what about the expense of those plans? I certainly have no money to spare.

Maybe I was a fool to even think I could get married. I had no idea what I was doing. I know how to grow beets and potatoes. And I understand livestock husbandry. I even know how to trap game. But the trapping of a mate is a whole other thing. Should I just ask Annie all these questions? That doesn't seem right to me. After all, what trapper in his right mind would ask his prey how it would choose to be trapped? I desperately need some sound advice. It at once occurs to me that Josef might be a good person to ask. After all, he succeeded in marrying Frantiska, and she's proven to be a solid, or rather, capable wife.

Early the next morning, I set about my daily chores, checking on the cows and goats that are out foraging in the brown pastureland. Then it's onto cleaning the stalls where Birdie and Daisy spend most of their days. It takes longer than usual to complete this task since I've been somewhat negligent about seeing to the cleanliness of the stable area. I eventually emerge from the horse shed, satisfied Birdie and Daisy will find their accommodations acceptable.

Standing for a moment, grasping my pitchfork, I scan the countryside beyond my modest farmstead. The trees on the distant hills are beginning to take on their autumnal hues of red and gold, their colors further radiant from the morning sun blazing through the branches. This is the season when I would normally be busy harvesting crops and storing hay for the winter. But the drought has guaranteed that no crop will be harvested this year. Still, I take some small bit of solace in knowing that I gathered a cutting of clover hay in June just as the drought began. That might keep the livestock alive for a while but I'll need to purchase more to sustain them through the winter. Where I'll buy it, I don't know.

That worry can wait for another day. I have much more important things to think about. My plan is to head back to Krouna this morning to consult with Josef. Perhaps my friend will have some answers for me. I lean my pitchfork against the side of the horse shed and head back toward the house. Pausing, as I often do, to take in a deep breath of the crisp autumn air rolling off the surrounding Bohemian hills, my nostrils are suddenly violated by the unmistakable stench of horse manure wafting upward from my shoes—

just a small souvenir offered by Birdie and Daisy in return for my efforts in their stable.

It doesn't take me long to make myself ready to travel. The sun is moving to a point higher in the sky by now, tempering the morning chill, and I decide to let myself relax and enjoy the ride to Krouna, allowing Birdie to find her own pace as she plods southward.

We finally arrive at the small town, and Josef is just leaving his hovel. He sees me and stands there holding his toolbox, waiting for me to approach.

"Well, well. Back so soon?" Josef calls to me as I get nearer.

"Hi, Josef. I was hoping you'd be here. I'd like some advice if you're willing to give it."

"Advice is about the only thing I have a lot of. You can have all of it that you can stand. What's this about, Vaclav?"

"I went to Jarošov to find Annie last night, just after I left here," I explain.

"And did you find her?"

"Yes, I did," I say, sliding off Birdie and standing momentarily, thinking about how I will present my dilemma to Josef. I have no choice now but to simply forge ahead. Looking around fearing that Frantiska might be close by, I approach Josef. He wrinkles his nose, glancing down at my shoes, and takes a step backward without commenting.

"I think we're getting married," I say.

"You think you're getting married?" Josef asks, shaking his head in puzzlement.

"What I mean is, I think we have a sort of understanding that we are going to get married."

"Well, that clears it up," Josef replies. "Why don't you start at the beginning and tell me about this understanding."

I explain the way Annie two years ago suggested we get married and go to America, and that last night when I found her again, I asked her if she had meant it, and she said yes. "Well, actually, she didn't say *yes* in so many words," I say.

"*Yes* is actually just one word, Vaclav. Did she say it or not?"

"Well, she kinda kissed me instead."

"Oh, well, now we're getting somewhere."

"The problem is, Josef, I'm not sure if that was a proper proposal. I mean, I didn't actually propose to her, if you know what I mean. She was the one who actually made the suggestion in the first place, and we more or less agreed to it. Is that a proposal? Or do I need to do something more formal?"

"This shouldn't be that difficult, Vaclav. Let's consider the essentials. Do you want to marry her?"

"Definitely."

"Good. That's good for starters. Now, do you think she wants to marry you?"

"She kissed me."

"That's true, so she still at least likes you a little bit, even though you ran out on her a couple of years ago. Remember that?"

"Hey, that's not how it happened. What happened was that—"

"Oh, never mind about that," Josef interrupts. "That must be water under the bridge, I suppose, seeing that she kissed you." He pauses a moment to gather his thoughts, and then continues, "Now, it's important to point out that the marriage was her suggestion in the first place, right?"

"Right!"

"Still, it would be good to get a definite confirmation, don't you think?"

"Yes, Josef. That's why I'm here. I want to know how to do that. And once I get that confirmation, then what? What about courting? How does that work?"

"Whoa, slow down. First of all, I think all that time you spent with Annie before you decided to disappear for two years is what I would consider courting."

"Huh?"

"Frantiska and I could see how much you two liked each other. You just need to continue where you left off. It's that simple."

"Simple? I doubt it."

"Look, here's what you do. First, ask Annie if it's OK with her if you talk to her parents about the two of you getting married."

"I've got to get their permission? I hardly know them."

"Doesn't matter. It needs to be done. Now, if Annie thinks that is a good idea, there's your confirmation, my friend. Also, consider that if Annie knows you are going to talk to her parents, she'll probably soften them up for you. That's the way it works. Then, of course, you'll need to follow through and do it. You need to go to their house, and ask them—and do it with confidence, acting like you know what the hell you're doing even though you don't. Got it?"

I ruminate on this for a moment, and say, "OK, so I talk to Annie, then talk to her parents, and then what?"

"The rest will take care of itself, Vaclav."

"Really?"

"Yes. Well, except for the actual wedding. You'll have to really be on your toes for that. But if you make it through the wedding, you'll easily slip into life as an indentured servant to a woman who will rule over you every moment of every day for the rest of your miserable life. That last part will just come naturally," Josef adds with a smile.

"Oh, OK. Thanks, Josef," I say, as if that made total sense. I stand there, processing all this information, and then nimbly slip back up onto Birdie, saying, "Wish me luck." Then, turning the horse in the opposite direction, I urge the animal forward.

"You're gonna need it," Josef mutters to himself.

"What's that?" I ask, pulling Birdie to a stop and turning back toward my friend and counselor.

"Well, Vaclav, as I've always said, nothing says *marry me* like the sweet smell of horseshit."

"What are you talking about?"

"Take a big whiff, Vaclav," Josef directs, pointing toward my shoes.

"Oh, that," I reply, looking down at them. I wonder if that is a subtle snort I hear Birdie uttering as we start back toward Budislav.

CHAPTER 35

I NEEDN'T HAVE WORRIED. Everything seems to fall into place after I speak with Annie and her parents. And why wouldn't it? I've observed much lesser men than me who've been successful in finding suitable wives. I should have realized my worries were blown far out of proportion. As it turns out, and as Josef promised, everything does indeed seem to take care of itself. The New Year comes and goes, and by February, Annie and I are officially engaged to be married. I now step back in the entire process, serving only as an observer, as Annie and her mother plan the wedding and prepare my house for Annie's arrival. During this time, it's all I can do to stay out of their way. I spend more time outdoors, tending to my animals and my various other chores.

In late May, just as I finish my planting, the wedding takes place. It occurs in Proseč on a sunny Saturday at the home of the ancient Pastor Kadlec, who baptized me two decades earlier in this very house. The wedding is a modest affair, attended only by Annie, me, Annie's parents and sister, Josef, Frantiska, Antonin, Vincencie, and, of course, the old pastor.

Annie is adorned dazzlingly, as is the tradition in most Bohemian weddings. She wears a colorful dress of red and green on white linen sewn by her mother and a bridal crown of fresh flowers from the family garden. I, on the other hand, don the best clothes I can find: pants borrowed from Josef and a mismatched jacket I inherited from my father. Still, my attire and the fact that I no longer smell of horseshit make my participation acceptable for the occasion.

Annie and I easily settle into married life, and soon the glow of nascent matrimony begins to fade. By the end of July, Annie suspects she's already with child, a development that immediately delights Annie and absolutely terrifies me. Annie reassures me that everything will be fine, though she warns that the new baby might postpone our plans for America. I consider going to Josef for advice regarding fatherhood, but think better of it. Instead, the worrying about the baby is left to my young wife, who doesn't appear to be worried in the least. Besides, I have enough to worry about, I figure, with the growing season just underway. And as the summer ensues, I'm heartened by the fact that the crops continue to thrive. By August, with harvesting underway, I am more and more confident I will be able to make my first loan payment in full to Solomon Wise. Maybe I'll even be able to save some money for our future trip to America, when and if it ever happens.

Vaclav Jr. is born on a stormy March morning after Annie suffers a long labor. I will not remember this ordeal with fondness. What I will remember is the combination of Annie's distressing moans accompanied by a violent spring storm, with ominous winds whistling around my house and through the many spaces I mistakenly thought I had filled in the walls. I will also remember the helpless feeling of standing around without a role to play, except for tending to the fire in the hearth and listening to the outside elements, wondering if the storm will prove to be a bad omen for our newborn.

Annie's mother is there, of course, to assist in the birth, as is the village midwife; I'm thankful for that, for I am of little help, having no experiential knowledge beyond the birthing of calves and goat kids. To be sure, the present situation is nothing even close to what I've been a party to out in the fields or in the horse shed. As Annie's moans ebb and flow throughout the night, I fear this is God's payback for all my past sins. And I feel guilty for the part I've played in bringing this undue punishment upon my wife. I vow not to put Annie through this again. I will add that to my long list of vows—the list, incidentally, which includes the vow promised after my night of debauchery with Josef.

As if on cue, the storm outside subsides in the early morning just as little Vaclav Jr. finally sticks out his head, presenting himself to his new life. Lovingly grasped by his grandmother's waiting hands, the babe is at once greeted with gleeful affirmations, none of which are uttered by me. I'm now spellbound by the sight of this wet, red, screaming creature, an apparent imp from the underworld. Are the two women possessed somehow in their elation over this misshapen, obviously abnormal wizard who seems to control the forces of the wind? I wonder.

Sitting by the fire, I'm transfixed by the display, watching the women fawning, cooing, tidying, and caressing this thing I helped bring into this world. Do you want to hold him? they ask. A shake of my head is all I can manage as I keep a safe distance from the scary creature, a fireplace poker gripped firmly in my hand and at the ready.

But soon—much sooner than I expected—I come around and warm up to this thing, as it quickly transforms itself from something otherworldly into a soft, unadulterated reflection of myself. Eventually, Annie's mother leaves us to our own child-rearing devices, and we fall into a routine of life centered totally around the nurturing of little Vaclav Jr.

As the year wears on, Annie spends her time attending to Vaclav Jr. and various household responsibilities as I oversee the weeding and harvesting of my crop. It's a balance of day-to-day living that Annie and I both embrace wholeheartedly. It takes me awhile to realize it, but one day in June, as I stand staring, as I often do, at my beloved

Bohemian hills, I realize I am happier than I've been my entire life. Annie's presence in my life has opened up a vista of possibilities for me. I feel like she's freed me from the chains of loneliness, fear, and despair that have long restrained me. It isn't that the conditions of my life are any less difficult now. In fact, the added responsibility of my new family brings yet more pressure to my everyday life. But it's that very family that now provides a purpose that heretofore eluded me. I find myself walking with more confidence and with greater optimism. The fact that my fall harvest produces enough income to cover my second loan payment and put away additional funds for the future doesn't hurt, either. But it's Annie who has made the biggest difference. My love for her seems to grow each day, and I revel in that love, realizing that Annie is making me a much better person—a person perhaps even worthy of her love.

CHAPTER 36
AMERICA

STANDING AT THE PULPIT, Reverend Francis Kun looks out at his expectant congregation. Their faces are bright—brighter than he's seen in a very long time. To be sure, this war against the South has taken a heavy toll, mostly on the families whose sons went off to fight. But today Francis doesn't see despondence; he sees hope. His twenty-five families of Brethren have come here to celebrate Good Friday, but they have also come to hear if the rumors are true—to hear if the war is really over.

Before the service even begins, Francis allows one of his elders, Frank Lorenc, to stand before the congregation to report recent events as he understands them. The rumors are indeed true, Lorenc says. Just last Sunday, the Federal troops trapped Robert E. Lee's forces near the Appomattox Court House in Virginia, forcing Lee to surrender the Army of Northern Virginia to General Grant, thus ending the bloody conflict once and for all.

The news is at once received with cheers and hollers, accompanied by considerable handshakes and backslapping. Francis finds the raucous celebration to be jarring. After all, this is the Lord's house. But he resists the temptation to quiet their revelry. He knows that seven of their young men are still deployed with their units in the Union Army—that is, except for the Vojtisek boy, who fell on the battlefield. As far as they know, the other six are still alive and well, and with God's help will soon be home with them again. Yes, this show of celebration is appropriate, he decides. On this day, when they honor the Christ crucified for their sins, it's appropriate to celebrate the redemption of their torn country as well.

Since accepting the pastorate here some five years ago, Francis has been pleased with his church's progress. What began as a congregation of five families has blossomed into a flock of twenty-five families. To be honest, though, he had hoped to do better, for there are many more countrymen living nearby who have not joined them in the sacrament. Early on, it became apparent that the war was hindering the church's growth. During the conflict, their community has seldom received any new Bohemian immigrants. Those who might have come are apparently fearful of leaving an oppressive old country for a broken new one. In addition, it seems to him, people who already live nearby have been falling from the faith in greater and greater numbers. He can only guess that the inhumanity of the conflict may be the reason. Perhaps the thousands of deaths on both sides have caused many of them to doubt there is a God up there watching after all.

Still, his small congregation has remained faithful to the Word. Just two years ago, they built a new parsonage for his family. This allowed them to move from their rented cabin to much better accommodations nearer the homes of his parishioners. Indeed, with the growing Kun brood, now two girls and four boys, Aneta finds their new home to be, relatively speaking, much more capacious than the old one. She seems much happier now. As for Francis, he is most grateful for the increased salary he now enjoys. It enables him to stable a horse, which helps him reach church members who live too far away to attend his services.

Yes, he's happy to say his life is much improved since leaving Tama County. Still, there's much more to be done in the name of God's glory. Most importantly, he dreams of erecting a church building of their own. But of course he knows his few parishioners cannot afford such an expensive undertaking. Sadly, for now they will continue paying the English Lutherans a small weekly sum for the use of their

Banner Valley Church on Sunday afternoons. This is an arrangement he finds more than a little vexing.

The rest of the Good Friday service goes smoothly, and after Elder Zvacek leads their small choir in the choral benediction, the Brethren begin to file out in two lines, men and boys on the right, women and girls on the left. Both lines converge at the door, where Francis speaks to each person briefly, saying things like "May God be with you" or "See you on Easter Sunday" or "My, how you've grown" or some such bit of encouragement. But there's little need for any kind of encouragement today. His parishioners need no words to heighten their sanguinity. The war is over. And even this day's reminder of Christ's suffering cannot deny the considerable raising of their spirits.

Two days later, on Easter Sunday, Francis approaches the pulpit once again. This afternoon he's surprised to see the sanctuary packed with people filling every pew, with an overflow standing in the back. He looks out to take stock of the unusually large congregation, possibly the largest congregation he's ever seen at Banner Valley. He knows why they are all here, and it's not only because it's Easter Sunday. Indeed, this is the most inconsolable and despairing congregation he's ever encountered. The packed sanctuary is silent but for the sobbing of women and sniffling of men. They gaze at him with reddened eyes and pleading hearts. What can he say? They are in pain, but his heart aches, too. How can he expect to fill these people with an understanding of God's grace on a day like this? How can he expect to ease their pain? This is supposed to be a joyous day, the day celebrating the ascension of Christ. Instead, it is a day that defies reason in its woeful comprehension. Mr. Lincoln is dead.

In front of him, the sermon that took him all night to write looks lifeless on the podium. As he stares at it now, he realizes how lacking it is, how void of any real consolation to their grief. Only a short time after the Good Friday service, the president was cut down by a Southern sympathizer. And as word of his death spread through the reverend's congregation, the elation of the war's end evaporated, and his flock plunged into an abyss of anguish. He wonders if this anguish is any different from the anguish felt by the few faithful kneeling at the base of Christ's cross on Calvary Hill. It occurs to him that, just as Christ gave his life to save his people, Mr. Lincoln won the war to set the negroes free and, like Jesus, was sacrificed days later. Both on the same day: Good Friday. This can't be just a coincidence. It must be a sign. But a sign of what? That He has a plan for what we can't possibly understand?

Francis looks up again at the congregation. He wonders if any of them have also made the connection between the Great Redeemer and the Great Emancipator. Mr. Lincoln was no savior, but he was America's most noble of men in their eyes. And now God has rewarded him by bringing him home. The sermon Francis wrote will do him no good now. He will speak of the sign that God has sent them. And he knows how he will begin. It's the way he begins every Easter sermon, but today the double meaning will not be lost on these people.

He clears his throat, blinks the tears from his eyes, and holds his head high, letting his voice resonate through the room as he pronounces, "He has risen." That's all he needs to say. And with those words, he sees the men sitting taller in their pews and the woman raising their heads from their damp handkerchiefs. He says it again, but more loudly this time. "He is risen, indeed." And then, "He has earned his great reward, has he not?" Is he speaking of Christ or Mr. Lincoln? Does it matter? Not to these people. Today, the two are the same. And for the rest of their years, his flock will consider Easter to be as much a celebration of President Lincoln's ascension as it is of Jesus Christ's.

The next day, at Francis's bidding, the congregation amasses at two o'clock at the parsonage. They are here to form a procession honoring the martyrdom of the slain president. They will march the entire distance to the Banner Valley Church, singing from their hymnals in honor of their fallen leader. Francis is heartened but not surprised to see how massive the assembling crowd has become. There are people here he's never seen before, even more than at the Easter service. It seems as though people from far and wide want to walk with them today.

Promptly at two o'clock, two standard-bearers take their places on the road. One carries the American colors, the other a plain black flag, the flag of mourning. Francis quickly gathers up his hymnal and Bible and takes his place just behind the flag bearers. Behind him come the church elders—Frank Lorenc, Josef Bures, Josef Zvacek, Josef Vojtisek, and Jan Janko. As they start down the road toward the church, the rest of the crowd follows. Soon, the entire procession is singing the Psalm *Grieving to Thee, O Lord We Call, Hear Our Pleading Words.*

Francis is singing at full-throat now, and the time passes quickly. With their three-mile trek at an end, the procession finally arrives at the Banner Valley Church. The church is situated in a bucolic valley from which the church received its name, and a small creek can be heard gurgling nearby. But no one stops to admire the picturesque setting or the gentle bubbling of the brook. Everyone's senses are dulled by their sorrow, and they solemnly file into the small building. The church soon fills to overflowing, and many people find places outside near the open windows to hear what the reverend has to say.

The pall of anguish is palpable across the assemblage as men and women alike weep openly in despair. Francis can't help but succumb to the grief that grips his parishioners, and he is forced to interrupt his opening prayer as he chokes up with emotion. The people before him are no less broken than they were at yesterday's Easter service. In fact, their grief seems to be heightened. But he must continue on; he must do what he can to reassure them of God's grace. Francis stands nervously at the pulpit, his Bible opened before him, and begins to struggle through a scripture reading. Soon he begins his message—a message not unlike the one he presented yesterday, for what else can he do to console the mourners in this moment of desolation? His message is that Lincoln was a man of faith, sent by God to rid our land of the injustice of slavery, just as Christ had been sent to free the people of sin. And that like Christ, President Lincoln was loved by the common people and despised by evil-doers. Francis continues with his comparisons of Jesus and Lincoln for he knows of no other message as powerful as this. And yet, he suddenly realizes that in this dark moment, his words fail to adequately assuage his suffering congregation. He suddenly stops and looks out upon the mourners, realizing what he must do. He slowly closes his Bible and retreats to the chancel chair sitting under the large wooden cross on the front wall. This is not a time for sermons, he knows. This is a time to internalize the pain, not as individuals, but together as a group—collectively, for he knows that feeling pain in commonality with others somehow makes one's own pain almost tolerable.

For several long minutes, the only sounds heard are the sniffles and mournful cries of the inconsolable and the mumbling of people praying quietly to themselves. Francis remains sitting with his head bowed, letting his people grieve together without disturbance. After what seems like a long time, when he deems the passage of time to be sufficient, he finally approaches the pulpit again and proclaims, "Death is swallowed up in victory. The Lord hath spoken. Go in peace."

And still, no one moves, all bound together in their sorrow. Many minutes pass, and eventually Francis notices one or two people outside who are peeling away from the crowd and heading for home. Soon, more follow, and after a while, the attendees inside the church begin to slowly file out.

Francis waits until everyone has exited the church and yet he sits there. He is tired, and he feels physically weak—so weak that he even wonders if he will be able to stand. What's wrong with me, he wonders. A rush of guilt assails him as he realizes how he has let the very thought of death somehow paralyze him. This is unacceptable, he thinks. He, above all others, should know better. Death is not the end of life. It's just the end of suffering. Hasn't Jesus shown us that death is but a portal to a better place?

With his strength returning, he abruptly rises to his feet. Gazing out at the empty pews, and in a voice that reverberates around the empty sanctuary, he makes a declaration that taunts death itself. "Death is swallowed up in victory," he bellows. "O death, where is thy sting? O death, where is thy victory?" Striding confidently down the church aisle, Francis steps outside to take his place at the rear of the procession, heading back toward the parsonage.

The walk home is a long one, or at least it seems so. There is no singing—only introspection. People eventually peel off in various directions, walking wearily toward their respective homes. They all walk in silence, wondering how their lives can possibly be reconstituted into something like they were before. As Francis approaches the parsonage where Aneta waits with the children, there remain only a few parishioners in the group. Most disappear back to their own homes, but Elder Bures hangs back and approaches him.

"Reverend. Could I speak to you for a moment?"

"Of course, Joe," Francis answers. Bures is a good friend and one of the congregation's most devout leaders. The very piece of land where the parsonage stands was indeed donated by him.

"I think it is finally time," he says.

"What do you mean?" Francis asks.

"For the church, I mean. It's time to build our church," he explains.

Francis finds this quite strange. Why is he talking about this at this particular moment? They are all in mourning for the fallen president. How can Joe be concerned about this? Why now?

"Joe, could we have this discussion later?" Francis says. "This doesn't seem like the time—"

"Hear me out, Reverend. This may be the exact time, the perfect time to be having this discussion."

"What do you mean? There is healing to be done now. We should give the people time," the reverend says.

"I agree. The people are hurting. Just look at how many showed up yesterday at our service, and even more today. All of them came because they are hurting. They came for you to help quell that pain. And most of them are not even from our congregation."

"And I did what I could to help them," Francis says somewhat defensively, wondering what Bures is getting at.

"Yes, and your words were very moving. You helped them. You helped them all."

"That may be so, but what does that have to do with the construction of our church? We are still a congregation of only twenty-five families. Hardly enough to think about such a project."

"But what about all those other people, those people who are not our members yet still came to seek your spiritual counsel? What about them? Don't you see, Reverend? Now is the perfect time to build. Now these people all know you, and they trust you."

"You think we should go to these grieving souls asking for a donation? Now? Is that what you're saying?" Francis asks, slightly perturbed by his suggestion.

"That's exactly what I'm saying."

"And take advantage of their vulnerability?" Francis asks, dumbfounded. There is something he's missing here. Joe Bures is not an insensitive man. On the contrary, Francis knows of no other man with such strong moral fiber, so attuned to the needs of others.

"Look, Reverend. In their time of sorrow, all these people sought spiritual guidance. They sought *your* spiritual guidance. Many of them haven't been practicing their faith and don't attend church at all, but they showed up for the last two days to listen to you. You've always told us we need to seek out our countrymen who are the lost sheep, the ones lost from the flock. And now, in the midst of this tragedy, many of those lost sheep have shown they are ready to come back to the flock. In a way, Mr. Lincoln's death set the stage for an awakening of their faith. Isn't it our duty to help them strengthen that faith?"

"By asking for money to construct a building?"

"The new church would be a strong symbol. A symbol of our resilience, a symbol of our ability to suffer any setback and come back stronger in our faith. We can't send that signal if we continue to meet at Banner Valley. It simply doesn't show a strong commitment to that faith."

Although he resists the notion, there's no doubt in Francis's mind that Joe is right. If their church is to grow, they need a temple of their own, one located more centrally in his flock's community, not one that's far down the road and leased week to week. What Joe is saying is that they would not be taking advantage of these grieving souls, but helping them process that grief. And, in doing so, rekindle their faith.

"Have you talked to the other elders about this?" Francis asks.

"No. Not yet. I just thought about it during the procession today."

"Go tell them we need to meet, Joe. Tomorrow if we can."

The next day, the six of them meet at the Bures home. The agenda for the meeting is clear. Joe has already briefed the other four elders regarding his idea, but Francis wants to hear what they have to say, and he wants to hear it directly from them. After all, this is their church more than it is his.

Although earlier he had his doubts about Bures's proposal, he's not surprised to find the other elders in complete agreement. Of course they are. They have longed for a church building of their own since before Francis even came here. So it's decided. But where do they go from here? he wonders. He knows the scripture inside and out, having read it in multiple languages. But this project has little to do with the Bible and much to do with fundraising, something he knows little about.

"Well," Francis begins, "it seems we're all in agreement, but shouldn't we first consider what this will cost?" Elder Jan Janko oversaw the building of the parsonage a couple of years ago, and Francis directs his question toward him.

"I've been thinking about this," Jan begins. "It all depends on how much of the work will be completed by our own people. We have some skilled carpenters within our numbers who can probably do much of the framing and siding and even the roofing, perhaps. But we may have to find someone from the outside to lay the foundation. We want that done right. And then there is the chimney. I don't know if we have anyone who's an expert at that kind of work."

"Of course," interjects Elder Lorenc, "we will need to furnish the interior. You know—pews and pulpit. That sort of thing."

"That's true," agrees Jan, "but even before we think about any of this, we need to find a place to build it."

That part hadn't even occurred to Francis. While it's true that Josef Bures donated the land for the parsonage, it's unrealistic to expect him to donate another lot, one large enough for the church. The land Elder Bures gave for the parsonage was a small timbered lot of no real use to him. But a church would require much more land to make room for the building and a cemetery. None of these poor farmers, who barely scratch out a living on their land, should be asked to give up a two- or three-acre piece of that land for free. Their land is vital to their futures, as far as they are concerned. Francis gets that. He'd feel the same way.

"We'll have to see about purchasing the land," he finally says. "I won't ask anyone in this room to donate part of their farm to this cause. It would be unfair—an excessive sacrifice, I think." And then he adds, "Unless I hear strong feelings otherwise." The room remains silent. He doesn't let the stillness linger too long before he adds, "OK then, that's settled. Jan, what do you think it might cost for the land, construction materials, and any labor necessary? The total cost."

Jan runs the numbers through his head for a moment before answering, "Maybe two to three thousand."

At that, the room goes suddenly quiet, until Frank says softly, "How in the world will we find that much money? None of our members can spare more than a few dollars, I would guess. And that would be a stretch for most of them."

Joe Bures is not to be dissuaded. "All we can do is try. And don't forget—a lot of those nonmembers who showed up the last couple of days would hopefully contribute."

"We'll just have to be persuasive," Francis says thoughtfully under his breath. "We should send out a letter."

"A letter?" Elder Zvacek asks.

"As Joe said, we need to reach a lot of people, not just our members," Francis says. "And remember, we don't need to acquire all the funding in one year. Maybe we can convince donors to spread their contributions out over a couple of years. Our letter should offer that option. At least, if we have some funds to get started, that might inspire more people to join us in this mission."

"But two or three thousand dollars?" Frank Lorenc repeats worriedly.

"As I said, we must be persuasive. Let me draft a letter. Then I'll bring it to you for your approval. How's that sound? Good?"

The elders nod their heads in unison, and Francis realizes they have just completed the first vital step toward the building of their temple: the First Bohemian Moravian Brethren Church.

CHAPTER 37
BOHEMIA

ANNIE AND I HAVE FALLEN into a comfortable routine of domestic and farm toil while looking after our little one. Vaclav Jr. is seven months old now and I'm satisfied that the child will survive under our incompetent care—or rather, *my* incompetent care, for this is all new to me. It's a good thing, however, that Annie seems quite competent in her motherly duties. I'm thankful for that, and I shouldn't have expected anything different.

By the end of October, Josef surprises us with the announcement that Frantiska is pregnant again, and on May 15, 1865, their fifth child is born. They name her Terezie, but Josef takes to calling her his *malíčká,* his little one. She is a strong and healthy baby, weighing about eight pounds, with the wide face and prominent chin of her mother. It's fortunate for her that she comes into the world so hale and hearty, for although she can't know it, her world is to be turned upside down. In a few short months, her parents will take her and her siblings from Krouna to Choceň in a horse-drawn wagon. Then to Bremen by train, to board a sailing vessel headed across the globe to America, only to be dragged on a dangerous trek across a wild and unyielding continent to her new home. But how would knowing that in advance prepare her for this adventure? How pointless to think a newborn could prepare at all for such a thing. She can only rely on good luck and the determination of her parents to get her there safely.

Josef and Frantiska, of course, are delighted at the child's birth but also conflicted about the prospect of yet another mouth to feed. This birth has come at an inopportune time for another reason, too. Although they finally have enough funds to embark on their voyage to America, they wonder how their *malíčká* will play into those travel plans. Can she survive such an arduous voyage, a voyage that can take over two months, confined to the bowels of a sailing ship? They're just not sure.

Still, the allure of America grows even stronger as news comes that the Great War between the North and the South has ended. Now, with the cessation of hostilities, the apprehension he once harbored is all but gone, making their dream of America more compelling. Indeed, how can it not be? For generations, his ancestors had never dreamed of a better life. Indeed, they didn't even understand the concept of dreaming. It was simply bred out of them with the many years of hopelessness. But when Annie first told Frantiska about that emigration poster at the mercantile shop, the seed of possibility was planted—a seed now sprouting into a dream, a dream that's found a cranny someplace in the backs of their thoughts, a dream routinely interrupting their daily lives with reminders of the promise of happiness. Or at least the possibility of something better. How can such a dream not push them forward with all haste, regardless of the risks involved? And now, with the end of the war, the risks seem so much diminished.

Josef ponders this dream on a daily basis through the winter months, and when spring approaches, he can resist the dream no longer. On a chilly day in March, he leaves his house and walks toward the village center and up the stone steps of the administrative building. He recognizes the woman at the front desk who is signing and stamping documents. She's the same woman who has treated him with such indifference on past visits. As he shuffles up to her desk, she looks up with a grimace, as if irritated by the interruption.

"I'm here to see the judge," Josef says matter-of-factly. He hasn't seen the judge in some time. In fact, Josef has taken great pains to avoid him, given the disappearance of Thomas.

"What is it you want?" asks the woman bluntly.

Josef hasn't really taken stock of her before. But he pauses to take note of her bulbous body straining against a dress far too small to adequately harness it. Josef notices also that he can smell her perspiration. Or is he simply smelling the dank atmosphere of the building itself?

"I need to speak with him about my emigration papers," Josef states plainly.

She makes no response, as if she's heard those words a hundred times. Josef realizes that she probably has, with the recent number of locals eager to follow the irresistible call of America. With considerable effort, she rises from her chair, turns, and walks toward the judge's chamber in the back. Josef hears her say gruffly "Follow me" as she walks away from him. He follows obediently in the wake of her fetidness.

Josef can see that Judge Spacek is not pleased to see him. As Josef enters, the man looks up from his paperwork and stares at him for a long moment over the rims of his tiny round spectacles.

"What is it, Josef?" he grunts.

"I'd like to see about our emigration papers."

"Uh-huh," is the bland reply. He continues to take Josef into account, then says, "I heard you were dead."

"Well, as you can see . . ."

"Yes, I see. I heard you were killed in Italia, but then I spotted you limping around the village. I was disappointed to see that," he says with a slight frown.

"Oh, the leg's not that bad. I can still get around OK."

"No, I wasn't referring to your leg. I meant I was disappointed you weren't dead after all," he says, now smirking slightly. "Have you learned your lesson?"

"My lesson?"

"You know what I'm talking about. Your lesson about poaching in the lord's woods."

"Oh, that. Sure, I learned my lesson just fine," Josef replies defiantly, trying to control himself.

"Good. Just don't let it happen again."

"Whatever you say. My papers?"

"So, you think you want to go to America, do you?" the old man says as he stands up and starts digging through files in an old wooden cabinet next to the window. "Well, I'll be glad to be rid of you." Finding what he's looking for, he sits back down in his chair, leafing through the papers.

"Hmm. Looks like you're up to date here. No debts or liens. I figure you've satisfied your obligation to the army, though there is nothing I'd like more than to send you back to the front. But I don't suppose they need a one-legged bohunk."

"I suppose not," replies Josef, trying not to let his temper get the best of him.

Judge Spacek fills out two forms, one of which he hands to Josef for his signature mark.

"Your family will need birth records. Also, you need to get your exit visas and your military release from the district office in Chrudim. Can you remember all that?" the judge asks, waiting for Josef's response.

Mentally reviewing this litany of items, Josef thrusts out his hand, replying, "Of course!" and abruptly snatches the form from the old man's grasp.

Josef is almost through the door when Spacek calls after him, "And don't forget to return all those carpentry and masonry tools before you leave, understand?" Josef keeps walking, hoping to never set eyes on the old man again.

CHAPTER 38

THE EMIGRATION DREAM CONTINUES to burn bright in Annie and me, too. And when Josef shows up at my house two days later stating his intent to travel to Chrudim for his family's exit visas, I am dead set on us going with him. Josef knows me well. He doesn't want his family to make the twenty-mile trip on foot, and he speculates correctly that I will insist on going, thus providing a suitable conveyance for his family on my wagon.

I've already paid my final military exemption fee and have only one more payment on the loan from Solomon Wise. Josef's family is intent on leaving as soon as possible, but we'll have to wait until fall after my crops come in. Then I'll be able to pay the remainder of my loan. Nevertheless, it will be good to have our papers in order ahead of time, so accompanying Josef on this trip to Chrudim doesn't seem like such a bad idea.

The forty-mile round trip will be a long way to drive my team in one day. I wonder if we'll require an overnight stay somewhere. In the chill of March, the prospect of staying overnight in the elements with the children doesn't seem acceptable. But the expense of renting a room in Chrudim doesn't seem acceptable either. We'll just have to bundle up in some of Frantiska's blankets for warmth and complete the trip in one day.

A few days later we're set to go, so I hitch up my team and drive my family to Krouna to pick up Josef, Frantiska, and the children. Then, huddled in our wrappings on the small wagon, we ride together, bouncing along on the dusty road toward Chrudim.

Chrudim is a large town, much bigger than Proseč, with a main road twice as wide as Budislav's. Many streets project out from the main street, with even more streets jutting further out beyond them. Churches, taverns, and shops are visible, and there is even a rather large brewery, where workers are loading barrels onto a large mule wagon. In the middle of town, we finally come to what looks like the district office, an imposing block building sitting amid an expansive maple grove. There is a considerable amount of activity on the training grounds beyond the building. It looks to be several infantry units engaged in drills, fully armed and dressed in dark blue tunics.

We all clamber down off the wagon in front of the office, shaking off the cold that's stiffened our legs. Climbing the stone steps, we proceed through the large wooden door into an office filled with uniformed soldiers and clerks, all busying themselves around rows of desks. A long counter separates us from these workers, and our two families take our places in a line of men who have queued up at the end of the counter. I assume them to be recruits who are waiting to be processed and assigned to their units. An officer directs the men one by one to various desks around the room, where clerks are busy taking down information and asking questions. Soon, our families are at the head of the line, and we're all directed to a desk near the window. As my family waits patiently, we watch Josef step up to the desk to stand in front of the man sitting there.

"Your name?" asks the young officer tersely. I know the man is an officer by the embellishments of his uniform, but considering his youth, I doubt he's been an officer for very long.

"Josef Zach. From Krouna," Josef replies.

"And what is your business here?" he asks, noting that Josef has two families surrounding him.

"Our families wish to emigrate, and we're here for our military service papers and exit visas," Josef replies. He hands over the form from Judge Spacek and the birth certificates, as required.

The officer immediately takes the documents, saying "One moment," and walks toward the file cabinets against the back wall. He comes back moments later and sits down with a look of puzzlement.

"Is something wrong?" asks Josef.

"It shows here that you were killed in action in Solferino. Did you say you're from Krouna?"

"Yes, that's me," Josef says. "And I'm clearly not dead."

"I see that. How do you explain this record?"

"It's obviously some kind of mistake," Josef replies, putting extra emphasis on the word *obviously*, and a rather sardonic emphasis at that.

The man ignores Josef's rudeness, saying plainly, "Well, you're not dead, that's for sure. But I can't give you your release." He then hands the form back to Josef, who stares at the man in disbelief.

"Why the hell not?" Josef protests.

"We need troops."

"Troops? What for?"

"The Prussians are threatening our northern borders. Haven't you heard?"

"You mean we're going to war again? Wait! You can't do this to me!"

"Well, actually, we can," replies the officer calmly.

"Look at this," Josef says as he suddenly unties his pants and lets them drop around his ankles.

Frantiska and Annie gasp in horror. "Josef, what in the world . . . ?" his wife shouts.

"What are you doing?" the officer cries. The attention of the entire room is on them now, aghast at the sight of Josef's bare backside. Many are thankful they aren't beholding his frontside.

The office is completely silent as Josef says, "Look at that leg." He points at his left leg, the one with a pronounced and abnormal angle to it. "Do I look like a soldier who can charge the Prussian line? Does that twisted leg show that perhaps I've done quite enough for the damn empire?" he shouts.

He glares at the man, waiting for a reply. By now, a senior officer has made his way next to Josef, who is fuming with his pants down, exposing himself to the entire office.

"What's going on? Who is this man?" the officer asks.

"Josef Zach, sir," says the clerk.

The young officer explains the situation and adds, "I noticed he had a definite limp as he walked over here."

Directing his gaze downward at the leg and trying hard to avoid the sight of Josef's privates, the senior officer asks, "How did you acquire that injury?"

Josef has calmed down a bit, even though he's still standing half-naked in a room full of people gawking at him.

"In Solferino, fighting the Sardinians and those damn French, sir," he says.

The officer looks down at Josef's leg and then up at his face, meeting Josef's eyes as he says, "Let him go, Ludwig. We don't need any cripples on the battlefield." Then, as he turns to walk away, he adds, "And pull up your drawers, Zach."

Josef does as he's told, and then waits for the young officer to peruse the birth records, fill out the release form, and stamp the visas for his family. As Josef takes his documents in hand and finally turns to walk toward the door, many eyes are still staring at him, and I watch as Josef finally decides it's best to do his waiting outside, quickly directing his family through the exit.

Fate can be unkind, especially to people like Josef and me. It can lift you up just before it cruelly drives you back down again, showing no pity and reminding you of your everlasting unworthiness. I know from experience that our lives will always hang precipitously in the balance between survival and ruinous downfall. At least, that's how it seems to me. And even though Josef has been lucky enough to obtain his release from further military service, fate chooses not to look as kindly upon me.

Instead of receiving my service papers and exit visas, what I receive is a possible death sentence. Even though I've completed the required number of years of exemption to military conscription, the dire circumstances of an imminent Prussian invasion now invalidate any earlier promise. Instead of the release I so desire, I've been ordered to report for training with a 98th Regiment stationed in Königgrätz. From there, I'll most likely be deployed to the front to fight the dreaded Prussians.

CHAPTER 39

AS WE HEAD BACK toward Budislav, the mood is somber. Both our families speak little as we sit on the wagon, bumping along the dusty road out of Chrudim. We ride on, moving at an easy pace, stopping only occasionally to rest the weary team. Traveling in the darkness, we are all deep in our own despondent thoughts. What can any of us possibly say? Nothing, really. So we sit in silence, listening only to the regular rhythm of the team's gait, with the half-moon our only light. It's nearly midnight by the time I've taken Josef and his family back home to Krouna and doubled back to Budislav. As Annie takes the boy inside to warm up, I methodically unharness the animals, provide water and feed, and then secure the door of the horse shed.

I remain there for a while. I'm in no hurry to enter the house and speak with Annie. What can she say that can possibly provide any solace? There's no real solution to my predicament beyond refusing to report for duty, and I know that isn't a good option. Sure, many men who've been conscripted for service have attempted to flee to America with their families, and a few have succeeded. But I've yet to settle up with Solomon Wise, and we don't have the necessary savings to pay for passage, anyway. Besides, my defection would make me a criminal, wouldn't it? And fleeing the country with my family in tow might put my family in danger. I can't let that happen. Jeopardizing the lives of Annie and Vaclav Jr. would be worse than taking my chances marching under Emperor Franz Joseph's flag. No, I won't defy the realm. I'll report to Königgrätz for training, and I'll fight, and I may even die, for I'm not much of a fighter. Never have been. And I can't imagine that some brief military training will change that.

I continue to stand in the night's chill, contemplating whatever's ahead. Soon, I see Annie peering out the door at me.

"Vaclav! What on earth are you doing?" she calls. "Come in and warm up!"

I offer a forced smile and trudge toward her. I'm sure she's taken notice of my demeanor, and I hope she'll tread lightly with me.

This changes everything. It puts a sudden halt to our dream of going to America. It even puts a halt to Frantiska and Josef's dream, for they can't imagine leaving Annie alone to face whatever fate might befall me. A disconsolate pall falls upon our two households. As much as Josef and Frantiska try to maintain a modicum of optimism, they sense that the flame once burning within Annie and me, the flame of hope for a new life, has been extinguished, perhaps for good.

Somehow, however, I finally find a way to move forward. Whether from a sense of fatalism or some latent bit of courage, I'm the one who finally speaks out loud about the chances, even the likelihood, that I won't return from the fighting. This is a difficult discussion among the four of us, but the discussion finally ensues, leading inevitably toward a plan for the future, a future without me. And so it's decided that, while I'm gone, Josef can help Annie see to the crops and animals on my farm. If I come home, Josef can simply hand it back over to me, and things can go on as before. If I lose my life during the campaign, Annie can sell the farm and accompany Josef and Frantiska to America, using the profit from the farm sale to fund her and Vaclav Jr.'s journey.

There are only two problems with this plan. One, Josef has never been much of a farmer. He's made it plain that he isn't sure he has what it takes to care for my crops, let alone my horses and goats. And how will he constantly travel the distance between Budislav and Krouna to complete his work? I'm quick to assure him I can tutor him in the two months I have left before leaving for Königgrätz, and I remind Josef that he will have Birdie or Daisy to make the ten-mile trek between locations. The second issue is that if Josef sees to the farm, he will sacrifice any income he might otherwise receive from his carpentry and masonry work, as well as his gig at Jakub's tavern. For this, there is no solution, although Frantiska assures him that her weaving enterprise can pick up some of the slack. And maybe he can even continue his gig at the tavern on a limited basis.

And what about Annie? Will she and the child remain in our home in Budislav? Annie is adamant in her decision to stay put, even given the dangers faced by women alone in this land. Frantiska has presented an excellent case for her moving in with her own family in Krouna. But Annie stands firm, her only concession being the possibility of her sister coming to live with her and Vaclav Jr. in Budislav.

"We can't impose on you, Frantiska," she says, "and besides, we should be with family during these hard times. We'll be nearer to my parents this way."

So, we have a plan in place—and while it won't make for happy times in the coming months, it at least will make them bearable.

It's early June when I finally leave for Königgrätz on foot. Annie walks with me to the edge of town carrying Vaclav Jr., and she stands there, her beautiful face now slack and her gaze empty. I walk sadly away, glancing back at her from time to time. But she doesn't move, standing vigil, as I disappear perhaps forever on that road into the Bohemian hills toward Königgrätz.

It takes almost three days to reach the fortification where I am to train. I spend most of that time preparing myself mentally for an undertaking so very contradictory to my nature. I can't imagine what battle will be like. Josef's advice could have been helpful on this matter, but he seemed reluctant to discuss it. However, he did tell me one thing, something a soldier once told him. He said that to survive in a battle, you must do whatever is necessary, whether moral or not, and you must do it shamelessly. Only then can you survive such an ordeal, he said. I've been repeating that as a mantra since I left Budislav, but no matter how many times I repeat it, I can't get myself to really accept it.

The training within the walls of the Königgrätz fortress is no worse than I feared. In some ways, the consistency of the daily routine is actually enjoyable: waking at dawn, eating the same food, training in marching and combat. Of course, I miss and worry about Annie and little Vaclav, but I soon fit in with the rest of my company, many of whom are green recruits just like me. Indeed, I find that I'm fit enough, more so than many other recruits, and I don't find it difficult to endure the punishment of the forced marches and other physical challenges the officers throw at our regiment.

The rifle I am issued turns out to be identical to the musket loader Josef told me he once owned. It has a remarkable kick, which totally takes me off guard the first time I fire it. But I soon adjust to the impact of the weapon's butt against my shoulder, and I even prove myself to be a marksman of above-average skill. At least that's how it seems to me. None of the weapons instructors ever actually tells me so. In fact, they rarely say anything to us during firing range training. I wonder if they even care whether our men can shoot straight or not. Mostly, they just stand there watching to prevent us from accidentally shooting each other. I finally decide that their strategy is a valid one; if the men aren't shooting at each other, they will most likely be shooting in the direction of the enemy. That makes some kind of sense, I figure.

The bayonet training is far less satisfying than the rifle training, and my efforts show it. I am regularly reprimanded for my lack of fervor in skewering the straw-filled enemy dummies they put before me. It isn't that I can't do it successfully. It's just that the dummies are a bit too realistic-looking. I'm not comfortable stabbing these Prussian dummies, each of whom I imagine is a father to a family of little dummies back in Prussia. I just don't have the stomach to impale them viciously with my bayonet, turning those little dummies back home into broods of fatherless orphan dummies. But if I have difficulty even impaling these straw dummies, how in the world will I be able to face real soldiers? How will I be able to shamelessly do what is necessary?

I soon make a new friend, a man named Pavel Krall, who sleeps in the bunk next to mine. He's a short, rather soft man, with slanting shoulders—a sharp contrast to my rangy physique. But I find him to be quite intelligent and easy to talk to. Like me, he's from a peasant background and was raised by cottagers in a town called Litomyšl.

Although Pavel doesn't look it, he proves to be a good soldier, adept with both his rifle and bayonet, and when he observes my half-hearted attempts to attack the straw dummies with my bayonet, he is quick to offer advice. "Kill that bastard!" he yells. "Run him through! If you don't skewer him, he'll surely skewer you!"

Pavel is so passionate in his urgings that Captain Bauer, our company's commander, takes a step back and lets Pavel take over the bayonet training exercises. Soon, Pavel is screaming at the top of his lungs at all the recruits, invoking the vilest and most disgusting commands:

"Disembowel that wretch. Skew the scoundrel. Slice out the rogue's gizzard!"

He is like a man possessed, but I understand clearly what Pavel is doing. Pavel knows, as I do, that in battle, we will have to shamelessly do what is necessary, just as Josef taught me. Soon, with Pavel's modeling, many of the recruits take to shrieking bloodcurdling screams as they lunge with their bayonets. This impassioned technique results in the destruction of so many straw dummies that soon there are no more dummies left to destroy.

The captain takes a liking to Pavel, and begins to share with him bits of information that is primarily shared only among the officers. This isn't information that will get the captain into trouble; it consists mostly of military updates that Pavel shares with me and the other men. I'm glad to receive this information, for otherwise I'd have no idea what is going on in this conflict with Prussia.

In mid-June, the company is informed that Prussia has declared war on Austria. This causes a palpable nervousness around the barracks, as the realization takes hold that we could soon be bayoneting real combatants, not straw dummies. The regiment receives no further information. We don't know how soon we'll be deployed, nor where the fighting will take place. Even Captain Bauer doesn't know for sure. All he can tell us is that the Austrian Northern Army is amassing to the southeast, near the military fortress-town of Olomouc. With the Prussians coming from the north and the Austrians moving to meet them, the fighting will commence somewhere in between. Maybe even near the Königgrätz fortress. So the regiment stays put, waiting to see where the two armies might clash, and wondering what part the 98th will play in the confrontation.

I continue to extract information from my friend, and he tells me that the officers have little faith in Ludwig von Bededek, the commander of our Austrian force. Bededek is new to his command and has not led such a large force before, and I've heard the rumor going around that he is a very cautious leader, perhaps to a fault.

It doesn't take long for the massive Austrian army to move northward, and on June 21, I can hear troop movement outside the walls of the fortress. We quickly scale the ramparts to watch as several battalions of infantry, cannoneers, and cavalry move across the countryside, all moving toward the Elbe River. I'm stunned at the size of the Austrian fighting force. I've heard it totals over two hundred thousand men, but to this point, that has only been a number. Now, seeing that many soldiers in one place is astonishing. I've also heard that the Prussian army moving toward us is of similar size, and I have trouble imagining two forces of such magnitude coming together on the battlefield. I wonder how many of these men will die in the upcoming battle. Too many to count, I suspect. I wonder if I will be one of them.

I don't have long to stand and ponder such things, as a bugle call soon signals our assembly. In very short order, the 98th Regiment marches out of the Königgrätz fortress toward the mass of Austrian troops, where we will join the 6th Corps. I'm happy to see that the 6th Corps is toward the rear of the fighting force. I hope that means we won't be in the thick of things as the armies first meet. Perhaps, I imagine, my regiment will be part of a reserve force to be utilized later on in the battle if needed.

As it turns out, I am correct, and when the massive army finally stops on July 3, 1866, just north of Königgrätz, I'm far to the rear, standing with my fellow soldiers on a hillside overlooking the incredible scene. The two massive forces of horsemen, infantry, and cannoneers halt and wait briefly before converging to annihilate one another. We all watch as the Austrian cannons suddenly begin to pummel the enemy. I count around two hundred cannons positioned in battalions spread across the Austrian line. They fire, sending projectiles down upon the Prussian soldiers, and I'm at once repulsed by the damage they cause—the screams of the wounded, the dismemberment, the death. The Austrian cannons are doing their job well, which doesn't surprise me. I've heard of the superiority they hold over the Prussian big guns, which lack comparable accuracy and range. But the Prussians keep coming, firing as they do. This puzzles me because they don't seem to stop to reload, but keep moving and keep on firing. Then I remember hearing about the Prussians' new breech-loading rifles that don't require them to stop and load in the muzzle. I watch with morbid curiosity as the Prussians continue to advance on the Austrian front, reloading as they go, pushing the Austrians back.

I stand, mesmerized by the scene. The sound of the cannons echoes among the nearby hills, veiling the constant chatter of rifle fire, and smoke hovers over the chaos in the valley below. I can smell and even taste the acrid odor of the guns. It wafts up the hill toward me, and I stand there in disgust, watching as the bodies of the dead accumulate at an ever-increasing rate in the killing zone below. I know I might soon become part of that, and my stomach churns in nervous protest.

The various battalions soon form fronts that seem to pulsate forward and back as they gain or lose the advantage. From atop the hill, the totality of it seems to resemble a living organism, moving and breathing, and leaving the excrement of human death in its wake. I make little sense of it all, not being able to tell who's winning the horrendous game being played in front of me.

The lines below undulate back and forth for a long time, while our 98th Regiment can do nothing but stand and watch. Suddenly, the cannon fire subsides, and I squint through the smoke to ascertain the reason.

"Look," someone shouts. "They've overrun our guns!"

We can now see the Prussians swarming past the cannons, picking up their pace as they penetrate the Austrian line. Among a cacophony of war cries, I notice that the right flank has completely crumbled. Thousands of Prussian cavalry and infantrymen are racing through the line of the Austrian 2nd Army, decimating it as they come. Above the cruel sounds of battle, I think I hear a bugle sounding. Then another one. It takes a moment for me to recognize the signal for retreat. And soon what's left of the Austrian fighting force is running back through the hills toward our regiment.

Pavel roughly grabs my shoulder and yells, "Come on, Vaclav! Run!" We both turn and sprint as fast as we can among the hundreds of other retreating soldiers, now at the mercy of the victorious Prussian army that is pursuing close behind.

CHAPTER 40

JOSEF WAS NEVER WELL SUITED for schedules and deadlines. He was never one to do things at the moment they needed to be done. So when Vaclav was considering who would take over his farm, Josef should never have been a candidate.

Josef is good at masonry work. Masonry jobs rarely involve repair work that can be considered dire. That kind of work can be done sometime in the future, not necessarily today or tomorrow, but sometime. And likewise with carpentry work. That barn wall that the bull knocked down is not a critical or catastrophic circumstance. Who cares if the bull roams around the yard for a while? He probably won't roam far.

Before Vaclav left for Königgrätz, he did his best to tutor Josef in the ways of farming. Together, the two of them saw the planting season almost to its completion. Vaclav was meticulous in his explanations regarding the techniques of grain harvesting and storing, including the timetables that had proven successful in the past. But Josef had always lived according to his own timetables, and that would not bode well for the success of his farming enterprise.

By mid-June, the oats, clover hay, and potatoes are doing well enough, but the vegetables are suffering, mostly strangled by the weeds Josef has neglected to extricate. After all, he figures, can't the vegetables and the weeds just coexist? It seems to him that there's plenty of soil to go around. And as the hay lies drying in the field, why is it so necessary to bundle it before the coming rain? Can't it just dry out again if it gets wet? The livestock also proves to be an annoyance for Josef. Why do the goats seem so out of sorts just because he forgets to milk them? He'll get to it eventually.

In spite of Josef's failings as a farmer, he does actually get a fair crop of hay put up. And he's also able to harvest a few bushels of oats and potatoes when he finally finds the time. As he takes stock in his growing season, he knows his crops don't look as good as the crops of farmers on either side of Vaclav's land. Still, they're good enough, he decides.

But then another drought strikes the region providing very little moisture for the area around Budislav. Suddenly Josef's prospect of a fair harvest becomes an expectation of a poor one. On a late afternoon, as he assesses the poor condition of the fields, Josef wonders how Vaclav will react when he comes back to discover the piteous job he's done. He finally walks gloomily out of the fields toward the horse shed and thinks that he might as well brush Birdie and Daisy down, a job he's put off for weeks. At least, he figures, he can do that job to Vaclav's specifications.

After he completes the job to his satisfaction, he leaves the horses inside and, with considerable effort, rolls a large stone against the door to hold it shut. The door's wooden latch split in two just a few days ago, and Josef hasn't gotten around to fixing it. He figures he'll get to it one of these days. In the meantime, he's been using a large rock as a doorstop. Now, as he rolls it into place against the door, he spots an odd-looking little man who is stepping down from a horse-drawn dray.

The visitor is rather squat in dimension, and on his head he wears a black hat with a round crown and a wide brim. "Is Vaclav around?" the man asks.

"Who's asking?" Josef responds brusquely. Today he isn't in any mood for small talk.

"I'm Solomon Wise. I have business with him. Could you go get him for me, please?"

"Sorry, can't do that. He's not here."

"When do you expect him back?"

"Maybe this month? Maybe never," Josef answers obliquely.

"Look, I just want to see Vaclav. Who are you, anyway?"

"I'm Josef. I'm taking care of Vaclav's farm while he is off fighting the Prussians. Does that answer all your questions to your satisfaction?"

"Hmm. So you're in charge here?"

"I suppose you could say that."

"Well, then, I'm here about the payment on a loan."

"Loan? What kind of loan?"

"Well, a couple of years ago, when the last drought hit, Vaclav took out a loan to tide himself over until the next harvest. Of course, his final payment is not due until September, but I was riding by and happened to notice that his crops aren't doing very well. I stopped to see if Vaclav will make his payment this year."

Josef is plenty irritated now. Not only has he not fulfilled his promise to grow Vaclav's crops, but now there is this loan payment that he won't be able to pay.

"It's not due until September, right? So why don't you go back under that rock you came from and come back in September?" Josef says venomously.

"Now, no need to be testy. I'm just a businessman taking care of my business. If I don't get payment, I'll have to call this loan in, you know."

"Can I see it?"

"See it?"

"The loan paper. Can I see it?"

"I suppose so," the man replies. He retrieves a briefcase from his wagon seat, opens it, and produces a single piece of official-looking paper. He hands it to Josef.

Josef looks down at it, pretending to read it. He says, "I can't see what Vaclav used for collateral."

"It's right there in the second paragraph," replies Wise impatiently.

"Well . . . er . . . I forgot my spectacles in the house," Josef says, still staring at the paper.

"He used that hectare of land on the east side of his property."

"But that's the most fertile hectare he owns. He can't lose that. Are you sure he specified that hectare?"

"I'm quite sure," Wise replies decisively.

"We won't pay it," says Josef with his usual defiance.

"But someone must, or we'll go to the town judge in Proseč to settle this," Wise spits back.

Josef glances toward the house, wondering if Annie or her sister can hear this conversation. Then he remembers he saw them a while ago heading with Vaclav Jr. out to the vegetable field. They are out there to see if there's anything to salvage from the withered plants. He figures they'll be out there for a while yet. Does Annie know about this loan? he wonders. How can she pay this money back? If Vaclav loses this hectare of his farm, the most productive parcel of land on his property, how will he and his family survive? Josef is at once infuriated, thinking that all of his work to maintain Vaclav's farm has been for nothing.

Wise suddenly reaches to take the loan paper back, but Josef wrenches the paper from Wise's grasp. The small man lurches forward, trying for the loan paper once again. The two men struggle, but Wise is no match for the feisty Josef, who simply shoves the little man deftly aside. This causes Wise to stumble backward, tripping over his own feet and losing his balance. He falls hard onto the ground, striking his head violently on the large stone doorstop. Josef watches in horror as blood pools around the man's head and onto the stone. The man is dead. Josef can see it immediately. He saw that same countenance on the faces of the dead on the battlefield at Solferino.

What is he to do now? Vaclav will never forgive him for this. And what of Frantiska? What will she do when they haul him off, charged with this crime? He shudders to consider it. But what choice does he really have? There is but one thing to do, he knows.

Soon Josef sits atop Solomon Wise's wagon as the dray horse pulls the rig down the dusty road. Wise's body, covered in a blanket, lies in a pile just behind Josef. The briefcase is there, too, and Birdie walks disapprovingly in the rear, tethered to the back of the rig. Josef grips the reins firmly, heading west on the road that goes to Proseč and eventually will turn south toward home. But first he has one stop to make on the way. Josef drives the rig toward the hills in the Mastale Woods, which separate Budislav from Proseč. He figures the wooded area will provide cover for his unsavory task. As he approaches the trees, he's glad he's seen no one on the road thus far, for if anyone catches him with Wise's body, he knows he'll be in trouble.

As Josef approaches the stream amid the forest, he slows to a crawl, surveying the area for any witnesses. Then he pulls the rig to a stop on the stream's bridge. After looking one more time up and down the road, Josef removes the blanket and slides Wise's body off the wagon and over the bridge railing. He watches it splash into the shallow creek below. Next, he opens Wise's briefcase and pulls out all the documents. Ripping them to shreds, he throws them into the stream and watches for a moment as the fragments float downstream.

There's something else in the briefcase, too—a bag of money tucked underneath the pile of papers. He guesses it to be close to 300 guldens. What is he to do with that? Who the hell is he kidding? Of course, he'll keep it. If Josef wants the authorities to assume Wise was attacked by road thieves, the worst scenario would be for them to find the bag of money washed up on the shore of the creek. What robber would toss that away? No, Josef will keep that money for the sake of concealing his involvement. And if he profits from the ordeal, so be it. He will do it for the welfare of Vaclav's family and his own. Frantiska would understand that, wouldn't she? Of course, he hopes she'll never find out.

When he finishes the unpleasant deed, he continues driving the rig to the western edge of the woods, where the trees give way to a wide expanse of pastureland. He parks the wagon on the side of the road and unharnesses the dray horse. Slapping it on its rump, Josef watches as it gallops off into the nearby field. Satisfied that no one has seen him, he unties Birdie and mounts her, steering her toward Krouna and leaving the moneylender's rig behind.

The next day, the rumors are already circulating around Krouna. Apparently, the body of a Proseč moneylender was discovered last evening, lying in the shallow Voletinsky Creek. His abandoned wagon, plus the horse roaming the neighboring fields, was the tipoff of something gone awry. Proseč officials report that Wise was probably accosted by robbers who murdered him and threw his body into the stream. An empty briefcase was found near the scene, but whatever was once inside, if anything, was not recovered.

CHAPTER 41

THE ONCE-ORGANIZED AND DISCIPLINED BATTALIANS, both Austrian and Prussian, are now fragmented into smaller units, fighting in small skirmishes as the Prussians push us deeper into the Bohemian countryside. Most of the men in my regiment peel off on their own to wait out the conflict in some place of refuge or to join up with other units. But Pavel and I are among the thirty or so that Captain Bauer still holds under his command. Astride his mount, the captain continues to direct us as we move from one strategic position to another, not in neat ranks, but as a disorderly throng, running in a crouch as we dodge the small-arms fire of the pursuing Prussians. In this fashion, we continue our retreat for most of the day until, with the Prussians in close pursuit, we find ourselves in the town of Vysoke Myto.

The town looks deserted aside from the soldiers immersed in house-to-house fighting. There's no time to form firing lines and fire in unison volleys. Each of us shoots and reloads at will, as we constantly seek new positions with better cover and sight lines. As my unit retreats south through the town, the townsfolk seem to be barricaded in their homes, hoping to spare their families the violence in the streets. I also note that none of the men of the town seem to show any inclination toward fighting the invading Prussians, and I understand why. To most of these civilians, one occupying force is no better than any other. Their only concern is for the safety of their families. That isn't altogether assured, however, judging by the screams of men, women, and children I hear coming from behind the Prussian advance.

Pavel is standing next to me, his back pressed tightly against a wall where I've positioned myself. "I've got to get out of here!" he cries.

I wonder what he means. My friend sounds frantic, but I've never imagined Pavel would be one to panic and run. He would always be the one to jump into the fray, I've figured.

"Just keep shooting, Pavel!" I cry. "We're better off if we all stay together."

"No. What I mean is I need to leave. I'm worried about my family in Litomyšl. What if more Prussian units are further south? Litomyšl is only a short distance away, directly in the path of the enemy advance. I'm heading there. Good luck, Vaclav."

Pavel doesn't utter another word, but simply slaps me on the shoulder and heads down a side street away from the fighting. I am never to see my friend again.

I think about Annie. Our farm is southwest of Litomyšl, but not that far beyond it. How will Annie, Vaclav Jr., and Annie's sister fare against the Prussians as they go door-to-door? I realize now that Pavel has done the right thing, and I begin to formulate my own plan. Leaving my unit will be desertion, will it not? Still, nothing matters more to me than my wife and child. I glance around to take stock of my unit. It's difficult to ascertain where all my comrades are positioned, except for the reports of their rifles. I do, however, see Captain Bauer firing from the corner of a mud home across the street, some twenty yards away. The captain's horse stands, tied to a nearby fence post, out of the line of fire.

Retreating further south along the back of several homes, I dart across the main street and backtrack to where the horse is tethered. As Bauer continues firing in the other direction, I'm now prepared to do as Josef instructed—to shamelessly do what is necessary. Despite a sudden wash of shame, I carefully untie the horse and lead it quietly down a side street. As soon as I'm out of Bauer's sight, I quickly mount the animal and dig my heels hard into its haunches. The horse bolts and races out into the main street and southward at a fierce gallop. I don't let the animal slow its gallop until we are well beyond the limits of the town. And even then, I urge the horse forward at an only slightly slower pace, testing its endurance for our dash toward Budislav.

My home comes into view, and as I approach, I can hear rifle fire. I fear I might be too late, and I quickly dismount, turning the horse loose with a slap on the rump. Bauer's horse can be of little use if I'm to take myself, Annie, her sister, and Vaclav Jr. to a safer location. I'll need my wagon and team to do that.

Behind the cover of a large oak tree, I reload my musket and secure the bayonet. Then, moving stealthily along the tree line skirting the road, I finally reach my house and stop to survey my surroundings. About fifty yards in front of me, there are what appear to be the bodies of Austrian infantrymen, all laid out on the road. Still further down the street, Prussian soldiers are moving from house to house. I feel a pang of dread, a dread that suddenly heightens to panic as I hear a gunshot very close, perhaps from my own home, I fear.

I edge nervously along the front of my house and notice the door is ajar. If I push it open, the squeaky hinge will announce my presence. I wish I had fixed that months ago when I had the chance. Annie is crying out, her words distorted by the terror in her voice, and I forcefully shove the door open, causing it to slam against the interior wall. Two soldiers stand over Annie and the boy. One soldier is holding a rifle whose muzzle is still smoking from the discharge a moment ago. The other soldier's rifle is leaning against the table Josef made for us on the occasion of our wedding.

The two surprised men whirl around to discover me with my Lorenz trained on them. The soldier with the rifle raises it toward me and I fire, hitting him man square in the chest. Without pausing, I then lunge forward, yelling as Pavel taught me, plunging my bayonet up to its hilt into the other soldier's abdomen. I'm struck by the ease with which the bayonet blade enters the man's midsection. It seems to be much easier than skewering a straw dummy, so for good measure, I twist the blade savagely before pulling it back out. I watch in fascination as the man crumbles, with his entrails spilling out onto the floor.

Breathing fast and hard for a moment, trying to get control of myself, I see another body lying on the floor. It's Annie's sister, who appears to have been killed moments earlier. Still, I have no time to linger.

"Are you and Vaclav all right, Annie?" I ask anxiously.

She can't speak, traumatized by the scene before her, but she manages to nod her head up and down.

"We have to go! Bring the boy and follow me!" I lean out the door, scanning the street in both directions, and then say, "Let's head back to the horse shed. We need the wagon and team."

"Where will we go?" asks Annie, her voice shaking.

"We'll figure that out later," I reply as I grab her arm, pulling them out of the house and toward the horse barn. There is a large stone holding the door shut, and I quickly move it aside with my foot to gain access to the shed. I shove Annie and little Vaclav through, slamming it shut behind us. That's when I notice that Birdie is gone.

"Where's Birdie?"

"Josef. He has her," Annie says. "He rode her home this afternoon. Took the dray, too."

I look at Daisy, who is moving about in her stall, distressed by the gunfire outside. Can the three of us all ride bareback on Daisy? I wonder. I now regret having set

Bauer's horse free. I have no choice but to take my chances with Daisy.

Soon, Daisy is bridled and trudging out of the shed with the three of us on her back. We ride with haste, westward away from town, pushing the horse as much as I think reasonable. It doesn't take long to arrive at the Mastale Woods, and we cross the small bridge spanning Voletinsky Creek. Turning south, we leave the road and weave our way toward Krouna through the fields of the outlying valleys, so as not to be spotted by any Prussians who might be about.

As we ride into Krouna, I am at once overtaken by an eerie unease. The only sound I hear is the clop-clop of Daisy's gait. Where is everyone? I wonder. Have the Prussians already been here? It doesn't seem so. There's no apparent evidence of damage or pillaging. It appears that the people of Krouna have simply left their homes. Soon, we arrive at Josef and Frantiska's hovel and bring Daisy to a stop.

"Wait here," I say as I hoist my leg over the mare's neck and jump to the ground.

Their door is open slightly, and I cautiously push it all the way inward to look inside. Everything is as tidy as Frantiska usually keeps it, showing no evidence of any kind of struggle. I take a cursory inventory of their belongings and then turn, returning to where Annie and Vaclav Jr. are sitting on Daisy.

"Where are they?" asks Annie.

"They're gone, Annie."

"Gone? Where could they have gone?"

My wagon sits next to Anton's stable, so I walk quickly to the stable door to gaze inside. Birdie is calmly standing next to the stanchion. "Where's Josef, Birdie?" I ask, but she offers no reply. Not even a discreet snort. I assume she's sleeping, and I bother her no further.

Returning to Annie, I say, "Birdie and the wagon are still here. Josef and Frantiska can't have gone far. The blankets are no longer on their beds, but I saw Josef's crank organ sitting in the corner. He wouldn't have gone far without that."

"But where do you think they are?" asks Annie.

"They might have heard the Prussians were heading this way and sought refuge elsewhere. That's all I can figure."

I gaze up toward Burnt Hill and offer a possibility, saying, "I don't know where all the other people in Krouna went, but I think I know where Josef took his family."

CHAPTER 42

THE SUN IS ALREADY SEEKING REFUGE over the distant hills, and I decide to wait until daybreak to search for Josef and his family. It seems pointless to be looking for them up on Burnt Hill in the dark. Besides, for all I know, Josef has procured another rifle since I saw him last. I certainly don't want him to mistake me in the dark for an approaching Prussian soldier.

In short order, Annie and the boy are safely asleep inside Josef's home, and I sit outside by the door, listening for small-arms fire and watching for any approaching troops. The time passes slowly, and I'm exhausted from the ordeals of the day. Still, I'm able to fight the urge to sleep, and as the morning nears, having heard no sounds of gunfire, I am heartened by the notion that the Prussians may have halted their push through my homeland. Of course, I realize that with daybreak the enemy may resume their movements south toward Krouna. Hopefully not, I think. What have they to gain by it? The Prussians have already defeated the massive Austrian Northern Army, thus throwing off the yoke of fealty to Franz Joseph. They weren't fighting to annex Austrian land, anyway; they were fighting for their freedom. What would they want with Bohemia, with its unproductive farmland and impoverished population?

I can hear Annie and the boy stirring now within the hovel, and soon Annie opens the door.

"Were you up the entire night?" she asks.

"Yes, of course. But I don't think we're in danger anymore. Look, do you see that?" I add, pointing toward a neighboring field. Some of Krouna's residents are returning from their hiding places in the wooded areas beyond the farmland. Annie walks to the corner of the house, gazing back toward Burnt Hill.

"Is that them, Vaclav?" she exclaims excitedly.

As we stand and watch, several figures appear from amongst the trees on Burnt Hill, heading in our direction. Annie sweeps little Vaclav up into her arms, and we walk quickly toward them. Vincencie has run ahead through the field to meet us. And in no time at all, both our families are standing in the middle of the parched oat field, exchanging hugs and vigorous handshakes.

At this moment, the fears we've all carried these last few months are no more. We are together again, and our joy is embraced in an odd juxtaposition to our otherwise bleak situation. We spend much of the morning recounting our experiences since last we saw one another: Josef's struggle with the crops, my flight from Königgrätz, and the tragic death of Annie's sister, Katerina. It is on this last point that we settle on our most immediate mission. It's decided that we must travel back to Budislav to provide a proper burial for Annie's beloved sister. Although Annie insists on being a part of this task, I deem it too dangerous for her to go. "We don't know if the Prussians are still in Budislav," I tell her. I suspect not, but I won't take the chance of putting Annie in harm's way. We finally decide that only Josef and I will see to the woman's burial.

Soon, Josef and I are atop Birdie and Daisy, riding toward Budislav. We ride along in silence for a long time before Josef says, "I have a notion, Vaclav."

"What would that be?"

"Now that you're back, I think maybe it's time to go to America. There is nothing holding us here."

"Nothing except not having the funds to make the trip," I counter.

"Hear me out," Josef continues. "A couple of weeks ago, we got another letter from Anton and Rose."

"Oh, really? How are they getting on?"

"They are doing well. Well enough, anyway."

"What did they say?"

"They gave us detailed instructions about making the trip, including specific costs and possible dangers along the way. They even provided directions to their home in a place called Iowa."

"Iowa? What is that? A town?"

"I have no idea, but Anton says they have very good farmland there. He thinks it would be to our liking. It reminds him of Bohemia in some ways, he said."

"Hopefully, without the rocky soil and droughts," I murmur.

"Anyway," Josef continues, "Frantiska and Annie did some figuring, and they think we have enough money accumulated to make the journey."

"Really?" I ask, surprised.

"Sure. If you sell your hectares of land, you should easily make it work."

Of course that won't be possible. At least not until I settle up with Solomon Wise. I hate to burst Josef's bubble of optimism, so I pause for a moment before saying, "Josef. There is something you should know. It's regarding that land. I used a hectare of it as collateral for a loan from a man named Solomon Wise. Anna is aware of this, but I guess I didn't think I needed to mention it to you. Anyway, I can't really leave until I'm released from that obligation."

At first Josef shows no reaction, which I find to be rather odd, and then I notice a slight smirk taking shape on his face. "Funny thing about that," he says finally. "Well, not exactly funny, but fortunate for you. You see, I know about that loan. In fact, Wise stopped by your farm a while back, asking about you. When I told him you were conscripted into the army to fight the Prussians, he felt so sorry for you that he decided to forgive the rest of the loan. He even donated 200 guldens to help out your family. Can you believe it?"

Pulling up on the reins, I turn to glare at Josef in disbelief, saying, "Frankly, no. I know that bastard very well. He would never do something as generous as that. Why are you even saying something so unbelievable?"

"He gave me your loan paper. I can show it to you. It's in my house under the bed. But here's the best part, Vaclav. Later, he was murdered by robbers who threw his body into Voletinsky Creek. Weird, isn't it?"

"He was murdered? Really? Murdered?" I exclaim in disbelief. "Wait, hold up here. Let me get this straight. That low-life Solomon Wise forgives my loan, gives you 200 guldens, and then conveniently gets murdered by thieves? I find that very difficult to believe."

"Well, that's what happened."

"Did you tell Frantiska and Annie about this?"

"Sure."

"And they believed you?"

"Of course they believed me. I mean, why wouldn't they believe me? It's true."

"But they don't know Solomon Wise as I do," I answer. "None of this sounds right to me."

"But why would I lie about something like that, Vaclav?"

"I'm not calling you a liar. It just makes no sense to me, Josef."

"Anyway," Josef continues, undeterred, "with that extra 200 guldens, we figure you have enough saved to make the trip, as long as you get a decent price for your land."

"And what about my obligation to the military? I haven't exactly left the regiment on good terms. Even if they accept my reasons for deserting, I still might not be released from my obligation."

"Oh, my young friend, but you are so wrong. Anton wrote in his letter that the German border authorities hardly check documents at all. He said the ship pursers at the port don't care about your military obligations as long as you have the money for passage."

I have no rebuttal for that, but I'm still suspicious of Josef's story about Solomon Wise. Still, if it's all true, could our dream truly be possible? Now, as Birdie plods along, I can't stop thinking about it.

Krouna to Budislav is not a great distance, and it doesn't take us long to arrive at the front of my home. The town still seems to be in shock from the Prussian incursion. There are a few bodies lying out in the street, and a few Budislav residents walk among them aimlessly, as though in a trance. The door of my house is still open, and as I enter, I see Katerina's body lying where I last saw it, next to the two Prussian soldiers I killed.

Josef and I drag the dead soldiers out into the street and then return to stand over Katerina's stiffened bulk, deciding what to do next.

"Do you want to take her back to Jarošov so her parents can bury her?" Josef asks.

"No. We don't know if it's safe in Jarošov or if her parents are even alive," I reply. "Let's just bury her here. We can find a pleasant spot near that big oak tree behind the house."

Together, we carry Katerina's body out the door and proceed to the rear of the house, where we lay her down gently next to the tree. I retrieve my shovel from its place in the barn, and we take turns digging. The ground is somewhat rocky and rootbound, but we are able to excavate a crater about four feet deep. It's not very deep, but it will have to do, we surmise. We quickly but carefully place her into the grave and cover her with a blanket from the house. Without ceremony, we then scoop the fresh dirt back into the hole, until a rounded mound of dirt covers Katerina's final resting place. I comment on the shallowness of the grave, and we decide to cover it with large stones that might deter any creature from exploring its contents.

Looking around, I notice the large rock holding the barn door closed. I remember seeing it there before, but hadn't given it much thought at the time. I wonder why Josef would have put it there. Regardless, I lean over to pick it up. That's when I notice something strange about the stone. Much of it is covered with something unusual: some kind of brown substance. What is that? I wonder. Is it dried blood?

I call to Josef, "Come, take a look at this. What is that?"

He walks over and stares down at the rock. "What is what?" he asks.

"What's all over that rock? Is that blood?" Josef remains silent for a long moment, running his fingers through the hair he's allowed to sprout on his chin.

"Uh, sure. That's what it is, alright. I guess I used the rock to decapitate some chickens Annie wanted for her cooking pot."

"That's an awful lot of blood for a couple of chickens, don't you think? And why would you do that on a rock instead of on that stump over there?" I ask, suspicious of his explanation. "Using this rock couldn't have been very good on my ax blade," I add.

Josef steps back from the rock and is now pacing back and forth, apparently frustrated by my observations. Finally, he stops and glares at me. His eyes show a distress I rarely see in my otherwise stoic friend.

"God damn it, Vaclav!" he shouts. "Why can't you just believe what I tell you and leave it at that? Why must you make this so difficult? I'm just trying to help you and your family. That's all. And here you are giving me grief." Josef looks nervous as he stands there shaking his head, staring down at his feet.

"What's wrong, Josef?" I ask benignly. "What's going on?"

Several uncomfortable moments pass before he finally looks up to meet my eyes. His ire has subsided, and he now has a look of sadness. Or is it something else? Remorse? Guilt?

What he tells me next is the most unbelievable story I've ever heard. But I can tell by Josef's demeanor that it's the truth. Josef even admits that the money bag he found in Wise's briefcase contained 300 guldens, not 200, and he'd decided to keep 100 guldens for himself as a finder's fee. He will turn that over to me as well, he promises.

"That was a careless thing you did," I say. "Covering up the accident that way, I mean."

"Under the circumstances, it was the only thing I could think to do," Josef insists.

"You can't kill someone, accidentally or not, and then just cover it up."

"If I had done otherwise, I might be in prison right now."

"There are right ways of doing things and there are wrong ways. God would say you chose the wrong way. God would say you're a sinner, Josef."

"Then you and your god are both stupid!" Josef blurts in frustration.

I choose to ignore his blasphemy and say, "This is going nowhere, Josef. Do you think I'm stupid because I'm wrong or because I disagree with you?"

"What's the difference?" he quickly responds, taking no time to reflect on the question I pose.

He is clearly entrenched in his own twisted righteousness, so I simply shake my head, answering with resignation, "Whatever you say, Josef."

Josef is my friend. That will never change. But he is not without his flaws, and I know that will never change either. Besides, what man leaves this world to meet his Maker still pure of heart and deed? Not many. Josef may not be the most honorable of men, nor the most commonsensical, and he certainly has that defiant streak that Frantiska complains about. But what he may lack in scruples, Josef makes up for in loyalty many times over. Was the moneylender's death Josef's fault? Probably. Well, not directly, but had Josef not scuffled with the man, Wise would be alive today. Still, somehow Josef was able to cover his tracks, and the result of the incident seems to have worked in our favor. I shouldn't feel glad about the result, but I admit that I do, for it may mean that we indeed can leave this godforsaken land. Does this make me less honorable, less pure of heart? Perhaps. But will I be lesser than any other man when I confront my Maker? I doubt it.

"Help me carry this rock over to Katerina's grave," I say plainly. Then, as we heft it up, I mutter, "Let's not mention any of this to Frantiska or Annie."

"I suppose there is no need for that," Josef agrees.

"And another thing," I add. "Let's just split those 300 guldens fifty-fifty, OK?"

Four weeks later, with all our emigration papers secured in my coat pocket and my land hurriedly sold off to a neighbor for a painfully low price, I pull my rig up to Josef's house. Their luggage sits outside the door, packed and ready. Josef's crank organ is there too. As I climb down off the wagon and begin hefting the luggage onto the dray, Birdie turns her head to watch me struggle with the largest of the trunks. She shakes away an annoying fly and offers me a slight snort of encouragement.

"Good old girl, Birdie. I know. I'll miss you, too. Who will I talk to when you're not around?"

"Are you talking to that horse again?" Josef asks as he brings another bag out the door.

"I figure this might be my last chance to converse with my like-minded friend. At the end of this trip, who will there be to share my most intimate thoughts? You?" I joke.

Josef ignores my comment and helps me lift the remaining bags onto the wagon. In short order, we load Frantiska and the children aboard the dray. And after a last look—hardly a sentimental one—at Josef's humble homestead, I snap the reins and let Daisy and Birdie take us toward Budislav, where Annie and Vaclav Jr. wait with our trunk and luggage.

From Budislav, it takes most of the morning to reach Choceň, and as we near the train station, there are several men loitering about. One of them is eyeing my rig as we approach. I pull on the reins, stop the dray, and ask him for directions to the ticket window. He points to the building not far away and then says, "You looking to sell that team and rig?"

"I guess I am, for the right price," I answer, indicating my intent to negotiate.

"I'll give you fifteen guldens for the whole rig," he offers matter-of-factly.

Chuckling, I answer, "It's worth at least four times that, and you know it."

That's all I have to say to the man, and I step down from the dray to help Josef with the luggage and the children. Josef and I leave the man behind as we herd our two families toward the train station. The August sun is upon us, and I find a shady spot where everyone can sit on the grass, waiting to board. Then I make my way back to my wagon, where the man is still standing, examining Daisy and Birdie. "I'll take thirty guldens, not a kreuzer less," I tell him sternly.

"See that rig coming down the street?" he asks as he points toward another family arriving with trunks and tied bundles. "I see about twenty of those every day, and you can be sure that they'll sell to me for the price I offer. What choice do they have? What choice do you really have? Fifteen guldens. That's a fair price. I would normally offer less, but this team is in better shape than most. Fifteen guldens is a fair price. Take it or leave it."

I didn't realize just how difficult this moment would be. Daisy and Birdie aren't just beasts of burden. They've become part of my family, especially since the death of my father. Fifteen guldens? That's all? I watch as the other dray draws closer, and I know that if I don't take the man's offer, the next person will.

Finally, I say, "OK, fifteen guldens," accepting sadly. The man hands me the meager sum, and I linger a moment in front of the team. "I'm sorry," I say softly, knowing how silly this must sound to the buyer standing nearby. But I don't care what he thinks. He can go to hell for all I care. I'm indeed sorry—deeply so. Not so much for selling at such a low price, but for leaving Daisy and Birdie in the hands of this stranger. Who knows what might become of them? But what am I to do? Finally, I turn to walk back toward the train station, and as I do, I hear a slight snort from Birdie. I can't bear to glance back in her direction, so I keep on walking, knowing I'll never be able to take counsel from her again.

The train carries us through the Bohemian and then German countryside for two full days. We sit on hard benches, silently watching as the landscape flies by, and we wonder if we've made the correct decision. Soon, we arrive in Bremen, and we know there is no turning back. For two days, we take refuge in a cramped boardinghouse. And then, with our luggage and extra provisions, we board the short train line to the port at Bremerhaven and find our places in line to register with the ship's purser. Before us sits the Barque Harzburg, a massive sailing ship that smells of the cotton and tobacco it just unloaded. Now it's ready for different cargo—human cargo.

Our queue soon shortens, and we approach the ship's purser. We're stopped by a man who insists on laying his hand on our foreheads, apparently checking for heightened temperature. Then he uses his finger, pulling down on our lower eyelids to check each eye, and finally adds a cursory gaze into our gaping mouths. This examination seems rather pointless, as he hardly takes any time at all before nodding to the purser, who's waiting impatiently to check our papers. This ritual is repeated for each family as they board. It seems to be more a ritual of expediency than it is of precision. Soon, all the passengers stand on the ship's deck taking their last look at Bremerhaven.

Finally, the Harzburg pulls away from the port into the North Sea, and I stand with the others, bracing myself against the wind, watching as the German coast fades behind us. When the port finally disappears from sight, I turn and gaze beyond the Harzburg's bow. Ahead is the English Channel, the vast Atlantic, and then, with God's help, the realization of our American dream.

CHAPTER 43
AMERICA, EIGHT WEEKS LATER

EASTERN IOWA IS AWASH in fall colors, and the leaves are falling faster now. It's already the end of October, and Joe Coufal wonders how long it will be until the first freeze. It doesn't really matter. He and Barbora are ready for the winter. Crops have been harvested and stored, and the apples, peaches, and plums from their orchard have been put up. His mules and cattle will be fine too, with clover hay and straw stored for winter feeding and bedding. Now it'll be up to him to keep the barns clean until spring.

For an October evening, it's quite temperate, and Joe decides to stand by the road, gazing out at the expanse of land that extends south to the Iowa River. There is a lot of fertile lowland out there, and he owns almost eight hundred acres of it, having purchased more and more parcels since arriving over fifteen years ago. It's proven to be quite productive, yielding abundant crops most of those years, except for the occasional season of flooding. But he doesn't mind the flooding so much. It brings nutrients to the land that further enhance subsequent crop seasons.

In the distance, he can just make out the old ferry moving across the river in his direction, bringing what looks to be a group of travelers from the south. Since he settled on the banks of the Iowa River, Joe has seen many travelers, mostly Slavs and Bohemians, passing by his homestead and heading for domestic and industrial work in Cedar Rapids. He's used to seeing these haggard sorts, stumbling along after weeks of torturous travel, with their vacant eyes and ragged clothes. Like the travelers who preceded them, this bedraggled bunch has probably spent their last few coins for the Rock Island train from Dubuque to Iowa City, and have come the rest of the way on foot. He continues watching as the ferry docks on the north side and the riders step off the ferry onto the bank. He can make out four adults and two children in the group, all carrying luggage with considerable effort. Joe raises his hand to his brow, shielding his eyes from the sun, and he now notices something else. Two of them are women, each carrying what seems to be a small child.

CHAPTER 44

"WATCH YOUR STEP," the ferry master warns as I step off his conveyance. "It's that road right over there," he points. "The first one on the left."

"Děkuji. Thank you," I mutter and head in that direction, with Annie and Wesley following close behind. Wesley—that's what we call him now. After the ship's German purser at Bremerhaven wrote *Wenzel,* the German equivalent of Vaclav, on the ship manifest, Annie decided it best to refer to Vaclav Jr. by a more American name. Wesley seemed to be a good compromise for the boy's new life in his new land. I, however, have resisted making a similar change to my given name. I figure if Vaclav was good enough in Budislav, it's good enough here in America.

We leave the river and the ferry master behind and start down the road, a road deeply rutted into wheel-carved grooves of now-dried clay mud. It's difficult to walk without turning an ankle, so I move over to the side of the road, now stepping through spent beebalm and goldenrod. Can our journey be almost at an end? It seems so surreal to imagine it after all these weeks, traveling across an ocean and half a continent. I should feel limitless joy, but my elation is tamed by the intense exhaustion that's been building since we walked from the train station to the river. As we trudge along in silence, I'm sure Frantiska, Annie, Josef, and the children are no less drained, their luggage being dragged more than carried along the rutted path. I raise my head against the weight of my bags and see Josef staring ahead, showing new vitality in his step. He is a man of remarkable strength, having limped along with his crank organ in one hand and his large case in the other for the entirety of the trip. He finally stops, staring down a connecting road.

"This must be it," Josef announces, setting his case on the ground, balancing his crank organ on top of it, and then bending over backward to stretch his ailing back. We all stop, breathing hard, yet somehow unwilling to believe our journey could be near its end.

Vincencie points toward a homestead not far down the road, exclaiming, "Look! There's a man watching us."

None of us responds, but instead we pick up our burdens and proceed in the man's direction. I wonder how we must appear to this man, having not had a decent bath for the duration of our trip. What must he think of us? I try to straighten my posture in order to make a better impression, but what's the use? With the weight of the luggage, I have to relent and trudge along, hunchbacked and weary, like the destitute and homeless peasant I am.

"*Dobrý den!*" the man calls as we approach, and I'm surprised that he addresses us in our native tongue. How does he know we're Bohemian? I'm almost afraid to answer my query. Do we all look the same? The same pathetic, downtrodden desperation in our demeanor? The same gray complexions and tired eyes?

"Hello, friend," Josef answers. "We're looking for the bottom road. I assume this is it."

"Indeed. Where are you folks headed?"

Waiting for Josef to answer, I'm surprised at my inability to come up with the answer myself. What's wrong with me? I suddenly realize that I'm rather befuddled, not knowing where I am or where I'm going. My recollections since boarding the train in Choceň are just a blur now. It's odd that I haven't noticed it before. My dream of America, once an image burning clear and bright, has somehow been reduced to a collection of dull distortions, representations of the stark realities of countless days trapped in the dank steerage of the ship, mesmerizing flashes of images seen through foggy train windows, and finally, the arduous lugging of our possessions from Iowa City. This dream, once ripe with hope and wonder, is now wrought with only the necessity for continued endurance—the requirement for me to just carry on. Where are we headed? I can't quite remember. And will we ever get there? I don't know if I even care anymore.

"The home of Anton and Rose Novak," Josef finally answers. "Do you know of them?"

"Oh, yes. They're just up this road. You should make it there by nightfall if you hurry," the man answers, pointing toward the west.

"By nightfall?" Josef replies, his voice faltering, showing his disappointment.

I feel the same way. I'm weak and I'm thirsty. Very thirsty. But we've come this far. I suppose we can endure just a bit further.

The man is looking at us now, gazing from one to the next, as if taking stock of the likelihood of us completing our trek. He must see our wretchedness, our misery, our waning fortitude. He finally says, "I'll go hook up my team. I'll take you there. See that well up by the house? Help yourselves to a drink. Wait there for me. I'll be right back." With that, he turns and walks quickly toward one of his barns.

It takes the man's hay wagon only a short time to carry us to the Novak home, and I'm suddenly disappointed. It's a humble abode made partly of sod, partly of logs, and covered with a thatched roof held down by large tree limbs. It's smaller than the home the Novaks left behind in Krouna. Somehow, I had expected the Novaks' living conditions to be vastly improved.

Anton's home is far too small to house all three families, and I'm suddenly attuned to the uncertainties of our immediate future. What are we to do? It's already far into autumn. If this land is anything like Budislav, winter will be hard upon us in a matter of weeks. There is no lord or town judge here to supply us with a hovel, and it's certainly too late in the season to complete the construction of a suitable home. Where will we live?

Standing next to the wagon, Annie and I watch as Josef, Frantiska, and the children greet the Novaks, their friends of many years, now reacquainted in this new land. I notice that Annie isn't watching them. Instead, she's surveying the Novak homestead, and I'm certain she's thinking the same thoughts I am.

"What are we gonna do, Vaclav?" she asks meekly.

"What do you mean?"

"You know what I mean. We can't all live here, can we?"

"I suppose not," I answer with a sigh. "We'll figure it out."

"We'll figure it out? That doesn't give me much reassurance," she answers, glancing up at me.

I know she's right, but what else can I say? At least I'm offering a little bit of optimism, sorely needed at this moment. As Annie leans into me, I put my arm around her and little Wesley, pull them close, and whisper, "We'll be fine. I promise."

PART THREE
REVEREND FRANCIS KUN
1866–1875

CHAPTER 45

BEHOLD THE BEAUTY of the Lord's creation! The shedding of the oaks, the blushing of the maples, the crispness of the autumn air—I love this time of year. Sure, I know what's coming. The winters in Iowa can be brutal, but they're not so different than in Moravia. I know what to expect—the blowing and drifting snow, the frigid temperatures, and the inherent dangers of winter survival. These are things familiar to me, and I'll suffer the upcoming winter just as I've suffered every other winter since arriving here. It's this suffering, after all, that will make the spring so much more gratifyingly welcome. Yes, this is all part of God's grand design: life, death, and then, with the returning spring, renewal.

The Coufal farm lies up ahead, but as I reach the corner to the bottom road, I turn my mare westward and continue riding. I might otherwise stop to visit with Joe and Barbora, but it's the middle of the afternoon and I want to give myself time to explore the river road in search of any new arrivals, any souls hungry for spiritual guidance, any recent settlers I might welcome to the area and possibly to my church.

I'm soon approaching the Novak homestead. I've visited the home of Anton and Rose before. Of course, that was after I first met them at the Coufal home a couple years back, when I preached there to a handful of Joe's neighbors. I remember that Anton seemed rather resistant to any commitment toward membership in our little congregation, neither dead set against it nor much in favor of it either. I'm used to encountering such a response. More so than people from Moravia and other regions, many Bohemian immigrants aren't anxious to pledge themselves to any particular church. There seems to be a liberal streak in these folks, probably born of the many years the Habsburgs tried to force Catholicism down their Hussite throats. I suppose I can understand their reluctance to join our church or any church. I'll continue to work on Anton, though, for I think Rose is a bit more enthusiastic, and maybe with her help, I can get Anton to see things our way. But that is for another day. Today, I'm interested in meeting people new to the area. So I keep riding.

As I pass the Novak homestead, I spot a man who seems to be digging a hole behind Anton's home. Who could this be? I wonder. I rein in my horse and turn back toward Anton's house.

"Hello, friend," I call as I dismount and walk toward him.

The man is sweating, and as I approach, he stops his digging and uses the back of his hand to wipe perspiration from his brow. "Do you need something?" the man asks. He doesn't seem very happy about the interruption, so I offer my very best effort at affability.

"Looks like you have a big job there, my friend. Why all the digging?"

"It's a well. Hoping to finish before the cold sets in. Is there something I can help you with? Anton is inside if you need to see him."

"Actually, it's you I wish to see," I say. "I'm Reverend Kun. I minister to a small congregation east of here. We are a congregation of Reformed Evangelical Brethren, and we're in the process of erecting a church building. I was hoping I could—"

"Not interested, Preacher. You can move along," the man replies gruffly before grabbing his shovel to resume his digging.

"If I could only leave this letter with you, you could—"

"I said I'm not interested. Please get yourself up the road. I'm sure there are some other victims further on that you can prey on."

"I'm not trying to prey on—"

"How can I say it more clearly?" the man says as he grasps his shovel in both hands, approaching me in what seems to be a threatening fashion. He isn't a tall man by any measure, but he is an imposing man, with wide sloping shoulders extending into muscular arms and large capable hands. His unkempt beard spreads out wildly, bordering from cheek to jowl along the perimeter of his face, a face brandishing a rather disagreeable countenance. He walks with a definite limp, but that doesn't seem to keep him from covering the distance between us in very short order.

"Please, sir. I don't want to make any trouble. I'll be on my way. Please tell Anton and Rose that I was here. May God bless you," I say.

"Right," the man utters derisively.

Leading my horse down the road, I watch warily to make sure the man isn't following. Seeing him walking back toward the house, I breathe easier and realize he's no longer a threat, so I mount up to consider which direction I'll explore next.

I'm only about a quarter mile down the road when I suddenly hear a voice in the distance behind me. It's a female voice, and I turn to see a woman in a long linen dress waving her arms and yelling frantically for me to stop. I turn my horse and urge it at a trot back in her direction. As we meet in the middle of the road, the woman is panting from her effort to catch up.

"Please, don't go," she pleads, breathing hard.

"I think perhaps I should. That man—"

"That's my husband, Josef. I'm Frantiska. Don't worry about him. Please, you must come back and join us inside."

"I don't know . . . he seemed quite agitated," I reply, thinking it might be best to just keep riding, for his sake and for mine.

"No, no. Don't worry. He talks big, but he's just a pussycat. Josef and God have a sort of on-and-off relationship, if you know what I mean."

"It appears so," I reply, trying not to roll my eyes and immediately feeling guilty for the very thought of doing it. "Don't worry," I say. "The Lord is patient. He'll wait. I'm sure they'll be friends one day soon."

"I hope so. Please," she says insistently, motioning back toward the small home.

"Well, OK. I guess I can," I say hesitantly, wondering if that pussycat has very sharp claws.

I follow the woman and notice that her husband has resumed his digging. Two small children play near him, and the man brusquely shoos them away from his work site, stopping only briefly to give me a disapproving look. I offer him a feigned smile and a nod—two gestures that go unanswered.

Entering the Novak home, I'm at once shaking hands with Anton and Rose. The place hasn't changed much since the last time I was here. When was it? Last summer? I wonder if Rose has made any headway with her husband. But this is not the time to ask. I've noticed on a couple of occasions that he has come with his wife to attend services at Banner Valley. I'm not sure if he was there simply as his wife's escort or as one of God's children interested in seeking spiritual nourishment. I will not pressure the man. He will embrace the Word or he will not, but it must be his own decision.

This other woman, though—what's her name? Frantiska, that's it. She seems eager to hear what I have to say, and I'm impressed that in spite of her husband's negative influence, she's evidently stayed strong in her faith.

"Good afternoon. It's good to see you again," I say to Anton and Rose as we meet. Rose is holding a young child, and I'm pretty sure it is not of her making. So I ask, "And whom do we have here?"

"This is Terezie, Frantiska's daughter," Rose says as she smooths down the child's dress.

"She's the reason I wanted you to stop in," Frantiska interjects. "She needs baptizing."

"Well, we can remedy that, can't we?" I reply.

"And my friend Annie also has a little one, Wesley. He needs baptizing too," she adds.

"Very good. We can do that any Sunday you'd like at the church. Or if you'd like me to baptize the children in your home, I suppose I could do it that way."

"How far away is your church?" Frantiska asks. "We'll probably need to travel on foot."

"Oh, yes. Well, that may be a problem then," I say. "Perhaps we should plan on the second option."

"I suppose so," Frantiska says with disappointment, "although it would be nice to do it at your church."

"Perhaps," I say to the woman, "but it's not really our church, anyway. It actually belongs to the Lutherans. We just rent it on Sunday afternoons for our services. But we're in the process of building our own."

"Do you think you'll build it closer to us?" Rose asks, showing interest.

"We're not sure yet. We're still raising the necessary funds to determine if the construction can proceed," I answer as I pull two pieces of paper from my coat pocket. "Here is a letter that I'll leave with you. It explains why our own temple is sorely needed. I hope you'll read it."

Frantiska takes the letter, but says sadly, "I don't think we will be able to offer any—"

"Oh, no, no," I interrupt. "I understand that having only recently come here, you may not be in a position to contribute. But I'll leave the letter with you anyway. Maybe Rose and Anton can take a look at it, as well."

Anton is looking sideways at Rose with a doubtful expression, and I realize that the man's earlier resistance still persists. I won't find any donors here today, I realize, but I nevertheless hold out the other piece of paper to show them the donor list. "Here are the people who have pledged funds thus far. As you see, there are about fifty signatures. There has been a lot of interest. Maybe in the near future, you might choose to help."

"We'll see," says Anton, his tone telling me I shouldn't expect his pledge anytime soon.

"I understand," I say. "Whether you can contribute or not, I hope you will still feel comfortable attending our services, whether in our new building or when I preach nearby at homes like the Coufals'. You are God's children, and I am his servant—and yours."

CHAPTER 46

VACLAV CAUTIOUSLY PUSHES the cabin door open. The door creaks inward, and he pushes away some bothersome cobwebs to peer inside. No rats scurrying about or raccoons rushing for cover; he's glad about that. The place is about the size of their old place back in Budislav, perhaps a bit smaller, but it will be sufficient for now. Hopefully, they won't have to rent it for long. Joe says there is land for the claiming just a short distance west of here. Come spring, Vaclav hopes to stake a claim and begin to build a proper home for Annie and little Wesley. In the meantime, though, he needs to find some way to generate an income. What he will do he doesn't yet know.

When Joe Coufal first settled here, he built this one-room structure nestled among the birches near the river. That was before he married Barbora and built the much larger stone home utilizing limestone from his quarry. Since that time, Joe has been renting out his small cabin to new immigrants who show up on his doorstep. But when the war came, the flow of immigrants slackened, leaving the place without tenants. The cabin has been vacant for five or six years now, and Joe has cautioned Vaclav about that. Who knows what could be living in the place now?

Vaclav and Annie step through the door to assess the condition of the neglected abode, taking note of rotting roof supports and a crumbling chimney. At least, the last tenants left a table and two chairs as well as a couple of pallets for beds. "Well, I suppose it could be worse," Vaclav says, knowing it couldn't be much worse.

"We'll make do," Annie says, not very convincingly.

Annie and Vaclav spend the remainder of the day cleaning the cabin's interior. As the day's light begins to fade, they decide that they have toiled enough for one day. They have improved the inside conditions considerably, and as they stand and admire the fruits of their labor, Annie says, "It'll do nicely for now, except for that chimney."

"I'll try to remember to talk to Josef about that. He'll know what to do."

The next morning, Vaclav arrives at the Novaks' house to help Josef with the digging of the well. He hopes he won't be here all day long, but he fears he will. That's OK, he thinks. Maybe he'll actually learn something about digging a proper well. Josef is an old hand at this, having dug several wells for Judge Spacek back in Krouna. Vaclav knows he'll need to dig one next spring if he makes a claim on his own piece of farmland.

Josef is already at the site digging away as Vaclav approaches. Vaclav can barely see the top of his friend's head as it bobs up and down in rhythm to the dirt flying up over the edge. Vaclav notices a pile of large stones stacked nearby and wonders where they came from and what they're for.

"Morning, Josef," he says cheerfully. "Struck water yet?"

"Very funny. We've got a ways to go for that."

"What's with this stone over here?"

"Joe Coufal brought a load of it from a limestone quarry he has on his property. I'm going to line the well with it. I think it will work nicely, much better than the stones I used to use in Krouna."

Vaclav is fascinated by Josef's process of laying stones along the sides of the well as he digs downward. Josef's winch is also of great interest to Vaclav, and he soon gets the hang of cranking the buckets of dirt upward with the winch, emptying them, and then lowering the stone blocks to the bottom. The two men work throughout the day, taking breaks only occasionally to rest. By late afternoon, the well is almost fifteen feet deep, and Josef is beginning to wonder if he's picked the right spot to dig. Fortunately, at the sixteen-foot mark, the soil suddenly becomes very moist, and soon he is hurriedly laying the final stones around the sides and on the bottom. Finally, Josef looks down with satisfaction at the incoming water as he nimbly climbs up the ladder out of the well.

"It must make you feel good when water starts pouring in like that," Vaclav says.

"I suppose, but it doesn't always happen that way," replies Josef. "Sometimes, when I'm down to about twenty feet, I have to decide if I should keep going or give up. At that point, I usually just find another place to dig."

"That must be frustrating."

"That's for sure. Talk about a waste of time."

"I've always wondered how well diggers know where to dig. How do you figure that out?"

"I just go by experience, the lay of the land, my gut feeling, that sort of thing."

"So you're saying that you just take a wild guess?" Vaclav jokes. "Seems like a *hloupý* way to do things."

"You calling me *hloupý*?"

"Yup."

"You're the one who's stupid, Vaclav, not me."

"No, I'm not *hloupý*. I'm not the one pretending to know the best place to dig when I really have no idea. That makes no sense." Vaclav is smiling now, beaming in the enjoyment of their verbal sparring.

"Hmm," Josef finally says, "Look down there, my friend. See that water gushing into the well? Now, who's the *hloupý* one?"

Vaclav can't argue with that. The well is taking in a considerable amount of water. Still, he can't let Josef have the last word. "OK, so you were lucky this time. Even simpletons like you can get lucky sometimes."

Josef sees no purpose in continuing this discussion any longer. He's made his point. It takes little time for the two men to clean up the worksite, and they stand there admiring their work. This well will make Anton and Rose's life so much better. No more trips down to the river to fetch water for drinking and washing. No more collecting of rainwater. Josef knows Anton will be greatly pleased. As he stands gloating over his workmanship, he suddenly can hear horses approaching, and he sees a rig coming down the road.

"Looks like Joe's coming by to check on our progress," Josef says. "I still can't figure why he's been so helpful, bringing me these stones from the quarry. He didn't have to do that, but it surely saved me the effort of finding large enough river stones to complete the job."

As Coufal arrives and pulls his rig to a stop at the house, Josef and Vaclav walk to meet him.

"How are things going?" Coufal asks.

"Come see for yourself," answers Josef, turning and heading for the well with Vaclav and Coufal following close behind.

Joe gazes down into the well at the rising pool of water. "That's really something, Josef. Really nice work. And the limestone seems to have worked well for this job."

"It sure has," replies Josef. "If I ever do another one of these, I'll probably ask for another load of the stuff."

Coufal shifts his gaze from the well to Josef, saying, "Well, it's funny you say that, Josef, because I was wondering if you'd like to dig another one, or maybe even several other ones?"

"What do you mean?" Josef asks, confused.

"How would you like to go into a little partnership with me? Several homesteaders around here have asked me if I know of an experienced well digger. It seems I do know one now. I could get you quite a bit of work doing this, Josef. I'm thinking you could charge enough to make it worth our while."

"Worth *our* while?"

"Yes. You supply the expertise and the labor, and I supply the stone, a wagon, and the use of a couple of my horses. What do you say?"

Josef and Vaclav stare at each other for a long moment, contemplating this offer. Then Josef asks, "Could we make enough to pay my friend here, too?" He's looking at Vaclav now for confirmation. Vaclav gives him a smile and an approving nod.

"Sure, I think so. Let me work out the details and get back to you. Sound good?"

Josef and Vaclav nod in unison, both already thinking about the possibilities for the future. Moments later, Coufal is on his way to the bottom road in the direction of his homestead.

"So that's why he was so helpful," Josef muses, watching Coufal's rig churning up dust in its wake.

"What do you mean?" Vaclav asks.

"Well, I wondered why he was so willing to bring me that load of limestone. I think maybe he was testing me, to see how I'd do, the old devil. He had this well-digging partnership idea in mind from the very beginning."

"So, what are you gonna do?"

"What do you think I'm gonna do, Vaclav? I'm gonna dig some wells, and you're gonna help me!"

Vaclav makes it back by midafternoon and sees that Annie has made several improvements to the area around the cabin. "She's been a busy one," he mutters under his breath as he walks through the door. Recalling how decrepit the cabin appeared when they first arrived, Vaclav is surprised at Annie's improvements to the place. This will be fine for a while, he thinks. At least, it will do until he can build a more suitable home.

"Done with the well?" Annie asks as he walks in.

"Yup. It's dug and producing water," he says, then adds, "I don't know how Josef finds the best place to dig. He claims it's a gut feeling. I say he's just plain lucky."

"What's that?" Annie asks, pointing at the paper in Vaclav's hand.

"It's from Frantiska. Some preacher stopped by Anton's place yesterday. Josef at first ran him off, but I guess Frannie took off running down the road after him and coaxed him back."

"Oh my, I bet that was embarrassing," says Annie.

"You could say that," answers Vaclav, shaking his head. "But you know how Josef is. Anyway, this is something the preacher left for them. It's some kind of letter, I think. I haven't really looked at it yet. Frannie said she tried to read it, but she thought maybe it would make more sense to you."

Annie gazes down at the page. "Francis Kun. That's the preacher's name. It says he's trying to build a church building."

"Yes. That's what Josef told me. And you can imagine he wasn't too keen on that idea."

"I don't suppose," she answers as she continues reading.

"It says he has a congregation of the Evangelical Brethren over past the Shuey homestead near a village called Banner Valley. I'm not sure where that is."

"Josef told me it's east of here. Too far away for us to be interested, as if Josef would be interested anyway. But Frannie showed interest, it seems."

Annie begins to read aloud. *"Dear Brethren and sons of Bohemian and Moravian kin. We turn to you in confidence, in hope that you will not deny your real brotherly attention to this proposition— —that we will put this affair, about which the minds of many of us from the very first step onto the soil of America were concerned, the realization of which we ardently desired, but until now without results, before you and upon your hearts."*

"What's he talking about?" Vaclav asks.

"Wow. This guy obviously has a lot of education. Perhaps too much," Annie says with a chuckle, adding, "Basically, he's saying that they—I guess he means his parishioners—are proposing something they've been wanting to do for a long time."

"Then why didn't he just say that?"

"And listen to this next part," Annie says. *"Brethren and descendants of the tribe, whose God-fearing deeds will forever remain written in the book of history with deserved recognition of praise, is it necessary to draw your attention to the need, to the advantage, and to the excellent influence of such a building upon the betterment of our community? Because this need speaks for itself, we omit all types of justifications and enticements and put before your loving consideration only the following.* There's a mouthful."

"I have no idea what he's talking about. Does he think people around here can understand that?"

"Well, apparently he thinks this will drum up support—money, that is—to build his church."

Vaclav shakes his head, saying, "Well then, maybe it would be better if he spoke like a normal person, don't you think?"

"It doesn't really matter, does it? Not as far as we're concerned, anyway," Annie says.

"What do you mean?"

"Until we get on our feet, we're not donating to anything. You can be sure of that."

"But I'd sure like to see a church built where we could attend regularly. Wouldn't you?" Vaclav says.

"Sure," says Annie, "but his congregation is well to the east, right? That won't do us much good, will it? Now if they were to have a church much closer, that would be different. Or maybe if we could someday get a horse team and wagon, we'd be able to attend the reverend's church at least once in a while."

"Well, it just so happens that Joe Coufal will lend us a team and wagon to use in our new business partnership," Vaclav says smugly.

"Business partnership?"

"Yup. We're gonna be digging some wells."

CHAPTER 47

IT'S A CRISP AND BRIGHT NOVEMBER AFTERNOON, and I stand in front of Banner Valley Church, greeting my flock as they happily file up the steps and into the narthex. The Bureses are here. So are the Lorenc and Janko families. Here comes the Zvacek clan, and soon, all the usual families have found their usual seats in the sanctuary. Joe and Barbora Coufal are here, too. Not a big surprise. I know they're close with the Zachs and Rejmans and wouldn't want to miss the baptisms.

It's almost time for the service to begin, but I continue to wait outside. They should be here anytime. At least, they told me they'd show. I hope Josef hasn't somehow disrupted the plan. That wouldn't surprise me. If that happens, I suppose we can . . . no, wait. Is that a wagon coming down the road? I watch as the rig finally nears, and I can see Josef and Vaclav with their families huddled together on the crude wagon, with the children all bundled up against the November chill.

I watch as Josef pulls up hard on the reins, bringing his team to a dusty halt. Vaclav quickly jumps off and helps everyone else off the wagon.

"Are we late?" Vaclav asks.

"Just in time," I answer as I direct everyone up the steps into the church. Everyone, that is, except for Josef, who remains sitting atop the wagon. "Coming, Josef?" I ask.

"Don't think so, Reverend."

"Suit yourself," I say plainly as I turn and ascend the steps.

Our small choir is singing *To Avert from Men God's Wrath,* one of my favorite hymns, written by our great reformer, Jan Hus. I direct Josef and Vaclav's families to seats in the front pews and then take my place next to the pulpit, waiting for the choir to finish the final verse, *". . . thus we may in all our ways show forth our Redeemer's praise."*

After short readings from Jeremiah 23 and Luke 1, I dive right into my sermon. It's the Sunday before Thanksgiving, and there is much to be thankful for. As I speak, I look out over my small congregation, a congregation that's grown steadily these past few years. They have grown in numbers, yes, but more importantly, in their faith—and this amid the efforts of the many nonbelievers who continually scoff at our devotion to God's word. Indeed, this devotion is something for which I give thanks, and as I preach about this, I see nothing but the radiant faces of the men and women sitting before me, awash in the promise of God's grace.

Then I see something else. As I glance out the side window, I see Josef still atop the wagon, a blanket wrapped tightly around him, sitting and watching his horses nuzzle in the dirt for grass. I'm at once sorry for him. And sorry for me too, for I have not been able to lead him toward the light, God's light. I feel somehow that I've let him down. Sadly, he just sits out there on his wagon, an outsider who doesn't realize that his redemption is just steps away.

I'm still thinking about this as I bring his family and Vaclav's family up to the front of the sanctuary for the sacrament of baptism. Terezie and Wesley will be baptized today, but Josef will not take part in it. I wonder if there will come a time when he regrets his absence from his daughter's ascension into Christ's care.

The service ends, and I watch as the wagons drive away carrying my flock, all satiated and replenished in their faith and hopefully girded against any temptations they may encounter in the coming week. I find it odd that our five elders have stayed behind, their families patiently waiting at their wagons for them. Joe Coufal is here, too.

"Is there something we need to discuss?" I ask, wondering if I've forgotten about a scheduled meeting.

"Well, not exactly discuss," says Jan Janko. "Just a possible solution to a problem."

"What do you mean?"

Janko signals for Coufal to join us, saying, "Joe here has a suggestion regarding our problem."

"Problem?"

Coufal explains, "I understand you're having trouble finding an adequate mason to supervise the laying of the foundation for your church."

"True," I answer. So that's the problem we're talking about.

"You may want to speak with Josef Zach about that. He's been digging wells for a few settlers around here. I've seen his stone work, and it's excellent."

"Josef?" I ask, surprised by the suggestion. I'm to ask him to do this? How will he react to that request? I wonder. He might just refuse. He certainly won't be offering his services for free, that's for sure. All of these things are crowding my thoughts as I struggle to make an appropriate response.

"What do you think?" Janko finally asks.

Presently having no other options, I answer, "Well, I suppose all I can do is ask him."

"You just baptized his daughter today," Janko reminds me. "Perhaps he'll donate his time or at least give us a good price for the work."

"We'll see," I respond weakly.

The next day, I ride toward Josef's place. No sense in putting this off. We've been searching for weeks for a competent mason. The only one we've found thus far lives in Cedar Rapids, and he's shown little interest in traveling so far to our work site with plenty of work in town to keep him busy. I wonder if Josef will show the same reluctance.

After all, it's about the same distance between the church and Anton's place, where Josef's family still lives.

Turning onto the bottom road, I see Vaclav and Annie's cabin across the field to the left, and I decide to pause to check in on them. As I approach their home, Vaclav is doing some work on the cabin's exterior. I know exactly what he's doing. It's the same thing I do about this time each year—check for openings in the walls that may have appeared over the summer. Leaving any of these cracks unfilled will serve as a hearty welcome for any insistent winter wind seeking to invade the inner warmth of the cabin.

"Hello, Vaclav," I say, dismounting.

"Reverend," he says as he continues poking at the gaps in the wall.

"Just thought I'd see how you all are doing."

"Annie and Wesley are inside. They're doing OK, I guess. You can go in if you want to. She's doing some mending, I think."

"Actually, I'm on my way to see Josef. We're looking for a mason to supervise the construction of the foundation for the new church."

"So, you found a place to build?"

"Oh yes. It's just up the road a piece from the parsonage. We bought a couple of acres from Frank Truhlar. Know him?"

"Afraid not. So you're looking for Josef? You won't find him at home. He's starting a well project over at the Dlouhy place. I'm going over there later to help him with it," Vaclav says, and then points. "If you keep heading down that direction on the bottom road, you'll go right by the place. It's not far."

"Let me ask you something, Vaclav. You know Josef better than anyone. Do you think he'll accept the job?"

"Um, I don't know. All you can do is ask him. But you know how he is. Josef won't do it for free. You can be sure of that."

"I'm not expecting him to. I just want the job done right."

"Well then, he's your man," Vaclav states. "I've been helping him with his well and chimney work, and he's quite good at it. If he does take the job, I'll probably be helping him, and although he won't offer it, I'll be happy to do the work for no pay. We appreciate you baptizing little Wesley."

"That's very generous. I'm sure the Lord will find your contribution more than adequate. Bless you, Vaclav."

I spot Josef standing waist-deep in a hole at the Dlouhy homestead. He's leaning against his shovel handle and seems to be talking to himself. I at once wonder if this might be a bad time to disturb him. But I've come all this way, so here goes.

"Josef, good day to you," I call from the road. I want to keep my distance in case he decides to throw something at me, like that shovel. He looks up but doesn't respond, and resumes his digging as if I'm not here. I cautiously dismount and lead my mare to where he's hard at work. "I've come at the behest of the church elders, Josef."

"Why is that?" he asks, looking up and finally acknowledging my presence. "Did I do something to offend them?"

He's sneering at me now, and I fear that his attempt at humor is also some kind of challenge. I'm not sure how to respond, so I change the subject. "It was good to see your family at our church yesterday. Your little Terezie is certainly a beautiful child."

"What do you want, Reverend?" Josef asks as he continues his digging.

All business. OK, here goes. "We're moving ahead with the construction of the new church, and we need someone who can help us with the foundation. I've heard that you're just the person to do it. Interested?"

Josef stops his digging and looks up at me. "Depends."

"We're willing to pay," I say, reading his mind.

"Seventy-five dollars," he says abruptly before he resumes digging.

He must be thinking that I'll go away if he gives me an outlandish price. I won't. We need the work done, and what Josef doesn't know is that the church may be a larger building than he realizes. We expected his price to be in this range.

"Done," I say.

He immediately stops digging and looks up at me, rather perturbed. "And that's not counting the cost of stone and mortar," he adds.

"Of course not," I say, knowing that Joe Coufal has already offered stone from his quarry for free. "We've got that covered."

"I'll want Vaclav to help me, too. My pay won't include his compensation."

"No problem," I say, smiling, knowing Vaclav will donate his time.

I can see that he's thinking about my offer as he gazes down the bottom road. Finally, he turns to me and says, "OK, I guess I can do that. Paid in advance?"

"How about fifty-fifty?" I answer, not wanting to be too agreeable. "Half up front, half when you're done."

"OK. I guess that's fair," he replies slowly. "We begin first thing next spring, I imagine."

"You imagine correctly, my friend," I say, extending my hand and waiting unsuccessfully for him to shake it.

I wonder why Josef is so angry. Why do I seem to offend him so? Is it simply because I am a preacher, representing the God he rejects? But his wife and his friend Vaclav are believers. Certainly, he doesn't treat them this way, does he? I've seen men like him in the past. Men in Moravia who came back from those interminable Austrian wars, men whose lives were forever changed. They too were angry, often aggressive, and prone to erratic behavior. Has Josef suffered as those men suffered? I have no way of knowing, and I will not ask him. Who knows? Maybe it isn't war that has done this to him at all. Maybe his defiance was bred solely by the persecution he suffered in the old country at the hands of those vile Habsburgs. Either way, it doesn't matter. I will do the only thing I can to help find the good in him. I will show him kindness and patience. And I will pray for him. I have to believe that there is a good man in there somewhere that's trying to get out.

CHAPTER 48

JOSEF HAS HEARD that the winters can be harsh on the plains of eastern Iowa. There's an Indian story he's heard recounting winter blizzards so fierce you could flush a prairie chicken out of the prairie grass and watch it freeze solid before it could land. He doubts this story's validity, and yet he understands the respect owed to the forbidding and often dangerous winter season. However, this winter has been different. As winters go, the winter of '66 has proven to be a mild one so far. So mild, in fact, that he and Vaclav have extended their well-digging enterprise into the first week of December, resulting in unanticipated income—additional reserves for their nest eggs.

Because of their savings, both men are already thinking about the genuine possibility of improving their living conditions come spring. Josef has suffered the strain of his family's cohabitating with Anton and Rose in that small sod hovel. And Vaclav has suffered no less in Coufal's ancient log structure, which seems to be in a continual state of disrepair. Even as the snow falls on the lifeless Iowa River bottomland, spirits are high for these two men, for they know their futures might be bright ones.

Their dream of a better life begins to take shape as April rolls around, and Vaclav gets word of a land agent setting up shop in Western, a small town located just to the northeast. Vaclav and Josef are soon on their way to Western atop Joe Coufal's wagon. They seek to find out whatever they can about this Homestead Act that they've heard so much about, and they hope they haven't missed their chance to claim some of the free, or at least cheap, farmland for their own.

They've both been through Western before. That was when they traveled to Banner Valley Church on the day Wesley and Terezie were baptized. Western is a small but impressive settlement with a few grand two-story houses and even a college, aptly named Western College. The extensive college grounds boast a large stone building, reaching three stories, surrounded by numerous smaller buildings. The post office in Western is much more modest, and they might have ridden right past it but for the flag displayed out front. Soon, Josef and Vaclav are inside the small building standing in front of a desk where a short man is filling out forms.

"We're here to claim some land. The government land?" Josef says.

"You're too late," says the land agent, curtly. "All the U.S. land has been claimed around here. You'd have to go much further to the west to find any of that."

"West? We don't want to go west. We want to stay right here!" Josef cries. "We were told there was farmland available for the taking!"

"Well, if you had shown up a couple of years ago, maybe…"

"What are we gonna do, Josef?" Vaclav asks with a look of despair.

The land agent raises both hands into the air with a submissive gesture, saying, "Hold on just a second. There are some tracts for sale by previous owners, people who decided to move on to the west or return out east. What area are you interested in? Here, take a look at this map," he says as he gets up and walks to a large table where a map is carefully displayed.

Josef tries but can't make sense of this intricate map, with all its undecipherable lines and numbers. "Can you figure this out, Vaclav?" he asks. Vaclav just shakes his head. He doesn't think he's seen a map like this before. Actually, when has he ever seen any map? he wonders.

"We live just west of the Joe Coufal place," Josef says. "You know the place?"

"Ah, yes. I know Joe," the man says as he puts his finger on the map. "His place is right there."

"Is there any available land near there that borders the river?" Vaclav asks.

"Afraid not. Joe owns a lot of that. Some speculators claimed more of it further west. But look over here," he points. "There are a couple of tracts for sale just north of the river. Here are two separate tracts, both about 80 acres. The owners are asking 15 dollars per acre."

Vaclav and Josef are silent for several seconds before the land agent loses patience and does the calculation for them. "That comes to $1200 for each tract. But you can pay it in four installments if you want."

Vaclav and Josef look at each other, both considering this unexpected cost. They had originally thought they would be able to claim government land for next to nothing. But now they wonder if they can afford it.

"We each have enough for the first installment, don't we?" Vaclav finally asks.

"I think so. It's a bit more if I remember right," says Josef.

"Can we purchase the land through your office?" Vaclav asks the agent.

"Yes, but don't you two want to at least go take a look?"

"Oh, I suppose we should. We wouldn't want to buy a piece of swampland or a mountainside," replies Josef, as Vaclav nods in agreement.

"You won't find either of those in these parts, but you should at least go look. I'll take you out there if you'd like."

Within moments, Josef and Vaclav are back on the wagon following the land agent on his horse. They head west past Isaac Shuey's place and further on across the stage line road. Then they turn south along a narrow dirt path.

They don't notice many homesteads along the road—only a couple of uncompleted cabins. Curious about this, Josef calls to the agent, "Where are the owners of those cabins?"

"Those are most likely abandoned. A lot of homesteaders have a tough time making it. Many of them just give up and leave, going back to wherever they came from."

"Can we buy these plots?"

"No. They've mostly been sold off to speculators or other landowners in the area. But we don't have far to go to the available lots I told you about."

Soon they arrive at the first location. This is rich farmland—Vaclav at once recognizes that. He'll be able to grow an abundant crop of whatever he chooses here in this fertile soil. As the agent leads them along the eastern edge of the property, Vaclav notes the rolling hills of the property, not unlike his farm back in Budislav. Yes, he thinks, this will be just fine. Soon they come to a stop at a tall wooden stake.

"This is the northeast corner," the agent says. "The tract stretches west and south of here—80 acres of somewhat hilly but tillable land, plus some timberland up on that hill."

Vaclav can't help but slip into a dream-like state, imagining what it would be like to live here—a small creek running through the length of the tract, a wooded area essential for his construction needs, a stand of oaks and maples by the road, where he could build a house for Annie and little Wesley. This would be just fine, he decides.

"Ready to move on to the next tract?" the agent finally says, stirring Vaclav from his reverie.

They travel down the road about a half mile to the next one. The topography is a bit flatter here, thus more easily cultivated, and there are fewer trees. Fortunately, the same creek running through the other tract also flows through this one on its way to the Iowa River.

"These are both 80 acres of really prime farmland. A bit hilly, but still very farmable," says the land agent. "So, what do you think?"

Josef and Vaclav have no need for a discussion. Both have already made up their minds. This will be perfect, they are thinking. There is only one question remaining.

"So, which one do you want?" Vaclav asks Josef. "The one with the better woods, or the one closer to the river?"

"I don't care."

"Neither do I. You pick."

"No. You pick. It's all the same to me."

"But why do I have to be the one to choose?"

"'Cause I said so, that's why."

"You're *hloupý*, Josef."

"I'm *hloupý*? No, you're the *hloupý* one!"

The land agent has had enough. "Look, I don't really have all day to listen to you two bicker," he says, reaching into his pocket. "Here—I have a coin." He points at Josef, saying, "Heads, you get this tract; tails, your friend gets it. OK?"

That settles it. The coin flip comes up heads, and Josef will claim the tract closest to the river. Vaclav will claim the land he's already daydreamed about. He's fine with that. Soon they are following the land agent back to Western to complete the paperwork for their claims.

They drive back toward Western in silence, Josef and Vaclav deep in their own thoughts: Josef hoping he will be a better farmer here than he was in Budislav, and Vaclav already making plans for the home he will build among the maples and oaks. They continue north to the corner that will take them east to Western, and Josef finally breaks the silence. "You're still *hloupý*, Vaclav," he says, smiling.

"Not as *hloupý* as you," Vaclav replies wryly.

"Well, Vaclav, we may both be *hloupý*, but at least we are about to be *hloupý* landowners. Just think about that," Josef replies as he snaps the reins, encouraging the horses on toward Western.

Back at the post office, Josef and Vaclav are soon filling out promissory notes for $300 and paying a few more for filing fees and to the land agent for his commission. Josef and Vaclav soon walk out of the Western post office and head for home with their documents proudly in hand. They're confident that they can continue digging wells to pay future installments, and in the meantime, can begin construction on their new homes. Josef and Vaclav have no doubt they can achieve all of this. After all, Josef has expertise in carpentry and masonry, and Vaclav can make sure they both get off on the right foot in their farming efforts.

CHAPTER 49

IT'S MID-APRIL, and I've seen neither hide nor hair of Josef's family. Of course, that's no surprise. While the winter was fairly mild, it was still winter, and traveling all that way to church during the cold season can be a significant dissuader, especially for someone like Josef, who can be dissuaded most easily.

I find it necessary to remind Josef about the church foundation, so I ride to Anton and Rose's house to prompt him a bit and perhaps suggest a date to begin construction—the sooner the better.

As I approach the Novak cabin, I can see Rose, Anton, and Frantiska working outdoors, cleaning up debris left by the swirling winter winds. I don't see Josef anywhere, but Vincencie and Antonin are there playing with Terezie near the open cabin door.

Dismounting, I greet Rose who is nearby raking up the scattered leaves and sticks in the yard. "Good afternoon, Rose. How's the spring cleanup going?" I say, approaching her.

"Hello. We're doing just fine," she answers with a bright smile.

"It's been awhile since I've seen you. Perhaps, now that the weather is more agreeable, I'll see you in church."

"Church? Oh, yes. We go to our church sometimes."

Confused for a moment, I wonder what she means. Of course she goes to church sometimes. I take note of her attendance whenever she does. In fact, I pay close attention to everyone who attends my church. It's not like I'm judging people by their attendance record; I just like to pay attention to things like that. OK, so maybe I *am* a bit judgmental with these observations. But isn't regular church attendance necessary to maintaining one's faith? Certainly, it is. Besides, if I note that one of my parishioners is faltering in attendance, isn't it my duty to make every effort to bring them back into my flock? It surely is. So, in the end, keeping close tabs on the comings and goings of my people is crucial to my godly evangelical mission, is it not? I have no doubt that it is. No doubt at all.

"Yes, Rose. And perhaps I'll see you at our church again soon," I offer.

"But we already go to another church. It's over near Banner Valley," she answers. "So we won't be going to your church."

"Banner Valley? That *is* our church. The church of the Reformed Brethren, right?" I ask her, confused by this entire conversation.

"Oh yes, that's our church. Yes, we'll be going there soon," she says.

"Hi, Reverend," Anton says as he approaches to join us. "Come, Rose. Let's go back to help Frantiska with that raking, shall we?" He grasps Rose's arm, directing her back to where she was raking up sticks and leaves when I arrived. I watch as she resumes her work, and Anton comes back to speak with me. "She's been like this lately."

"She didn't seem to recognize me. Is it her eyesight?" I ask.

"No. She can see just fine. It's her memory. She doesn't seem to remember things. She even forgets who I am sometimes."

"Oh my," is all I can think to say.

"I hardly noticed it at first. It kind of grew worse over the winter. At first, I thought things just slipped her mind. You know, things like tasks she had planned to do or the name of a neighbor. But this past winter, I've noticed it getting much worse. I'm not sure what to do about it."

I really don't know what to tell him. I, too, once had someone in my life who began forgetting things. It was my dear mother, in Moravia. There was nothing we could do about it but watch her gradually drift further and further away from reality. By the time she died, I don't think she knew any of the family members surrounding her deathbed. It was heartbreaking.

"I'm so sorry, Anton. Maybe now, with spring here, she will show some improvement. But you can be sure, Anton, that I shall pray for her," I say, knowing this is of little consolation to him.

Frantiska lays her rake against the house and walks to join us, saying, "Beautiful day, isn't it, Reverend?"

"It surely is. How was your winter?"

"Oh, you know. We made it through, I guess, and everyone is doing well," she says, then adds, "Well, except for poor Rose."

"Yes, I understand," I answer.

"What brings you around today?" Frantiska asks.

"Oh, I was hoping to speak with Josef about the church foundation. Is he around?"

"No, sorry. He left this morning to get some supplies in town. He should be back soon. Would you like to have me give him a message?"

"Oh, I suppose you could just tell him I'd like to get started on the project as soon as we can."

"OK, I'll tell him. But I wouldn't be surprised if you meet him on the road, and you can tell him yourself. As I said, I expect him back any time now."

"Thanks. I'll be watching for him. It was good seeing you. And I hope to see you at church soon," I say as I look toward Rose to give her a wave. She waves her hand in return, offering a smile—the kind of smile I imagine she might offer to any friendly stranger.

As Frantiska predicted, I ride no further than about a half mile when I see Josef driving in my direction. His wagon is loaded with a variety of shovels, picks, and something else——some kind of contraption I don't recognize.

"Hi, Josef," I call as he pulls his rig to a stop.

"Afternoon, Reverend," Josef replies bluntly.

"I just came out to see you."

"I figured you'd be here any day now. I guess you want to know when we can get started on the church. Don't worry, Vaclav and I will get over there in the next week or two."

"That's good news, Josef. I'll let the elders know."

"I'll also need my first payment, of course."

"Of course."

I look at the contraption in the back of the wagon and ask, "What's that thing you've got back there?"

"It's a drill. I got it from a guy in town who showed me how to use it for construction. It's for putting in wooden pegs to secure wall beams."

"What're you building?"

"Vaclav and I purchased some farmland just to the west of here. We'll be building there soon, but don't worry. We'll make sure we divide our time between our homesteads and your foundation."

"OK, I guess that's fine. But I hope we can finish the foundation and start on the church building itself sometime this summer."

"Shouldn't be a problem, Reverend."

"OK, good. It was nice to see you, Josef. I'll look forward to seeing that foundation take shape," I say as I dig my heels against my horse's haunches.

"I got something in town today," I hear Josef say, and I pull the animal to a halt, looking back.

"Oh?" I answer, wondering where this is going.

"I stopped at a tavern for a refreshment—"

"You mean a beer?" I interrupt.

"Yes, a beer. You're not going to give me a sermon, are you?" Josef asks defensively.

I decide not to rile him. What would be the point? "No, Josef. I'm not," I say.

"The bartender gave me this," Josef says as he pulls something off his wagon seat, handing it to me. It seems to be some kind of newspaper. It's entitled *Pokrok*. I haven't seen this before, but I immediately recognize the name of the publisher—Frank Zdrubek, a man who has come to my attention as one who's been spreading anti-religious ideas. I've been hearing a lot about him lately. He calls himself a freethinker, and I've heard he's been presenting public speeches at the new Reading Society Hall in town.

"Is this new? I haven't seen this publication before."

"The guy said it just started coming out this week."

"Have you read it yet?" I ask, knowing what it must contain.

"No, but the bartender told me a lot about Zdrubek. I find his ideas quite interesting, and I have to say that I agree with a lot of 'em," Josef says. "Do you know of this Zdrubek?"

He is staring at me, waiting for my reaction, so I say, "I do, Josef, and I will tell you I disagree with most of what he professes. If I'm not mistaken, he seems to think that religion is unnecessary, and that man, not God, is the ultimate being in this world, the central figure. I don't believe that, do you?"

"I don't know for sure. But it makes a lot of sense to me."

"Hmm, well, just be careful, Josef. This stuff may sound compelling, but it can't answer all of life's questions."

"Like what?" Josef asks.

Now what do I do? I ask myself. Am I to sit here on this horse all day addressing the multitude of life's questions I'm thinking about at this moment? I say, "Look, Josef. This is probably not the time for this discussion. To be quite frank, you are probably going to like a lot of what Zdrubek has to say. It will seem logical to you, but remember this—man did not create this world. And if man didn't, then who did? Think on that for a while, and then we'll talk again, OK?" I encourage my horse forward, only to be interrupted by Josef once again.

"Hmm. But where's your proof? You don't have any. Hell, it could have been God, or it could have been the man on the moon. Who knows?" he continues, forcing me to pull back on the reins again.

I'm getting impatient now. I shouldn't let impatience affect me, but I see so much evidence of God around me every single day that I find Josef's question of proof to be a bit irritating.

"Open your eyes, Josef! The proof is all around you."

"It is? Where?"

"Look, Josef. I'm sorry. I can't convince you of God's grace any more than you can convince me otherwise."

"I suppose not."

"But before I ride on, I have one question for you."

"What's that?"

"Have you ever sinned?" I ask him.

"Uh, well, let's see . . . I'll have to think about that . . ."

"Of course you've sinned, Josef," I declare, exasperated.

"How could you possibly know that?" he protests.

"Because every man has sinned, Josef. And if you fail to ask Jesus for the forgiveness of those sins, you'll carry those sins with you for the entirety of your life. Frank Zdrubek won't be able to help you with that, will he?"

One last time, I urge my horse forward, and this time I keep on riding, hoping that I've at least planted a small seed in Josef's mind. While my godly faith resonates in me with the visceral reverberation of a Magyar drum, Josef's faith is something he examines with curiosity and trepidation, as if he's holding a sleeping opossum by the tail at arm's length, afraid of looking too closely, lest the creature might awaken and bite him on the nose. I have no doubt that Josef and I will speak again, and I hope that when we do, I can bring him closer to seeing God as I do.

A week later, I'm standing outside the parsonage, avoiding the commotion caused inside by the children. It's impossible to write my sermons under these conditions. So these days, when the din of the children's play overtakes me, I just come outside to clear my head and put my thoughts in order before returning to my desk to jot them down. Our family has grown considerably in the last several years since we arrived here. Six children—that's the size of our brood now. Karel, Julie, Vilim, Ludvik, Sophia, and Godfrey. And now Aneta is with child again. Sometimes I wonder if it will ever end; other times, I am thankful to the Lord for the blessings of these little ones.

I see a wagon approaching from the south, and soon I recognize Josef driving his team and wagon with Vaclav sitting next to him. Why didn't they stop at the site of the new church and get to work on that foundation? I wonder.

"We have a problem," Josef says as he pulls the team to a halt, failing to exchange any niceties.

"What do you mean? Didn't you see the supplies we put there for you? The stone, lime, and sand?"

"Sure, we saw 'em. But there's no water. We need access to water for the mortar."

"Oh. I hadn't thought about that. Let's see," I say, thinking. "I could maybe bring some buckets of water from the creek behind my house."

"Or we could just dig a well," Vaclav suggests matter-of-factly.

"A what?" cries Josef. "We don't have time for that. We need to get going on that foundation!"

"You'll need a well eventually, won't you, Reverend?" Vaclav asks.

"Well, yes, I guess we will," I answer.

"We could dig that for you. Then we'll have plenty of water for our work on the church foundation."

"Now wait, Vaclav," Josef exclaims. "That wasn't part of the deal."

"What would it cost?" I ask, knowing that money is the source of Josef's protest.

"Oh geez. I don't know," says Josef, sounding less hostile. "I suppose we could do it for . . . maybe . . . thirty bucks, but it will put us back a few days."

"How about twenty-five? That'll bring your total to an even one hundred. Deal?" I bargain.

Josef thinks for a moment, and then says, "No. I don't think so. Maybe you could get one of your flock to dig that well. Otherwise, it's gonna cost you thirty." Josef knows as well as I do that competent well diggers are in short supply these days.

"Oh, come on, Josef," Vaclav says. "It's for the church, for goodness' sake."

"Thirty bucks. Take it or leave it," Josef declares defiantly.

"OK, fine," I say with a sigh. "Thirty dollars."

"In advance," Josef adds.

"My God, Josef," cries Vaclav. "Give the man a break!"

"No, it's OK, Vaclav. I'll pay him in advance. No problem," I say, knowing I'll receive no favors from Josef today—or maybe ever.

CHAPTER 50

SOON, JOSEF AND VACLAV ARE BACK at the construction site exploring the area for the location of the new well. Suddenly, Josef stops dead in his tracks, saying, "This spot will do. Go get the shovels and then tote some of those blocks over here while I start digging."

"What's so perfect about this spot?" Vaclav asks. "It's no different from any of the other spots we've looked at."

"I just have a good feeling about this spot. I just know things you wouldn't understand."

"I wouldn't understand? That's *hloupý*!" Vaclav challenges. He's having fun now.

"You calling me *hloupý*? Look, we've been through this before, Vaclav, and I think I've clearly proved that you're the *hloupý* one."

"Why am I the *hloupý* one?"

"Because if you had it your way, we'd be digging this well for free! That makes you *hloupý*."

Vaclav can't argue any further with Josef. It's true. He is willing to dig this well for free. Does that make him *hloupý*––make him stupid? He wonders about that as he turns to walk back toward the wagon in search of the shovels.

For most people, a considerable amount of animosity would linger after such an exchange. But there are no hard feelings between these two men. They have been together for enough years to develop a relationship that withstands any personal affront from such verbal jousting. To them, these arguments have simply become a sport, an entertainment that helps them pass the time and, in doing so, further cement the strength of their friendship. In no time at all, they are working together as usual, taking turns digging the new well as if nothing unpleasant has been said between them.

It takes four days to dig the well and construct the well winch. To Vaclav's surprise, and admitted disappointment, the well yields some water at only a nine-foot depth. It's not much, but it will be sufficient for their needs, and the work on the foundation can begin.

The next day, they arrive early to get started. They will have additional help tomorrow from some parishioners, but today Josef and Vaclav will dig up enough sod to mark the entire perimeter of the foundation. That will make for more efficient excavation tomorrow by the additional workers. It's the perfect time of year for this type of labor. The sky is clear, exposing the full intensity of the sun, but a cool April breeze seems to negate its effect. Josef and Vaclav work throughout the morning and afternoon, mostly in silence, until Vaclav says, "I have something to ask you."

"What?" Josef says, without looking up from his digging.

"I don't mean to pry, but Annie tells me you and Frannie are having some problems. What's going on, Josef?"

"Oh, it's nothing really. Frantiska and I . . . you might say we had a bit of a spat."

"What brought that on?"

"It all started when I brought that newspaper home for her to read to me."

"Newspaper? What newspaper?"

"Oh, it was just a thing published by a guy named Zdrubek. He's one of those freethinkers you've probably heard about."

"What happened?" Vaclav asks.

"Oh, you know Frantiska. She gets all worked up over nothing. She didn't like what Zdrubek wrote in the newspaper. We had a bit of a tiff, and she ended up throwing the paper into the fireplace. She made a big thing of it and said if I brought anything like that in the house again, I'd be sleeping outside. She's kind of a hothead sometimes."

"Well, at least she didn't throw you out."

"No, but now I find myself sleeping on the floor instead of in our bed."

"Hmm, that must have been quite a spat."

"I guess so, but I should be able to have my own opinions, shouldn't I? This whole religion thing is for the birds. I told her so."

"Uh-oh. I'll bet that went over big with Frantiska," Vaclav says with ample sarcasm.

"I should have a right to express my beliefs just as she has a right to express hers, don't you think?"

"Well, that depends, Josef."

"On what? What Frank Zdrubek has to say makes perfect sense. And I figured Frantiska was a reasonable person. I figured she'd get it. But as it turns out, she's as brainwashed as all those other fools in Kun's church."

"Fools? Who are you calling fools?"

"Oh, you know, Vaclav. Those fools who will do whatever that preacher says, and do it for free, like those guys coming tomorrow to help us. You can bet they're offering their labor for nothing. At least you and I have smarts enough to demand a fee for our work."

"Uh, well . . . you see, Josef . . . about that . . ." Vaclav stammers.

"What? What about that?"

"Well, I may have agreed to help out by—."

"Please don't tell me you're one of those fools," Josef interrupts with obvious disgust.

"We need a church, Josef. It's my moral duty to help make it happen."

"Is it your duty to let that preacher have control over you, just like those priests back in Bohemia? When will you ever learn that it's all about power?"

"Power? I don't think so."

"Vaclav. Of course it's about power. But you don't need to do that anymore. We live in a free country now. You're a fool for falling for Kun's scam."

There's a long silence as the two men stand glaring at one another. Then Vaclav finally lays his shovel down and approaches Josef. Josef at once steps back, wondering if Vaclav might do something rash. But his friend will do him no harm. He simply wishes to make his point clear.

"Look, Josef," Vaclav says softly. "You may think we're all fools, but what does it matter if Frantiska or I or Annie or anyone else believes in the worth of Reverend Kun's vision—the worth of his church? If it makes us happy, what harm is there in that? Look at yourself. Are you happy? There you are, because of your beliefs, forced to sleep on the floor out of reach of the wifely pleasures you would otherwise enjoy. There may be a fool standing here, but it clearly isn't me."

CHAPTER 51
OUR TEMPLE RISES

THE COMPLETION OF THE CHURCH foundation takes much longer than I hoped. The work should have been finished by June or July, but with their own construction underway on their homesteads, Josef and Vaclav have other ideas. Sharing their time between the church's foundation and their own construction causes progress to proceed in fits and starts throughout the summer months. And despite my discreet encouragements, Josef continues to show up at the work site according to his own schedule, a schedule that continues to delay the installation of the walls and roof far into the future.

As late September soon arrives, the foundation is finally almost finished. And on October 1st, I stand with a small group of my parishioners, our coats wrapped snugly around us as we brace ourselves against the fall chill. Assembled next to the church foundation, we wait patiently for the stoneworker and his assistant to show up for our ceremony——the ceremony of laying the cornerstone for our new church.

Finally, as my patience begins to wane, I spot Josef and Vaclav coming down the road. I note that Josef isn't driving his team with any urgency. He's just taking his own sweet time. He must know that the ceremony won't start without him, and he's in no hurry. They finally arrive, and after I offer a prayer and join in the unison hymn-singing by the attendees, we watch as Josef and Vaclav position the stone, mortaring it securely in place. It's a brief ceremony but a significant one. It will only take a couple more days to finish the foundation, and then we'll be ready to build the rest of our temple. Then Josef's employment will come to an end, and he'll receive the last installment of his payment. In the future, I won't be seeing much of him and Vaclav, I'm sure. They no doubt will be committed to the work on their new farms.

As for me, my attention will be directed toward the building of this church. Of course, my direct involvement will be limited. I'm not much of a carpenter, after all. Fortunately, a couple of my parishioners excel at that type of work, and many others are willing to help them. I'll simply stand by, providing encouragement and spiritual guidance—things I do best.

We're far behind schedule, and I've been much disappointed by Josef's lack of urgency with the foundation. I doubt that Vaclav had anything to do with it since Josef was the one in charge. It had to be Josef's doing. As it stands now, we'll be lucky to have the walls up before the first snow falls. After that, who knows how much we can accomplish before spring?

The winter proves to be a harsh one, and construction comes to an abrupt halt in mid-November. For the next 3 months, it's almost unbearable seeing the structure standing there without improvements. If not for Josef's delays, the church walls and roof would be completed by now. But all I can do is sit a wait for the weather to improve. As April finally arrives, the church walls aren't in place yet, but at least we've resumed construction. Unfortunately, as May arrives, suddenly no one can be seen at the construction site. I find the inconsistencies of our efforts quite annoying to say the least and on the following Sunday, I strongly implore my parishioners to rededicate their efforts to our temple. I make a special point to stress their duty as faithful followers of God to make the Church construction their first priority. My frustration must be fully on display, for I notice a certain aloofness from my flock as they shuffle out of Banner Valley

Church. Were my exhortations excessive? I wonder. Certainly, they were warranted, weren't they?

Joe Bures is the last to leave the sanctuary, and he pauses just long enough to offer the explanation that suddenly explains everything. "It's planting time," he says, and adds, "Questioning our faith might have been a bit harsh, Reverend."

I'm struck speechless by his comment, not for any disrespect he's shown, but by the painful realization that I've failed to demonstrate one of the most essential traits of any good preacher—patience. For the last several months, I've allowed my frustration to grow, oblivious to the everyday responsibilities of my parishioners. What right do I have to question their contribution to our church when their first obligation is to see to the welfare of their families as they struggle in their day-to-day survival? What good would a church edifice do them if they didn't get their crops planted? Even my earlier criticism of Josef appears unwarranted now that I think about it. Didn't he also have an urgent need to build a proper home for his family? I'm at once ashamed. I've been selfish and vain, putting my wants above everyone else's.

The week passes slowly as I devolve into a depressive state of self-pity. I feel unworthy of my calling as God's representative. Who do I think I am? I'm nothing, really. A man of God? Hardly. Preaching is all I've ever known how to do. But now I realize that I've failed in that calling. Aneta and the children sense my despair as they keep their distance, so as not to rile me. They don't know what might be wrong, but they leave me to work it out on my own. They are wise to do so, seeing me spending most of my time in prayer, for they know God is my best counselor now.

Fortunately, as Sunday approaches, I find myself in a better emotional place. I'm only human after all, I've realized. How can I not exhibit the human frailties of any other man from time to time. Humility is a difficult lesson to learn, but an important one—one especially essential to a man of the cloth.

Sunday finally arrives after a week of painful self-reflection, and I speak to my flock with earnest contrition. I did not recognize their needs—only my own—I tell them. As I stand there speaking, I lay myself bare, for I have wronged them, and I beg for their forgiveness, offering my sincerest apology. I also offer them the promise that, in the future, I will be a worthy partner in our common quest to serve the Lord.

With planting season behind us, the work on our temple resumes with a flurry of activity and our church finally begins to take shape. Joists and rafters are all in place, and the men begin work on the strapping that will support the flat boards for the roof surface. Finally, it's June. The cedar shingles are installed and the wood floor is nearly finished. Pulpit and pews will be arriving soon, much of it donated by other area churches. Things are progressing nicely and it's time for me to decide on a date for the dedication service. I settle on Sunday, July 5, in the year of our Lord 1868. This is just one day shy of the anniversary of the death of Jan Hus, the great founder of our faith. On that day we will dedicate our temple to you, Lord. It will serve as a monument to your abundant grace and guidance, and a testament to our continuing commitment to your Word. O Lord, have mercy on us all, remain that we fear you, recite your commandments, that we reach the goal of our faith, the redemption of our souls, that we soon triumph in heaven where you dwell and reign greatly.

It's early in the morning, and I'm walking the mile from my parsonage to the church. Though excited about the dedication, my excitement is tempered by woozy grogginess from my sleepless night. There's no doubt that today is one of the most important days in my life, and I'm now thinking of the people who came before me—my forebears. I'm sure that the dedication of my First Bohemian Moravian Brethren Church would greatly please my father, the deceased Reverend Charles Kun, who was my most important teacher in all things, both linguistic and spiritual. And I think it would also elicit pride in my grandfather, Count Alexander Kun, one of the brave Magyar Reformed ministers who defied Emperor Joseph's persecution of Protestants in Bohemia and came from Moravia at great risk to minister to the spiritual needs of the people there. My ancestors have indeed set a very high standard for me, but I hope with all my heart that they are smiling down on me today.

I leave Aneta and the children behind, as it's not yet time for them to leave for the service. It's early yet, but I've decided to be the first to arrive in order to spend some time alone in the new sanctuary, reflecting on this important milestone and also taking time to commune with my Lord.

As I approach the church, I am surprised to find that some people have already gathered in the churchyard with their horses tied nearby. These are people I don't recognize. They're huddled together in a group, taking directions from a tall, bearded man. Why are they here so early? Don't they know the service won't start for quite a while?

Several of these people are holding signs, and I now know why they have come. As I walk up to them, the tall man turns and comes to greet me.

"Ah, Reverend Kun. It's so nice to see you. We are—"

"I know who you people are! Why are you here? I hope you don't plan to disrupt our dedication."

"Disrupt? Oh, of course not, Reverend. We're just here to offer another side to your story."

"My story? Do you mean God's story? The true story?"

"As I said, we are here to remind your people that there is an alternative to the hogwash that you are offering them. It's the alternative of reason and logic. Don't you think they should be able to hear it? Don't you think they should be free to choose?"

"I insist that you take your freethinkers and leave the church grounds immediately. You are not welcome here. Go back to Cedar Rapids and stir things up there if you'd like, but not here. Not like this. Please." I'm not sure why I added the pleasantry at the end. Just habit, I guess, but if it helps, so much the better.

"I think we'll stay awhile," the man says. "Maybe hand out some leaflets to your members. How's that sound? Don't worry. We're not here to start a ruckus. Just to inform and teach, like you do."

"This is hardly how I do it," I reply angrily. "Please take your people and go home!"

"I think not," the man answers, calmly but firmly.

"Then at least promise that you won't try to enter our church and that there will be no violence on this holy day."

"There won't be any trouble unless your people start it, Reverend. We're just here to encourage freethinking. That's all."

There's nothing more I can do, so I turn and stomp off without another word, heading up the steps into the church. I walk up the aisle to the first pew and sit down dejectedly. This was going to be a celebration of our big triumph, a triumph for me, my Brethren, and especially for the Lord. But now I have the terrible feeling that our dedication might devolve into something quite ugly. I have faith that my people are peaceful, nonaggressive citizens and won't start anything. But if these freethinkers rudely encroach into our celebration, the celebration that has been so long in coming, I'm not sure what may happen. But what am I to do? All I can do is pray, so I begin, "Dear Lord . . ."

Soon, horses and wagons are arriving, and I rush to the front of the church to greet them. The people file into the church, and I welcome each one of them, while at the same time keeping an eye on the group of protesters who stand nearby with their signs and leaflets. It's a wonder to see the sheer number of faithful arriving. Maybe we should have built a larger church, I think. More and more people tether their horses and teams and join the queue that extends down the road and up the steps to where I stand waiting for them. They all look with concern at the freethinker protesters, but I'm glad to see that they generally ignore them. And when an occasional freethinker tries to hand a leaflet to a parishioner, they are met with a stern refusal. My congregants know what these people are all about. I've warned them. They've heard about their blasphemy and bully tactics, and have no patience for them.

Most of my own parishioners are here, but there are others as well including several members of the Lutheran Church at Banner Valley who have come to join in our celebration. This pleases me greatly, as they have been very supportive of my efforts to serve the faithful. There are also a few people to whom I have preached in homes in and around Cedar Rapids.

As I continue to welcome attendees into the church narthex, the families of Josef and Vaclav arrive, and soon they are standing in line with everyone else. I'm especially surprised to see Josef standing with them. I would have expected him to stay on the wagon waiting for the service to be over. This is encouraging at first. But he's begun to edge his way over to where the freethinkers are assembled. Frantiska follows him and has what she must think is a discreet argument with her husband. But their raised voices defy discretion, and now many people in the queue are staring at them. Abruptly she walks back to her children, leaving Josef behind with his like-minded mob. Poor Josef. When will he see the error of his ways? I wonder.

Soon, the last person enters the portal to the church, leaving just me, Josef, and the protesting contingent outside. I scowl briefly in their direction before I turn and walk through the door, making sure to close it securely before I proceed up the aisle to the chancel.

The church is filled to near capacity, taking my mind back to the day last year when the Banner Valley Church was overflowing with mourners for our dead president. Today is a much more joyous day, and I hope the freethinkers, assembled just outside our open windows, don't change that.

Despite the presence of the freethinkers, spirits are high throughout the congregation this morning. For many of these people, this church is a dream come true, something they worked long and hard to achieve. Their dream has now been realized, and despite the chanting that has begun outside, the excitement in this sanctuary will not be dampened. After a brief call to worship, we plunge headlong into the first hymn, all of us singing loudly in an attempt to drown out the chanters in the churchyard. The hymn finally comes to an end, and it is time for me to proceed with the service. But the chanting continues, and I have no hope of competing with the freethinkers' shouts of "Be free to choose!" or "Don't believe his lies!" or "Be free of religious bondage!"

Elder Bures finally rises from his seat and walks up to the pulpit where I stand in silence, not knowing what to do. He suggests that we shut all the windows, a suggestion that seems logical. But with the church packed to the brim with people, the temperature in the sanctuary is rising rapidly. Without open windows, the stifling heat will become oppressive indeed. I stand there looking at Bures, trying not to stare into the faces of the confused parishioners. What am I to do? I ask myself.

Suddenly, I hear the unmistakable sound of a horse team pulling a rickety wagon, and then the shouts of the crowd outside as the rig drives directly through it, forcing the protesters to run in every direction to escape injury. The rig passes beyond the church windows, out of sight, and the crowd begins to reassemble, but the wagon soon reappears, causing the freethinkers to run to safety yet again. Much of the congregation is standing now, trying to get a glimpse of the goings-on outside. I move closer to the window in time to see the rig pass for a third time, and I can see Josef snapping the reins, urging his team through the group of protesters, making them scatter with exasperated shouts. Soon, several of the men in attendance leave the church, running to their own rigs. They follow Josef's lead, circling the church with their wagons and preventing the mob from taking other positions. Frustrated, the protesters have no choice but to retreat to their horses and head home.

Soon, a general calm has replaced the din of the earlier mob action, and everyone is sitting in their pews as if nothing out of the ordinary has happened. They look at me with fresh expectation, waiting to hear what I have to say.

"This is a joyous day," I begin. "The day the Lord has made. On this glorious day, we worship in our own temple. Not under a tree, nor in a rented building, nor in one of your homes, but in the Lord's house, a product of our enduring faith, built by our sweat and toil, ensured by our prayers. Let us, in this momentous occasion, turn to God. Lord, please be open-eared as we invoke you to bless your holy church here on Earth and make it victorious against the devil's deceit, sin, and power. Glorify it within all nations so that the world may be filled with your glory. O Lord, have mercy with us all, remain that we reach the goal of our faith and soon triumph in heaven, where you dwell and reign greatly. In the name of the Father and Holy Spirit. Amen."

The rest of the service goes without a hitch, and I am satisfied that we have properly consecrated our holy place. As I watch the people file out of our new church, I am confident that this edifice will be a haven for our faithful for many generations to come. I realize how truly blessed I am to have come to this place to lead this small flock, and I have every confidence that it will soon grow to fill this building for the glory of God.

As the last congregant leaves the church, I scan the grounds to see if Josef has left yet, and can see that he's just now helping his family onto the wagon. Hurrying down the steps, I walk quickly to catch him before he drives away.

"Josef, excuse me—just a moment, please," I call as I approach.

He holds his team in place, waiting for me to catch my breath, and I say, "I want to thank you for what you did today. You saved the day. Saved the dedication."

"Don't think too much of it. I just thought they were being rude, that's all," he says plainly. "It doesn't mean I don't agree with their ideas. I just don't think they need to express them in that way."

"Well, thanks anyway, Josef. You know, they say God acts in mysterious ways. It seems to me that perhaps God was working through you today. What do you think of that?"

"What do I think? I think it's nonsense. That's what I think. The way I see it, I put about as much work into this building as anyone. I just figured it deserved a proper dedication, that's all. Don't build my actions up to be anything beyond that, Reverend."

"OK, Josef, whatever you say," I state, smiling. Turning to Frantiska, I ask, "So what do you think, Frantiska? Was Josef acting at God's behest?"

She glances over at Josef and replies glumly, "It seems to me that if Josef is doing God's work, perhaps the Almighty should reconsider his hiring standards."

"Hmm. I don't know, Frantiska. I think this man may surprise you one day."

Josef has had enough, and he grunts, "Are you two gonna keep talking about me, or can we leave now?"

I step away from the rig, saying, "God be with you, Josef. I'll see you soon." Without a word, Josef snaps the reins, and the wagon bolts forward onto the dusty road. Standing in the middle of the road, I continue to watch until their wagon disappears over the rise.

CHAPTER 52
SEVERAL MONTHS LATER

I WONDER WHAT IT MUST BE LIKE. How is it that Aneta —my dear Aneta —can go through life this way, bearing child after child in rapid succession over the course of a decade? Her body barely recovers before repeatedly burgeoning with new life, year after blessed year, like the lactating cow in the back pasture.

Last summer, Aneta revealed that she was pregnant once again, and when spring came, the child arrived. This is number eight! Thank you, Father, for the blessing of my children, but perhaps eight is enough for your humble servant, a servant who wishes to expend more energy spreading your word, and less energy disciplining a throng of children.

With the appearance of this one, I must admit my joy was tempered significantly by the routine nature of it all. It seems so commonplace now, so unremarkable. After seven previous births, Aneta herself neglected to conceal a kind of indifference toward the entire affair. After this birth, she took hardly any time at all to linger before cleaning herself off and going about her household chores with the child suckling at her tired breast.

Anna Katherine, we named her. As newborns go, she is as handsome a creature as one might expect, I suppose, but after the children and I gazed upon her for only a short time, we too resumed our daily activities, expecting Anna Katherine to dutifully take her place at the rear of the pecking order.

Despite this additional mouth to feed, I take some comfort in the fact that the church elders just a week ago granted me a pay raise, not exactly a significant one, but a pay raise just the same. One hundred and forty-eight dollars is the figure they came up with. While it's not much, it's over twice the meager sixty-dollar sum I received when I first arrived here. In addition, I'll receive a year's supply of wheat, rye, potatoes, and corn—the total value of my annual pay being around two hundred fifty dollars. No, I shouldn't complain. It'll be sufficient for the ten of us, especially if I can earn a bit more from my preaching to other congregations in the area and beyond.

The Lord provides for me, and I will not ask for anything more. I have my faith and my work to sustain me, which is more than I can say for poor John Novotny. It's not his faith that's waned, but his livelihood. I knew John was struggling to support his family. I just didn't understand the extent of it. Unable to prosper on his thirty acres of wooded land, he was forced to give up on farming and work as a hired laborer. Even then, he continued to volunteer in the construction of our temple. But sadly, his livelihood as a laborer was too much to bear, and he finally sold his land, bought two covered wagons, and made plans to travel westward with his wife and six children.

Just yesterday morning, they began their journey, stopping at our parsonage to say goodbye. John didn't know exactly where they were going—only that he had heard of available land, free of timber, on the Nebraska grasslands. It was disappointing to see them go, since John was such a committed member of our new church. But this is a common story. I've witnessed the departure of many souls, either traveling further west to find more opportunities or returning east to an earlier existence. The Novotnys and I prayed together for a long while before Aneta and I reluctantly bid them a tearful farewell and *God be with you.* We watched them drive off with the sun at their backs, my thoughts shifting to the many other Bohemian immigrants I know who have found themselves in similar straits.

I find myself wondering about the Zachs and the Rejmans. Will they suffer the same fate as John Novotny and his family? Only time will tell. I haven't seen them at church for quite some time. That makes me worry, so I've been planning to ride out there sometime to see how they are doing. Of course, with Anna Katherine's arrival, my travel plans will have to wait.

It's a full week later before I feel it prudent to visit the homesteads of Josef and Vaclav. It is my curiosity that takes me there, but my ostensive motive will be to deliver Bibles to their families. This is a gift our church elders decided should be extended to all those who contributed to the building of our temple.

I'm not sure if the two families have moved to their new homesteads, so I decide to first stop at the old Coufal cabin, where Vaclav and Annie had taken up residence. When I arrive, the place is deserted. This could be a good sign, meaning they are settled in their new homes further to the west, or a bad sign, meaning they've left the area completely.

I continue down the bottom road and turn right on the path to the home of Anton and Rose Novak. As I approach, I see no sign of the Zach family anywhere. Dismounting, I approach the rustic domicile just as Anton opens the door wide to greet me. Gazing past him, Rose is in plain sight, sitting in her rocking chair, slowly rocking back and forth, staring straight ahead with vacant eyes.

"Hello, Anton. How are you folks doing?" I ask, noting Rose's unresponsive state.

"Oh, we're fine, I guess, Reverend."

"And Rose? How's she doing?"

"See for yourself, Reverend," Anton says, turning to look at Rose. "She seems to be slipping further into herself."

"I'm so sorry, Anton," I say sadly.

"Oh, it's OK. I take her out for a walk every day and read to her as often as I can. It's hard, though, since I'm now responsible for all the chores around here. I'm sorry we haven't been to your new church, Reverend. I've wanted to come, but it's difficult, you know, to get out, and . . ." his voice trails off as he looks at his wife sitting silently in the dim room.

"May I sit and pray with her?" I ask. That's all I can offer. What else is there to do?

"That would be nice," Anton replies softly, wiping the moistness from his weathered cheek. "That would be really nice, Reverend," he repeats.

The Zach homestead is right off the bottom road, about a mile beyond the Novak homestead. Of course, the last time I rode by, it was just a section of undeveloped land. As I turn off the bottom road onto the dirt path to Josef's claim, I am at once surprised by the improvements to the property. The house is visible from the corner. It's a simple house, certainly not what I'd call grand. But it is a step above most of the sod and log houses around here. Josef's house seems to have three rooms and boasts clapboard siding and a shingled roof. An impressive chimney stretches up the entirety of the east side and extends several feet above the roof into the Iowa sky. It's certainly not as impressive as many of the homes I've seen in Cedar Rapids or Iowa City, but it is totally commensurate with the construction capabilities Josef possesses.

There are a couple of other crude structures nearby, too: an outhouse, a small barn with a fenced enclosure, and a shed probably utilized for storage. And, of course, Josef has dug himself a well not far from the house. It seems that Josef is doing quite well on his new homestead.

I stop on the dirt road directly in front of the house and dismount. There's Josef helping Antonin fill a large bucket at the well. When Josef sees me, he strides resolutely in my direction, and I wonder what kind of reception I will receive from him this morning.

"G'morning, Josef," I call to him cheerfully as he approaches.

"If you're looking for a donation, maybe you should keep on riding, Reverend," Josef replies in a manner to which I've become accustomed.

"Not asking for one, Josef. I've got something for you and your family," I say as I hand him the Bible.

"What's this for?" Josef responds brusquely.

"We're giving these Bibles to families who contributed to the construction of our church. It's our way of thanking everyone."

Josef gazes at me with puzzlement, saying, "But, as you must recall, we didn't actually contribute. You paid me fair and square for the foundation work."

"True, Josef, but we couldn't have done it without you, that's for sure. And then there's that other thing."

"Other thing?"

"You know, when you saved our dedication ceremony from those protesters."

"Oh, that. I told you why I did that. It was no big deal. Look, I really have no use for this book. It's all made up, you know," he says as he holds it out to me.

Taking the Bible back from him, I suggest meekly, "What about Frantiska? Do you think she'd like to have it?"

"Oh, I suppose so," he replies hesitantly. "She's in the house with the girls if you want to give it to her."

"You don't mind?" I ask, surprised that Josef would make the offer.

"No, I don't mind. If that book will make her happy, that's OK by me, I suppose."

I'm momentarily taken aback by this conciliatory concession, half expecting him to refuse to allow the Bible anywhere near his home. "Well, that's big of you, Josef," I reply.

"Don't take too much meaning from it, Reverend. I'm just trying to keep the peace around here."

"No, I understand completely. Keeping the wife happy is important. And sometimes you just need to do what needs doing, even if it's against your liking, I guess."

"Huh," Josef chuckles.

"You find that humorous, Josef?"

"Oh, not exactly, Reverend. It just reminds me of something someone told me while I was in the Austrian army. He said that when it comes to surviving in battle, you must do what is necessary whether you think it's right or wrong."

"Well, I've never been to war, Josef, but I can see how that kind of thinking might help you survive in battle. Of course, hand-to-hand combat is hardly comparable to maintaining domestic bliss."

"You don't know my wife very well, do you, Reverend?" Josef responds dryly.

I decide to leave that comment alone and change the subject. "You've done a nice job with the house, Josef. I'm looking forward to seeing the inside."

"Go right ahead. I'm sure Frantiska will be happy to see you and show you the place," Josef says as he abruptly walks toward the barn.

I lead my horse toward the house and rap on the thick wooden door. The door quickly creaks open, but only a crack, and I look down to see the familiar face of a small girl. She gazes up suspiciously at me as I say, "Hello, Terezie."

"Hi. You here to see Mama?"

"Who are you talking to?" comes a voice from inside the house.

"It's just me, Reverend Kun," I call through the opening.

Frantiska is at once at the door, opening it wide and ushering me into her home. "Please come in, Reverend. I'm so sorry for the mess. We just moved in last week, and Josef hasn't yet finished the cupboards. We're lucky to have beds to sleep on."

"Oh, don't worry about that. I bet it's nice to finally have a home of your own."

"For sure. Anton's place was getting pretty cramped."

"Here, I've got something for you," I say as I hand the Bible to her. "I hope you'll share it with Josef and the children."

"Oh, how nice! You can be sure I'll share it with the children. But Josef? Well, you know that story."

"That may be so, but I was pleasantly surprised. He didn't seem to mind my giving it to you."

Terezie interrupts, announcing, "I know how to count. You wanna hear me?"

"Uh, sure. That would be fine," I say hesitantly.

"Sorry, Reverend," apologizes Frantiska. "Annie's been teaching her, and now she has to count for everyone she meets."

"OK, so here goes," announces Terezie as she begins, "*Jedna, dvě, tři, . . .*"

I wait patiently until she reaches ten, and then she says, "Do you want me to do it again?"

"Well, I suppose you can if you—"

"Maybe later, Terezie," her big sister thankfully interrupts.

"I can write some letters, too. Wanna see?" the younger girl persists.

"Let the reverend and me chat awhile, Terezie. Then maybe you can show him," Frantiska says.

Frantiska spends some time speaking of their new farmstead and their hopes for the future. I then take a few moments to bring her up to date on church affairs, hoping to convince her to bring their family to Sunday worship sometime soon. Finally, after we pray together and I watch Terezie write part of her alphabet, I'm out the door, riding my mare up the dirt road toward Vaclav's farm.

As I approach his place, I am not surprised that the place mirrors Josef's homestead almost exactly: the same small clapboard home, outhouse, crude barn, and shed. Why would it not? Josef and Vaclav have been partners in all things since I've known them, and that partnership has apparently served them quite well. It seems the challenge of settling in an uncompromising wilderness is best overcome with the help of friends. How many times have I seen families trying to go it alone, only to desert their claims for the promise of a more hospitable life elsewhere?

As I walk my mount up to the house, Vaclav is harnessing his team in the fenced enclosure near the barn, so I head in his direction. His team of horses seems different from what I remember when he and Josef were working on the church foundation. "Hi, Vaclav," I offer as I tie my horse to the fence. "How are things?"

"Just fine, Reverend. You?"

"Couldn't be better unless I saw you folks at church more often," I answer, immediately regretting my pushy comment. "Sorry, Vaclav. I know you've been busy here."

"That's OK, Reverend. Annie and I have been talking about coming, but with the baby and all . . ."

"The baby?"

"Oh, yes. Little Franz was born just last month. Annie and the baby are doing well, and Wesley has been a good little helper, so we're all doing fine."

"Well, congratulations, Vaclav. That's great news. So we have another baptism in our future."

"Guess so. And now that we have our own team and rig, we should be able to attend more often."

"I thought they looked different from Coufal's team."

"Joe finally lost patience with us using his horses. I can't blame him. Josef and I got a good deal on these two. We got 'em from a settler nearby who couldn't make a go of it."

"Oh, before I forget, here's a Bible for you folks. It's thanking you for your help with the church," I say, handing him the book. "I stopped by to give one to Josef, too."

"How did that go?" Vaclav asks dubiously.

"Somehow, better than I expected. He seems to be, how can I put it, . . . somewhat softening in his worldview."

"Well, I don't know about that. He might just be trying to avoid conflict on the home front, if you know what I mean. When he's out of earshot of Frantiska, he still talks a lot about that Zdrubek bunch and their weird ideas. I'm tired of hearing about it."

"I've noticed a lot more of those freethinkers around. I think they're becoming quite a problem, especially in town."

"Josef is trying to talk me into going to a lecture this coming Saturday."

"Lecture?"

"Apparently, Zdrubek is lecturing for some group at the Reading Society Hall. I think it's over on Commercial Street."

"Josef didn't mention the lecture to me when I spoke with him."

"Well, that's not a real surprise, is it?"

"I suppose not."

"Plus, he didn't want Frantiska to catch wind of it. There'd be hell to pay if that happened," Vaclav says before he realizes his error. "Oh, sorry about that, Reverend. You know what I mean."

"It's fine, Vaclav. No need to apologize. The devil may indeed be Josef's final arbiter."

CHAPTER 53

IN THE DAYS THAT FOLLOW, I think often about Josef and Frantiska. Their relationship must be a strained one, with Josef's radical beliefs existing in stark contrast with Frantiska's strong faith. I know them both to be quite strong-willed, even self-righteous, in their individual convictions. And though Josef may try to appear less contentious to his wife, I'm sure there's a battle of wills, albeit a subtle one, being waged in that household. I also wonder if there's another battle, a battle of ideas, being waged in Josef's mind as he continues to make sense of the world. This must be hard on him. I shouldn't forget that. But I can't help but recognize the evil nature of this freethinker movement. It seems to gain momentum with many others like Josef, who see simple reason as an alternative to faith.

The devil is at work here. This is becoming clearer to me with each passing day. I've watched it take hold like a plague in the town of Cedar Rapids, but I've recently seen it spread to the outlying areas as well, where people, mostly men like Josef, have taken the notion of individual freedom to a new level of freedom from spiritual pursuits. And while there are plenty of devout Reformed Evangelicals, Lutherans, and Catholics who continue to worship in their own ways, there is still much cause for worry. If something is not done, this freethinking may soon erode the faith of more of my flock, causing them to follow men like that vile Zdrubek. It is said that he speaks with great eloquence—that his orations are compelling in their passion and logic. Who will stand against him if not me? It is I who must be the champion for the faithful. How can I not be? Isn't that what I've been doing my entire life?

On Saturday, this is on my mind as I travel to Cedar Rapids to preach to a small, but growing, group of Evangelicals on the east side of town. They've noted the success of my congregation, and they too have a dream of building their own church. Some of them have even traveled to my church to hear me preach the Word, but today I am traveling to see them. I will offer spiritual guidance, to be sure, but also inspiration to energize their desire to make plans for their own temple. I have prepared a sermon that should satisfy their need for inspiration. But I also plan to speak strongly against the insidious danger of the freethinker movement.

Around twenty congregants are in attendance as I open the service with a prayer. The proceedings take place under the shade of a small group of oak trees. It's mid-June, and the grass is fresh and moist with morning dew. A cool breeze gently wafts through the trees, offering an idyllic setting, and I look out on bright and expectant faces. These are believers eager for my assurance of their salvation, and they hang on my every word. Why do I feel so threatened by freethinkers when Christians of such devotion stand before me? In these faces, I see no cause for worry. But just to be sure, I forge ahead, cautioning them against the menace now existing in their community. I speak with as much passion as I've felt in a long time. And as I come to the end of my homily, I'm satisfied that I've made a satisfactory, even moving, argument against the evils of the anti-religion movement. After the service concludes, I stay to speak informally with some of the attendees and am happy to hear many enthusiastic reactions to my words. This tells me I have hit the mark squarely, perhaps assuring that these people, at least, will not be susceptible to the threat they face.

It's early afternoon when I finally leave for home. I make my way along dirt streets lined with modest log homes until I turn onto Commercial Street on the southwest side of town. This is a route I have taken on several occasions in the past when I've preached in this growing town. As I head southwest, I encounter a noisy crowd standing in the street. I can see no way of getting around them, so I sit on my mare wondering what is going on. The crowd, consisting mostly of men, appears to be filing into a tall building of recent construction. When I read the name above the door, I realize what it is I've happened upon today.

As the crowd on the street thins, I continue to ride south, wondering if it's wise to do what I am considering at the moment. Then, about a block down Commercial Street, I abruptly stop and tie the horse to a nearby hitching post. I stand there watching until the line disappears into the tall building. I'm still not sure I'm doing the prudent thing, but I walk back down the street until I'm gazing up at the sign above the door that reads *The Reading Society*. Then I step inside.

The hall is packed with rowdy men—rough men who are all remarkably fluent in colorfully crude language. Many of them are smoking, and a gray haze hovers above the boisterous crowd. The combination of the smoke and men's sweat produces a stench that forces me to cover my face with my handkerchief, and I wonder if I might become ill. But my stomach soon settles down, and I find a place to stand near the door in case I want to make a quick exit from this squalid scene. Soon, a man I presume to be Frank Zdrubek mounts the small wooden stage and places his hands firmly on each side of the lectern. The unruly crowd quiets itself, waiting to hear his message. This strikes me as not so different from my service this very morning. But instead of twenty Evangelicals listening to my sermon, this crowd numbers well over one hundred, and they are every bit as eager to be inspired.

"We are here today," Zdrubek begins, "to proclaim our place in our community as the custodians of truth. The ones who know the difference between facts and fairy tales."

Affirmative shouts begin to resonate around the room. Responses such as "hear, hear" or "that's right" or "tell 'em, Frank" are clearly heard at each pause in his oration. I recognize the power of these pauses. I use them myself to add weight to points I want to stress in my own sermons.

"We are religious independents," he continues. "Do not be ashamed, for what is there to be ashamed of? Our belief in natural law? Was Thomas Jefferson ashamed to be an independent thinker? Or Ben Franklin? Or Thomas Paine?"

Shouts of "No!" erupt from the crowd as Zdrubek waits patiently to continue.

"Or what about the greatest of all our leaders, President Abraham Lincoln? He, too, was a freethinker, a believer in the need for a secular government and religious liberty."

Is that true? I wonder. Certainly not. Not President Lincoln. He, of all people, must have believed that religious faith is the proper compass of men. I'm not sure I will be able to stand much more of this, and I'm grateful I decided to stay near the exit.

"Shame should play no part in our mission to doubt the dogma of religion. Instead, we should take pride in our recognition of what is. Of what we see in plain sight before our eyes. This is where the truth abides. Not in the stories of popes and preachers."

"Hear, hear! Damn right!"

"Let's stand with pride to proclaim our belief that all things exist at the directive of natural law. At the behest of an intelligence not of the heavens but right here on Earth."

"Yes, yes!"

"Let us also state that the most developed of all the creatures is clearly the human being, representing the most perfect culmination of all things. And that the only thing higher than man is his spirit, the beautiful emanation of his mind and will."

"Blasphemer!" It comes out of my mouth before I can stop it, and it echoes about the room and hangs there in a vacuum of silence, as if uttered by the voice of God Himself. Of course that's only how it seems to me. Apparently, the rest of the crowd hears it quite differently. This time, there are no affirmative responses to be heard. Only angry mutterings, starting as whispers and then growing to include shouts of "Get him outa here!" and "Who is that?" and "Throw him out!"

Suddenly, a man standing near me shouts, "I know this man! He's the preacher from that church out in the country south of town! Let's get him out of here!"

"Now just calm down, everyone," Zdrubek shouts. "There's no need for violence. This is a public forum. All are welcome. Even preachers, I suppose. Who knows? Maybe he's here to learn something." This generates some laughter around the room.

But I'm not laughing. I am now worried. Frightened, even. What have I gotten myself into?

"Bring him up closer, so we might have a chat," Zdrubek instructs, as if this is some kind of lighthearted social gathering. Suddenly, I find myself surrounded by several men who push me roughly through the crowd to the front of the room.

"So, you seem to disagree with me. Is that correct, Preacher?" Zdrubek asks, smiling with contempt.

"The highest, most exalted entities in this world are God and His Son, Jesus, who reigns with Him!" I reply with ease, as if I'm quoting a line from some past sermon. "To say anything different is utter blasphemy!" I add. I'm feeling less frightened now, emboldened by my intoning of the words *God* and *Jesus*.

"Well then, Preacher, I guess you can consider me a proud practicing blasphemer. What do you think of that?"

"Indeed you are, Mr. Zdrubek! But I'll pray for you," I answer. This brings more than a few chuckles and derogatory asides from the people standing around me.

"No need, Preacher. There's nothing to pray to. What would you pray to? A golden calf? A statue of Zeus? Your invisible god? Don't waste your ignorant breath on make-believe idols," he says, his voice indicating an annoyance, perhaps with the notion of my praying on his behalf.

I'm greatly offended by his referring to the Lord as invisible and can't help but shout in return, "You will burn in hell for your words!" Then I immediately turn to Revelations 21:8, adding, "But for the cowardly and unbelieving and abominable and murderers and immoral persons and sorcerers and idolaters and all liars, their part will be in the lake that burns with fire and brimstone, which is the second death!"

I now realize that this may have been a mistake on my part, for the entire crowd begins to shout and move toward me, surging like an ominous wave, back and forth with fists raised high. I'm being pushed about at the mercy of this wave of outrage when a rather large man suddenly grabs me and shoves me violently to the floor. As I glance up at him, I see a large knife, sheathed and strapped to his waist. His hand is gripping the knife handle, and I wonder if he intends to use it. The weight of his boot is pressing down on my neck as he constrains me there, laughing as if fed by the violent fervor of the surrounding crowd. I flail about among trousers and boots with my head pinned rudely to the wood floor, and I can hear faint cries from the now-distant stage, where Zdrubek pleads for calm. But it is to no avail. He has lost control of his disciples, and my fate is now in their hands.

My breathing is labored, and I fear I may pass out, maybe even die. Thrashing about frantically in an attempt to free myself, I feel myself weakening with each breath. God, help me! I have so much more work to do on your behalf. It can't stop here. Not like this, I plead.

Suddenly, I hear a forceful grunt from my assailant, and his boot releases its pressure on my neck. I look up with blurred vision just in time to see a stick of some kind shoved into the man's belly. Then the same stick comes down on the side of his head, sending him to the floor on top of me.

Coughing and spitting, gasping for air, I struggle to get out from under the man's bulk, finally pulling myself up on my hands and knees.

"Get out of the way or you'll get the same," a gruff voice bellows to the surrounding crowd.

I'm now being pulled by my coat collar toward the door along the wooden planked floor. "Let's get you outa here, Reverend," the voice says.

As I'm being dragged along, it is difficult to see who my rescuer is. His voice is obscured somewhat by the din of the crowd, but I manage to notice that he's using a cane for balance, and he's walking with a limp. "Josef? Is that you?" I exclaim.

"Shhh. Don't talk. Let's get the hell outa here," he responds as we finally reach the door and he pulls me to my feet. He pushes me down the street and then into an alley where we stand, breathing hard, staring at each other. "Are you OK, Francis?" he asks.

I've never heard Josef use my first name before, and I wonder if the disrespect should offend me. But I'm at once ashamed. The man just risked his life for me, after all.

"I think I'm fine, Josef, thanks to you," I answer.

"How's that neck?" he asks, moving closer to get a better look. "You'll definitely have some bruising there. I imagine it hurts?"

"A bit."

"It's not safe here. We need to get you as far away as possible. Those thugs may come looking for you. Looking for me, too. My rig is down the street there," he points. "Where's your horse?"

"It's down in that direction, too."

"Let's go." That's all that needs saying as we bolt out of the alley and hurry down the street toward my mare and his wagon. Soon, we're on his rig with my horse tied behind, riding out of town at a good clip.

We reach the outskirts of town before he speaks again. "What the heck were you trying to accomplish in there, Reverend? That was a really *hloupý* thing to do."

"*Hloupý*?" I ask, looking sideways at him. Again, I feel a pang at his disrespect.

"How would you describe it?" he asks, still staring straight ahead.

I hesitate a moment before saying, "Yes, I suppose that's an accurate way to put it. It was pretty *hloupý*, alright."

"That's a pretty rough bunch in there. It's a good thing I was here to help you. That Emil Pavlista is the worst of 'em. I've seen him around town before, and most people do their best to avoid him. When I saw Pavlista going for his knife, I knew he was gonna use it."

"I'm glad you intervened, Josef. Otherwise, who knows what could have happened?"

"I think I know, and it's not good."

"You know, Josef? You've developed quite a habit of rescuing me from freethinkers. Don't you think that's a bit odd?"

"Odd?"

"Well, you always seem to be in the right place at the right time. You think that means something?" I'm looking at him now, expecting his response to be a negative one.

"Doesn't mean a thing, Reverend. It's just that if something happens to you, my wife will be hard to live with for the foreseeable future. She thinks a lot of you," Josef says, then adding, "…for some reason."

"That may be true, but if you keep this up, those freethinkers aren't going to want you around, are they?"

"You're probably right about that. I may have to do my freethinking all on my own from now on."

"Seems so. It's just as well, Josef. It doesn't seem that all the freethinking Zdrubek preaches is turning his followers into very nice people."

"I can't say you're wrong about that, Reverend."

CHAPTER 54

IT'S BEEN SEVERAL WEEKS SINCE MY ENCOUNTER with the freethinkers and my subsequent rescue by Josef. As frightening as that was, I have put it behind me, not that I've ended my campaign against Zdrubek's movement—I haven't. But at least I've stopped worrying that Emil Pavlista is hiding in wait for me around every corner. In fact, I hardly think of Pavlista at all anymore.

Unfortunately, that changes one morning when I hear a rapping on my door. A town marshal named Marek Holub stands there telling me that Emil Pavlista has gone missing.

"What's this got to do with me?" I ask. "Why would you think I know something about this man?" Holub is a tall, imposing man who appears to have led a rough life, from the looks of him. In some ways, he reminds me of Pavlista who attacked me at the Reading Society lecture hall.

"I was told by one of his friends that you two had a bit of a fight back in June; it was June 12th over on Commercial Street if I'm not mistaken," he says, looking down at a piece of paper.

"It was hardly a fight. The man attacked me for no reason. He was getting ready to pull his knife and kill me with it," I say.

"Well, he's known to be a bit of a rough character. Anyway, he vanished sometime after that. We're not sure of the exact date. Nobody seems to care much about Pavlista, so it took some days before anyone bothered to mention he was missing."

"That's no surprise, I suppose," I say.

"Normally, I'd just assume the guy left town, except that one of his so-called friends noticed that he left all his belongings behind. So, have you seen Pavlista since June 12th?"

"No, sir."

"Hmm. What about that other fella?"

"Other fella? What other fella?"

"I was told that another fella was helping you—a fella who knocked Pavlista silly with some kind of cane. Who was that?" Holub asks.

"Another one of those freethinkers, apparently," I say. It isn't a lie, after all. And I see no reason to get Josef mixed up in this.

"Did you catch his name?"

"I didn't ask, and he didn't offer," I say, again satisfied that I'm answering truthfully.

"Can you describe him?" the marshal asks.

"Well, let's see. I think he had a beard," I say.

"So do 80 percent of the men I see in town. Any specifics that might help?"

"I really didn't get a good look at him. Pavlista had been standing on my neck, so my vision was sort of blurred at the time." Just a slight exaggeration, I'm thinking.

"I've been told the man who helped you had a visible limp. Is that right?"

"I guess so. He did have a cane, you know."

"So, you'd swear that this man didn't accompany you to the event?" Holub asks dubiously.

"He definitely did not. I was as surprised as anyone when he came to my aid." Also, not a lie.

He stares down at his paper, considering his next question, if any. He can't be happy with the information he's extracted from me, and the look on his face shows it. Finally, he says, "OK then, Reverend. I thank you for your time. I hope you'll let me speak with you again if I have the need."

"Sure. Come back anytime," I say, feigning nonchalance. Then I point, saying, "Sunday services begin at nine sharp down that road at the church. You're certainly welcome to come."

"Uh . . . , sure. Thanks, Reverend."

I have nothing in particular scheduled for the afternoon, so I saddle my horse and head toward the Zach homestead. I'm curious to find out if Josef knows anything at all about Emil Pavlista's disappearance. That's highly doubtful, I think. Why would he? But at least I should let him know that the town marshal is looking for him. I owe Josef that much, don't I?

I turn into Josef's yard and stop at the house, dismounting my horse and leaving it to graze freely in the yard. It's already late in the afternoon, and I can see smoke wafting in puffs out of the chimney. Frantiska is most likely in the midst of cooking. I knock firmly on the front door.

When Josef opens the door, I see the entire family assembled within, hurrying about doing their assigned jobs. "Hey, Josef. How are you folks doing?" I ask.

"We're OK, I guess. What do you need, Reverend?"

"I'm here to talk to you about Emil Pavlista," I say. Josef and Frantiska give one another a concerned look, and I wonder what that means.

Josef suddenly turns to his daughter, saying, "Um, Vincencie, would you and Antonin take the little one outside for a while? This won't take long. We need to speak to the Reverend about something."

"OK, Papa," she answers obediently, shepherding the younger children out the door and closing it behind them.

This is puzzling to me. Do they know something about Pavlista's disappearance? How could they? Are they involved somehow?

"What about Pavlista?" Josef finally asks.

"Well, a town marshal stopped by asking about him. It seems that Pavlista disappeared recently, and the marshal heard about our little encounter with him back in June." Suddenly, I wonder if Josef has told Frantiska about that incident, and I look at Frantiska for her reaction.

"Don't worry, Reverend. She knows all about it," Josef says.

"Whew, that's good. Anyway, he thought there might be a connection, and he was asking me about you, and—"

"What did you tell him?" Josef interrupts.

"Oh, nothing really. I played it like I didn't know you. I think he bought it."

"You mean you lied to him?" Josef exclaims, a sly grin planted on his face.

"Well, no. At least, not exactly. Why? Do you know anything about his disappearance? Is there something I should know?"

"No. Nothing about his disappearance," says Frantiska. "But Pavlista did show up here after that thing in Cedar Rapids."

"He showed up here? At your house? When?" I ask, alarmed.

"It was about a week after that freethinker meeting. He must have taken the mud wagon from Cedar Rapids to Coufal's way station and then walked the rest of the way here. He just stormed right into the house. Scared the hell out of us," Josef says.

"He was angry—furious," Frantiska adds.

"He sure was, and he reeked of alcohol. He was holding a bottle in one hand and that knife of his in the other."

"Oh, my goodness," I blurt. "What did you do?"

Frantiska answers, "I was kneeling down by the fireplace beginning to prepare supper, and Vincencie and Antonin were still outside doing some chores. But poor little Terezie was inside with us. Pavlista started shouting at Josef about how he was going to make you and Josef pay for what happened that day at the lecture hall. It was really scary. The man was wild-eyed. Real wild-eyed. Like a madman. Terezie was terrified!"

"I'll bet she was! And you say he threatened both of us——Josef and me both?" I ask worriedly. I now realize I had every reason to worry about that man, and I'm relieved to know that he has disappeared, hopefully forever. "So what happened?" I ask, eager to hear the rest of the tale. "What did you do, Josef?"

Josef gives a half-chuckle, saying, "Huh, well, it really wasn't what *I* did. Maybe you should tell him, Frannie."

"He was coming toward Josef," she says, "and I could see that Josef had no way to defend himself, except with his bare hands. And Pavlista had that big knife."

"It was a Bowie knife, like the ones they sell in town," Josef adds.

"Yes, I know. I saw it the day he attacked me," I say.

"Anyway," Frantiska continues, "I had to do something, so I grabbed the only thing that was within my reach. It was my iron skillet, and I just swung it as hard as I could—"

"She swung that thing around," Josef interrupts, "and she nailed Pavlista square in the knee. It made the most revolting sound you could imagine—and the man's knee smashed into an ugly mess. He went down like a load of bricks right there on the floor, where you're standing now."

"And poor Terezie," Frantiska whispers.

"Terezie? Was she alright?" I ask.

"Well, physically, yes," Frantiska says. "But she was in a state of shock. We were watching Pavlista groaning there on the floor for a while before we realized poor Terezie had picked up Pavlista's knife and was holding it in her little hands, as if in a trance. And she was reading the letters carved on the knife handle, reading them aloud over and over again: *E-P-E-P* . . ."

"*E-P?*" I ask.

"Pavlista's initials, I guess," says Josef.

 "So is Terezie all right?" I ask.

"Yes, I think my *malíčká* is fine."

"And what about Pavlista?"

"I finally dragged him out of the house, which was not an easy job, as big as he was. And I somehow got him up on my wagon and drove him back to the way station, leaving him there with five cents for his fare back to town."

"Do you know for sure if he made that stage?" I ask.

"No idea," answers Josef.

"You didn't check?"

"Nope. Why would I?"

"Didn't you worry he'd be back to finish the job?" or come after me, I'm thinking.

"Not in his condition. He won't be walking out here anytime soon. I don't think we have to worry about him anymore. I think he learned his lesson," Josef says with confidence.

"How can you be so sure?" I ask.

"I just think we've seen the last of him. That's all."

"I hope you're right, Josef," I reply, far from convinced.

CHAPTER 55

MARSHAL MAREK HOLUB ARRIVED in Cedar Rapids almost five years ago. Originally, he came from a small Bohemian town called Lukavice and arrived alone at New York's Castle Garden docks on a sailing ship. Holub quickly made his way west, but only as far as Pennsylvania, where he found himself working long days in the coal mines.

Having no wife or children, he figured he could endure anything for a while, until he got his bearings in this new land. But he soon realized that he wasn't suited for work in the mine shafts. It wasn't that he didn't have the strength or fortitude to tough it out as a miner. The problem was his height. At six-five, Marek was the tallest man on the crew, and though his strength far exceeded that of most of the other men, he found it increasingly difficult working under the low ceilings of the shafts. Having to work while hunched over caused him considerable back pain, and within a year on the crew, he knew his mining days were over.

He set off again, traveling west until he arrived in Cedar Rapids, where he intended to stay only a day or two before continuing on. Where would he go? He wasn't sure. Maybe he would head further west—buy himself a ranch and raise cattle or horses. But he hadn't as yet saved enough to buy himself a spread and purchase livestock. Besides, what did he really know about ranching? Not much. This ranching notion was absurd. He didn't know where he would go or what he would do.

But that changed when he walked into a tavern in Cedar Rapids to have a beer and encountered a drunk who tried to pick a fight with him. By nature, Holub was not an aggressive man—not that he couldn't handle himself, but he avoided conflict when he could. On that day, however, he was confronting an inebriated bully who took pride in fighting the biggest man he could find. And Holub was a big man. The two ended up out in the street, surrounded by a small crowd of curious onlookers who watched as Marek easily dispatched the man with a stiff upper hook. One of the onlookers was a town alderman, who wasted no time in offering Holub a job as one of the town marshals.

Five years later, he's all but forgotten about his plans to move on. In many ways, this job suits him. His imposing frame earns him the respect of everyone he meets, whether law-abiding or otherwise, and his talent for de-escalating conflict usually makes it unnecessary to introduce offenders to the business end of his marshal's baton, the intimidating club he carries on his belt.

The only thing he hates about this job, the thing that he had not counted on, is the loneliness. Since becoming one of the town marshals, he's found it almost impossible to make friends. No one seems to want to associate with an officer of the law, no matter that the laws in this town are loosely enforced. Apparently, a friendship with a town marshal makes one a potential snitch by association, and nobody wants any part of that. Even relationships with women are almost impossible. After all, being a lady friend of a marshal would prevent a woman from being privy to most of the juicy gossip around town. And if, heaven forbid, a woman married a town marshal, she'd have to worry constantly about the dangers inherent in his day-to-day job.

No, the life of a town marshal is not conducive to widening one's social circle. Holub has come to terms with that, and he hardly tries anymore to encourage social affiliations with anyone besides other lonely marshals. If only, he thinks, there could be some good-looking females among the handful of lonely marshals in this town. Women marshals? Huh—that's a laugh, he thinks.

Holub's beat is the southwest side of town, populated mostly by Bohemians. Most of them have shown resistance to learning English. Why shouldn't they? Everyone around them, from merchants to harness makers to teamsters to bartenders, is Bohemian. Most of these people can go for weeks or even months without hearing English spoken. Marek's facility with the language makes him a perfect fit for this area, and he's happy to do his part in keeping the peace for his countrymen. Actually, peace is a rather relative term. While most of the Bohemian immigrants here are hardworking and law-abiding citizens, a few ruffians keep him very busy—mostly small-time petty thieves, drunk-and-disorderlies, and the occasional horse thief or murderer. Many of the latter, more serious, cases go unsolved since many are the work of itinerants who disappear after the deed is done.

Marek Holub hardly expects to attain any closure in the case of Emil Pavlista's disappearance. After all, it's been several months already. Besides, while it's true the man disappeared, leaving his belongings behind, that doesn't mean he didn't just run off with someone's wife. It could have been any number of things that forced him to flee the area. Pavlista's case isn't of any real importance to Holub. Now the case file is crammed into his desk drawer, and he's almost forgotten about it.

So he isn't thinking about Emil Pavlista when spring arrives, and he receives word of a body found south of town near the Iowa River just off the bottom road. It's most likely some immigrant who lost his way out in the countryside, he suspects, or perhaps a farmer who got disoriented in a blizzard last winter.

Holub rides south along the stage line to a farm owned by a man named Joe Coufal. The marshal has gone by here before, on his way to Iowa City, but he's never bothered to stop and meet the guy. Coufal is just another poor farmer living along the river. Why would he bother to stop?

As he turns off the stage line road and rides up to Coufal's home, Holub can see that the man's house is not the domicile of some poor farmer. The house is constructed of stone and surrounded by several outbuildings. Apparently, this Coufal fella has done pretty well for himself, Holub thinks. As he dismounts, he can see the farmer walking out of his house in his direction.

"You Mr. Coufal?" asks Holub.

"Yes, sir. And you?"

"Town Marshal Marek Holub, from Cedar Rapids."

"Ah, this is about the body, I suppose."

"That's right. Can you show me where it is?"

The two of them ride into the woods to examine the site. The marshal can see that the body wasn't buried deeply at all. It appears to have been here awhile and isn't in very good shape, having been partially exposed to the elements. To make matters worse, it appears to have been dug up by something, perhaps a coyote. It will be difficult to identify this victim, he thinks, but as he examines the body, he notices a knife sheath strapped around the waist of the unfortunate soul. He remembers Reverend Kun mentioning his assailant's knife. He also remembers one freethinker describing Pavlista's knife as inscribed with the initials *EP* on both the knife handle and the sheath. Holub looks more closely at the sheath, scrubbing some caked mud aside to reveal those very initials. This must be Pavlista's body. He discovers something else, too. Holub can see several stab wounds in the dead man's torso. These aren't wounds made by some scavenger. These are puncture wounds.

"Did you see a knife when you came upon the body?" asks Holub.

"No, Marshal. But I wasn't really looking."

"Can you help me look around to see if we can find it? Don't touch anything. Just look around the area over there." He points, and the two men search meticulously for the murder weapon among the weeds and dead leaves before Holub finally says, "OK, that's it for now. I'll send a wagon out here to retrieve the body."

"The sooner the better, Marshal. I'm ready to get him out of my woods. This guy's really stinking up the place."

This case is perplexing for Holub. If this is Pavlista's body, and he thinks it is, why is it buried almost ten miles south of town? Marek realizes that he'll need to pull that case file back out of his desk drawer and review it. Was there something he missed? He has to admit that Pavlista's disappearance hasn't been at the top of his priority list. But it's time to put it there. He will need to re-interview some men who were at that lecture hall on June 12. If those were the closest thing Pavlista had to what he could call friends, Holub knows they'll be his best chance of gaining new insight on the case and learning more about the man who incapacitated Pavlista and rescued that preacher from the mob.

CHAPTER 56

STANDING AT MY DOOR, the marshal looks much more imposing this time. Has he grown since last I saw him? Of course not. That would be impossible. No, it's my sudden anxiety that exaggerates my perception of the marshal's stature. Why would he be here at my door if not to question me further about Emil Pavlista? He must have realized that I was holding back information. Marshal Holub's presence here can't bode well for either my reputation or Josef's involvement in the case.

"Can I help you?" I ask meekly.

"Morning, Reverend. Could I have a few moments of your time?"

He sounds friendly enough, I think. Perhaps this will go better than I expected. "Of course, Marshal. I'm always willing to help. What can I do for you?" I reply.

"Well, I don't know if you heard, but we've found what I believe to be Emil Pavlista's body."

The man pauses, studying my reaction, trying to read something by it. I try to present a neutral expression. Why would I react any differently? It's not like I would know anything about that. Finally I say, "Oh, that's a shame. How can I help?"

"Well, here's the thing, Reverend," he says, sounding much less friendly in my estimation. "I had a chat with one of Pavlista's friends who was at the Zdrubek lecture last June, the day you had that altercation with Pavlista."

"Not an altercation. He attacked me," I say, knowing this detail is not important to him.

"This fella told me something about the mystery man who rescued you that day. It seems this fella saw him before, at your church. This guy said he was there with some freethinker protesters. Apparently, he noticed this same fella standing outside the church before your service. He was arguing with a woman, and he later drove a team and wagon through the group of protesters to move them away from the church."

Holub is studying me again, and I'm less than confident that my countenance reflects the innocence I'm trying to maintain. "So?" I ask timidly.

"Well, Reverend, I find it difficult to believe you didn't know this man since he was evidently attending your church service. And then he showed up on June 12th to help you when you needed him at the Reading Society Hall."

"I didn't exactly say I didn't know him," I reply in my weak defense.

"You most certainly did."

"No, I didn't. As I recall, you asked if the man gave me his name, and I told you he did not, which is true."

"But you know who he is, don't you?" the marshal asks in a frustrated and threatening tone.

"Yes, I guess I do."

"So your previous statement was misleading?"

"Perhaps, but I didn't lie to you. Hey, the guy saved my life that day, OK?" I say, thinking he will understand the reason for my deception.

"So?"

"So what?" I ask.

"So who is this mystery man that you've been protecting, Reverend?"

I decide not to take issue with his question. Protecting? Not exactly protecting. Or was I? Sure, I guess I was. I wasn't forthcoming about Josef's identity. I suppose I was protecting him. And I'll do my best to do the same in the future.

"Well?" Holub prods with considerable frustration. "What's the name of this buddy of yours?"

"It's Josef Zach. His family comes to my church sometimes. But he's not exactly my buddy," I say, knowing that this is another unimportant detail.

"Do you know where I can find him?"

"Yes. He lives up the bottom road from the stage line."

"You mean near the Coufal place?"

"Yes. Just up the road."

"That's curious because that isn't far from where we found Pavlista's body." He's watching me again for my reaction.

"Doesn't really implicate him," I answer stoically.

"I need you to give me specific directions to his place."

I'm worried about where this is going. What will happen when the marshal confronts Josef with all his questions? I know Josef to be rather unpredictable. Could this encounter escalate into something regrettable? And will Josef find out that I gave the marshal his name? That I ratted on him? I saw how Josef stopped Pavlista at the lecture hall. Pavlista was a large man, but Josef had no problem bringing him down. As imposing as Holub seems, he won't intimidate Josef, that's for sure.

"I'll do you one better," I say. "I'll take you there." This seems like the way to assure that Holub treats Josef fairly, and also that I'll be there to mediate if any conflict arises between them.

"That is unnecessary. If you'd just tell—"

"No, I insist. After all, don't you think Josef might be more truthful with you if his preacher is listening in on the questioning?" I know this isn't true. I'm really not Josef's preacher. Josef knows it, and I know it. But Marshal Holub doesn't know it.

"OK. I suppose that would be alright," the marshal says.

By the time we come to the bottom road, it's almost noon, and I'm thankful that a thin cloud cover eases the effects of an otherwise oppressive sun. We ride on, side by side, passing Joe Coufal's place and eventually his quarry.

"Found the body up there," Holub says, pointing up at the wooded area to the right of the road. I don't know if he expects a response, but I offer none. Instead, I try to appear disinterested. After all, I have nothing to do with it.

"Joe Coufal found it half-buried and defiled by some critters, probably coyotes," he continues.

The image of that moment of discovery makes it impossible for me to remain silent. I respond, "Poor Joe. It must have been terrible to see something like that up in your timber."

"It isn't what he expected, I'm sure," the marshal answers.

That's the extent of our conversation until we finally arrive at Josef's homestead. As we ride up, we spot Josef cleaning out his horse shed, heaving soiled straw out of the pen onto a pile. I'm glad that Josef's wife and children aren't nearby, for I know Josef will have to give the marshal his account of the day Pavlista barged into his house with that knife. I don't think the children, primarily Terezie, need to hear it.

"Hello, Josef," I say as we dismount. "We're here in order to—"

"Please, Reverend. Let me handle this," Holub says, asserting his control over the situation. "Are you Josef Zach?"

"Who's asking?" Josef replies with his usual curtness, thrusting his pitchfork into the soft ground but keeping his grasp on the wooden handle.

"I'm Town Marshal Marek Holub. I need to ask you some questions about Emil Pavlista."

"What about him? Why do you think I can help you?"

"Well, we found him a few days ago, dead and buried down by the quarry. You may be the last person to have had a scuffle with the man. That makes you a person of interest."

"A person of interest, you say? Well, that is great," he says with sarcasm. "Most people don't think I'm interesting at all. Just ask my wife, or maybe talk to Vaclav down the road. He doesn't think I'm interesting. In fact, he thinks I'm a bit *hloupý*. What do you think of that?"

"Josef, please," I say. "Just let the man ask you some questions, OK?" Josef is picking an odd time to make jokes. This is serious. A marshal has come all the way out here to see him, and he's making light of the situation. He can't possibly think the marshal finds him amusing, can he?

The marshal stands stone-faced, silent for a moment, and then says, "Look, Mr. Zach, here is why you are a person of interest. You disrespected the man by giving him a beatdown at the freethinker lecture. And now we find his body out in the country, just down the road from your house. That's quite a coincidence, don't you think?"

"Yup—just a coincidence. I had nothing to do with it," Josef says.

"Did you ever have contact with Pavlista after that encounter on June 12th?"

"June 12th?"

"The day of your encounter at the Reading Society Hall. The day you rescued the reverend here from that mob and knocked Pavlista senseless," Holub clarifies.

Josef hesitates. Of course they had contact after that. Josef told me himself. Why is he hesitating now? I wonder.

Josef looks over at me as if guessing what I'm thinking, and says, "Yes, I did. He came here and stormed into my house with a knife, making all kinds of threats."

"When was that?" the marshal asks calmly.

"It was about a week after that encounter in Cedar Rapids. I can't remember exactly."

"Can you tell me about it?" the marshal asks.

Josef relates the same account that he told me, including every detail from the man's threats to the iron skillet to the crushed knee to Terezie holding the knife and reading the man's initials over and over. Then he explains how he took Pavlista to the way station to await the stage back to Cedar Rapids.

"Do you still have the knife?" Holub asks.

"Of course not! Why would I have the knife?"

"Because I didn't find it on his body. Someone apparently stabbed him to death, possibly with that knife, and then took it. Maybe that person was you."

Josef is agitated now. I can't blame him. I'm hoping he doesn't do or say anything rash. It won't surprise me if he does. I wonder if the marshal notices that Josef's knuckles are whiter now, showing the increased strain of his grasp on the pitchfork handle. Suddenly, he takes a threatening stride toward the marshal, and I quickly step between them, forcing Josef to halt his progress. I look him square in the eyes saying "Josef, this man is merely doing his job. There's no need to take offense to his questions. Just answer them the best you can, and soon he will be on his horse riding away from here. You'll probably never see him again."

The pause is long, and I worry about what Josef might do. Finally, he speaks to the marshal, his eyes still planted squarely on me, "Well, I didn't kill him, and I didn't take the knife. I gave it back to him when I left him at the way station."

"Gave it back? Why would you do that? Weren't you afraid he'd come back to your house with the knife in hand?" Holub asks.

"Not in the shape he was in. He was in a lot of pain, and he couldn't walk on that damn leg at all. Besides, I wasn't sure of the evening stage schedule. I thought maybe the scoundrel would have to sit there all night waiting for a ride.

To be honest, I hoped that would happen. But as much as I hated the bastard, it didn't seem right to leave him there without a means of self-defense. I hear a lot of criminals hang out down around the river bottom."

"So you just gave the knife back to him?"

"Yep, plus I gave him five cents to pay for the stage back to town."

"Really? So let me get this straight. Pavlista assaults your family, and then you take the guy to the way station and give back his weapon—plus five cents for stage fare. Is that accurate?"

"Yup. That's what happened."

Holub studies Josef's face in disbelief for a long time, and then asks, "So, what do you think might have happened to Emil Pavlista?"

I think this is an odd question. How would Josef know? The marshal should be the one to figure that out, not Josef. But now I realize Holub is keeping Josef talking to test the consistencies in his story.

"How should I know?" Josef blurts. "Maybe some criminal came along and killed him. Like I said, there are a lot of road agents to be found along that route. He was injured, after all, and easy prey for those types."

"So some thief came along, robbed him, and then killed him just for the five cents you gave him?"

"Maybe they wanted that knife. Did you ever think of that?" Josef asks defiantly. "Come to think of it, maybe it was one of those Indians I see floating up and down the river near there. They'd certainly like a knife like that."

I think about disagreeing with that point but realize this might not be the time to contest Josef's argument.

"Hmm. Indians, huh? Maybe," Holub says, glancing my way as if to solicit my take on Josef's testimony.

"Satisfied?" I ask him.

"For now," he says to me. Then, turning to Josef, he adds, "If you think of anything you might have left out . . . er, forgotten, I mean, be sure to let me know."

"Oh, you can be sure of that," Josef answers, his tone seething with sarcasm.

"You know, Zach? I don't like your attitude much. And there's something a bit fishy about this whole thing." Without another word, the marshal turns and pulls himself up onto his horse, heading at a trot back onto the bottom road.

Josef and I watch him ride away without speaking, until I say, "Josef, I want you to know that I didn't willingly lead that man out here. Someone connected you to our church, having seen you at the church's dedication. I couldn't deny that I knew who you were, so I had to give him your name."

"I understand, Reverend. It's OK. I think he bought my story."

"Story? Don't you mean your account of what happened?"

"Sure, that's what I mean. Of course that's what I mean, Reverend. Now, if you'll excuse me, I have a lot more shit to scoop here."

Lord, is it not right to seek the best in men instead of pointing to their failings? Can sinners not be redeemed? Of course they can be. Through Christ's sacrifice, you have shown us the true meaning of redemption. But does redemption erase all evidence of past transgressions? Or are past sinners always marked somehow and susceptible to more sinning?

Josef has forced me to ask all these questions and more. I have tried to believe in his goodness. I have tried to see the best in him, and I believe that in some small way I may have helped to strengthen his faith. It makes me wonder, though, if I am blinded by naïveté to think that he is truly redeemable. Lord, let my faith in him be justified and his redemption attainable.

CHAPTER 57
TWO YEARS LATER, 1872

IT'S BEEN ELEVEN YEARS since I accepted the call to service by this tiny congregation. For eleven years, I've been preaching to my church of devout Brethren. And not only this congregation, but many others who have invited me to preach for them, whether nearby in Cedar Rapids or as far away as Wisconsin and Illinois. These days, I receive far more of these invitations than I can accept, my reputation having spread far and wide to souls seeking spiritual nourishment. Of course, it's for God's glory, not for my own. But I admit I find it gratifying that so many people are so receptive to hearing God's Word. In fact, I recently received a letter from my old friend John Novotny asking if I would travel to Nebraska to preach to his group of Bohemian believers. That would indeed be a lengthy trip. I wonder how Aneta would react to that. Not in a positive way, I imagine. A trip like that could take more than a month to complete on horseback. And Aneta left here with our eight children? I just don't know. Of course, the older children could help, couldn't they? Karel is already almost thirteen, and Julie isn't far behind. They could pick up much of the slack, I figure. Of course, my opinion and Aneta's would most likely be miles apart on this point. I'll not propose this trip just yet, but I will be patient. I can wait. For when I propose it, it will need to be at just the right moment.

Looking back over the past decade, I'm proud that my little church has grown considerably. My congregation began with only five families and now numbers almost forty. It isn't my work alone that's accomplished that. The construction of our own temple played an important role, there's no doubt. Now I've been getting correspondence from other groups of believers to whom I have preached. They are telling me of their plans to build their own churches. This heartens me and causes me to be much less worried by anti-religion forces like the freethinkers. These forces will always work against our crusade to save souls. But I am convinced that the Lord will prevail, and I will stand as one who will help to guarantee it.

Time passes quickly, and the four years that follow produce several more letters from John Novotny. His small but devout congregation near Clarkson, Nebraska, is struggling. He's written that there are no proper preachers to be had. Still, they carry on, meeting regularly in John's home, reading the scriptures, praying together, and singing hymns. This year, John wrote that land has been donated for a cemetery, and he hopes that I will come to dedicate it properly. I am inclined to do so. I believe that this could be the first step, a kind of impetus for the construction of their church building, and my presence could be a true inspiration to them.

Timing is everything. What's folly today may be a necessity tomorrow. A trip to Nebraska might have been folly four years ago, but I feel that it is a necessity now, considering the current needs of John's Evangelical congregation. The timing may be perfect. Aneta has been in high spirits of late, mostly because of the expansion of our parsonage. The house now boasts an extra room to better accommodate her many domestic activities and our large family. Also, and of no less relevance, four of our eight children are now in their teenage years and capable of fulfilling many responsibilities.

On a bright mid-June morning in 1875, I finally pack my saddlebags with provisions for the trip, including my Bible, a communion cup, a baptismal bowl, and several of my written sermons. Then I begin my 300-mile ride westward, heading through my old environs of Tama County and onward over the grassy plains of Iowa.

These plains seem to stretch for mile upon mile of grassy tedium. The land is nothing like the rolling hills near my home. I see no hills here at all. In fact, I have never seen such an expansive land of flatness as western Iowa. But I continue undeterred, riding as far as I can each day, avoiding the tall grass by finding various deer and Indian paths that crisscross the land. I finally come upon what appear to be wagon ruts, and I wonder if the Novotnys traveled on this trail. It proves to be a fortuitous route, as I find a few settlers along the way who have staked their claims after deciding they could travel no further. I'm able to stop at many of these homesteads, where I am offered sustenance in the way of water, food, and companionship in return for a scripture reading or a prayer.

It takes six days to reach the Missouri River because of difficult weather and my aging mare. Eventually, I find the ferry and cross the river to the town of Omaha, eager to connect with civilization once again. To my dismay, I am at once sorry I didn't take an alternate route around this miserable place. Heavy rain last night resulted in streets now almost impassable with mud. And as my horse sloshes into the center of the town, I'm repulsed by a stench someone tells me emanates from the meat-packing plant recently built there. But that isn't the worst of it. The main street seems to be lined with tavern after decrepit tavern full of rowdy customers, all engaged in foul language so loud I can hear it from the middle of the street where I sit on my horse. Are there any preachers in this town? I highly doubt it, judging from the apparent low moral fiber of these people. I make up my mind then and there to spend as little time here as possible, lest someone determine my vocation and string me up.

Finding a boarding house that seems halfway respectable, I stable my horse and then bed down for the night in a lumpy but acceptable feather bed. Fortunately, the bed comes with a morning breakfast. And after a restless night's slumber, I eat and make a beeline out of this serpents' nest, riding westward to the Platte River. As per John's directions, I follow the riverbank northwestward. Then I veer to the north until I finally arrive at Clarkson, a settlement that is hardly a town at all. It doesn't take me long to find John's claim, which is just a few miles from there.

I'm drained from my journey, but the reception I receive more than recoups my energy. I am at once welcomed into the embrace of the Novotny family's hospitality. The following day, a grand feast appears out of nowhere. Members of John's congregation converge on his sod house bringing food of all types, ranging from salt pork to potatoes to wonderful pastries. They are all pleased that I have arrived, and we spend the evening eating and visiting at outdoor tables. We do a lot of planning too, for there is much to do in the days to come.

Two days later is Saturday, and it's time for the dedication of the new cemetery, which is named the Zion Church Cemetery. That is curious, since there is no Zion Church. But there will be, I've been told. The name of the cemetery will be a reminder of the goal they have set for themselves, the goal of building their own church edifice.

The dedication proceeds with all the pomp and circumstance these settlers can attain, and when the ceremony is completed, the celebrating continues with more food and socializing. This is indeed a vibrant Evangelical community, and I am greatly impressed by their joy of life and Christian fervor.

The next day, the Sunday service is held in the barn of one of John's neighbors. The people gathered here are eager to hear me preach. But first, there is the sacrament of baptism, the sacred ritual that I gladly confer upon ten eager souls. Soon, it is time for my sermon, and I have chosen it wisely. I speak about the need to build on one's own faith, something these people excel in, but something that continually requires reinforcement. I also speak of the need to build a community of faith, a community of faithful who have their very own place of worship. I even speak at length of the steps that led to the construction of my own church, from practical steps such as fundraising and planning the building to the more spiritual steps of evangelizing and praying. I am impressed that, although I speak longer than I usually would, covering things that some might find mundane, these believers seem to be captivated by my every word.

The service concludes with John leading the congregation in unison singing of a favorite hymn. Soon after the benediction, the people surround me, wishing me well and thanking me for what they say is the honor of my presence. Before long, it is time again for a festive meal and plentiful Christian fellowship.

The ride home seems much easier than when I came. Indeed, the glow of Christian love from those believers sustains me as I ride south along the Platte River. I am surprised to find that I am still smiling when I pass through the Gomorrah they call Omaha. I'm not sure about the reception I'll get from Aneta when I arrive home, but it doesn't really matter. This is the reason I travel to preach in faraway places. There seems to be a void, a spiritual void that needs to be filled. It exists everywhere that God's children thirst for His love, and His love is best expressed to them via God's messengers, like me. I will never stop this evangelizing. I can't stop. I won't stop. Not until it's time for me to meet my Maker.

It's been twenty-four days since I left the parsonage, but as I approach the stage line road, I decide to take a detour south past Vaclav and Josef's homesteads, looking for new settlers down along the river. I pass Vaclav's farm, where I see him out in one of his fields, hoeing weeds between the rows of corn sprouts. I ride toward Josef's farm and notice something interesting out by his creek. It's a small, pointed structure, similar to a Plains Indian teepee. And there's a child sitting by it. A girl? Her arms are moving back and forth like she's rocking a baby—or maybe a doll. Is that Josef's daughter Terezie? Suddenly, the girl sees me riding by on the road and she stands up, vigorously waving. Yup, that's Terezie, alright. I wave back.

PART FOUR
TEREZIE
1875–1884

CHAPTER 58
IOWA

I LOVE PLAYING DOWN HERE BY THE CREEK, so this is where I spend a lot of time in the summer. Here I can do anything I want, or do nothing at all. I can just be myself, or be whatever my imagination will let me be. Today it's hot. Mama says July is always this way, so get used to it. That's what she tells me. I don't mind. Just lying here all day on the bank of the little stream, looking up at passing clouds, and listening to the birds sing is my idea of the best day ever. I can't imagine anyplace better than this. But, of course, I don't know any other place. My mama often talks about the way it was in Bohemia, in little towns like Krouna and Jarošov. She talks about the Bohemian hills, the way the sounds of hawks, wolves, and hungry farm animals would echo among those hills. But I know nothing of those hills. Even though I was born in Bohemia, I don't remember a thing about it. Maybe Bohemia was like paradise. Maybe not. But I don't see how it could have been any better than this place right here, right now.

As I said, I've been spending a lot of my time down here by the creek during the summer months. That is, unless Mama finds something for me to do around the house. Then I complete her task as fast as possible so that I can sneak off to resume my play. I suppose it would be nice to have other kids to play with, but there just aren't many around. Vincencie and Antonin are already nearly grown. These days, Vincencie always seems to be doing chores for Mama or spending time with a boy named Jan who lives further down the bottom road. The other day, I even heard them whispering about marriage. Antonin is eighteen now, so he'll have nothing to do with me. Papa keeps him real busy around the farm, which really irritates him. I think Antonin's kind of lazy, if you ask me.

I used to play with Wesley, but lately he doesn't seem to want to do the same things I like to do. I'm not sure why that is. I still see him quite often, though. For the last couple of years, his mama has been letting me watch Franz, Wesley's little brother, during harvest season when the adults are out in the fields. During those times, I see Wesley quite a lot. He's usually hanging around when I watch Franz. I think his mama trusts me with Franz more than she does Wesley. That kind of makes him mad, though I don't know why. I don't think he likes playing with Franz, anyway.

It's fun pretending to be Franz's mother, doing all those things that mothers do, like feeding him and teaching him stuff and reading to him. Wesley would never wanna do that. Playing house is what I do down here by the creek sometimes, too. In fact, that's what I've decided to do today.

I'm imagining that I'm the wife of an Indian brave. They call women like me *squaws*. I don't know why, but they do. I've built a little shelter out of tall branches that I've tied at the top with twine I brought from home. This is a perfect home for me, my Indian brave husband, and our daughter, Running Fawn. Our little home is right next to the embankment of the creek, and as I sit next to it, rocking my Indian baby, I can hear the rustle of the flowing water and the sound of birds and frogs nearby. I wonder if my Indian husband is out hunting bison for our evening meal or if he's somewhere attacking a cavalry fort with his band of Indian friends. Either way, I'm sure he'll come home soon, victorious.

Suddenly, I hear a voice. Is it someone singing? Perhaps my husband is singing an Indian war song on his way back from ambushing some blue-coat regiment. I step out of my stick home and gaze in the direction of the sound. Nope, it's not my Indian husband. It's just Wesley walking across the field, heading back toward his house from our place. I saw him there earlier, helping my brother Antonin with the horses. I wonder what tune he's singing. If he thought someone was listening, he'd be embarrassed, that's for sure. I think I'll be very still and see if I can surprise him if he comes near. He's following the creek now, and just at the elbow curve he leaves it behind, heading for his house about a quarter mile further on. He's nearer to me now, so I let out my best Indian whooping display, hoping it'll scare the britches off him.

"Woop, woop, woop, woooooop!" I yell. I'll bet that'll do it. He'll probably pee his knickers, thinking I'm a real Indian.

"Hi, Terezie. I know it's you," he calls to me. "Papa said there aren't any Injuns around here."

"Darn. I thought I'd get you this time." I suspect he might keep walking toward home, but he veers from his path and approaches my Indian stick home.

"What are you doing?" he asks.

"What's it look like? This is my Indian encampment. Wanna play?"

"Play how?" he asks.

"Well, you could be an Indian brave, and I could be your wife. Oh, and we have a beautiful little Indian daughter. Running Fawn is her name. I'm just getting ready to make supper. You wanna come in here and maybe smoke your peace pipe or something before we eat?" I ask. I realize I'm trying a little too hard to make it sound fun, for I already have a notion of how he will respond.

Sure enough, he says, "Nah, I don't think so. Playing house isn't my idea of fun. Now if you wanted to have a fight to the death with Indian lances, I'd wanna do that."

"I don't think so, Wes," I say. "Maybe another time. I'm expecting my Indian brave husband home at any moment.

You might want to get on your way, being a white man and all. If he finds you here talking to his beautiful Indian wife, that might not end well for you, if you know what I mean."

"Whatever you say, Terezie," he says as he walks away. That's Wesley for ya. He never wants to have fun anymore. Maybe I'll just stop asking him.

Wes is almost out of shouting distance when he turns back toward me and hollers, "Hey, Terezie!"

"What?" I yell back.

"I forgot to tell you something. Your mama said if I saw you, I should tell you to get on home. She has work for you to do."

"OK, thanks."

"See you later, Pocahontas!" he yells as he again turns toward home.

CHAPTER 59
THREE YEARS LATER

THINGS HAVE CHANGED around here quite a lot lately. These days, I spend much less time lollygagging around the creek pretending I'm someone I'm not. After all, I'm thirteen now—almost grown up, I figure. My body is changing too, but not nearly fast enough if you ask me. My hips seem to be widening, but my chest? Well, that's another story. What's wrong with my bosom? Hasn't it got the message? Recently, I've taken to checking my breasts regularly to see if they've shown any improvement. At first, I checked them about every week, but now I do it almost every morning when I get out of bed, hoping they had a growth spurt during the night.

A couple of weeks ago, while Mama was out working in the garden, I snuck into her room and looked at myself in the mirror to judge my progress. It's a mirror Papa found in town at the mercantile store and brought home to surprise Mama. I pulled my dress over my head and stood in front of the mirror in my panties, staring sadly at my unremarkable body. I took to poking and prodding at my breasts, thinking that perhaps some stimulation might spur them into action. "Come on, get on with it," I scolded. "I don't want to end up as some flat-chested spinster who lives alone the rest of her miserably flat life!"

Last week, Mama caught me in her room staring at myself in the mirror. I was standing there half-naked taking stock of things when I heard the door creak open slightly, and there she was peeking through the opening at me. "I heard someone talking in here," she said. What a sight I must have been, standing there in my panties with my hands cupped under my uncooperative breasts, pushing them skyward. I just froze, not knowing what I could say. There were any number of ways she might have reacted. She could have shrieked, "What in the world are you doing in here?" Or she could have laughed her head off at me. But she didn't. Instead, she quietly muttered, "Don't worry, Terezie. They'll grow soon enough." Then she closed the door, leaving me standing there with my small breasts cupped in my hands. As she walked out the front door, I could hear her call back to me, "Now get out here and feed those chickens!"

These days, although he comes to our farm regularly to help Papa, Wesley doesn't talk to me much. That could be because he's noticed my unimpressive breasts. That's probably it. Or he could just be shy since I do notice him looking at me once in a while. I don't know why he's doing that. He just looks at me kind of weird-like, without saying anything.

I'm not gonna spend my time worrying about Wesley, though. I've got plenty to do around here with all the tasks my mama gives me from day to day. I'm happy to do all of this. Well, not exactly happy, but I must take on more responsibilities since I'm older now, I guess. And of course, with Vincencie getting married to that Jan boy last year, I've had to take on most of her duties around here. I still see her all the time since she's living just down the road a bit, but she has her own home to take care of now. She won't be helping me around here, that's for sure.

I've even had to help Papa out in the fields recently. That's because Antonin got it into his head that he hasn't seen enough of the world. That's how he puts it: *haven't seen enough of the world.* So he got a job at that new Sinclair plant in Cedar Rapids. It's a meat-packing plant. Apparently, they slaughter animals there, which is pretty gross. The way Antonin stinks when he comes home from work almost makes me vomit, it's so bad. He's been working there for about two months now, and he already complains about that place. I doubt he'll be there for very long. It appears he's seen quite enough of the world already. When he quits, I think Papa will be glad to have him at home again to help with the farming, although we'll certainly miss the extra money Antonin has provided.

Reverend Kun stopped by the other day with some exciting news. He told us of a celebration happening in town on the anniversary of Jan Hus's death. Mama says that we should go, but Papa isn't too sure. I'll let them hash it out, but I hope she gets the upper hand. She usually does. I really want to go, since I rarely get to go anyplace. The event is going to happen on July 6—that's coming up just a week from now. If we go, it'll most likely be with Wesley's family. I guess I'll have to put up with Wes's weird looks at me. That's OK. I'm getting used to it. In fact, I kind of even like it. At least he notices I exist.

When July 6 finally arrives and we prepare to leave for town, I put on my best dress, the only one I have that doesn't make me look like an orphan. I can tell that Mama is pretty excited because she has gone to extra lengths to fix herself up as best she can. Her dress is much more colorful than mine, and I'm sort of jealous, I have to admit. Finally, we are ready, except for Antonin, who is working—still *seeing more of the world* at the slaughterhouse. We clamber onto the wagon and head up the road to pick up Wesley, his little brother Franz, Uncle Vaclav, and Aunt Annie. Of course, they're not my real aunt and uncle, but that's what I've always called them.

Finally, we find ourselves in Cedar Rapids, riding down Sixteenth Avenue. Many people are out on the street, and I can see flames reaching skyward from a bonfire they've built in a nearby grove of trees. A crowd is assembling by the fire, and soon I can hear them singing. It sounds like a hymn I've heard before, but I don't know its name.

"Mama, is it OK if I wander around a bit?" I ask.

"I don't think that would be a good idea," she responds. "You had better stay close by."

Uncle Vaclav interjects, "Maybe if Wesley went with her, they'd be OK."

I hadn't figured on that. I'd rather go wherever I want to go and not follow him around. But if that's my only option, it will have to do. "How about if Wes comes with me?" I ask my mother.

Soon, Wes and I are walking along Sixteenth Avenue, gazing into the storefronts of shoemakers, dress shops, dry goods stores, cigar shops, and bakeries. Papa has given me a few coins to spend, and the smells coming from the bakery make me stop to ponder if my money would be well spent here.

"Wanna go inside?" I ask Wesley.

"Nah. I'll be across the street. You can find me there when you're done."

That's fine by me, I think. Now I won't have to share my money with him. As I walk into the shop, the smell of freshly baked bread and pastries is intense but not altogether unfamiliar. After all, Mama bakes bread regularly, and I love it when she does. It makes the entire house smell like this. But bread is not what I'm after today, and I soon find myself in front of the kolache case.

I stand there considering which kolache to select. Cheese? Prune? Fruit? There are just too many possibilities, and I can tell that the lady behind the counter is getting impatient with me.

"They're all good," she says. "You can't go wrong with any of them."

"I just can't decide," I say, noticing that someone is standing right behind me, waiting to order. I glance back in that direction and see it is a boy a couple of years older than me.

"She's right, you know," he says to me. "They're all fantastic. I like the apricot ones the best, though."

"OK, I'll have one of those," I say to the lady.

"Me, too," says the boy. "I'll pay for them both." He reaches into his pocket and pulls out the coins, handing the exact amount to the clerk as if he comes here all the time.

"I have my own money," I protest.

"That's OK. It's my treat."

"Thank you. That's really nice of you," I say, blushing. "My name's Terezie. What's yours?"

"Edwin, but you can call me Eddie."

We walk out of the shop with our treats in hand, already sinking our teeth into the delectable pastries. We stand for a moment in front of the shop, enjoying our kolaches. Then he gestures to a bench outside the shop, saying, "You wanna sit for a while and finish these off?"

"Sure," I say. This is all new to me. Is this boy interested in me? I'm not sure how to act. My simple dress must look terrible to him. What must he think? I catch myself eating with my mouth open, so I instantly close it and continue to chew my sweet delight. Don't be such a country girl, I tell myself. Suddenly, I remember Wesley and look around until I see him on the other side of the street. He's watching a button accordion player who's standing on the sidewalk punching out a lively polka to the glee of bystanders. What will he think if he sees me with this Eddie boy? But what does it matter? This boy has shown more interest in me in the last few moments than Wesley has shown in the last month.

"I haven't seen you around here before," Eddie says.

"I'm from south of here, just over the stage line down near the Iowa River. We're here for the celebration," I explain. I wonder what he must think of me—this simple farm girl who knows nothing except milking cows and beheading chickens.

"You wanna come with me to the bonfire? It's just down the street," the boy says.

Wesley is staring at us now from across the street, and I wonder what he's thinking. "I don't know," I answer. "I promised my mother that I'd stay with my friend."

"Like I said, it's just down the street. We can come right back. Come on, let's go. It'll be fun," he says as he stands up and offers me his hand.

"Uh, OK, I guess," I say as I stare back in Wesley's direction. My hand seems sweaty in Eddie's grasp and I wonder if he notices, but I let him lead me along the street, winding our way through the crowd toward the bonfire. I glance back and see that Wes is following us. He doesn't look thrilled, but I feel somewhat safer knowing that he's keeping an eye on me. Having him follow us means that I haven't actually gone against Mama's wishes. We aren't really separated. At least, not by more than shouting distance.

Eddie and I arrive at the bonfire, and the crowd that is amassed in the grove soon swallows us up. We stand shoulder to shoulder as someone gives a speech about Jan Hus. But I'm not really listening. My attention is on the boy's hand that is grasping my own. I'm feeling something quite odd, a sensation new to me. What it is I'm not sure, but all I know is that I'd like to hold his hand forever. Soon, the speech is over and the crowd is singing *Jesus Christ, Our Blessed Savior*, one of Hus's hymns that I actually know. The two of us stand there holding hands and singing for a long while, until Eddie suddenly puts his arm around me and pulls me close, laying his hand on my small breast.

"What are you doing?" I yell, but my yell is hardly audible above the unison singing. I struggle to escape his grasp, but I'm helpless against his superior strength.

"Don't you like it? Being touched like this?" Eddie says with a roguish smile. "I know a place where we could go—."

I rip his hand off my breast and finally squirm out of his grasp, but he grabs my wrist and won't let go. "What? I'm not good enough for you, you cheap bohunk?" he shouts. "I'm the best you're ever going to find, so you should get it while you can."

Wesley's fist comes in hard, making contact with Eddie's eye, and the boy goes down in a heap. Without a word, Wes grabs my arm and pulls me through the crowd as fast as I can keep up. We reach Sixteenth Avenue, and even then, he keeps pulling me along until we reach where Papa has hitched the wagon and team. Wesley pushes me under the wagon, and after looking to see any signs of Eddie, we sit together hiding there in relative safety.

Breathing hard from our running, Wesley asks, "Are you OK?"

"I think so," I answer. "You're bleeding!" I exclaim as I stare down at his hand.

"Oh, it's not too bad. Just a scratch. Your friend had a hard face, I guess," he says, smiling.

We sit there in silence, for we don't know what else to say to one another. But something needs saying. "Thanks, Wes," I finally offer. "I'm so sorry. That was all my fault. Please forgive me." I'm looking down at my lap, unable to look him in the eyes.

"That's OK, as long as you're not hurt. You sure you're OK?"

"Yeah, I guess so. That Eddie guy was kind of rough, though. He really had a grip on my arm, and he squeezed me really hard…up here," I say as I lay my hand on my chest, at once embarrassed that I even mentioned it. Why am I drawing attention to my tiny stunted breasts? I ask myself.

Wes seems very concerned now, asking, "Does it hurt? Are you injured?"

"No, Wes," I laugh. "I'm not that fragile. I'll live."

"You sure? Maybe I should go find your parents," he says glancing down at my bosom, the absolute worst part of my body.

"No, I'm fine. It hardly hurts at all," I assure him.

For a long moment, we sit there in uncomfortable silence, until Wes finally says, "I'm glad you're not injured. Your mama would never forgive me."

Then, I do something that comes from somewhere deep inside of me, a place so unrecognizable and new that it seems to be done by a complete stranger. I lean toward him and plant a hard kiss square on his cheek. "Thanks for helping me today, Wesley." I say coyly. "You're kind of my hero."

As I draw back again, a wide smile appears on his face, and he slowly puts his arm around me, pulling me close to him. Laying his other hand on mine, he begins to stroke it ever so gently, as if he's comforting a newborn bird just fallen from its nest. The rest of the world drifts away now, and all that's left is the sound of our breathing.

After a while, I wonder how long we've been sitting here. Two minutes? Ten? I'm not sure. It doesn't matter though. In fact, nothing else really matters. My sore wrist doesn't matter; that boy Eddie doesn't matter; my small breasts don't even matter. Nothing besides the stroke of Wesley's gentle hand on mine matters anymore, and we sit there a while longer, wondering what's happening to us. Things seem very different now between Wes and me, and it suddenly occurs to me that maybe I'll never need to poke at my breasts again—not if Wesley likes me the way I am, tiny breasts and all. Perhaps, no pokes or prods or pleas will be necessary. Maybe Mama was right. *Don't worry, they'll grow,* she said. And when has she ever been wrong about anything?

We sit there under the wagon for a while longer, both of us wondering what we should do next. What is there to do or say? We don't know. So we just sit there—his hand caressing mine—his arm pulling me close. And while it's nice to sit quietly like this, the silence eventually becomes far too awkward. Still more time passes until I can't stand it any longer, and I finally blurt out, "You wanna go for some ice cream?" Not giving him a chance to answer, I exclaim, "Let's go—my treat!" I immediately grab his hand, pull him out from under the wagon, and we head down the street in the opposite direction from the bonfire so as not to run into Eddie.

We walk hand in hand about two blocks when we happen upon a large building with a sign above the door. *Bohemian Dance Hall*, it says. Many people are going in and out, most of them stumbling from drunkenness. A bulletin board plastered with posters stands in front of the building, and we stop to read some of them. Several of these posters promote churches located nearby, while others advertise job openings. Several are for a new oatmeal factory, and others are for the Sinclair meat-packing plant where Antonin works. There are also several positions advertised for women: domestic jobs like clothes washing, cleaning, cooking, and that sort of thing. I think to myself that I might one day work here in Cedar Rapids. I can do all these tasks that they are requiring, and it would be exciting to work in town, as long as I could avoid people like Eddie.

As we gaze upon the bulletin board, a ruckus suddenly erupts inside the dance hall. I hear a lot of shouting and swearing, as if a fight is about to start. Wes and I certainly don't want any part of that, so Wesley grabs my hand, and we hurry down the street in search of our ice cream.

It's late afternoon when we get back to the wagon, where my mother is already waiting with Aunt Annie and little Franz.

"Did you have fun?" Mama asks as we approach.

"Yes. We just had some ice cream. Yum," I say, and that's all I intend to say about our day.

"What happened to your hand?" Aunt Annie exclaims as she grabs Wesley's hand to examine it.

"Uh . . . it was sort of . . . an accident," Wesley answers, not very convincingly.

"It looks like it's swollen. What happened?" his mama presses.

I'm not about to let Wes lie for me, so I say, "It was my fault."

"Your fault?" Mama asks.

"Kind of. There was this boy who tried to sort of touch me, and he wouldn't let me go."

"Oh, my goodness," Mama exclaims. "Are you hurt?"

"No, I'm fine. But Wesley hit him. He hit him pretty hard. That's when his hand got bruised."

Mama and Aunt Annie are speechless, not something I often see. Finally, Mama says, "I knew we shouldn't have let you go off by yourselves."

"No, no," I protest. "Wes was there. He protected me. It was OK, Mama."

Mama grabs me, squeezing me tight, saying sadly, "My poor Terezie."

Suddenly, we see Papa and Uncle Vaclav walking in our direction. Their wobbly gait tells me they've had a couple of drinks, and I wonder what Mama will say to that. Their voices are loud and raucous like I've heard Papa speak when he comes home from the tavern. I notice that Papa's shirt is badly torn, and I also see that Uncle Vaclav has a split lip that has deposited some blood onto his shirt.

"What in the world?" Mama screams.

"Lord, have mercy!" is Aunt Annie's response. "What on earth happened to you two?"

Uncle Vaclav touches his lip and then looks at his finger to see if he sees any blood. He says, "Oh, it was just a misunderstanding. Well, not actually a misunderstanding. More of a difference of opinion, I would say. Well, no, not even that, since no opinion was really given. You might say that—"

"Oh, for cryin' out loud," says Papa. "Just tell 'em!"

"Well, we were at the Bohemian Dance Hall just minding our own business, enjoying ourselves, when some troublemakers came in. It was a group of about five Americans who started insulting some of our people," explains Wes's papa.

"Let me guess," says Mama. "Josef hit somebody, didn't he?"

"Now wait, Frannie," Papa pleads.

Uncle Vaclav comes to his aid, saying, "Not exactly."

"Not exactly?" Mama asks. "What's that mean?"

"Well," continues Uncle Vaclav, "one of the Americans pushed me against the bar and then tore Josef's shirt. Then Josef took a swing at him."

"So he did hit someone, then," Mama declares, exasperated.

"Well, yes. Sort of. But the American ducked, and Josef nailed me square in the face."

"My Lord. What is wrong with you people?" cries Aunt Annie. "Can't we just commemorate Hus's death like normal people instead of trying to relive it?"

This brings out a burst of loud laughter, but I notice that the only people laughing are the men. Between guffaws, Papa sputters, "Well, if I'm not mistaken, Annie, Hus was burned at the stake, not killed in a bar fight." Then he resumes his laughter, proud of his historical clarification.

Wes and I are soon giggling along with our fathers. But that comes to a sudden halt when Mama declares, "How dare you speak of Jan Hus in that fashion? You should be ashamed of yourselves! I don't want to hear another word. Get on the wagon. We're going home!"

That would be the last time we'd ever attend the Jan Hus celebration as a family. And Uncle Vaclav would forever carry that scar on his lip—a reminder of the homage he and Papa paid to the great Bohemian reformer on the anniversary of his martyrdom.

CHAPTER 60

ANOTHER WINTER HAS PASSED on our farm. It's been so very boring to be stuck in our farmhouse during the cold weather, struggling to keep up with my chores and look after the animals. Of course, Antonin is still away since he hasn't quit that job, which surprises me. I thought he hated it so much. He still rides the mud wagon into town most days. They call it a mud wagon for good reason. When it rains, the road between Iowa City and Cedar Rapids is near impassable. It has been especially bad this spring, with the snow melting and all. Antonin tells me that sometimes the team gets so mired down in the mud that the passengers have to get out and push the coach to get it going again.

When it's raining hard or particularly cold, Antonin just stays overnight in town at Frank Horak's boardinghouse. That way, he doesn't have to deal with the mud wagon or take the time to come home and then get back to work in the morning. That's good in one way and bad in another. When he stays in town, Antonin tends to visit the local taverns after work. Mama worries that he's been drinking as much as Papa. She also complains that he's spending too much money on brew when he should be bringing that money home to us. I agree with her. Why should he be getting drunk on our money?

It's the middle of April, and Papa is already out in the fields planting his crops. With Antonin gone, I'm the one left to help him, but I don't mind. Springtime is especially beautiful here, and I'd rather be out in the open air than cooped up doing housework or tending to the animals. Of course, there really isn't that much livestock, just the two horses, the milk cow, and the chickens. But that is soon to change. Papa has purchased a few beef calves that are soon to be delivered by a local farmer. This came about because Antonin told him how much he could make from them at the Sinclair plant. Of course, we'll need some feed and bedding for all this livestock, so Papa's been cultivating clover hay, corn, and oats. This will take some time, and I'll probably have to help with it. And then there's the garden that Mama takes great pride in. That will require more work than she has time for, so guess who'll provide a lot of that labor? Me, that's who!

It's well into May now, and the crop seedlings are emerging in the fields. The vegetables in Mama's garden are popping up, too. It won't be long until we're eating fresh tomatoes, my favorite. The rain that's been coming down for the last two days should really help guarantee a good crop for our family.

I've been seeing more of Wesley recently. He's much more attentive to me now. Last winter, he even walked from his house to mine in a snowstorm just to give me my birthday present. That was sweet. He gave me a little bird that he'd carved out of a piece of wood. He did a really nice job carving it, and it must have taken him a long time. It's hanging on the wall next to my bed, and I stare at it each night as I go to sleep. Sometimes I imagine it will awaken from its slumber and fly off while I'm sleeping.

It's been raining off and on for a couple of weeks now, and Papa is worried. He heard from Joe Coufal that the Iowa River is cresting early because of the combination of the snowmelt from the north and the heavy spring rainfall. Several of Mr. Coufal's fields are already flooded. Those crops are gone, and if the waters don't recede soon, it might be too late for Joe to replant, Papa says. Much of our cropland is also in a low area, but not as close to the river, and Papa thinks it's less likely to be affected by the rising water.

I think he was a bit too confident, for now, not three days later, flood waters enter Papa's cropland and cover the oat field and half of the clover field. This isn't water from the Iowa River—it's from our swollen creek that feeds into it, but it's no less damaging. This is bad—really bad, Mama tells me. Without those crops, how will we feed the livestock, or ourselves?

I can tell that Papa is depressed, and Mama is worried, too. I often hear them talking about how dire things are. How will we make it? How will we eat? What about the animals? Papa asks. Joe Coufal assures Papa that flooding rarely happens around here, so the future should bode well for us, but what about right now?

I hear Papa talking about getting a job in town, maybe at the Sinclair plant, but Mama talks him out of it. She points out that we have some other acreage on higher ground that we haven't yet cleared for crops. "Couldn't we get to clearing that so we could plant it for at least a small late crop?" she asks. He agrees, but he wonders if that will be enough to make it until next year.

It is during one of these discussions that Antonin mentions a job opening at the boardinghouse in town. They're looking for a domestic worker to help wash bedclothes and clean. "Maybe Mama could earn some money doing that job," he suggests.

"Or maybe I could do it," I offer, suddenly entering the conversation.

There's a long silence as the three of them ponder the possibility. Then Mama says, "No, that's not possible. You're only fourteen. I don't want you traveling to Cedar Rapids alone. Remember last year when you were there?"

"But I'll usually be with her on the stage," says Antonin.

"*Usually* is not good enough," she replies.

"Look," Antonin says, "I understand why you're worried. There are a lot of questionable sorts in town, and she's only fourteen. But Frank Horak and his wife run a very respectable boardinghouse and attached grocery as well. She will be safe there. And she will be fine on the mud wagon whether or not I'm there."

"That would help bring in some income," concedes Papa.

"And I'd be really careful, Mama," I assure her.

"Like the last time?" Mama replies with sarcasm.

"That won't happen again," I say. "I promise."

"I'm gonna have to think about this," she finally says. She thinks about it, and after further urging, she gives in to my pleading and agrees to take me to town to discuss the job with the Horaks.

The next day, Mama and I board the mud wagon, pay our five cents apiece, and endure the ride along the muddy road to Cedar Rapids. When we get there, we walk toward the boardinghouse, taking note that it's very near to the stage office. I can see that Mama's reassured by that, and soon we are standing on the porch of Frank Horak's establishment, rapping on the door.

The door opens and a smiling Mrs. Horak appears to greet us. She's a plump woman with a pleasant disposition, and I can't help but stare at the bright cherry-colored cheeks that protrude from her otherwise pallid face. She invites us in, and we sit, having coffee and talking about the job requirements, none of which seem very hard to do. Mrs. Horak tells us that the boardinghouse has ten rooms but seldom has more than eight rented out on any night. My job would be to clean the rooms after the boarders leave and then wash the bedclothes. I'm sure I can do that, I tell her.

"I'm sure you can too, dear," she replies kindly.

We spend a long time discussing my duties and my pay until Mama and Mrs. Horak finally settle on my schedule and salary. It will include free boarding for Antonin when he stays there and a discount on goods from their grocery store. With all the arrangements complete, Mama and I walk down the street to the stage station. We board the mud wagon and ride home, satisfied that the Horaks will take good care of me.

Mama and I arrive home in the late afternoon, and it surprises us that Papa is nowhere to be seen. In fact, it isn't until evening that he shows up with his breath smelling of beer.

"Where have you been?" Mama asks, as if she doesn't know. She knows exactly where he's been. He's been at that new tavern up the road that he's been talking about, the one just north of Vaclav's place about half a mile.

"I went up to the new tavern. That's where I've been," Papa answers defensively.

"Was it wise, do you think, to spend our money on beer when we don't even know if we'll survive the year?"

"Actually, yes," he replies with a slightly inebriated smile. "I was seeking an employment opportunity."

"Huh? What do you mean?" she asks, confused.

"Well, I noticed he had a fairly decent-sized crowd there, so I asked the owner if he'd like to have some music at his establishment. I told him about my crank organ that I played in taverns in Wien and Krouna. I think it impressed him."

"Really? So, did he hire you?"

"He was open to the idea. He said I could play for tips, but he warned that if it cut into his beer sales, he'd have to let me go. I thought that was fair. It's worth a try, anyway."

"So, when do you start?"

"Whenever I want, I guess. He says most people are there on the weekends, so that's when I'll probably make my big debut. But first I need to get the contraption out to see if it still works."

"Big debut?" I hear Antonin scoff under his breath. I haven't heard Papa play his crank organ, but I guess Antonin has. He must know something I don't. That something soon becomes clear to me. As I crawl into bed that evening, I am shaken by an assault of noise coming from Papa's room. It bears a slight resemblance to music, but only slight.

Things are looking up for the Zach family. Sure, it will be difficult to keep the farm running, but we'll get by somehow. Maybe next year things will be back to normal and I'll be back home attending to my same old chores. Of course, that is, unless I prefer town life. We'll just have to see how that goes, won't we?

CHAPTER 61
WINTER OF 1881

ANTON NOVAK BURSTS through the door of his small house, accompanied by an intrusion of wind and blowing snow. A storm has been bearing down for several long days, one of many such storms this winter, and Anton expects that when all is said and done, this winter of 1881 will rank as the worst yet since he and Rose arrived here. He stomps his feet as he slams the thick wooden door behind him and sets down the load of firewood he brought inside.

"Whew, it's really nasty out there," he says as he brushes snow from his shoulders and sleeves. Rose does not respond, but Anton doesn't expect her to. These days she doesn't respond to anything that he says. He's used to it. Now he talks to himself most of the time.

But he senses that something is different this time. He glances over at the rocking chair where Rose spends most of her days. She's not there, and he scans the inside of the cabin. It isn't really much of a cabin, comprising one room, and it doesn't take but a couple moments for Anton to realize that his wife is gone. Where could she be? he wonders. Did she leave the cabin to look for him? Why would she do that? He'd told her where he was going and that he'd be right back.

Suddenly, Anton fears that Rose might be out looking for him in the subzero blizzard conditions. He opens the door and calls out frantically, "Rose . . . Rose . . . are you out here?" The dense and blowing snow makes it difficult to see more than a few feet in front of him, and he looks at the ground to see if he can see tracks showing where she went. But the snow has already covered his own tracks, and he realizes that there will be no chance of following any path she has left.

"Rose!" he calls as he begins circling the exterior of the house to see if he can spot any sign of her. The snow around the house is piling up near the roof, amassing so quickly that even walking is becoming nearly impossible. But this does not deter Anton. He plows through it as best he can. But there's nothing! Nothing but blowing and drifting snow. "Rose! Where are you? Rose! Follow my voice! Rose!" he cries.

Anton steps back into the house to think for a moment and to warm himself. He knows Rose can't survive long out in this weather. He'll have to head back out to look for her, but he knows he could lose his bearings and not find his way back. Still, he has to try. Stepping out of the cabin again, he walks in as straight a line as possible toward the grove of trees behind his house, calling Rose's name. He loses sight of the house in a matter of a few yards, but he continues on to the trees, knowing that he can't allow himself to get disoriented or he won't make it back. He moves on a little further and then, worried he'll lose his way, doubles back the way he came. Luckily, though the snowdrifts impede his progress, he finds the cabin and then directs his search in another direction. This time he heads toward the woodpile where he just retrieved his load of firewood. Perhaps Rose headed in that direction, knowing he was going there.

Anton struggles through the drifts and finally reaches the woodpile. No Rose. Using the woodpile as a reference point, he searches frantically to see if she is anywhere in this area of his property, but it's to no avail. Now Anton is getting quite cold, and he knows Rose must be in imminent danger from the frigid conditions if she is out here wandering about. He takes a long time—too long, he thinks—to get back to the cabin and head out in another direction. This time he thrashes through the snow toward the road. He realizes he has been searching far too long. And who knows how long Rose might have been out here before he even realized she was missing? Anton is beside himself with fear as he flails about in the drifts with numb fingers and failing limbs.

Suddenly, he stumbles onto something, and he stoops down to find Rose lying there, not moving. He notices she didn't even bother to bundle up before leaving the house; she's wearing only the thin housecoat she often wears as she rocks by the fire. "Rose!" he cries. "Why did you come out here? What were you thinking, Rose?"

Anton tries to gather her up, but she's encrusted in snow and ice. He finds it too difficult, his hands being numb and his weakened body unresponsive to his urgings. He crouches next to her, with the snow lashing horizontally against his face. Anton tries again to pull her up toward him, but finding it impossible, he leans over her, attempting to warm her with his own body. But it's too late. Rose is dead. He can see it on her face. "Rose, Rose," he cries. "You can't be . . . Rose, wake up!"

Anton now realizes that he too will perish if he stays here much longer. He is shivering and tired. Exhausted. There's no point in trying to carry Rose or even drag her back to the cabin. He knows he can't do it. But he can't leave her here in the snow either.

"Rose," he says finally, "don't worry. I won't leave you. I love you, Rose." He is calm now as he slowly unbuttons his coat and lies down in the snow, embracing his wife, trying to cover the two of them with it. In a matter of a few moments, the snow has almost completely covered them in a drift, not unlike all the other drifts forming near their modest pioneer home.

It isn't until two weeks after the blizzard that we find their bodies near the road in front of their homestead. It's a frosty February morning, and Papa is driving me with his wagon to the Coufal way station, as he often does during the winter months. I've been working fairly regularly at the boardinghouse for two years now, taking time off only during terrible weather or during harvest season. With the severe winter we've had, I've been staying home most of the time these days. Mrs. Horak doesn't mind too much when that happens. After all, there aren't many travelers renting rooms during the coldest months, anyway.

The snow from the last blizzard is disappearing now, and we decide to stop by the Novak home to check on them. When we arrive, we at once see their bodies partially exposed in a snowdrift by the road. Papa makes me stay on the wagon as he approaches them. I sit and wait, trying not to watch, but I find it impossible to avert my gaze. Poor Anton and Rose. I wonder what happened. Soon Papa comes back and climbs up on the wagon, staring straight ahead.

"Is it them?" I ask, already suspecting the answer.

"I'm afraid so, my *malíčká*," he replies, clearly shaken.

"What happened to them?" I ask, trembling, with tears finding their way down my cold cheeks.

"Not sure, but if they were out in that blizzard for long, they didn't stand a chance, I suppose," he answers as he puts his arm around me.

"What are you gonna do?" I ask.

"I'm going to take you to the way station so you can go to work. Then I'll take care of Anton and Rosie on my way home." With that, he snaps the reins and the team bolts forward, heading for the stage line road.

I spend the day at work cleaning and washing bedclothes, but I can't stop thinking about the Novaks. All our work on the homestead has made it hard to keep in touch with them, but we still thought of them as two of our closest friends. In fact, until Rose's condition worsened and took her mind away, I thought of her as my *babička*, the grandmother I never knew. I will miss her.

The day drags on, and I'm eager to get home to be with Mama and Papa. When I finally return from work, Papa is there as usual to pick me up at the way station. I'm eager to know what he did after he left me off this morning, and I ask, "Papa, what did you do about Anton and Rose?"

"I have them at home. I spent the day building caskets out of the wood left over from the house floors. Your mother thinks we should take them to the church tomorrow to ask the reverend what we should do with them. She's hoping they can bury Anton and Rose in the church cemetery. You can come with us tomorrow if you like."

"I'd like that, Papa," I say sadly.

CHAPTER 62
TWO YEARS LATER, MAY 1883

"WHAT IS THAT?" I ask, standing behind Wes's wagon and gazing into the crate.

"What does it look like?" Wesley replies.

"It looks like a pig. Why did you bring it here?"

"It's for you, Terezie. Happy Birthday!"

"You're giving me a pig for my birthday?" I ask in disbelief. "You gave me a bouquet of wildflowers last year. That was nice."

"You're eighteen now, so I figured it was time for me to give you more grown-up gifts."

"How do you figure this is a grown-up gift?"

"You like salt pork, don't you?"

"Sure. Who doesn't?"

"Well, I figure this is something you can contribute to your family. You can raise it, then butcher it for meat. I'm sure your folks will really appreciate it."

"But Wesley," I cry. "What am I supposed to do with him, for pity's sake? How do I take care of him? I have enough to do around here without looking after your pig!"

"It's your pig, not mine. I bought five for myself and one for you. They're weaner pigs, just weaned about three weeks ago. Got 'em from a fella over past Vincencie's place."

"What am I supposed to do with him?" I ask again.

"He's not a him. He's a her. Not a he."

"Huh?"

"A female pig. She's a she. And you won't need to take care of her. I'll turn her out in our timber with the rest of my pigs. I built them a little shelter among the trees. They'll be fine up there. They can root around foraging for acorns and stuff, and maybe wander in the fields for some ear corn. As I said, they'll get by just fine."

"Where did you get the notion to get pigs, anyway?" I ask, confused by this recent development.

"Antonin told me how much they were paying for live hogs at the Sinclair plant, so I thought I could make some money. And you, too."

I'm looking at the weaner pig now as she stares back at me with large, clear eyes. "She's kind of cute," I hear myself saying aloud, mostly to myself.

"Well, don't get too attached, Terezie. You realize what'll happen to her at Sinclair's, don't you?"

"Gross!" I protest. "There's no way I'll take her there. She's a female, right? Instead of taking her to Sinclair, couldn't I just let her have more little piggies when she's grown?"

Wesley considers this and then shakes his head, asking, "But Terezie, what about her *little piggies*? What are you gonna do with them? You gonna keep them all?"

"Hmm. I don't know. I'll have to think about that," I say.

"I don't know, Terezie. Maybe this was a bad idea," Wesley admits.

"A bouquet would have been nice, Wesley, but I suppose I could get used to my cute little pig," I say as she sadly gazes at me through the crate's slats. "What should I name her?"

"Oh, for cryin' out loud! She isn't a pet! You're gonna eat her!"

Ignoring him, I suggest, "Maybe I'll call her something like Katerina or Aneska."

"This is ridiculous! What was I thinking, bringing you a pig for your birthday?" Wes turns to climb up on the wagon. "Just never mind, Terezie. I'm taking her back up to the timber with the rest of 'em. You can just forget about this whole thing."

"Oh no you don't, mister!" I protest. "I'm coming with you. I need to see where little Aneska will be living."

"This is unbelievable," I hear Wesley blurt in frustration as he climbs onto the wagon.

"Just wait a moment. I need to tell Mama where I'm going," I say as I turn and head into the house.

With a needle and thread in hand, my mother is intent on fixing the hem of her housecoat, and she doesn't even look up as I step through the door into the kitchen.

"I'm going for a ride with Wesley. I shouldn't be long," I say.

"That's nice, dear," she says, still looking down at her sewing.

"Wesley gave me a pig," I say as I turn to leave.

"That's nice, dear," Mama replies distractedly. I know she isn't listening. It's probably just as well. She'll find out soon enough.

The door slams behind me, and soon I'm up on the seat of the wagon, sitting next to Wesley. We ride about a half mile toward his family's farm and turn left to climb the steep road leading to the timber. Wesley is silent, probably still frustrated by my playful banter regarding the pig. Perhaps I've overestimated his patience, I'm thinking, so I turn and give him a loud kiss on his cheek. He smiles as he continues staring ahead, giving a quick snap to the reins.

Since our first kiss at the Jan Hus celebration in Cedar Rapids, Wes and I have taken to kissing one another quite often—mostly in playful ways, and usually on the cheek. Sometimes he kisses me at the most unexpected moments. I like that. And once, entirely by accident, he turned toward me to say something just as I was about to plant one of my kisses on his cheek, and our lips met. I think he was as surprised as I was, but our surprise didn't prevent us from letting the kiss linger awhile. It lasted much longer than what my mother would have considered appropriate, that's for sure.

We finally arrive at the top of the hill and turn off the road and into the woods. I spot Wesley's pig shelter, and as the team clatters to a stop, his five pigs burst out of the structure, heading in our direction.

"They probably think I'm going to feed them," Wesley says. "I've been doing that the last couple of days, so they get used to staying up here and not wandering off somewhere. Don't worry, they won't hurt you. Just shoo 'em away."

"I think I'll stay right where I am, if you don't mind," I say.

"Suit yourself, Your Highness," he says as he grabs a few ears of corn from behind his seat and throws them several yards away to distract the insistent swine. Then he walks to the back of the wagon and opens the crate, letting my pig jump out to join in the fray.

Wesley climbs back onto the seat next to me, and we watch as the pigs fight for every last kernel of corn. I try to figure out which pig is the one Wesley gave to me, but I can't do it. They all have the same black-and-white coloring. "Which one is mine, Wesley?" I ask.

"Look at their tails."

"What about their tails?" I ask.

"Just look, Terezie!"

"Oh, that one over there has part of its tail missing. There's just a stub left," I say, pointing. "Why is that?"

"Who knows. Maybe it got stepped on when it was younger, or maybe some other pig bit it off."

"Really? They do that?" I ask, horrified at the thought.

"I guess so. That's what I've been told. Anyway, that's your pig. That's how you can tell which is yours."

"So, you gave me the one with the deformed tail?" I ask, looking at Wesley accusingly. I wonder if I'm pressing Wesley's patience.

"It doesn't really matter, Terezie. At butchering time, they'll taste just the same," he replies, grinning at me.

"Stop saying that about Aneska!" I protest.

"You realize she's just a pig, not a pet, don't you?"

"Well, that's yet to be seen, isn't it? She's mine, after all."

"If you say so," Wesley says as he turns and plants a kiss on my cheek.

We continue watching the critters eat, and after a long moment, Wesley says, "So, what do you think? Do you want to go into pig farming with me?"

"What are you talking about?" I answer.

"Well, I think it might be a good way to make some money. In about a year, we can sell some off and breed the others so they can birth more pigs. Pretty soon, we could have quite a herd of pigs. Then you could quit that job in town and spend your time helping me out here on the farm."

"Whoa!" I exclaim. "Are you crazy? I like my job in town. The Horaks have me working in their grocery store now. No more washing of bedclothes. You can get Franz to help you out here this summer if you need him."

"I'm talking about the long term, Terezie. I'm talking about your life beyond this summer. These pigs and horses and crops and everything else will need our attention. You can't just go off to town every day, can you?"

Now I am wondering what the heck Wesley is yammering on about. Then it hits me. "Wes, it almost sounds like you're asking me to marry you!"

"Well," he says, hesitating, "I guess that might be a good idea, you know, with the pigs and all."

"You really are something, Wesley! Aunt Annie warned me about you Rejman men. She told me the story of how your father proposed to her. It seems the apple doesn't fall far from the tree."

"I have no idea what you're talking about."

"Never mind, Wes. But if you want to marry me, you will need to talk to my father about it first."

"Do I really have to?" he grumbles.

"Yes, and if he agrees, I might consider it."

"Consider it?" he asks, looking worried.

"Don't fret, Wesley. It won't be so hard to convince me, I promise. But please don't use the pigs as a selling point, OK?"

"OK."

The next day, Wesley shows up in his best pants and shirt. I spot him through the window as he walks down the road toward our house, and I know why he's come. He's here to speak with Papa about marrying me. I've already warned my parents about this imminent visit, but at the moment, I'm the only one in the house. Papa is gone. I don't know where. He's probably at the tavern down the road. And Mama has gone out to her garden to check on her seedlings. They're just beginning to poke out of the dark soil.

"Hi, Wesley," I say as I step outside to greet him. He looks rather ridiculous the way he's all dressed up. "You going to church or something?" I ask him, smiling.

"No, silly. You know why I'm here. Where's your papa?"

"Hmm. If you didn't see him at your place, he probably went right past your farm to the tavern down the road. But don't tell Mama, or she'll have a fit."

"I suppose I could come back tomorrow," Wesley says.

"You don't seem very disappointed, by the looks of it. You aren't afraid of him, are you?"

"Of course not!"

"Well, if that's true, then why don't you go find him at the tavern and ask him what you wanna ask him?"

"Maybe I just will! And you know what? I think you're kinda bossy sometimes. That's what I think!" he says defensively.

"I suppose that might be true, but you still like me, don't you?" I ask.

Wesley hesitates and then says, "Sure I do. I like you quite a bit, Terezie. I bought you a pig, didn't I?"

"You might even say that you love me, right?"

"I suppose so."

"Then why don't you ever tell me that? Go ahead and say it, Wesley."

"There you are getting all pushy again."

"Why don't you just say it?" I press on.

"OK, OK! I'll say it," he says. I watch him as he swallows nervously and then looks at me, saying slowly and awkwardly, "I lov—"

"Yahee! Help!" It's my mama, screaming at the top of her lungs. I at once race out the door toward the garden, with Wesley following close behind.

"Ahhhhhhhh! God help me!" My mother is screaming and staring in anguish at her garden with her hands cupped over her mouth.

"What is it? What's wrong?" Wesley asks as we reach her.

"There's a giant rodent in my potato patch. Look!" she points. "Get him out of there! He's a monster!"

"That's no monster, Mama," I say, amused at her panic. "That's just a little pig!"

"Where in the world did he come from? Look there! He's rooting up my potato starts!"

"That's one of Wesley's pigs. He's raising them up in his timber," I explain.

Wesley walks up behind the animal, which ignores him and continues to feast on the treasures it just dug up. Wes notes the stub tail before saying, "This isn't one of my pigs. It's yours, Terezie."

"You have a pig?" Mama asks me, confused.

"I'm afraid so. Wesley gave it to me."

"Well, get him out of my garden. Now, before I have no garden left!"

Wesley and I chase Aneska out of the garden, trying to steer her across the yard, past the horse barn and eventually into the oat field to the north of our house. "Can't we put a rope on her or something?" I ask Wes.

"That doesn't work well. It's best if we just herd her in the general direction of the timber."

Of course, that's easier said than done, and I soon learn that a pig can have a mind of its own. Aneska has no intention of moving toward the timber and instead keeps trying to double back toward Mama's garden. It seems like it takes forever to get her to zigzag across the field, up the hill, and into the woods to join the other pigs.

"How will we keep her from going back to chomp on Mama's garden?" I ask Wesley as we watch Aneska lie down with the other pigs.

"I don't really know. You'll just have to keep a sharp eye out for her, I guess."

"Great! That's just great!" I say, wondering if this pig business Wesley has in mind is such a good idea after all. How in the world am I supposed to guard Mama's garden all day and night?

CHAPTER 63

IT'S TWO DAYS LATER, and Wesley and I are finally engaged to be married. I have to give Wesley credit, for he did in fact find my father at the tavern and boldly ask for my hand in front of all Papa's drinking friends. At least, that's what Wes told me. I doubt he asked as boldly as he led me to believe, but still, I'm happy to say that Papa approved wholeheartedly. It may have helped that Wesley promised not to tell Mama that Papa was drinking at the tavern in the middle of the day. But if that's what it took, then that's OK with me.

It's kind of strange to think about those earlier days when I played house down by the creek and Wesley never seemed to show any interest in spending time with me. But now that's all he wants to do. These days, he delivers me to and from the Coufal stage station whenever I go to work at Horaks' grocery. When we ride on his wagon, he makes me sit next to him, real close, apparently so he can feel my body next to his. And he gives me a kiss when I leave for town and then again when I return. He doesn't often say it, but I can tell that he really loves me. That's good because now that I think back over the years, we were probably destined to be married from the beginning. After all, who else was around that we could marry? Neither of us often saw other people our own age, unless at a church gathering. I've run into a few young men at the grocery store that might have been possibilities. But there have been very few potential female candidates for Wesley to take an interest in—besides me, that is. That suits me fine, and I'll just take it upon myself to keep it that way. The fewer temptations he encounters, the better.

Marrying Wesley will be the easy part, I'm thinking. All the stuff surrounding it will be the hard part. One of the more challenging things will be that we'll live with his parents for a while, and I have no idea what *a while* really means. It's not like their house is all that huge. Up to this point, Wesley and Franz have shared the same room. What will happen now? Are they going to shove Franz out into the horse barn? I rather doubt it. I suppose Franz could move in with my mama and papa and stay in my old room. But that would be kind of weird, I think. The one thing I know for sure is that I will not share a room with both Wesley and Franz!

Another worry is how Mama and Papa will get along when I'm not there to help them. I won't be there to take care of the chickens or help with chores or provide my grocery store earnings. Sure, Antonin might help them. He's still working at the packing plant and isn't married yet. He should keep sharing some of his earnings, shouldn't he? I'm not so sure, though. Lately, he's been less willing to do that—probably because of his growing tab at his favorite tavern. Regardless, Mama and Papa will just have to learn to get along without me, I suppose. Now that I think about it, as weird as it sounds, maybe Franz moving in with them would be a good trade after all. The Rejmans get me; the Zachs get him. Sounds fair to me.

Wesley and I spend the remainder of the year helping our families with farm work that's become routine for both of us. I spend most of my time washing clothes, tending the chickens, helping at planting time and butchering time, and cleaning the house; of course, I complete this work on days that I'm not in town working for the Horaks. Wesley is his father's right-hand man, taking care of the horses, tending the crops, and seeing to his pigs. It seems like nothing has really changed, but of course it has. There's a definite excitement brewing within both of our families. So when the planting season is past and it's time for Wesley and me to go visit with Reverend Kun about the wedding, we can barely contain ourselves.

It's the middle of the afternoon when we arrive at the parsonage. We are quick to climb down from the wagon and retreat to the shade of a nearby oak tree, where we use Wesley's handkerchief to wipe off the sweat and road dust. Then, as we walk toward the parsonage door, it suddenly swings open and there stands Reverend Kun, saying jovially, "Well, if it isn't the two lovebirds!" That brings a smile to our faces, and we forget all about our arduous trip. The reverend invites us in, and we're soon sitting at the kitchen table making plans. Wesley and I are eager to start our lives together, and when Reverend Kun inquires about the timetable for our planning, we inform him we are aiming for an August wedding.

"But that's next month!" he states with surprise.

"Is that a problem?" I ask. I can't imagine this would matter to him. After all, all he has to do at the wedding is stand up there and say all the right stuff, and that's the end of it for him, right?

"Yes, there is a problem with that. We're moving the church," he says.

"What?" Wesley exclaims. "Where? How? Is that possible? Can they move a building so large?"

"The church is going to be moved closer to the parsonage," Reverend Kun explains. "We've found a gentleman from Iowa City who knows how that's done. I guess they'll support it on wood timbers and pull it to the new location with a couple of oxen teams."

"But why?" I ask. "It's just fine where it is!"

"We have decided that it should be more centrally located among our churchgoers," Reverend Kun explains.

"But what about our wedding? Will the church be ready by next month?" Wesley asks.

"I'm afraid not. Maybe if you could delay the wedding a couple of months, that would be best," he suggests.

I don't have any intention of putting the wedding off just for the convenience of his congregation. "Could we be married here in the parsonage?" I ask.

Wesley immediately protests, "But I thought you wanted a church wedding!" I can see that he'll need some convincing.

"A church wedding would be nicer," agrees Reverend Kun. "It will only be a couple of months later, after all."

"We've been planning to marry in August, and that's what I want to do. Tell him, Wesley. Isn't that what we planned?" I insist.

"Uh, I guess. But you want to get married here? In the parsonage?"

"We planned for August, so I want the wedding in August," I declare with finality.

"Why?" Wesley asks, apparently still confused by my suggestion.

"I have my reasons. Can't you just agree to keep to our planned date? For me?" I plead, looking at him with imploring eyes. I know this will sway him. It always does. And I have good reason for insisting on sticking to our plan. Wesley doesn't know it, and I don't intend to tell him yet, not until the right time, but we share a secret, a secret that has born fruit, and if we wait too long to get married, our inconvenient little truth will be clear to everyone.

On Wednesday, August 27, it's midmorning when things start to get busy at the church parsonage. My parents and I arrive first, trying to beat the sweltering afternoon heat. Soon, Wesley drives up with his parents and Franz, with Vincencie and Jan arriving just behind them. After we wait awhile for Antonin, the wedding is ready to begin. This is the extent of our attendees. To be sure, it's just about all that can fit in the parsonage, which greatly limited our guest list. Who else would we have invited, anyway? Sure, we could have invited a couple of our neighbors or one or two of Papa's drinking friends, but in the end, we settled on family members only.

Wesley is attired in his Sunday best, the same outfit he wore the day he came to ask Papa for my hand. I can see that his coat and vest are making him notably uncomfortable. I expect his string tie will immediately disappear once the ceremony is finished. I am proudly wearing the wondrous dress that Mama wore when she married Papa. It fits me perfectly, and I am wondering if one day my own daughter might don this same dress for her wedding. I dearly hope so.

Soon, Reverend Kun walks to the front of the room, where Wesley and I are standing. I can see Mrs. Kun standing in the back, not wanting to intrude, but with a countenance of high anticipation. The reverend takes his place and looks briefly at both Wesley and me. He is ready to begin, and I take in a big breath, exhaling it as I turn my face up to smile at him.

The ceremony is brief, but it's not without adequate solemnity and pomp. The plainness of the venue does not affect the reverend's demeanor. He conducts himself as he would at any wedding in his church. After we finally complete the exchanging of the vows and kiss, Reverend Kun offers a prayer conceived especially for Wesley and me. He speaks of the many years of our friendship that has grown into love, and the closeness of our families that will provide support for our love to endure. He speaks of the dignity of working the soil and digging wells and building chimneys. He speaks of the joyous sounds of Papa's crank organ, and he even mentions Aneska's continuing visits to

Mama's vegetable garden. How he knows about that, I have no idea. When he finishes, I think what a wonderful prayer it was, personal and moving in its delivery. And I am mightily grateful that the reverend is the one we asked to bind us together in matrimony.

Finally, the ceremony ends, and a flurry of hugs and kisses begins as Wesley and I are inundated with well-wishes. Soon, Wesley and I are alone on his family's wagon, driving southward. I glance back to see Wesley's parents and brother riding with Mama and Papa behind us. Wes pulls me closer to him on the wagon seat, just like he always does when we ride together. He says nothing. He doesn't have to. Everything is perfect. No need to look for words at a time like this.

Aunt Annie has prepared a nice meal for both of our families, and when we arrive back home, we all sit to eat and enjoy each other's fellowship. But my mind is already focused on what is to come next. This afternoon, Wesley and I are planning to move all my things from my parents' home to his. This will be both joyous and sad, I realize, and I wonder how Mama will survive it. But it must be done, and I resolve to offer her all the kindness and understanding I possibly can.

By two o'clock, Wesley and I arrive on his wagon at what I will now consider my *former* home, the home of my parents. We quickly go about the task of gathering all my things and loading them onto the wagon. Mama is there helping us, and I can see that she is full of emotion. I take her in my arms and squeeze her tight. "I'll be here for you whenever you want," I say. "I'm just down the road, you know."

"I know, Terezie. I love you, my *maličká*, and your papa loves you too," she says tearfully.

Continuing to hold her close, I ask, "Is Papa coming to say goodbye?"

"He was here a while ago, but I don't know where he's run off to. It doesn't surprise me, though. He's not good at this sort of thing."

"*This sort of thing?*"

"You know—sentimental moments like this, like saying goodbye to his daughter. He seems like a cantankerous old man most of the time, but he's just a big pussycat. Maybe the thought of you leaving is just too much for him to handle. But don't fault him for that. Remember how he blubbered his way through the wedding?"

"He did?"

"Well, maybe *blubbered* is putting it a little strongly. But I can tell you that he had trouble getting through the ceremony, that's for sure. He's always been that way with you."

"He has?" I ask dubiously. I've always found him to be kind enough toward me, but he's never been one for kisses and hugs and stuff like that. And I can't imagine him in an emotional state like the one Mama is describing.

"Oh, for sure. You must know that. He doesn't show it very much, but you are his *malíčká*, after all."

I have difficulty picturing Papa getting emotional about anything at all. He's always been so steady, so unflinchingly stoic. How did I not notice him at my wedding? Now that I consider it, though, he did give me a particularly big hug afterwards, letting it last longer than I expected. Perhaps Mama is right about Papa. Maybe, under that grumpy exterior, Papa is just a big old pussycat. A pussycat who loves me, who loves his little one, his *malíčká*.

As Wesley and I prepare to leave for his house, Mama walks back inside and comes out carrying a rather large trunk. As soon as we see her struggling with it, Wesley rushes to help. "What is this?" he asks.

"It's for you, Terezie. When we were going through Anton and Rose's things, I found this trunk, and when I opened it, there was a note inside that said *For Terezie*. It looks like Rose's handwriting. I'm not sure why she wanted you to have it. I'm even kind of surprised she had the wits about her to do it."

"What's inside?" Wesley asks.

"I haven't looked through the whole thing, but it seems to be blankets and linens, things like that. Things you'll surely need for your home," Mama says.

"But why did she leave it for me?" I ask.

"I don't know, but I'd like to believe she was thinking ahead and giving you a wedding present. That's why I kept it from you until now."

"I really miss her. Her and Anton," I say tearfully.

"Me too," Mama answers. "I think maybe they're smiling down at us right now. What do you think?"

"I hope so," I answer as I watch Wesley hoist the trunk up onto the back of the wagon with our other things. Then I give Mama one more long hug and kiss her gently on the cheek. "I'll see you tomorrow, Mama," I say. She doesn't answer, but steps back to let me climb up on the wagon next to my husband.

CHAPTER 64

AFTER UNLOADING ALL MY WORLDLY THINGS and moving them into the house, Wesley goes back outside to tend to the team. I remain standing in Wesley and Franz's old room—the room that now belongs to Wesley and me. And as I peer down at the old trunk given to me, I consider how it has traveled all the way from Krouna, where Anton and Rose once lived. I unlatch the lid and open it, only to be met with the musty fragrance of bygone days. Is this the smell of the old country? I wonder. Continuing to push the lid all the way back, I reach inside and pull out a large woolen blanket woven in intricate patterns of greens, yellows, and reds. Examining it, I'm grateful that it shows no sign of moth damage. Was this blanket woven by my mother on the loom she owned back in Krouna? I wonder.

I set the blanket aside and continue exploring the contents of Rose's trunk. I find a linen housedress, and I hold it up to my body, determining that it will fit me just fine. Next are about ten linen towels that will definitely come in handy. I find other treasures, too: an assortment of mittens, aprons, tablecloths, and nightwear, all items that will be useful to me in my new life with Wesley.

Wesley has returned and is standing in the doorway now, watching me examine the trunk's contents. "Aren't these great?" I say to him. "I'll be able to use every one of these things."

Wes peers into the trunk and says, "What's that on the bottom? Are those books?"

"Let's take a look," I say, reaching to the dark nether regions of the trunk. "Let's see here. This looks like a school writing book, and . . . oh, look! It's a Bible. She gave me her

Bible. How sweet," I proclaim gleefully as I lift it up from the shadows of the trunk's innards.

"What's that?" Wesley asks as he reaches to retrieve one last item that was hiding under the large tome. "It looks like a—"

"Oh my God!" I scream as I stare in disbelief. I've seen this before. It's part of a very distant memory, but my mind has no trouble reconstructing it.

"What's wrong?" Wesley pleads, as I stand dumbfounded by the item he holds in his hand.

I can't stop staring at the letters etched into it, and I can hear myself muttering, "*E-P-E-P* . . ."

I feel Wesley's grip on my shoulder. He's shaking it. "Terezie, what's the matter? Terezie!"

"Emil Pavlista," I say finally.

"What? Who?" he asks.

"Don't you remember Mama talking about the man whose body they found over by the quarry?" I answer, my voice trembling.

"The guy who attacked your family?"

"Yes, he's the one. I remember his knife as clear as day. I'll never forget it as long as I live. They found him later, stabbed to death and left up near Coufal's quarry. But they never found that knife," I say haltingly, "until now."

"Are you sure it's the same one?" Wesley asks.

"I'll never forget it, Wes. Yes, it's the very same one."

"But why would it be in Rose's trunk?" Wesley asks.

That's the question, alright. Why there? I wonder. With Anton and Rose both gone, I wonder if we'll ever know. But that doesn't prevent me from speculating. "Was it Anton? Could he have killed Pavlista?" I ask Wesley.

"This is Anton you're talking about. Do you really think Anton would have been capable of such a thing?"

"But why else would the knife be in Rose's trunk? Who else would have put it there if it wasn't Rose or Anton?"

I can see from Wesley's expression that he agrees with me. "What do you want to do about this?" he asks. "Should we take it to the authorities?"

"I suppose that'd be the right thing to do," I answer, adding, "though I hate to implicate Anton or Rose when they're not alive to explain any of this. I'm not sure what to do."

We decide not to go to the authorities—not yet, anyway. This is too big a responsibility to be determined in haste, for there may be a very logical explanation that we're not considering. After all, Wes and I were mere children when this incident took place. We really don't know all the details surrounding Emil Pavlista's demise. Of course, no one else does either, but there are two people who know far more than we do. Unwilling to wait for Wesley to harness the team and hitch them up, I suggest we just walk the half mile back to Mama's house. It strikes me as odd that I refer to it as Mama's house when, just a day ago, I lived there too. How quickly one can change one's point of view, I think to myself. It doesn't take us long to reach Mama's door, and when she sees the knife in Wesley's grasp, she stares at it, stunned.

"Where did you find that?" she asks with a bluntness that surprises me.

"It was at the bottom of Rose's trunk," I say, waiting to judge Mama's reaction.

Mama stands without uttering a word for a long while before she finally poses a possibility. "Anton?" she offers.

"Do you think that's possible?" I query, but she seems afraid to answer. Is it because she believes he actually could have killed that man, or is it because she now thinks it was a mistake to even suggest it?

Finally, she says, "But even if we think he could have done this, why would he keep the knife? Why wouldn't he just dispose of it, bury it, or even leave it at the scene of the killing?"

I have no answer for that. I hadn't even considered it. How am I supposed to imagine the contemplations of a murderer's mind, anyway? There might be many reasons that a mad killer would keep a murder weapon. How would I know? Wait! Did I just call Anton a mad killer? I push the thought out of my mind, reminding myself that Anton was one of the kindest people I ever knew.

"What do you think we should do with it?" Wesley asks. "Should we take it to the marshal's office in Cedar Rapids?"

Papa steps through the door and asks, "Take what to the marshal's office?"

Wesley places the knife in Papa's hands, and he stares at it as if he's holding something handed to him by the devil himself.

"Where did you find this?" he asks.

Wes and I explain that we discovered it in Rose's trunk, and then I ask him the same question Wesley posed to Mama. "What should we do with it?"

"Well, I definitely wouldn't report this, if that's what you're asking," he says, as if unwilling to consider any other option. That seems odd to me.

"You wouldn't, Papa?" I ask incredulously. "Why not? It might help solve the mystery of that killing after all these years."

"What's the point? If Anton did it, what good would it do to accuse him? He's dead and gone. Who really cares anymore?"

To this, Wesley objects, "But I would think it right for Emil Pavlista's killer to be identified."

"Pavlista was a thug," Papa says. "He doesn't deserve what you say is his right. Besides, Anton isn't responsible. We can't let him take the blame for something he didn't do."

"How do you know he isn't responsible? The knife was in Rose's trunk. If Anton didn't do it, then do you know who did?" I ask.

"No, but I know for a fact that Anton is innocent."

This makes absolutely no sense to me. If Papa doesn't know who killed Pavlista, then how would he know for sure that Anton didn't do it? Papa is looking at me as if reading my thoughts, and he states, "I gave Anton that knife. I told him to hide it somewhere. I guess he just chose the wrong place."

A cold pause descends over our family as we stand there considering the words Papa just uttered.

"Y-y-you gave him the knife?" I ask in disbelief.

"Yes," he answers. Then, noticing the expressions on our faces, he quickly adds, "But no, I didn't kill Pavlista. How could you even think that? I found the knife on the bottom road some weeks after Pavlista's death."

"You found it," Mama says, more an affirmation than a question.

"That's what I said. I found it, but I figured that whole Pavlista thing was just a thing of the past. So I thought it best to just let sleeping dogs lie, and I gave the knife to Anton to store away for me."

"Why would you want to keep a thing like that?" Wesley asks.

"It was a perfectly good knife. I didn't want to just throw it away!"

The warped logic in Papa's response stops us in our tracks, and we utter not a word for a long moment. What is there to say? It makes no sense, and we all know it. That *perfectly good knife* was a murder weapon. Papa must have known that. What good could possibly come from holding onto it?

As much as I love my papa, I know that he sometimes behaves in unexpected ways, letting cautious restraint fall prey to impulsive instinct. At times, this works out for him, but sometimes it doesn't. And I've noticed that when regret follows in the wake of one of his rash actions, he often manages to find solace in some peculiar rationalization— one that makes perfect sense to him but to no one else.

Still, regardless of Papa's reasoning for his actions, I can't help but feel obligated to turn this evidence over to the marshal's office. It's the right thing to do, isn't it? The marshal will certainly believe Papa's account of finding the murder weapon on the road, won't he? And then, perhaps, the Pavlista case can be solved.

CHAPTER 65

THE NEXT DAY, Wesley harnesses the team and the two of us climb up onto the wagon. It's early morning, a bit humid but still cool, and we know the August heat will return as the sun rises higher in the eastern sky. Hopefully, we'll come back from Cedar Rapids before midafternoon, when the sun is most oppressive. It shouldn't take long to run this errand, after all. We'll stop at the marshal's office just long enough to turn over the knife and explain where we found it, then be on our way.

Wesley remains quiet as he drives the rig onto the bottom road, and we head eastward with the sun glaring in our faces. Finally, he asks, "Are you sure about this, Terezie?"

"About what?" I ask, knowing well what he's asking.

"You know—turning this knife in to the authorities," Wesley answers impatiently.

"I don't know how we can just pretend we didn't find it, do you?"

"I don't know, maybe?" he answers.

"As I see it," I say, "whoever killed that man should be held accountable. The knife is evidence. It just wouldn't be right to conceal it."

Wesley doesn't answer, but he pulls up on the reins, bringing the team to a dusty stop in the middle of the road. Turning toward me, he says, "I've been thinking about this, so hear me out. Your papa said that he found the knife on the road near the murder scene, right?"

"So?"

"Have you considered that he might be covering for Anton? Isn't it possible that Anton was indeed the killer, and your papa wanted to divert the blame from his friend?"

"I suppose that's possible," I say, realizing that Wesley has a point.

"And have you considered that if your papa maintains that story, the marshal might not believe him and might instead accuse him of the murder?"

"Why wouldn't the marshal believe him?" I ask. Suddenly, this is all beginning to sound more complicated than I'd earlier thought.

"Well, your papa's reason for keeping the knife, that *perfectly good knife*, would most likely sound just as unreasonable to the marshal as it did to us. That might put him under suspicion, don't you think?"

Wesley snaps the reins, and the team lurches forward once again. He continues, saying, "It seems to me there are three ways this can go. One, the marshal will believe your papa and the case will most likely go nowhere, since I doubt there are any suspects after all this time. Two, the marshal might think that your papa is covering for Anton and name Anton as the killer. That will taint Anton's reputation, whether he was guilty or not, since he's not alive to contest his involvement. And three, the marshal could accuse your papa of the crime since he admitted to having the knife in his possession. The first option would be an acceptable outcome. But the other two? Well, either of those would bring nothing but pain to our families. Do you see what I'm saying?"

I do indeed understand what he's saying, and I sit silently, thinking about this for several moments as we near the Coufal corner at the stage road. Suddenly, Wesley turns the rig to the right and drives on the path toward the old Coufal cabin where he once lived with his parents. I know this path very well, for Wesley and I have visited the cabin many times in the last year. Sometimes, after he picked me up from the stage station, we'd stop here to be in private, away from curious eyes and ears. We'd talk and hold each other and kiss. It was romantic to be together for a while, even if it was in an old, decrepit cabin. But we haven't been here for a couple of months now. I remember the exact date we were here last. The twenty-third of June. I remember it clearly because that's when I let Wesley make love to me for the first time. If that's his intent today, I'm having nothing to do with it.

"What are you doing? I don't feel like going to the cabin today, Wesley," I say with obvious irritation.

"I'm not going to the cabin," he says, not looking at me.

He drives on, past the cabin, down the narrowing trail toward the bank of the river. Wesley brings the rig to an abrupt stop as the path becomes too narrow for the wagon, and he jumps down, offering me his hand.

"What are you doing?" I ask, confused.

"Come with me, and bring the knife," he directs as he helps me down from my seat.

He takes my hand and leads me under the shade of two large basswood trees and through some bothersome elderberry bushes. We arrive at the riverbank and stand there watching as the Iowa River moves by us in an intricate array of currents and eddies. We look westward and see the river narrowing as it recedes upstream, its banks lined with birches, maples, and cottonwoods. Looking in the opposite direction, we spot the ferry docked on the north bank. It's the same ferry that carried our families across the river years ago.

"What are we doing here?" I ask Wesley.

"I really don't want to go all the way to Cedar Rapids until you're sure about all this."

"I thought I was sure, but now . . ." I say softly, "I just don't know. Do you think Anton could have done such a thing? Do you think Papa may be lying?"

"It really doesn't matter what you or I believe to be true. It's what the marshal will believe." Wesley pauses and then adds, "Your father once told me something that made little sense at the time, but now I think I understand it."

"What was that?"

"He said that, when deciding between right and wrong, it's often best to just shamelessly do what is necessary, regardless of its rightness or wrongness."

"Papa said that? That sounds like something he might come up with, alright," I say sarcastically.

"But don't you see some wisdom in it? It's about survival. Whether something is right or wrong means little when the practicality of survival is at stake. Don't you think it might apply in this case?" Wesley asks as he extends his hand.

"I don't know, maybe," I finally concede.

I gaze down at Pavlista's knife, thinking about its significance not only to our past but also to our future. Why should that make any difference? I wonder. Isn't the truth all that matters? I'm not sure anymore. Why should I feel so compelled to search for the truth? As Wesley said, even if seeking the truth is the right thing to do, why should I risk endangering my family? Pavlista is dead and gone, so who really cares?

Either Papa found that knife or he's covering for Anton. Certainly, he had nothing to do with Pavlista's death. I'm just sure of it. He said so himself, and I believe him. After all, he's my *tata*, and I'm his *malíčká*. But the marshal doesn't know Papa like I do. He might not see the good that I see in him. It's suddenly clear to me that Wesley is right. There is only one thing that truly matters to me, and whether right or wrong, I finally decide to shamelessly do what is necessary to keep my family safe.

Slowly I place the knife into Wesley's outstretched hand, saying, "Here, Wesley. Go ahead. Get rid of it. Then let's go home."

I watch as Wesley rears back and throws the knife with all his might, sending it high over the churning waves. Then we stand, my hand in his, as we watch the knife disappear with a splash into the river's channel.

CHAPTER 66

MARSHAL MAREK HOLUB HAS HAD ENOUGH of Cedar Rapids. For two decades he's been breaking up drunken brawls at the Bohemian Dance Hall, patrolling Sixteenth Avenue and Commercial Street, and, lately, riding herd on the ruffians arriving to take the new factory jobs. All of it has taken its toll. This kind of work is for younger men, he thinks. It's for men who find joy in mixing it up; it's for men who like dominating others, bringing their clubs down on the heads of any societal miscreants who look at them sideways.

Holub is tired of it all, and he wants to forge a better direction for his life while he has a bit of life still in front of him. What he'll do next, he doesn't know. All he knows for sure is that it's time to hang up his badge and club. He'll head west in search of a place to settle, even if it's only temporary, and find some kind of paying job to wait out the winter before he moves further on.

He rides south out of town, not even bothering to look back. He has no regrets about leaving, nor does he feel any sentimentality toward the many people left behind. Most of them don't care if he stays or goes anyway, so why should he glance back to see if they even notice?

Marek is eager to embark on a trip with no set itinerary. This makes him think back to when he ventured westward from Pennsylvania some two decades ago. He had no itinerary then either. That was an exciting time, full of possibilities, and he wonders if he should have just kept on riding when he first rode into eastern Iowa. It's too late to worry about that now, he decides. What's done is done.

Holub rides on along the stage road, finally reaching Joe Coufal's homestead. Pulling up on the reins, he brings his mount to an abrupt halt at the intersection with the bottom road. He hasn't been in this area for quite some time, and the thought of Emil Pavlista's corpse half-buried in the woods suddenly takes shape in the back of his mind. It's a dim memory, one that's faded over time—so much time, in fact, that he hasn't given the Pavlista case much thought in recent years. He now wonders again how Pavlista ended up in that shallow grave. How did this man, who had the wherewithal to travel from the old country across the world to a new continent, have the misfortune of suffering such an ignoble death so soon after arriving here? Just bad luck, Marek figures, and he realizes at once that he shouldn't be surprised by that. After all, for centuries, bad luck has been the touchstone of the Bohemian's existence, stalking him like an opportunistic predator as he agonized under the heavy hand of the Holy Roman Empire and then the Habsburgs. Why shouldn't some of that bad luck follow him regardless of where he runs off to?

Holub sits there pondering how countless generations of his people have suffered and continue to suffer in his native country. They had their chances, he knows, such as that fateful day in 1620 when hundreds of Bohemian rebels mounted a desperate attack at the Battle of White Mountain to preserve their religious freedom. And then, some fifty years later at Chlumec, they tried again, this time using farm implements as improvised weapons, attempting unsuccessfully to throw off the shackles of serfdom. In both of these revolts, the bad luck of the Bohemians prevailed, as the rebels were easily dispatched by the Imperial Army. Both of these defeats were blows to Bohemia's dream of freedom, offering proof of its people's unworthiness. They would remain unlucky peasants living in poverty for generations—to this day, and who knows how much longer?

Holub is thankful that he finally escaped Bohemia where he lived as a forsaken soul under the callous guardianship of the Habsburgs. He knows he was one of the lucky ones, having escaped all of that. But what of those left behind? They're all still orphans of White Mountain; that's how Holub thinks of them now: living in poverty, existing like helpless children, forced to work and worship as they are told.

But isn't he just another orphan of White Mountain? he wonders. Wasn't he pushed away by his beloved motherland, orphaned out of desperation to fend for himself in this new land? Perhaps he and his countrymen, wherever they reside, will always be orphans of White Mountain, destined to carry centuries-old scars and the bad luck that caused them.

Marek shakes himself free from his ponderings and gazes ahead at the Iowa River and the ferry moored there, standing ready to transport him to the other side. While it is tempting, he decides instead to save his money and locate a shallower spot downstream to cross through the swift current. Finding a suitable place, he urges his mount into the river, through the muddy water, onto a sandbar on the other side, and finally up the opposite bank. His plan, if you'd call it much of a plan, is to follow the south bank of the Iowa River westward as far as it goes and then continue on toward Nebraska. Beyond that, he has no particular travel plans. Maybe he'll work as a hand at a cattle ranch, or perhaps he'll find another marshal job in a frontier town. No, that's one thing he definitely will not do, he promises himself. More likely, he figures, he'll find a nice piece of land that he can claim for himself to farm, and maybe even find a woman and raise a passel of little Holubs. That sounds better to him.

This puts Marek in mind of that guy down the bottom road—what was his name? Josef Zach, that was it. He seemed to have carved out a pretty good life for himself and his family on his homestead, despite his contrarian nature.

Thinking of Josef Zach reminds him of that preacher. Kun was his name, he remembers. Marek smiles, thinking the absurd notion that he himself might take up a career as an evangelist, sermonizing across the Colorado and Wyoming territories. That seems to him like a pretty comfortable job. What a laugh, he thinks, chuckling to himself. Given his sordid past, he figures God would sooner send down a lightning bolt to smite him than let him serve as the Lord's representative even for a moment.

Holub rides on, but before he rides very far past the ferry dock, he notices that the duffel bag he has secured to his saddle has come loose and is flopping around on the horse's hindquarters, so he stops to refasten it. He dismounts and ties his horse to a nearby cottonwood tree beside the roiling river. As he works to re-secure the loosened tether, he glances beyond the horse to something on the far side of the river.

He can see two figures standing next to the riverbank on the opposite side. One is a woman, he is sure, and he assumes the other, taller one is a man. What are they doing over there? he wonders. Are they fishing? Having a romantic rendezvous, perhaps? What does he care, anyway? he thinks as he struggles with the ties on his duffel bag. Suddenly, a reflection flashes across his face, and he looks up again at the couple still standing there. He can see the woman handing something shiny to the man and then the man heaving it in a high arc across the river in his direction until it splashes into the water.

"Whatever that was," he mutters, "it's gone forever."

He gazes at the two figures for a moment more, and then, with the duffel bag once again secured, he climbs back onto his horse, snapping the reins and spurring the animal forward through the trees. Whatever that man threw into the river might have interested Holub last year, last month, or even last week. But it's of no interest to him now, he decides. It's just none of his business anymore. So he rides on toward the western plains, to vanish like that blade disappearing into the murky river's undertow.

AUTHOR'S NOTES

The main characters in *From the Bohemian Hills* lived in the times and places depicted throughout these pages. However, as peasants in Austrian-controlled Bohemia, they left very little written account of their lives in the old country. Was this simply because many were not literate, or was it perhaps because they considered their lives of such little worth? It could be a bit of both. So with so few written accounts to go on, many of the storylines herein are purely speculative, based on conditions as I understand them in east-central Bohemia and eastern Iowa in the late nineteenth century.

The Austrian Empire at War

The descriptions of the battles at Solferino and Königgrätz are central to Josef's and Vaclav's narratives. Did these two actually take part in these conflicts? That remains unknown. However, the conscription of Bohemian men into the Imperial Army was a constant source of anxiety. The Crown demanded a military obligation of about ten years, during which Bohemian men could be called up at any time to fight in some conflict or other. It was one of the primary reasons they so readily fled their homeland, some doing it legally when their term of service was finally completed and some choosing the riskier option of seeking passage without official military release documents.

The Austro-Sardinian War of 1859, in which Josef Zach may or may not have taken part, began as an effort by the Kingdom of Sardinia to wrest control of northern Italia from the Habsburgs. It eventually developed into a bloody war that pitted the Austrian army against not only the Sardinian military but the formidable French army as well.

Though the war lasted only about two and a half months, it was a terribly bloody affair that resulted in massive casualty counts on both sides. In many ways, it marked the beginning of the end of the Habsburg monarchy. This *little war*, as Emil Spacek called it, was nothing of the kind.

On the twentieth of May, in and around the town of Montebello, an army of twenty thousand Austrians suffered well over one thousand casualties in the first real battle of the war. The Austrian army was out-maneuvered and out-reinforced by the more mobile French blue-coats, who effectively used their railway system to bring in fresh troops. The Austrian army finally retreated from Montebello northward to Magenta, where they dug in to take a stand. They had hoped to protect Milan, the capital of Lombardy. But once again, the French force threw itself fiercely against the Austrian front. The Austrians were overwhelmed by the well-trained French fighters, who used their state-of-the-art rifled cannons to decimate them. Overpowered and exhausted, the Austrians pulled back into Milan and fought desperately as they continued to retreat eastward through town. It is at this moment that our story inserts Josef Zach into this war.

It should be noted that the depiction of Henri Dunant at the battlefield near Solferino is factual. He indeed did happen upon this horrible sight of dead and injured soldiers, and his efforts that day to enlist the help of military doctors and local citizens helped save the lives of hundreds of injured men. This act inspired Dunant to later play an important role in establishing the Red Cross.

The Austro-Prussian War struck much closer to home for the Zachs and Rejmans. The battle in which I inserted Vaclav Rejman in the summer of 1866 took place only about thirty-eight miles north of Budislav in a town called Königgrätz, now called Hradec Kralove. Well over four hundred thousand combatants clashed in the battle, resulting in over fifty thousand casualties. It was one of the bloodiest conflicts of the nineteenth century, in which the Prussian alliance utilized superior strategy, logistics, and weaponry to soundly defeat the Austrian army, thus gaining independence for the new North German Confederation.

Reverend Francis Kun

Of all the characters in *From the Bohemian Hills*, Reverend Francis Kun is the most factually documented and depicted. Kun is recognized as the first Czech settler to engage in missionary work in the midwestern United States. A descendant of a long line of Moravian Magyar religious men, he decided in 1856 to start a new life in America. As my narrative describes, he indeed settled in Tama County where he may or may not have encountered Meskwaki people who reclaimed part of their homeland about this same time. But given Kun's frequent forays out into the countryside evangelizing to his flock, such an encounter may easily have occurred.

The Cedar Rapids freethought movement is well-documented in historical accounts, and Reverend Kun was an important opponent of this movement, often writing and preaching in opposition to Frank Zdrubek and his followers. While the depiction of Zdrubek's lecture at the Reading Society Hall is a point of fact, the altercation between Kun and Emil Pavlista is purely fictional, as is the involvement of Josef Zach.

The growth of Reverend Kun's Bohemian Reformed Evangelical congregation takes center stage in my narrative, and the timeline of events surrounding it is portrayed accurately according to numerous historical accounts. It may be of interest to know that the Bohemian Moravian Brethren Church that Kun helped to found continues to thrive today, though it is now known as the First Presbyterian Church Near Ely. Much of the church's current membership is of Czech descent, with some being descendants of its founders. The church stands as a proud tribute to the early Bohemian immigrants who settled in the Cedar Rapids area to live and worship in freedom.

The Luck of the Bohemians

Bohemia suffered for centuries under the thumb of the Habsburgs. Finally, with the defeat of Austria-Hungary in 1918, Czechoslovakia came into being as an independent state under the leadership of Tomáš Garrigue Masaryk. It appeared that the Bohemian bad luck had changed. But after only two decades of freedom, Czechoslovakia was sacrificed to Germany in 1939 by a group of European allies who hoped this would dissuade Hitler's aggressive ambitions. With the end of World War II came the hope of freedom once again, but it was not to be, as Czechoslovakia was subsumed under the communist control of the Soviet Union from 1948 to 1989. It seemed that the luck of the Czechs would never change.

Finally, after all those years of oppression at the hands of the Habsburgs, Nazis, and Russians, the nonviolent Czech Velvet Revolution threw off the shackles of communism, and Czechoslovakia became a parliamentary republic in 1989. Then, four years later, the country split peacefully into the Czech Republic and Slovakia. Both nations thrive today as members of NATO, and it seems as if their luck has finally changed for the better.

A Musical Note

Little is known about these families' voyage from Bremerhaven to New York City. But one thing we do know: Josef did indeed take a crank organ with him across the ocean to his new home in America. I can't help but think that Frantiska would have considered this an unnecessary burden for their arduous journey, and no one really knows why Josef insisted on bringing it—it only played two tunes, after all. But I would like to believe that this one act signaled the beginning of a vibrant family music tradition that has endured for five more generations to this day.

The storyline of *From the Bohemian Hills* encompasses a period of only twenty-five years, from the spring of 1859 to the fall of 1884. Of course, the lives of the Zachs and Rejmans would continue. Wesley and Terezie would later have five children. The youngest of these would be born in 1902, and they would name him Joseph. Joseph Rejman, who later Americanized his surname to *Reyman,* was my grandfather. As a young man, he inherited the home farm, later handing it down to my father. I was raised on that 160-acre farm of grain crops, pigs, chickens, and Angus cattle, and spent many hours as a boy playing alone down by that creek, pretending I was somebody I wasn't.

ACKNOWLEDGMENTS

I want to express my sincere appreciation to all the people who helped bring *From the Bohemian Hills* to completion.

First and foremost, I must thank my wife, Tina, for her patience and encouragement during the writing of this book. There were so many times that I might have stopped short, letting this project languish unfinished in my computer, but she was always there to spur me onward.

I must also credit David Muhlena at the National Czech & Slovak Museum and Library in Cedar Rapids, Iowa, for his generous help while conducting my research there and John K. Novak at Northern Illinois University for his help with the Czech dialogue in my narrative. No less notable, the staff of the 1st Presbyterian Church Near Ely (current visage of Reverend Kun's church) generously accommodated me with important details of the church's early history.

I owe a special debt of gratitude to the people who spent so much time scrutinizing my manuscript for inconsistencies in my narrative. Their insights were immensely valuable in helping me tell this story. Thanks go to Shelley, Steve, Laurie, John, Michael, Ron, Susan, and Claire.

And many thanks to Becky Rauff, my editor, who did such a magnificent job tightening up my manuscript. Becky, you're the best!

Finally, I must express my appreciation to all my ancestors who took the chance to make the dangerous journey from Bohemia to America and realize their dream of freedom. This book is dedicated to those daring souls.

FROM THE BOHEMIAN HILLS— DRIVING TOUR

Exploring the setting of *From the Bohemian Hills* is easy, as long as you restrict your exploration to the American portion of the narrative. The entire journey is only about 20-25 miles in total after you exit Interstate 380 between Iowa City and Cedar Rapids. Let's get started.

Whether traveling on Interstate 380 south from Cedar Rapids or north from Iowa City, take the Swisher exit, Exit 10, and head west toward the town of Swisher. You are now on the Swisher blacktop (officially named 120th Street NW). Proceed through Swisher and turn left on Falcon Avenue NW (this turnoff is about 3.5 miles from the Interstate exit). Falcon Avenue is a gravel road, somewhat hilly and a bit dusty. While it is quite drive-able, keep to the right and watch for oncoming traffic over the hilly terrain. Just about two miles ahead you will see the farmstead on the right (to verify the location, type "1557 Falcon Ave NW, Swisher, Iowa 52338" into your GPS app). This is where Vaclav and Annie Rejman farmed, as did their four generations after them. In 1907, Wesley built the home that you see now. Behind it, you can see various buildings in various states of decay or restoration. The old farmhouse has been renovated nicely inside by the current owner, but the exterior is still much the same as when Wesley and Terezie built it in 1907.

Continue southward on Falcon Avenue NW for about 2/3 of a mile and you will encounter a stop sign. You have now arrived at Amana Road NW. As you turn right you will immediately see Dupont Cemetery on your left. Turn into the parking area and search for the graves of Josef and Frantiska Zach. It won't take you long to find them. Wesley and Terezie Reyman are also buried here. Take time to notice all the other graves, too. Note that they display names primarily of Czech heritage. Facing the cemetery, if you look to the left, you will see a grassy area next to the cemetery where Dupont School once stood. Until the mid-1950s, this school was attended by children from the farms of the surrounding area.

Now, it's time to proceed to Blain Cemetery, which is not far away. Proceed back in the opposite direction on Amana Road, going past the intersection of Falcon Avenue heading east. Incidentally, Amana Road is the same road referred to as the *bottom road* in *From the Bohemian Hills*. A bit over 2 miles from the Falcon Avenue intersection turn left (north) on Blain Cemetery Road. Proceed on this winding road for about 2 miles, and you will arrive at Blain Cemetery on your left. In this bucolic cemetery you will find the gravesites of Vaclav and Anna Rejman. Leaving the cemetery, you can continue onward on Blain Cemetery Road and soon intersect with Greencastle Avenue. Go right on Greencastle and you will meet the Swisher blacktop (120th Street NW) where you can turn right toward Swisher.

As you go through Swisher, you may want to explore the small town and even stop at its charming café for a snack before proceeding. Driving onward out of town, proceed past Interstate 380, driving eastward toward Shueyville where you will need to stop at the Shueyville intersection before continuing straight on. Continue for about a mile and a half and turn left on Fisher Pond Road NE. This road will become Spanish Road at the next intersection, and you will immediately see Truhlar Cemetery on the left. Stop and explore the site of the first location of Reverend Kun's Bohemian Moravian Brethren Reformed Church. Kun's grave is there, too, as well as the graves of many of the church's founders. Continuing up the road a bit, you will encounter the church, now known as the 1st Presbyterian Church Near Ely, at its present location.

Getting back to Interstate 380 is easy. Simply continue northward on Spanish Road. It will take you to Wright Brothers Boulevard E which will take you westward (left) to the interstate.

This entire excursion of discovery will not be complete without a visit to the two historic neighborhoods on the south side of Cedar Rapids, namely Czech Village and Little Bohemia. The Czech Village & New Bohemia District comprise a vibrant 40-block district straddling the banks of the Cedar River. New Bohemia, on the east side of the river, is on 3rd Street E south of 8th Avenue and includes the old Sinclair Packing House site. Czech Village, 10 blocks on the west side, is centered on 16th Avenue SW from D Street SW to the river. Next to this historic district sits the must-see National Czech & Slovak Museum and Library. This fabulous facility adeptly fulfills its mission statement of engaging the community "with unique Czech, Slovak, and American stories to inspire individuals with universal themes of culture, freedom, democracy, and immigration."

Josef and Frantiska Zach, c. 1890

Reverend Francis Kun

Wesley and Terezie Rejman with children, c. 1890

Wesley and Terezie Rejman family
in front of their new house, c. 1907

The Bohemian Moravian Brethren Reformed Church,
c. 1931.

www.ingramcontent.com/pod-product-compliance
Lightning Source LLC
Chambersburg PA
CBHW020336010826
48970CB00012B/922